Published Internationally by Tema N. Merback

CA, USA

belleamiauthor.com

Copyright © 2024 Tema N. Merback

Exclusive cover © 2024 joannadangelo.com

Interior book design and formatting

Editor: Joanna D'Angelo

EBOOK: 979-8-9899811-0-6

PRINT BOOK: 978-1-7359423-9-1

She would risk everything

to protect her daughter...

BELLEAMIAUTHOR.COM

Mona Lisa's DAUGHTER

A Heart-wrenching World War II Novel

BELLE AMI

PRAISE FOR BELLE AMI

THE LAST DAUGHTER

This amazingly written book was more in depth than any I've read before! And then to find out that it's the author's mother's story of survival of the largest genocide ever in history is truly remarkable!

— ANGIE SIMMONS (VERIFIED PURCHASE REVIEW)

I've read many WW2 era novels but this one touched my heart like nothing else I've read...Grab a box of tissues and get ready to be amazed...

— JODIE54 (VERIFIED PURCHASE REVIEW)

This was a book that moved me to tears. Beautifully written and hopefully a lesson for us all...

— A READER OF BOOKS (VERIFIED PURCHASE REVIEW)

THE GIRL WHO KNEW DA VINCI

...Carefully planned and beautifully executed work of fiction.

— MARINA OSIPOVA (VERIFIED PURCHASE
REVIEW)

...This was a great read. Kept me guessing and wouldn't let me put it down. A great romantic mystery. Anxious to read the next one.

— ZANNIELL ZEVENBERGEN (VERIFIED
PURCHASE REVIEW)

...Based on an entirely original concept, *The Girl Who Knew Da Vinci* will take readers who love romantic suspense, mysteries, and fast-paced thrillers on a ride they'll not soon forget.

— FRANCES (VERIFIED PURCHASE
REVIEW)

THE BLUE COAT SAGA

...I love how the author weaves in present day, history, and time travel. It is not only enjoyable because of the story itself but because it leaves the reader with something to think about long after the book is read...You will definitely want to read this one.

— MARTHAEZT (VERIFIED PURCHASE
REVIEW)

...Belle Ami is an amazing writer. Time seems to slip away as you get caught up in each of her books.

— ELIZABETH KANE (VERIFIED PURCHASE
REVIEW)

...Belle has done it again using meticulous research woven into a captivating story.

— SALLY BRANDLE (AUTHOR)

MONA LISA'S DAUGHTER

A GRIPPING AND GUT-WRENCHING HISTORICAL
NOVEL ABOUT WORLD WAR II FROM THE AUTHOR OF
THE LAST DAUGHTER

BELLE AMI

I dedicate this book to my mother Dina Frydman Balbien, and my late father Leo Balbien. Your courage and strength took you down separate paths during one of the darkest times in history. But you both ended up in the same place, together in America, where you forged a new life and created a new family.

I also dedicate this book to the tenacious spirit of so many Italians, who, in World War II did everything they could to help their fellow Italians. With courage and determination, they hid Jewish families and children in convents, schools, hospitals, secret rooms inside their homes, and even the Vatican. They tried to save as many Jewish people as they could, and for this, they were a blessing.

ACKNOWLEDGMENTS

I poured my heart and soul into this book, but none of it would have been possible if not for you, my dear friend Joanna D'Angelo —developmental editor, story consultant, cover artist/book formatter, cheerleader, and proud daughter of Italian immigrants.

"Wisdom is the daughter of experience."
"Truth was the only daughter of Time."
~ Leonardo Da Vinci

PROLOGUE

JUNE 20, 1882 ~ SANTA MARIA DEL CARMINE ~
FLORENCE, ITALY

ever try to wake a sleeping mule with a song. Suor
Maria Vittoria learned that valuable lesson when she
was ten years old. Il Cocciuto did not appreciate her wobbly
mezzo-soprano and let her know it with a swift kick to her shin.
Her old injury throbbed on rainy days, such as today, making her
limp more pronounced as her clogs thumped out an uneven
rhythm on the stone floor. The teapot and cup rattled on the tray
as she tried to keep them balanced. When she reached Suor Ursula
Botti's door, she set the tray on the floor and knocked softly.
"Posso entrare?"

"Avanti!"

Suor Maria Vittoria opened the door and carefully picked up

the tray. She nudged the door closed with her rear end. *"Come ti senti?"*

"How should an old woman on her deathbed feel?" Suor Ursula grunted. "The only thing worse than dying is a coffin full of regrets." She frowned, making her wrinkled face resemble an apple left out in the sun. "And leaving so much unfinished."

Suor Maria Vittoria had no answer to that. After all, what possible regrets could a nun have when she lived most of her life within the sacred walls of a nunnery? Besides, it was a little late to rewrite the page. "May I help you with something, Sister?"

Suor Ursula cackled like a witch from a fairy tale about to eat a pair of lost children. Unfortunately, the old nun's laughter released a most unseemly smell from the other end of her body. Out of politeness, Suor Maria Vittoria refrained from covering her nose. Instead, she opened the small window and prayed for a breeze.

Suor Ursula patted the bed next to her. *"Per favore,* pour me a cup of tea and sit down, *mimma."*

Suor Maria Vittoria helped Suor Ursula raise the teacup to her lips.

"Ah, peppermint, so fragrant." The old woman smacked her lips and grinned, displaying a set of yellowed teeth. "I have been putting this off for some time, but I'm afraid I can no longer delay."

"Delay what?"

"Initiating you into the sisterhood."

Suor Maria Vittoria feared the old nun's senses had taken flight. "But I am already a nun. I was consecrated five years ago."

Suor Ursula sighed and pursed her lips as if she'd been forced to taste a wedge of lemon. "I have not lost my wits, girl, just my strength. If I could choose anyone else, I would do so."

Suor Maria Vittoria tried to ignore Suor Ursula's insult. After all, she was old and frail and would not be long for this world. Age and frailty called for patience and kindness from the young. But it was difficult not to be hurt by the dying nun's harsh words after a lifetime of kind deeds. "I'm sorry if I have not met your expectations, Sister. Perhaps my work in the convent library has not been to your satisfaction?"

"No, no, no, you misunderstand. Your work is exceptional. You have a clever mind and have learned much in your young life."

"Then what is at issue here?"

"I worry because you are too good, too kind, and too trusting. I fear the task before you requires a more devious and cunning nature."

"May I ask what this task is?"

"Another sip of tea first, *per piacere*."

Suor Maria Vittoria lifted the cup again to Suor Ursula's lips, then placed the cup aside and clasped her hands in her lap.

"Much better." Suor Ursula sighed and laid her hand over Suor Maria Vittoria's. The old nun's protruding blue veins twined up her forearms like vines up a tree trunk. "You are very dear to me, child."

Suor Maria Vittoria swallowed the lump in her throat, regretting her earlier reaction to Suor Ursula's words. She grasped the old nun's hand between hers. "You have always been more like a mother to me than a mentor."

"*Piccolina*, we have had many adventures, have we not?"

"We have, indeed." She chuckled.

"God has a sense of humor, I think."

"What do you mean?" Suor Maria Vittoria pulled a handkerchief from her pocket and wiped the tears from her friend's eyes.

"God has given us strength, stamina, and beauty when we are too young to appreciate it and wisdom when we are too old to put it to good use."

"I am certain you have many more days of sunshine—"

"Hush, little sparrow, I do not. But you do. As I have told you, I came to Santa Maria del Carmine from Sant' Orsola when that horse's ass Napoleon went on a spree, deconsecrating convents. But that is neither here nor there.

"I brought with me a small chest containing private correspondence that belonged to a patroness of the convent four hundred years ago. That blessed lady's dying wish was for the preservation and safekeeping of the contents of this chest from prying eyes forever. The patroness's daughter, Suor Ludovica, made a sacred promise to God that generations of nuns have upheld, including me. And now, so will you."

"But why? Are these items of immense value?"

"Priceless."

"Would it not be wiser to preserve them in a great library or a museum? Think of all the good that could come from sharing this remarkable find with the world."

Suor Ursula shook her head. "No, you must never, ever, make known the existence of this treasure. Not to anyone. It would cause a catastrophe that would shock the entire world. Besides, a vow to God cannot be broken. It is not up to you, nor me, nor anyone else to decide the fate of this chest. We are merely its caretakers."

Suor Maria Vittoria thought for a moment on this. "You are certain there is no other way?"

"There is an old saying, '*Vecchi peccati hanno le ombre lunghe.*'"

"Old sins have long shadows?"

"*Sì, precisamente.* Our job is to keep this treasure trove safe and out of the grasping hands of greedy fortune hunters. I assure you it is a worthy duty." She smiled, transforming her face into a map of fissures and crevices. "Before I tell you where to find this precious chest, you must swear before God to uphold the promise and protect it with your life."

"Should I not see it before I make such an oath?"

"No. *Ogni promessa ha un debito.* Every promise owes a debt. Once made, it cannot be broken. *Capisce?*"

A rumbling toot and the wafting smell of rotten eggs accompanied Suor Ursula's declaration. Suor Maria Vittoria shot up, backed herself up to the open window, and inhaled a breath of fresh air.

The old nun erupted in laughter. "*Mi dispiace.* If it were not my own gas, I would probably take leave of my senses." She waved her hand in front of her face to dispel the pungent odor. The moment of laughter passed, and her eyes narrowed, a steely glint reflected in their filmy gray depths. "Your promise, Sorellina."

Suor Maria Vittoria returned to the bedside. "I promise." It did not matter what the promise was for. She loved the old nun and did not want worries plaguing her heart in the final days of her life.

"*Bene, molto bene.* You must not forget what I am about to tell you."

"Why would I forget?"

"Because your mind is like a butterfly, forever flitting about, Sorellina."

Suor Maria Vittoria smiled. "I promise I will never forget."

"*Brava*." The old nun patted her hand. "Fetch me the treasure, and I will tell you a story."

CHAPTER 1

*V*alentina Amato saw only blackness. She shivered, huddling deeper into the folds of the damp blanket. She couldn't tell whether the frigid temperature or her fear of the unknown caused her to tremble. Rain battered the tarp she sheltered under, and she worried the heavy winds would carry it away. She prayed for the old farmer who drove the cart and the old donkey who pulled it. She tried not to think of their destination or why she was forced to leave her home in Fiesole. In her short life of only fifteen years, Valentina could not imagine why she deserved this fate.

"Hai portato vergogna alla famiglia! Dio mio, che maledizione!" Her mother's screams had shaken the walls of their house. "You have brought shame on our family! Dear God, what a curse!"

Her mother, Giulia, had repeated the words over and over as she tore at her hair and rocked back and forth in her chair. Giulia never held anything back when it came to her temper. Her outbursts were legendary. Valentina often wondered if her mother believed she stood on a grand stage with an audience watching her perform.

For Valentina's crime, Giulia had declared banishment was the only recourse—both for her and her bastard unborn child.

"Mamma, please," Valentina had begged. "Let me stay. I promise to hide in my bedroom until the baby is born. No one will know. I promise not to tell a soul."

But Giulia would not be dissuaded. Valentina was to blame for the tragedy that had fallen upon their heads and must pay the consequences.

The pelting rain and icy wind certainly felt as if God agreed with her mother's punishment. Valentina wiped her tears with the back of her hand as she contemplated why her mother hated her. Giulia's anger seemed to have simmered for years, just beneath the surface, like a dormant volcano. Valentina's pregnancy had caused the volcano to erupt, giving her mother license to proclaim what an ungrateful, wretched girl she had for a daughter.

The more Valentina had pleaded and wept, the angrier Giulia had become until the words between them became a flood of rebukes and vituperations that neither mother nor daughter would ever forget.

Hateful words, once spoken, can never be forgotten. It was a lesson Valentina would always remember.

The cart came to a stop, and Valentina's heart wrenched. Tommaso pulled back the tarp to help her descend. In an instant, the rain soaked her. At least the nuns would think her face was wet from the downpour and not from tears.

"*Madre di Dio*, what a storm," Tommaso said, the rain spilling over the brim of his hat. "Come, girl, make haste. I must find shelter for the donkey and myself on this wretched night."

He held her by the arm, escorting her to the massive double doors of the convent. He pressed a button, and a bell echoed on the other side of the thick, heavy wood. Valentina's legs shook, and she pulled the wet blanket tightly around her with one hand and clutched her small suitcase with the other. Finally, the door groaned open, and a nun appeared, holding an umbrella.

"Don't just stand there, girl, come in. Come in. We've been expecting you." A flash of lightning lit the sky, illuminating the nun's face. Valentina's gaze skittered away at the condemnation she read in the sister's eyes. Her gut twisted in despair. *Am I to be judged guilty without the benefit of a trial, even here under God's own roof?*

Tommaso lifted his hat respectfully. "Where might my donkey and I find shelter?" he shouted above the thrashing rain.

"The caretaker's cottage is behind the church. Giuseppe will put you and your donkey up for the night."

"*Grazie, grazie.*"

The nun shut the heavy door, sliding the bolt in place. She hurried through the cloister, her black habit billowing in her wake. Valentina scampered behind, trying to keep up. She caught a shadowy glimpse of frescoes on the walls while the sweet scent of grass and freshly tilled earth hinted at the presence of a nearby garden.

The nun broke the silence by introducing herself as Suor

Emilia. "Get a good night's sleep. Tomorrow, you will learn your duties."

"Duties?"

"Yes. Everyone here works, and so will you." Suor Emilia glanced back at her. "Of course, we will take into consideration your condition." She shook her head, her gaze dropping to the barely visible bump of pregnancy. "Why you girls don't realize that your silly fancies will lead to ruin is beyond me."

Valentina said nothing. She would not give this black crow the satisfaction of a reply. She may have been ruined, but not by her own silly fancies.

THE MORNING SUNSHINE streamed through the sheer lace curtains on the window. Valentina sat up and rubbed her eyes. She blinked several times, confusion muddling her thoughts. Spying her small, unopened suitcase on the chair in the corner of the room brought her mind back into focus.

Her mother's bitter parting words, the frightening cart ride through the storm, the nun's scorn, and her own exhaustion had all but overwhelmed her last night. She'd barely stumbled into bed before blessed sleep had claimed her. Valentina surveyed the cramped room, her home for the next few months. A small table with a washbasin and pitcher sat against the wall. Above the headboard hung a wooden crucifix.

She got out of bed and padded to the window. Moving the curtain aside, Valentina gasped at the view below. The storm had run its course, and a well-tended garden glowed in the brightness of day, water drops still clinging to the leaves glittered like polished gemstones. Neat rows of colorful vegetables poked through the rich black soil, and fat red tomatoes drooped on staked vines. Unlatching the window, she breathed in the morning air filled with the tangy scent of lemons, and her heart felt a little lighter.

Leaving the window open to air out the stuffy room, she washed hastily, using the water in the basin, and unpacked her few belongings. She slipped on a simple brown shift dress with buttons down the front that fit loosely in anticipation of the baby. Over that, she pulled on a sweater she'd knitted out of remnants of yarn. Valentina was clever with a needle and thread, but she could only hide her growing girth for so long. Her other day dress, the color of green figs, she hung in the narrow armoire along with her best for Sunday mass, a dark blue dress with a crisp white collar.

A few minutes later, Valentina was tucking the corner of the blanket neatly under the mattress when a gentle knock sounded on the door. "Come in," she called out, hoping it wasn't Suor Emilia from last night. The door opened, and a young nun stepped into the room. Dressed in a freshly starched habit, pristine white scapular and veil, a welcoming smile twinkled in her eyes.

Hope swelled in Valentina's chest. Unable to hide her joy at seeing a friendly face near her age, her enthusiasm burst forth. "Good morning! My name is Valentina, and I'm so happy to see you."

The nun set the tray on the bed. "*Buongiorno a lei!* My name is Suor Teresa, and I will be helping you settle in here at the convent."

Valentina's stomach growled at the aroma wafting up from the tray. Her cheeks flooded with heat in response. "Excuse me."

Suor Teresa giggled. "My stomach growls too when I'm hungry," she said in a conspiratorial whisper. "Sit and enjoy your meal. Suor Elena is the best cook in all of Italy. She told me specifically to make certain you eat everything on your tray. Your child needs nourishment as much as you do," she added with a gentle nudge.

"Please, can you keep me company while I eat? I have so many questions."

Suor Teresa grinned. "I was hoping you'd ask."

Valentina sat beside her new friend, sipped the rich coffee, and sighed.

"Suor Elena also makes the best espresso."

"It is delicious," Valentina agreed. She tasted the porridge and almost sighed again. Thick cubes of hearty bread soaked in a milky custard with currants and sweetened with honey.

"Once you're used to things here, you can join us in the dining room for breakfast at six," Suor Teresa said. "But if you like, you can join us for Vigil and Lauds prayers before that at five." She fingered the gold cross on the chain hanging from her neck. "You are always welcome."

"Thank you. I will do my best to fit in and not cause any trouble." Valentina had known more than her share. Her mother's parting words echoed in her mind: *You have too many airs. Just like your father. I should have taken a stronger hand with you…*"

Valentina pushed the dark thoughts away and took another sip of coffee. "You look so young, Suor Teresa. Have you been a nun for very long?"

Teresa beamed, and a glow lit her features. "I took my first vows three months ago."

"I can see by your smile that you are happy here."

"It's a freedom and a blessing I never expected to feel."

Valentina found it an odd declaration. She considered the life of a nun anything but free. Then again, what did she know about freedom? Here she was, pregnant and far from home.

"Last night, when I arrived, Suor Emilia mentioned I would have duties, though she did not tell me what they might be." Valentina scooped up another spoonful of the porridge. The baby growing inside her was as hungry as she was.

Suor Teresa bounced on the bed, bubbling with exuberance. "Can you read, Valentina?" There was no judgment contained in the young nun's question. She was as guileless as a child. "If not, you can work in the garden."

Considering the view from her window, the thought of working outside was tempting. On the other hand, the question about literacy pricked her curiosity. "Yes, my father made sure I could read and write." Valentina swallowed the lump in her throat. The thought of her father made her sorrow surge, reminding her of all she had lost. "I am quite well-versed in history, literature, and art—my father always read to me, and we talked about many subjects."

"I can see you are sad to be away from home," Suor Teresa said gently.

Valentina could only nod as she sipped her coffee. *Home.* Where was home now? Her mother had all but banished her... *"I can't even stand to look at you,"* Giulia had spat when Valentina could no longer hide her burgeoning belly.

Valentina's brother, Rodolfo, had begged their mother to let Valentina stay until he could make inquiries for a suitable place for her to give birth. Thankfully, the convent had agreed to take her.

"Then please consider this your home."

"You are so kind, Suor Teresa."

"*La gentilezza è più importante della saggezza.*"

Kindness is more important than wisdom. As unaffected as Suor Teresa might be, she seemed to possess a knack for seeing into a person's heart. Valentina had always hidden her feelings behind a stoic face. Something she'd learned from her father as well.

"Perhaps you might consider working in the library with Suor Maria Vittoria. She oversees the convent's collection. Our library is quite extensive—many of the books came from Sant' Orsola, a convent founded in the fourteenth century. Sadly, Napoleon deconsecrated it in the 1800s."

"That's wonderful—" Valentina said. "I mean about the books, not what Napoleon did." She shook her head at her misspeak.

Suor Teresa giggled and patted her hand. "I know what you meant to say. Suor Maria Vittoria says it is unfortunate that we are forced to live at the whim of political leaders."

Valentina agreed with a solemn nod. Her father had often shared his views about politics and society. He was self-educated and had instilled a love of learning in her.

Giulia did not share Enrico's love of books. She would sit with her sewing every evening, mending socks or shirts for Rodolfo or the twins, and say cruel, hurtful things to Enrico as he read the newspaper. "*So many opinions on such important matters,*" Giulia would goad, "*and yet, no ambition to put those grand ideas to any use other than boasting to your cronies.*"

Valentina could not fathom the reasons for those verbal lashings. Her father was a gentle man. Oh, how she wished he'd stood up to Giulia, but all he did was turn the page and keep reading.

Even worse, her mother's mood could be measured by how late her father got home from work. Did Enrico stay away because he couldn't bear Giulia's harping or because he lost track of time, immersed in lively discussions with his friends?

Even with Giulia's mercurial temperament, Valentina had inherited her father's patience to balance it out. But all of that changed almost a year ago when her father, once again, failed to come home in time for supper. Giulia's temper had been on full display as she ranted to Rodolfo and the twins. Valentina had washed the dishes and slipped away to bed. At dawn, realizing their father had not yet come home, Valentina and Rodolfo had gone to the shop searching for him. They found him there face down on the floor. The doctor's pronouncement had been death from a massive heart attack. *A heart attack or a broken heart?*

"Valentina, are you all right?"

"Pardon me?" Valentina looked at her new friend in confusion.

"I asked if you were ready to meet Suor Maria Vittoria, and you were far away again."

Valentina felt her cheeks flush with embarrassment. "I am sorry, my mind wandered for a moment. Forgive me. I am not usually an absentminded person."

"That is a relief." Suor Teresa's eyes looked up at the heavens.

"Why is that?" Valentina asked as they gathered up her breakfast dishes and went downstairs.

"Because Suor Maria Vittoria is..."

"Absentminded?"

Suor Teresa sighed. "Truly, she is the smartest nun at the convent—her mind is brimming with stories and ideas, but sometimes..."

"Sometimes she can forget a boiling pot on the stove?" Valentina finished.

"Luckily, Suor Elena is in charge of the cooking." Suor Teresa giggled.

"I can cook as well, but I much prefer to be surrounded by books. I hope I will be of good use to Suor Maria Vittoria."

"I am certain you will. When I stepped into your room, I could not help but notice how neat and tidy you have made it."

"I think everything should have its place, don't you?"

"Assolutamente!" Suor Teresa nodded vigorously. "I think you will be perfect for Suor Maria Vittoria."

"Thank you for the compliment." The library would be a lovely place to pass the remaining months of her pregnancy. "Is Suor Maria Vittoria kind? I only ask because Suor Emilia—" Valentina struggled to put into words her first impression of the old nun who answered the door and couldn't hide her contempt.

"Oh, don't mind, Suor Emilia. She's a curmudgeon but harmless. Suor Maria Vittoria is a saint. You will love her."

Valentina breathed a sigh of relief as she rubbed her abdomen.

Suor Teresa's gaze followed her movements. "Do you know what you will do after the baby is born?"

Valentina shook her head. "Not yet..." Would Giulia allow her back home? Did she even want to go back? What if she crossed paths with *him* again? The one who had altered the course of her life. Knowing he lived on the other side of Fiesole, how could she reclaim any semblance of an everyday existence? "I hope God will provide an answer."

"I am certain He will."

CHAPTER 2

"*A*t last, you are here! I have waited a long time for you to arrive."

Valentina was taken aback as the diminutive nun's arms wrapped around her with surprising strength. She had no idea what the nun was talking about, nor did she know how to respond except to return the embrace. Valentina glanced at Suor Teresa, who winked, her hands coming together in prayer.

The petite nun finally released Valentina and stepped back to look her in the eyes. "My dear girl, I can see you are confused by my greeting, it's just that when I found out you were coming to stay with us, I knew my prayers had been answered. God speaks in profound ways."

"You prayed for an unmarried pregnant girl to work in the library?" Valentina blurted.

Suor Maria Vittoria's laughter chimed like a cuckoo clock sounding the hour. She wagged her finger. "A sense of humor, *bravissima!* I can tell you will have me laughing until my eyes pour tears. No, my dear child, I prayed for a pure heart to assist me."

Valentina's smile came unbidden, warmed by the nun's kind words. "I will do my best, Sorella."

The nun's glance swept the room. "So, what do you think of our little library?"

Valentina had paid scant attention to her surroundings, so engrossed was she by her conversation with the nun. She looked up, admiring the high barrel-vaulted ceiling painted a snowy white. For a fleeting moment, she imagined it adorned with a beautiful fresco. She shook off her musings and surveyed the entire room. Shelves holding hundreds of leather-bound books lined the walls, tables cluttered with piles of more books speckled the ample space, and next to an old desk stood a pushcart loaded with another mountain of books, waiting to be sorted.

"I think you need assistance," Valentina said.

The nun winked. "Yes, we have much to do, and you have much to learn."

STANDING on the top rung of the ladder, Valentina stretched on tiptoe, one hand on her belly and the other holding an ancient text about miracles. She tried to slip the book into its allotted spot, yet the space was tight. "Stubborn book. Why won't you fit?" Something was preventing it from sliding in completely.

Setting the book on the ladder's shelf, Valentina felt around for whatever was causing the obstruction. The wall seemed to jut out in a particular spot. She shifted books to either side of the shelf to create more space and traced her fingers along the odd protrusion when it suddenly gave way and popped out of the wall.

A gasp escaped her as she realized it was an enclosure that housed a small chest. She pulled the box out and noted it resembled a miniature version of a *cassone*, a chest used to hold fineries for a bride. A wave of sadness engulfed her. Given her condition, she doubted her fate would ever lie in marriage. She blinked back tears and examined the pretty box.

The beautiful object was made of wood and carved with an inlay of two birds in flight. Its metal hinges were free of rust. No dust nor any cobwebs covered its exterior. It was not overly heavy, but it was locked, so she stretched her hand again to the back of the secret compartment, seeking a key to unlock the chest.

"I see you've discovered our treasure," Suor Maria Vittoria's amused voice floated up the ladder.

Valentina gasped again and would have lost her footing had the nun not steadied her.

"Careful, my child."

"I—I'm sorry, I did not know the chest was meant to be hidden. I was only trying to fit *The Book of Miracles* into its proper slot because I thought somebody had placed it on the wrong shelf."

"Ah yes, that was my doing." The nun shrugged. "There are so many miracles in that book. You would think one miracle could have been put to good use in getting rid of that *pomposo buffone*, Il Duce."

Valentina's eyes widened at the colorful comment about Italy's autocratic ruler.

Suor Maria Vittoria put her finger to her lips. "My fellow sisters feel the same," she said, "yet we must guard our tongues these days. There are ears everywhere." She took the box from Valentina's hands and set it on the desk. *"Eh, beh, Il gatto è fuori dalla borsa."* The cat is out of the bag. "Come, I will help you down and tell you a story."

Valentina wondered what possible treasure might be tucked into the chest. "Is this story true or fictional?" She eased down the ladder and followed Suor Maria Vittoria to a small table where the nun had set a tray of biscotti and coffee.

"True, of course. I never lie...Well, that is unless I need to." She chuckled as she filled two small cups with the steaming brew and set one in front of Valentina.

Taking a biscotti, Suor Maria Vittoria dipped it into her cup and took a bite. "Ah, Suor Elena is truly the best baker in all of Italy. Here, child, enjoy." She pushed the plate of treats toward Valentina. *"Mangia, mangia."*

Valentina helped herself and dipped the cookie into the aromatic brew. She closed her eyes, savoring the swirl of vanilla and tang of lemon that tickled her tongue.

Suor Maria Vittoria sipped her coffee and heaved a deep sigh. "You were just a child, *piccola*, when the Spanish flu ravaged the world, claiming the lives of so many of our brothers and sisters. May they rest in peace. Death chose no favorites—snatching both old and young, rich and poor. For many, it was a time of questioning the existence of God. I found purpose during those dark times in my work and keeping a sacred promise."

"A promise, to whom?"

"Suor Ursula Botti...she died many years ago. God rest her soul." Suor Maria Vittoria made the sign of the cross. She looked at the wooden chest as if gazing at an old friend. "I'm the current caretaker of the precious contents of this box."

"What is inside?"

Suor Maria Vittoria leaned forward and said *sotto voce*, "A correspondence that lasted almost twenty years between Leonardo da Vinci and Lisa del Giocondo."

"The Mona Lisa?" Valentina asked, her eyes wide. "You mean there are letters in that box written by Leonardo da Vinci to Mona Lisa?"

"Yes, and she to him."

"But how did you come to possess such letters?"

"They were entrusted to a nun named Suor Ludovica, who was Signora del Giocondo's daughter. The signora gave them to her daughter on her deathbed and asked her to keep them safe. Nuns have guarded these letters for almost four hundred years."

"Incredibile."

"Yes, it is."

"But there is something I don't understand. If the box holds Leonardo da Vinci's letters to Mona Lisa, how does it also contain her letters to him?"

"You are a clever girl." Suor Maria Vittoria tapped the side of her nose.

Valentina beamed at the praise.

"I suspect he must have returned them to her at some point. Perhaps they argued, and she asked for them back."

"You don't know for certain?"

A flush of pink tinted Suor Maria Vittoria's cheeks. "Unfortunately, I do not."

"You have never read them?"

"I have not."

"But why? Is that part of the promise?"

"No, however, you must understand that education in Italy was not widespread until this century, and even now, many Italians can barely sign their own name, let alone read and write."

Valentina had been lucky that her father had encouraged her love of books and learning.

"Many nuns who cared for the chest before me were either illiterate or could barely read."

"But that is not true of you."

"It is true for me as well. You see, I cannot read—at least not the way you can." A blush crept across her cheeks.

"But you're a librarian. You have kept this library for years."

"Suor Ursula entrusted this library and these letters into my care. She was my mentor and dearest friend, taking me under her wing when I was only a girl. She taught me to read differently, which suits how my mind learns and my eyes see. I have learned to read books printed on a printing press; alas, handwritten letters are difficult for me, especially ones as old as these."

"But it is a blessing that you were able to overcome your problem and take care of these wonderful books," Valentina said.

"Yes, my time in this library has brought me boundless joy. One is never alone when surrounded by books."

"Oh, Suor Maria Vittoria, I agree. Books are like dear friends."

"I have noticed you take pleasure in reading. Many afternoons, I see you sitting under the olive tree in the garden with a book in your hands. Yesterday, it was *Romeo and Juliet* by Shakespeare, was it not? You are thirsty for knowledge." She tapped her temple with her index finger. "Perhaps..." Her eyes twinkled. "Perhaps God meant for you to find the box."

Valentina's gaze strayed to the chest. She was not a nun and had not made the sacred promise to guard the treasure. She could not possibly ask Suor Maria Vittoria's permission to read the letters...could she? "I thank you for the compliment, Suor Maria Vittoria. I have always enjoyed reading and learning about the world... I am drawn to love stories, even the ones that do not end happily." She stared down at her empty cup. "I cannot help but wonder at that kind of bond...that transcends every obstacle hurled in its path," she said softly. "Even tragedy."

Suor Maria Vittoria sniffled, drawing Valentina's notice. The nun wiped away a tear that slipped down her cheek.

"I'm so sorry. Did I say something that offended you or caused you pain?" Valentina reached for the nun's hand.

She shook her head, gifting Valentina with a gentle smile. "Whether won or lost, love is always something to be cherished. Although a happy ending does not await all who journey down the path of love, opening one's heart to another is worth the pain that sometimes follows. Stories are wondrous, indeed. They help us see the world in a different light and perhaps help us better understand our place in it."

"Do you have a love story?" Valentina asked.

Suor Maria Vittoria's eyes clouded momentarily, and she stared past Valentina beyond the library's four walls. "One day, I will share it with you." Her gaze met Valentina's. "You might think it a tale of sadness; however, I cannot utter a single complaint about how my life has turned out." She smiled and patted Valentina's hand. "Would you like to help me with this treasure?"

"Oh, I would be honored to help you in any way I can."

"Good. There is an important task that I require assistance with. Given the fragility of these letters and how much they have degraded over the centuries, I think it would be a good idea to copy them. A transcript, if you will."

"I think that is a wonderful idea."

"You can copy them by hand, and I would also like you to make a typewritten copy."

"But I do not know how to type."

"I will teach you. Now, there is another mystery that I must tell you about—one that will make your task quite challenging."

"I will do my best, whatever it is." Valentina gave a firm nod.

"I knew you would say that." Suor Maria Vittoria grinned. "You see, Leonardo da Vinci had a particular way of writing, a code if you will—no doubt one of his eccentricities. Suor Ursula, God rest her soul, nor I could make heads or tails of it. I can see how clever you are. Would you like to try to decipher this code and translate the letters?"

"I would indeed."

"I am pleased to hear it. I will give you the first letter to transcribe. If you are successful, I will give you another one."

"But why are you entrusting me with these letters? I am not a nun. I have made no sacred promise."

"Do you promise me that you will not tell anyone what I am about to show you?"

"I–I promise. I will not tell a soul."

"There, now you have made a sacred promise."

"But how can it be sacred?"

"You have given me your word."

"But how do you know you can trust me?"

Suor Maria Vittoria placed her hands on Valentina's shoulders and looked into her eyes. "Do you want me to trust you?"

"Yes."

"Tell me why I should trust you."

"Because..." Valentina hesitated, not knowing what to say. Tears sprang to her eyes, and she blinked them back. "I don't know..."

Suor Maria Vittoria laid her hand against Valentina's cheek and said gently, "You have a good soul. I already knew that from the first moment I saw you. And that is why I trust you."

Valentina nodded, tears pouring forth. "Thank you. Thank you for trusting me."

Suor Maria Vittoria removed a neatly folded handkerchief from her pocket and handed it to Valentina. "There, my child, dry your eyes." The nun pulled a chain out from around her neck. A simple chain of gold with a key. "Now, come with me and bring the box." The nun got up and made her way to her desk. "You will need a pair of special gloves to use when you handle the letter."

"Special gloves?" Valentina picked up the box and held it carefully against her chest as she followed Suor Maria Vittoria across the room.

"I wear clean white cotton gloves to protect the delicate paper because it is hundreds of years old." Suor Maria Vittoria smiled over her shoulder. "I know you will be careful. And I trust you will find sympathy and perhaps a common thread to the answers you seek."

"I do not seek—"

"Ah, my dear child, you are very young...Eventually, you will realize what it is that will bring you peace. In the meantime, reading is always time well spent."

CHAPTER 3

*G*entile Signora Giocondo,

*The first time I saw you, time stood still. Do you remember
that day? If only I had wings, I would have followed you home.
Your beauty had arrested my senses, nearly stealing my voice...*

The Mercato Vecchio teemed with Florentines who walked
about smelling and sampling the vast array of fruits, vegetables,
olives, cured meats, and cheeses on display. Every few feet, a
vendor called out, hawking his wares.

"*Fichi* with pulp as sweet as sugar!"

"*Pesce fresco!*"

"*Polli* for sale!"

"*Formaggi* fit for a king!"

Their voices raised in a cacophony, each trying to outdo the other, competing to grab the attention of prospective buyers. Many of the vendors called out to Leonardo by name, having known him since he was a boy. His father, Ser Piero, had brought him to Florence at the age of twelve and apprenticed him to Master Verrocchio's workshop when he was fourteen. Leonardo's genius drew recognition early on, surpassing his master, and he reveled in his status as Florence's favorite son.

But not all boys are created equal in temperament. Leonardo, as a youth, was nothing like his companion Salai. The beautiful boy with curly hair and hazel eyes who'd arrived at Leonardo's household when he was ten had grown into a fetching albeit vexing young man. Leonardo couldn't help shaking his head as he recalled Salai's impish behavior from that morning.

The young man had strolled into Leonardo's private rooms with a sly grin. "Shall I go to the mercato, Maestro? We are running low on food." In addition to serving as his assistant, Salai took on duties that would otherwise cost Leonardo precious time away from his work.

For fourteen years, they had been inseparable. A devoted attendant and student in his household, Leonardo had used Salai, now twenty-four years old, as the model for his Vitruvian drawing of a man encircled by a square—well, not quite. In his quest to draw a masculine figure that would symbolize a blend of art, science, and perfect proportion, Leonardo combined Salai's splendid physique with his own in one unique sketch. The drawing was based on first-century Roman architect Vitruvius' treatise *De Architectura* and his principle that architecture must reflect man and nature in its harmonious proportions.

"Maestro, I am here only to serve," Salai had said as he leaned down to give Leonardo a playful tug on his beard while his other hand had slipped into Leonardo's pocket as stealthily as a seasoned pick-purse.

"Yet you often serve yourself first," Leonardo had countered, slapping Salai's hand and gently cuffing him on the head. "I will go myself and find the most perfect eggplant for our meal."

"*Ahi!* You wound me, Maestro," Salai had huffed, his hand going to his chest in a show of pretended innocence. "Besides, I was hoping for a juicy roast."

"No one I know has a taste for meat as you do," Leonardo had said in irritation.

Salai had erupted into a ripple of giggles, and Leonardo couldn't help smiling at his unintended double *entendre*. But the truth was, the young man was as defiant as a toddler when it came to eating any vegetable or legume. And yet, Leonardo found it impossible to deny Salai much of anything. His friend's real name was Gian Giacomo Caprotti, but Leonardo had nicknamed him Salai—*little devil*. The moniker had fit like a pair of new silk tights, as the hellion loved to stir up trouble and reveled in the nasty habit of stealing.

"You will turn my hair white before its time," Leonardo had warned with a shake of his head.

"And yet, what a splendid mane it would be, Maestro," Salai had quipped. Kissing Leonardo's forehead, he spun and danced out the door.

Leonardo expelled a deep breath as he strolled by the meat

seller stalls, knowing his precocious friend would pout for a fort-
night if he did not buy him the *spiedini di carne.* He would give
in, as always, but only after purchasing his own dinner. He
stopped at a vegetable stand and picked up a dark purple *melanzana.* The skin of the voluminous gourd-shaped fruit was as
smooth and shiny as a newly minted florin. He held it to his nose,
inhaling its ripe scent. Giving it a gentle squeeze, he tested it for
firmness. *"Squisito, amico mio*—such vivid color. As beautiful a
specimen as I have ever seen," he proclaimed.

The vendor took a bow. "Perhaps you will paint this perfect
eggplant, Maestro."

Leonardo chuckled. "It will be painted in *olio d'oliva* and fried
to perfection for my dinner." He patted his stomach. "A glorious
end for a glorious creation." Paying the merchant, Leonardo
tipped his hat and slipped the melanzana into the cloth sack with
his other purchases.

His mood had much improved, a welcome relief, as his
thoughts often shifted like the moving parts of the machines he
designed. Leonardo's endless curiosity supplied the replenishing
fount from which his innovations took shape. But such boundless
inquisitiveness exacted a price—principally the continual strife
between creativity and completion. The excitement of a nascent
idea called to him like a siren's song, luring him away from one
project to embark on another, stealing from him what he desired
most—time.

He continued his stroll, his senses attuned to the sights, smells,
and sounds floating around him. A distant chorale of angels
tickled his ears. The Santa Maria del Fiore Cathedral bells rang for
the Angelus at noon. Despite the tension between his religious

convictions and his feelings about the Church, hearing the familiar bells further buoyed his disposition. He hoped his decision to return to Florence after seventeen years under the patronage of Duke Ludovico Sforza would prove a wise one for both his financial and artistic standing.

Rounding a corner, Leonardo came face-to-face with a winged orchestra of caged birds. The percussive honking of geese and quacking ducks underscored the symphonic squawking of quail, partridge, pigeons, and doves. Lending a dramatic crescendo to the performance was the robust flapping of wings of hawks and falcons, as though the large predators lamented their frustration at being so close to plump prey and yet hindered from hunting it.

At that precise moment, he saw her through the cloud of floating feathers. A young woman stood as still as a statue, watching a pair of turtledoves cuddling like lovers. The young woman watched the birds, her gaze enthralled. The feathery lovers cooed and fluttered, fluttered and cooed. Their wings, the color of roasted cinnamon bark, touched and glided in a delicate dance. A few feet away stood her maid, holding a basket. The servant shifted her feet and leaned the basket against her hip. She heaved a sigh, clearly chafing at her mistress's delay.

Leonardo bit back a smile and resumed his study of the lady. She wore the latest fashion from Spain, a forest green gown of silk. He observed the swelling of her bosom pressed against her bodice and the fecund fullness of her face and surmised she had recently given birth. With his painter's eye, he subconsciously calculated the miracle of muscle, skin, and bone that resulted in such an unusual face. A delicate auburn wave of hair fell across her high forehead. Leonardo followed the course of the curl that meandered like a river through pristine countryside. Her bold, high cheekbones lifted her eyes into an intriguing slant, forming a shadowed surround that, had he not known better, would suggest she'd applied ancient kohl to enhance them. His gaze traveled to her mouth, and he lost his breath. While not overly full, her lips curved up in a gentle arc. Gentle and yet sensual at the same time. *A smile that is not quite a smile.*

"I feel such profound sorrow when I see winged creatures so confined," she said in a mellifluous voice. "To be deprived of flight, once having tasted it, seems cruel beyond reason."

He hadn't expected her to speak, and even less did he expect her words to match his sentiments.

Her eyes met his, their burnished beauty pensive.

Struggling to put thoughts into sentences, he answered, "Animals, like us, reflect the perfection of nature. And yet, they survive only at the whim of men. It is an affront to imprison any creature. But I will further suggest that killing and eating them is an even greater tragedy. It is for that reason I consume neither meat nor fowl nor fish of any kind—" He stopped himself and mused that for a man who had trouble conjuring clever words to say to this young woman, he'd managed to provide a loquacious revelation and a heart-held truth about himself.

Her fine, dark brows rose. "How curious you should say this, for I, too, have lost my ability to consume animal flesh." Her lips turned up in that shadow of a smile. "Unfortunately, my husband —indeed my entire household—is not convinced that a diet composed of pasta, beans, vegetables, and fruit could be sufficient to placate one's hunger."

Leonardo laughed. "Alas, my own household would concur. I

have come to learn that one cannot force a belief or a way of life on another."

"I could not agree more. Better to keep one's counsel if one wishes to preserve a happy home." Her eyes dropped to his hands, covered in red dust. "You are an artist."

Looking down at his hands, he grinned. "It seems I have betrayed myself." He hadn't realized he'd plucked a piece of chalk from his pocket and had been fidgeting with it. "Among other things, I paint." He patted the sketchbook that hung at his waist, generating a cloud of chalky dust. "Forgive me." He rubbed his hands together, brushing it away.

"You do not use a stylus and ink?"

"I find the chalk more conducive to capturing a moment, especially when away from my desk. I can model the features more accurately with chalk, something impossible with ink. It allows me to create greater dimensionality to the face in the fullness of the moment. I call the process *sfumato*—to evaporate like smoke." His hands circled expressively, causing more puffs of red dust to float around him.

She watched the floating swirls and then met his gaze. They both burst into laughter.

The birdseller interrupted their shared mirth, his broad girth suggesting that a good amount of meat formed the foundation of his diet. "Maestro, may I ask your patience while I see to the lady's request?" At Leonardo's nod, the vendor turned to the young woman with a deferential smile. "Signora, how may I be of service?"

Leonardo took the opportunity to study the olive-skinned beauty more closely. She carried herself as regally as a queen, yet she possessed an intriguing spirit that captured his inquisitive nature. He found himself drawn to her pleasing manner and the way her midnight eyes focused intently on the vendor as she coaxed him into giving her the best price. Her high forehead spoke of intelligence, while the gentle slope of her aquiline nose gave her profile an elegant silhouette. But it was the pertness of her rounded chin and the teasing curve of her rosebud mouth that captured his artist's eye. He was mesmerized by how her lips almost, but not quite, committed to a smile. What thoughts lay behind her curious expression?

Leonardo had an overwhelming desire to sketch her—quite surprising since portraiture was his least favorite medium. He pondered if he should ask her to pose for him. Would she think him impertinent? He quickly dismissed the notion as inappropriate, given her obvious standing as a lady of quality.

Even so, he'd rarely met a woman who reflected his own thoughts so well. He would have leaped into a lively discussion if she had been a man. He was used to men's blunt and often coarse camaraderie; women, on the other hand, required a more delicate dance. While the lady's candor bemused him and her beauty enchanted him, other qualities fascinated him as well—the cadence of her speech and, more subtly, the pauses between her words. And, of course, her attentive regard as he spoke attracted him most of all.

"Will you purchase any birds today?" she asked Leonardo as the vendor disappeared to the back of his stall. "What will you do with them since I know you do not eat them?"

"Why do you ask?"

She shrugged, and yet her eyes held a challenging sparkle.

Leonardo recalled something his friend Machiavelli once said:

*Men generally judge more by the eye than by the hand, for
everyone can see, but few can feel. Everyone sees what you
appear to be. Few really know what you are.*

Leonardo sensed this woman was unlike most people.

The birdkeeper returned and opened the cage that held the
turtledoves, scooping them into a small, slatted box. The signora
pulled an intricately embroidered *borsetta* from a pocket in her
skirt and removed a florin, handing it to the vendor. He counted
out her change, and she thanked him, dropping the coins into the
small, draw-stringed pouch and tucking it back into the folds of
her gown.

She turned to Leonardo once more and inclined her head in a
slight nod. "I bid you a good day." She turned to her maid and
said, "Come, Estella, we must be on our way."

"Sì, Signora." The young woman bobbed her head, seeming to
snap out of a dazed reverie.

The lady hesitated as though she might say something more to
Leonardo but then seemed to change her mind, offering up one
more almost-smile instead as she picked up the box with the
turtledoves and walked down the lane of stalls, her maid, now
rushing to keep up.

The impression she made might have ended at that moment,
yet Leonardo's gaze followed her as she stopped at a quiet spot
where no vendors hawked, no buyers gathered, and no awning
cast a shadow. The servant girl, once again, stood a few feet away
from her mistress, holding the basket on her hip.

The warmth of the sun's rays bathed the regal lady in a golden
glow. She slid open the wooden slat and coaxed the turtledoves out
with a few whispered words of encouragement. They hovered

before her, cooing as their wings flapped in tandem. It was as if they thanked her, and he half expected them to embrace her with their wings. She waved them off, wiping her tears with a handkerchief. Leonardo watched, mesmerized not only by the duo that took wing and disappeared into the blue sky but also by the woman who freed them.

CHAPTER 4

APRIL 7, 1926 ~ FLORENCE, ITALY

Suor Maria Vittoria pushed open the library door with her rump, balancing a tray laden with a steaming pot of chamomile tea and a cake.

Sitting at the desk, hunched over a magnifying glass, Valentina glanced up. "Let me help you," she said, heaving herself up from the chair.

The contents of the tray rattled. "Stay where you are. I am fine. It's just my limp."

"Does it pain you?"

"It only bothers me when it rains, and getting old doesn't help." Suor Maria Vittoria set the tray on the table and unwrapped the dishtowel encasing a golden lemon cake.

Valentina sniffed the air. "What a delicious aroma."

"Suor Elena couldn't sleep last night. That unfortunate

circumstance resulted in a heavenly gift. She was up before dawn and baked six cakes. May God bless her." Suor Maria Vittoria went to the cupboard and took out two cups and plates. "Come, *dolcezza*, take a break from your transcribing."

"*Grazie*, Sorella." Valentina stifled a yawn with the back of her hand as she padded to the table, her pregnant belly leading the way.

"I see that you, too, had a restless night," Suor Maria Vittoria commented as she set down the plates and cups. Her bedroom was next to Valentina's, and she could not help but hear the girl's pacing and muffled weeping. Worried, she'd knocked on Valentina's door, but the stoic girl told her she had merely stubbed her toe.

Valentina bit her lip as her finger traced along the embroidered flower pattern of the tablecloth. "Sometimes I have bad dreams."

Suor Maria Vittoria cut a large slice of cake for Valentina and plated it. "My dear mentor and friend Suor Ursula always said that sharing a burden with a friend halves the load."

Valentina gave a little shrug as she poured them each a cup of chamomile tea. "I don't know if someone could ever lighten this burden."

Suor Maria Vittoria cut a smaller slice of cake for herself. She hoped the child would one day confide in her. She would have to be patient even though patience was never one of her greatest virtues. "Suor Ursula also said that lemon cake was as close as one could get to tasting a ray of sunshine."

Valentina took a bite. "Mmm..." she said with a sigh. "Suor Ursula was right about that. This lemon cake is the best I have ever tasted."

"Indeed, it is." Suor Maria Vittoria took a dainty bite, savoring the blended aromas of citrus and vanilla. "The dear Sister has truly outdone herself."

"Is it wrong to hope for Suor Elena to have difficulty sleeping every night?" Valentina giggled and took another bite.

"I will refrain from telling her you wish her insomnia to continue," she said with a chuckle. In any case, I do not think you are the only one. My fellow sisters and I always say a silent prayer of thanks when we awaken to the aroma of Suor Elena's fresh-baked creations."

"Perhaps I can convince her to teach me her recipe."

"I am certain Suor Elena might be willing to share a few culinary secrets with you." Suor Maria Vittoria took a sip of the fragrant tea and set the delicate cup back down. "Now tell me what you were working on so studiously when I came in. Have you cracked Maestro da Vinci's code?"

Valentina quirked a half smile. "I proceed at the pace of a turtle crossing the Apennines. Even so, I have made some progress." She leaned forward conspiratorially. "A mirror does the trick."

"What do you mean?"

"I discovered that Maestro da Vinci wrote from right to left. I can see a reverse image of his words with a mirror and re-write them from left to right."

"But that is wonderful news!"

"Yes, but even with the mirror, it takes me almost an hour to do a few lines because the words are so faded. And I am still practicing on the typewriter as well. I worry that I will not be able to complete this duty for you before..." Valentina glanced down at her belly, her hand smoothing over the protruding bump. "I don't want to disappoint you, Sorella."

"My dear child, you could never do that. These letters have been sitting for centuries; they can certainly sit for a few more years until the next caretaker."

Jarring sirens and angry shouts from the street startled them from their seats—a banging followed, loud enough to wake the dead.

"*Dio mio*, what a cacophony," Suor Maria Vittoria said.

"What could it be?"

"I'll go and find out," she replied as more shouts and what sounded like gunshots boomed outside. "Fold those letters away, child. One never knows."

Valentina nodded and rushed to the desk.

Suor Maria Vittoria pulled open the library door just as Suor Teresa burst into the room. "Il Duce has been shot!"

"Sorella, you almost gave me a heart attack." Suor Maria Vittoria patted her chest.

"Forgive me. I ran from the Mercato Nuovo when I heard the news."

"Was he killed?" Suor Maria Vittoria crossed herself.

"No, he's fine. The bullet just grazed his nose." Suor Teresa bent over, dragging in deep breaths, her hands on her knees.

Suor Maria Vittoria shook her head as she opened a side cupboard and took another cup and plate from the shelf. "*The Book of Miracles* must be more powerful than I thought."

A bubble of laughter burst from Valentina's lips. "Oh, pardon me."

Suor Maria Vittoria tossed a wink at her.

"What does the *Book of Miracles* have to do with Il Duce being shot?" Suor Teresa asked, joining them at the table.

"Never mind. Sit, and I will pour you a cup of tea. Suor Elena baked the most beautiful lemon cake. And you know she is the best baker in all of Florence."

Suor Teresa raised the cup to her lips and sipped, sighing.

"You must tell us everything about what you learned and spare no detail," Suor Maria Vittoria said, placing an extra thick slice of cake in front of Suor Teresa. The young nun favored sweets with a passion beyond anyone she had ever known. Lucky for her, she was thin as a beanstalk.

Suor Teresa clapped her hands, picked up her fork, and took a bite. Her face took on a glow of beatification usually reserved for saints. "*Madonna mia*, I think Suor Elena might have outdone herself." She laid her fork down. "I will try to eat slowly. I want to savor each bite."

"Don't worry, there is plenty, and God will not punish you if you indulge in another slice. We can talk about the cake later. Tell us what happened to Il Duce."

"I am on pins and needles," Valentina chimed in.

Suor Maria Vittoria suppressed a smile as the young nun turned her head left and right, then leaned forward, cupping her hands around her mouth as if she were a spy for the Medici. "Mussolini had just given a speech to a massive crowd assembled on the Capitoline Hill in Rome. Hundreds of people came to see him, and afterward, he walked among them, as the crowd cheered."

"What happened next?" Valentina scooted to the edge of her seat.

"A woman pulled a revolver from beneath her shawl and shot him!" Suor Teresa stopped to take another bite of cake.

"And you say he wasn't hurt?" Suor Maria Vittoria asked, refilling her cup.

"No. The bullet merely grazed his nose."

"Who would dare such a thing?" Valentina asked.

"Who, indeed?" Suor Maria Vittoria shook her head. "Our boastful leader has many enemies, although a bullet-riddled nose is not what I would wish for him. Maybe now he will reconsider his future and retire to Naples and open a pizza parlor."

Valentina giggled. "You are so irreverent, Sorella. But why all the commotion here in Florence?"

"Vengeance!" Suor Teresa slapped her hand on the table, making them jump. "Crowds began forming in our city streets, and there were many cries for revenge. The *polizia* showed up and made everything worse. I hurried back as soon as I could. I did not want to get caught in the thick of an angry mob."

"You were wise to do so," Valentina said, protectively resting her hands on her belly. "Who was this woman?"

"The woman who shot Mussolini was Irish. A Catholic, no less!"

"Do you think they will blame the Church?" Valentina's eyes were wide.

Suor Maria Vittoria patted her hand. "I think we are safe."

"*Che Dio ci protegga!*" Suor Teresa placed her hands together in prayer.

"*Non fare una montagna con una collina talpa,*" Suor Maria Vittoria chastised. "Don't make a mountain out of a molehill and imagine problems where there are none. I do not think Mussolini would be foolish enough to take vengeance on Catholics. He needs to remain in the Pope's good favor. Who was this Irish assassin who made such a lousy shot?"

"Her name is Violet Gibson, and she is the daughter of a

baron. Imagine. From an aristocratic family. Rumors were flying that she shot Mussolini to glorify God."

"Aah, I see."

"The crowds wanted to lynch her, but Il Duce calmed them down, professing it was nothing, and once they arrested the woman, he resumed marching in the parade."

Suor Maria Vittoria huffed, "I'm sure he will use this to show the people he is a brave leader and to crack down on dissenters, giving him even more power over the populace."

"I wonder why she did it?" Valentina continued to rub her belly.

"No one who would perpetrate such an act, especially a woman, could be in their right mind. Who's to say what sort of fragility took hold of her?" Suor Teresa took another huge bite of cake.

"We mustn't assume she is *pazza*. I'm sure she had her reasons." Suor Maria Vittoria would not allow fear to cloud her judgment.

"Oh, no—" Valentina's face drained of color.

"*Piccolina,* what is it? Do not worry about a few *ignoranti*. We are safe here."

Valentina stood and looked down. "No, it's not that—it's...I don't know."

Suor Maria Vittoria saw the small puddle of liquid on the floor. "My dear, it's all right. It's your water." She stood and wrapped her arm around Valentina's shoulders. In her calmest and most reassuring manner, she turned to Suor Teresa. "Go to the Holy Mother and tell her to call the midwife. Valentina's water has broken. The baby has decided to make its entrance into the world. I will see her to her bed."

"But the baby—will she be all right?" Valentina's eyes filled with tears.

"There is nothing to be worried about. A woman's water breaking is a natural occurrence. God speaks in mysterious ways."

Suor Teresa ran from the room as Suor Maria Vittoria escorted Valentina at a more sedate pace. She thought it sweet that Valentina referred to her unborn child as *she*. *God will reveal all in His good time.* Wisely, she would wait to tell Valentina about the letter Mother Superior Busnelli had received from Rome. It might cause the girl more distress. Padre Anthony D'Angelo, a dear friend of the abbess, had written of a family he knew in Rome who would welcome Valentina's unborn child—a true blessing. However, Suor Maria Vittoria worried about Valentina's attachment to the baby. She noticed the constant caresses of her belly and the whispered endearments.

"Breathe deeply, my child," she said.

First, the birth, and then we will deal with what comes next.

CHAPTER 5

FLORENCE, ITALY ~ APRIL 5, 1503

*G*entile Maestro da Vinci,

    The feeling of finding a kindred soul has remained with me since we met in the mercato and warms me as the rays from the sun warm my face...

"Piero, *per favore,* do not pull your sister's braids! If your father finds out you are teasing Camilla again, he will take only Bartolomeo to the Mercato Nuovo, and you will be left home with the women." *Madre di Dio, have mercy on me.*

"Why do you make your life so difficult?" Her mother's calm question resounded like a drum in Lisa's ears.

"What do you mean, Mamma?"

"You know full well what I mean." Lucrezia pierced her with a sharp look as she jabbed her needle into her embroidery and set the tambour frame in her lap. "You have a blessed life. Healthy children, a beautiful home, a strong and successful husband—"

"You do not need to remind me of my blessings, Mamma."

"Did I overly indulge you as a child? Perhaps I encouraged your curiosity too much?"

"Why do you say that?"

"Because you are so far away."

"I am right here, seated beside you."

"When you smile, it never quite reaches your eyes."

"Mamma, how many times have we had this discussion? What is this obsession you have about my smile?"

"Because you do not smile as you used to."

Lisa clucked her tongue, shaking her head at her mother's whimsies. "I have the worries and cares of a woman with a large household to manage and children to care for—"

"And yet, you do not mention Francesco," Lucrezia interrupted.

"If you would let me finish speaking, Mamma, I was going to say—and a *husband* to keep content."

"And yet, I remember how you glowed with happiness in those first few years of marriage. When Francesco looked at you, it was as though the sun itself shone upon your face. Even though you are his second wife, he was as besotted with you as a youth with his first love."

Lisa watched her children kick a *calcio Fiorentino* ball made of rags and leather around the garden. Piero, Andrea, and Bartolomeo played as if their lives depended on winning while Camilla, with her plump little legs, chased after her brothers like a baby chick. "Mamma, I am a busy mother with many duties on my shoulders," she repeated.

"My beautiful daughter. Life can be as simple as a stroll through the Piazza della Signoria on a sunny afternoon or as difficult as carrying a basket of stones up Monte Ceceri. Whether it is one or the other depends on you."

Lisa's eyes glistened with tears. "My life is blessed..." *But not entirely.* A beautiful stepson from her husband's previous marriage and four lovely children in eight years of marriage, her youngest a true joy...*But it should have been five.*

Her sweet daughter Piera was born just eighteen months after Piero. So close together it was as though God had gifted her with twins. *Why did God take you, my lovely Piera?* The pain of loss was still with her. She carried it in her heart even now.

"We cannot fathom His infinite wisdom," Lucrezia said, as though reading Lisa's mind. "Look at God's blessings before you. Look at your beautiful children and the baby, Giocondo. Are they not enough to ease your grief over Piera? Look how rosy Giocondo's cheeks are, how sturdy those little legs are when he kicks in his basket, and he is only six months old. He will be playing *calcio* with his siblings before we know it."

Lisa knew her mother was right, but grief could not simply be eased away with the brush of a hand. "You sound like Francesco. He expressed more sorrow from a water-logged shipment of silk than the death of his daughter."

"That is unlike you, Lisa. You are never unkind. You should not say such things. It invites the Devil to your door." Lucrezia made the sign of the *cornicello* behind her back. "And never say it to Francesco's face. It is merely the way of men."

"What do I care of the way of men? I will not make excuses for him or anyone else's insensitivity."

"I know you suffer from the loss of our precious Piera, although you know it is a woman's lot in life to rejoice in motherhood and bear its sorrows. Nearly every woman in Florence, or the world, for that matter, has lost a child. We can only take solace in believing we will one day reunite with them in the afterlife."

Lisa placed her hand on her mother's. "I know you mean well, Mamma."

"It worries me, this perpetual sadness within you. Do you not see it will damage your marriage and hurt your children?" She nodded toward the three boys, Camilla, and the baby, sitting on a blanket at their feet. "Would you bring sorrow upon them as well?"

"My children know how much I love them. And I would protect them with my very life. I would never foist my pain on them." How could she explain to her mother that her world had shifted when Piera was taken from her? That her husband's reaction was the last straw. In the privacy of her heart, she had stopped pretending. The truth was that her marriage no longer fed her soul.

Lucrezia slapped her hands on her knees. "You will be the death of me, Lisa."

"Mamma, please do not say such things."

The ball rolled toward her, and Lisa lifted her skirt and kicked it back to Piero, her mischievous, curly-haired son. Giocondo clapped his hands in delight. Lucrezia blew him a kiss and clapped her hands in unison.

Lisa breathed out a sigh. *Good, focus on your grandchildren and not me.*

"Mamma, Mamma!" Camilla ran to her and buried her face in Lisa's skirt. "Bartolomeo is mean! I hate him!"

"Sh-sh. Do not speak so about your brother." Lisa smoothed her hand over her daughter's sleek black hair. "I am certain he meant no harm."

Her ten-year-old stepson, Bartolomeo, giggled. He was even more mischievous than Piero. The two brothers resembled Francesco and looked like identical twins, except for the difference in their height. Andrea, on the other hand, favored her. Camilla stuck her tongue out at Bartolomeo.

"Camilla," said her grandmother, "that is no way for a lady to behave."

Camilla looked down, scuffing the toe of her shoe on the grass. "Sì, Nonna, perdonami."

Lisa kissed the top of her daughter's head. "Boys are silly pranksters, and sometimes they act without thinking," she said reassuringly. "It's best we humor them because we ladies know better."

Camilla nodded in wise understanding. "Is Papà a prankster?"

"Good heavens, child, no," Lucrezia said, picking up her embroidery.

Lisa chuckled and hugged her daughter close. "Your grandmother is right, tesorina. Papà is a gentleman. I am certain Bartolomeo will grow up to be just like him."

Bartolomeo stuck his hand under his armpit and made an unseemly noise.

Perhaps I spoke too soon.

Piero erupted into a fit of laughter. "Teach me how to make farting sounds!"

"Me too," yelled Andrea.

"*Basta*, Bartolomeo!" Lucrezia called out, shaking her hand in a chopping motion as a warning.

"Why don't you teach Piero and Andrea that clever trick of bouncing the ball on each knee," Lisa encouraged. "I've seen you do it at least *eight* times without dropping it."

"It wasn't eight. It was at least *ten* times, Mamma," Bartolomeo corrected.

"Really? I could have sworn it was eight." She suppressed a grin. "Well, then show us again. Maybe try for eleven times."

"I will do better than that, Mamma! I will do it twenty times in a row!" Bartolomeo turned to his brothers. "Keep your eyes on the ball and watch exactly how I do this trick."

Piero and Andrea plunked down on the grass, their gazes glued on their older brother, their idol, at least for the time being.

Lisa cupped Camilla's chin in her hand. "Go now, *tesoro mio*, go and watch Bartolomeo and count how many times he bounces the ball. Make sure he doesn't cheat."

Camilla lifted her skirt, her sturdy legs propelling her toward her brothers.

"A little firmer hand with the children, Lisa. You don't want them growing up like wild animals."

"Sì, Mamma."

Lucrezia must have realized she was harping too much. She glanced around as if seeing the garden for the first time. "Everything is blooming beautifully this year."

Lisa took in the greenery with its lush fruit and olive trees. "Yes, I could not want for a lovelier place to spend time with the children."

"*Cara*," her mother continued, "I forgot to tell you about the latest scandal. Oh, what a tale."

Lisa was relieved the conversation had shifted to something other than herself. There wasn't a woman alive who loved gossip more than her mother. "Pray tell, Mamma, what have you heard?"

Lucrezia leaned forward and said, *sotto voce*, "It concerns *La Balbi*."

"Really…" Lisa was intrigued; no love was lost between her mother and Signora Claudia Balbi.

"You may recall, her daughter Rosetta is wed to Secondo Lombardi—such a lazy young man. He's lucky his father-in-law handed him a job on a golden platter. He clerks at the Balbi bank —*ma veramente*, all he does is greet the customers. What else can he do with no skills or trade to speak of?" She lifted her shoulder in a dainty shrug. "Not even two years they are married, and Rosetta begins to whine to her mother that she wants a companion to help ease her boredom throughout the day."

"How can a married woman be bored?" Lisa shook her head. "Does she not have a household to run? And is she not yet with child?" Lisa had given birth to Piero precisely one year after her wedding to Francesco. It was a tremendous relief as she had worried she might be barren, a terrible fate for any woman, let alone one who yearned for children as profoundly as she did.

"The Balbi family is richer than the Pope," Lucrezia continued. "They probably have three servants for every room in that massive palazzo."

"What happened? Did she get her companion?"

"I will tell you what happened. Signora Balbi allowed her daughter to hire a young woman named Allegra Fontana. For three months, Allegra was Rosetta's companion, devoted and attentive. Then, one day, Rosetta arrives at her mother's doorstep, sobbing! The poor girl was in complete hysterics. She told her mother she had awakened from her afternoon nap early and went in search of her dear companion, Allegra. As she approached the young woman's quarters, she could hear such terrible shrieks and howls; she feared the poor girl was being murdered in her bed! In a panic, Rosetta burst into the room and received the shock of her life—her sweet, devoted companion was screaming like a she-devil, gripping the headboard as Secondo rutted her from behind!"

Lisa's hand flew to her gaping mouth. "*Madre di Dio.*"

"Signora Balbi gave the girl a thrashing to within an inch of her life and threw the harpy out. And then she warned Secondo she would chop off his *pisello* if he dared be unfaithful to her daughter again," Lucrezia said with a clap of her hands. "Two months later, Rosetta was pregnant with her first child. It was no wonder the poor girl hadn't conceived. Her louse of a husband was spilling his seed on that tart's backside. And let me tell you, this is what comes of marrying a man with too much time on his hands. Secondo was always a man of leisure with only his two *palle* to rub together."

"Mamma! Such language." Lisa chuckled.

"As I said, Rosetta was determined to marry him because of his handsome face and form. The Balbi family always indulged her whims, and this is what comes with poor choices. *Il Diavolo* will always tempt a man with no purpose to his days."

"And did Signora Balbi herself share this with you?"

"You know very well Signora D'Amico told me all."

Lisa shook her head. "That poor girl. I hope her husband has truly reformed."

"Signora Balbi made certain of his reformation—she hired a *devoted* companion for Secondo. A big brute of a man who keeps a watchful eye on the golden-haired Adonis and his golden *palle*."

Lisa threw her head back and laughed. Her mother's sense of humor never failed to lift her spirits.

Anna, her nursemaid, jumped up and ran to separate Bartolomeo and Piero, who were fighting over the ball. Her mother leaned forward and whispered, "It is fortunate Anna is homely, or we might have had the same problems as the Balbi family."

"*Roba da matti.*" Lisa pursed her fingers, shaking them at such an outrageous notion. "Anna is a good and kind-hearted girl. Besides, Francesco would never bring scandal to his family's name."

"I'm sure you are right, but it is better not to tempt fate." Once again, her mother made the sign of the *cornetto* to ward off the *malocchio*.

Lisa sighed, her attention returning to her embroidery. Her thread had run out. She sorted through her bag and searched for the matching rust-colored skein. "Mamma, I need to go inside and see if I have more of this thread color." She held up her needle, where a short piece dangled. "*Per favore,* keep a close eye on the children."

Lucrezia flicked her wrist. "*Madonna mia!* After raising seven children, do you think I need lessons in childrearing?"

Lisa kissed her cheek. "You are a loving mother and a devoted grandmother." Taking her tambour, she swept across the lawn and into the house. Alone in her *salone,* she picked through her skeins of silk thread until she found a close match to the color she'd been embroidering with. Walking to the window, she scrutinized it in the light. The cinnamon color reminded her of the wings of the turtledoves she'd set free. It also reminded her of the painter.

Her lips curved into a smile as she recalled their encounter and pleasant conversation. It surprised her how engaging he was. She'd immediately known it was Leonardo da Vinci. Everyone in Florence knew of the great Maestro. She had thought of introducing herself to him during their exchange at the birdseller's stall, although she changed her mind. *Nor did he seek to find out your name.*

Her mother's story of the Balbi family flashed through her mind, but she pushed it away. *There is nothing wrong with an enjoyable and enlightening conversation between a man and a woman. Where is the harm in that?*

Lisa had never been unfaithful to Francesco, no matter how her feelings toward her husband had changed. Besides, she had heard rumors about the Maestro over the years that he preferred the company of men. *It is no concern of mine what people do in the privacy of their bed chambers, provided they do not hurt anyone.*

"Bah, it makes no difference," she said aloud. It was unlikely they would meet again. In any case, if they did, the maestro would probably not remember her. She returned to the garden, the cinnamon-colored thread held tightly in her hand.

CHAPTER 6

APRIL 7, 1926 ~ FLORENCE, ITALY

The pain was unbearable.

"Short breaths and push. Don't stop, *ragazza*. The child will soon be here."

After twelve hours, Valentina was beyond exhausted. The arduous labor felt as though it would never end. Suor Maria Vittoria wiped her sweaty brow while Beatrice, the midwife, rubbed her distended stomach, urging her to breathe and push harder. She tried her best until another shattering contraction wiped all reason from her mind. She wanted to believe the nun's comforting words that all would be well, but she was frightened and couldn't think beyond the agony that stole her breath and left her soaked in sweat.

"I can see the crown of the baby's head," the midwife encouraged.

A scream erupted from Valentina's throat, so great was the pain she could not keep it in. "I hate you, *bastardo!* May you burn in the fires of hell!" The blasphemous words had escaped her lips before she realized she had uttered them.

Suor Maria Vittoria and Sour Teresa exchanged glances with Beatrice.

"*Boh*, I've heard worse," the midwife said with a shrug.

"Oh, *Dio mio*, forgive me—" Valentina gathered her breath, preparing for the next contraction. "*Benedici questa bambina!*" She prayed her child would not be born with a dark cloud hanging over her because of that demon. And then all thoughts flew from her mind as the scorching pain burned through her again. Her scream reverberated off the walls so loudly it was no doubt heard as far away as the Duomo.

Then, as if God had heard her, she felt a gush of fluid and a relief beyond imagining as the child released itself from the confines of her body into the waiting arms of the midwife.

"Congratulations, you have a daughter," Beatrice announced, taking the newborn to the table in the corner.

"*Brava ragazza.*" Suor Maria Vittoria wiped her forehead. "You did it, my child."

"She doesn't cry. Why doesn't she cry?" Valentina sobbed, trying to sit up.

"Hush, it's all right," Suor Maria Vittoria soothed. "Beatrice knows what to do."

"Everything will be fine," Sour Teresa echoed, handing the older nun a soapy wet cloth to wash Valentina.

Valentina watched as the midwife held the babe upside down and gave her a good whack on her bottom. A moment later, a wail echoed around the room.

"*Grazie, Dio.*" Valentina closed her eyes and relaxed as the nuns changed her sheets while Beatrice bathed the child and wrapped her in a downy blanket. With God and the good nuns' help, she'd given birth to a perfect life. Pride warmed her heart even though she had no loving husband or family to celebrate with.

"She has the face of an angel," Beatrice said as she placed the swaddled infant in her arms. Valentina marveled at the miracle. She remembered something Mona Lisa had written in her correspondence...

In times of darkness, the light of love will always lead the way...

"Chiara..." she said aloud, trying it out on her tongue. "We will name you Chiara. You will always be my light of love." She nuzzled the wispy curls atop her daughter's head. Was there ever a scent more divine than that of a baby?

"She needs to feed. Here, let me help you," said the midwife. She positioned the baby to Valentina's breast, and Chiara wasted no time fastening her lips to the nurturing font of milk.

"Thank you, Beatrice."

"It is my pleasure to do whatever I can for the good nuns of Santa Maria del Carmine," the midwife said. "I'll be back in the morning to check on you." She brushed her knuckles against the baby's cheek. "Be well, little one."

"I'll see Beatrice out and return later to visit you," said Suor Teresa.

Valentina studied her daughter's face as she nursed. The straight brows and pointed chin resembled *him*, yet when the baby opened her eyes, Valentina could see a similarity to hers. Chiara would have hazel eyes rimmed with blue like her. She felt sure of it.

A rush of love filled her, and with that flush of emotion came a torrent of tears. Although she knew Chiara would have a better life in a home with a mother and a father, the thought of giving her baby away and never seeing her again seemed too much to bear. She hated to cry when she should feel grateful and joyous.

Suor Maria Vittoria, who remained at her side, rested her hand on hers. "Why are you crying?"

"I think giving her up will kill me," Valentina said in a broken voice.

The nun's expression turned solemn. Her fingers brushed the dark, downy hair on Chiara's head. The baby had fallen asleep, her lips slightly open. "Do you recall asking me whether I had a love story?"

"Yes, you said you would share it with me one day."

"I think this may be a good time for you to hear it."

"All right."

"First, let me wrap Chiara snuggly and put her next to you."

Valentina reluctantly released the sleeping infant and watched the nun lay Chiara in a small basket on the bed.

Sitting in a chair beside the bed, Suor Maria Vittoria folded her hands in her lap and closed her eyes.

"It was long before the Great War. I was about your age. His name was Alberto, and he was a university student from Bologna visiting Lake Como. I was from a small village nearby, a farming community called Schignano. I worked for an innkeeper in Bellagio. Even in those days, there was a lot of tourism. The beauty of the lake and the mountains drew people from far and wide.

"We could not have been from more different backgrounds. Alberto was an intellectual studying for his professorship. I was *un analfabeta,* uneducated in every way. Who can say what brings two hearts together?" Suor Maria Vittoria beamed a smile like sunshine. "Alberto's friends teased him over how he flirted with me when I brought their meals, and yet nothing they said dissuaded him from the attentiveness he bestowed upon me. Then, one evening, he asked to see me home after work. I was flattered by his attention. He was so handsome and so polite. Never had a young man treated me with such deference. I did not know he had delayed his return to Bologna. I just assumed he was on an extended break from university."

Suor Maria Vittoria breathed out a deep sigh. "Before too long, he declared himself to me. Alberto told me he loved me, which was music to my ears since I, too, was in love with him. We courted for weeks until he finally said he had to return to Bologna. Tearfully, we parted; his promise to return was my only solace. One month, then two months went by with no word from him. I was heartbroken, and then I grew worried and afraid when I realized I was pregnant. I prayed to God for an answer.

"After three months, Alberto returned, and my heart took wing. The love between us was real. When I told him of the child, he was overjoyed. Alberto had so many plans. We would marry, he would finish school, and I would live with his family in Bologna, where his father was a well-respected doctor.

"He talked, and I listened, hardly believing my good fortune. Our passion for each other was something I'd never dreamed of— all-consuming. Nothing on earth could keep us apart.

"He traveled home two weeks later to tell his family about me and our child. He promised to send for me as soon as he made all the arrangements...I never heard from him again."

"My goodness, what happened?"

"Again, weeks went by with no word from my Alberto. The baby grew inside me, and my family, having discovered my transgression, shunned me. I could not blame them. They were ashamed. I was afraid and did not know where to turn. With nowhere else to go and no one to help me, I did the only thing I could do. With my savings, I packed my suitcase and boarded a bus to Bologna. Alberto's last name was Brunotti. I did not think it would be too hard to find a Dottore Brunotti in Bologna, and it wasn't." Suor Maria Vittoria's eyes glistened with tears. She paused to wipe them.

Valentina grabbed her hand and held it in hers. She could only imagine what Suor Maria Vittoria must have felt. "Did you find him?"

The nun shook her head. "It was an accident, you see. One-in-a-million. My beloved Alberto had been killed by a horse-drawn tram on the Piazza Maggiore. I collapsed on the steps of his parents' home when his father told me."

"But they must have helped you?"

"They were grieving. Alberto was their only child. They took me in, but not happily. I think they believed I was the cause of his ruin. I was inconsolable, and the situation was intolerable. Our son came into this world stillborn, and I knew they were relieved. They had no desire to raise a *bastardo*. I named the child Amadeo, love of God." Suor Maria Vittoria wiped away the tears that escaped her eyes.

"As soon as I was well enough, I packed my bag and returned to Schignano. Of course, things were not better there. I knew I could not remain in a place where everyone looked at me as if I were tainted. Besides, everywhere I looked, I saw Alberto, and it tore me to pieces. So, one day, I stood over a map of Italy with a pencil in my hand. I closed my eyes and made an X on the map. When I opened my eyes, I saw that I had left my mark on Florence. I packed my bag and said goodbye to everything I had ever known. Seeking shelter, I arrived here. I have never regretted my decision."

Valentina was in awe of Suor Maria Vittoria's fortitude. Could she find that kind of inner strength? "I am so sorry."

"Don't be. I found peace and an unexpected joy in my life here. I do not regret having loved Alberto. I was fortunate to have loved him and even luckier to have been loved in return. I came to terms with the loss of my child long ago. I feel certain Amadeo is with Alberto, safe in the arms of our Lord."

"Yes, but..."

"I told you this story for a reason, *piccolina*. You, too, will come to terms with your past and discover your path. Chiara will always be a part of you. She is a precious gift, and now you will bestow that gift on a young couple who are not as lucky as you."

"How am I lucky?"

"Because you have brought life into this world. And your sacrifice is a bond of love that will connect you forever." Suor Maria Vittoria caressed Valentina's cheek. "Now you must rest. You will need your strength. Chiara will awaken in a short while and will need her mother's milk."

VALENTINA HAD NEVER FELT this kind of love before. A mother's love. A love that filled her soul to overflowing. With each passing day, Chiara grew plumper, her cheeks rosier, and her disposition sweeter. But even the most well-tempered infant's needs are taxing, especially when she awoke in the middle of the night demanding to be fed. Valentina never complained of the interruption or her stolen sleep. She would simply roll over and scoop up her daughter from the cradle beside her bed, settling her against her breast. She cooed and rained kisses on Chiara's downy head, savoring every precious moment she had with her.

A week after giving birth, Valentina sat in bed gazing down at her beautiful child as she nursed. Although none of the nuns had confided anything about Chiara's adoption, Valentina knew the time must be nearing. She would have given anything to keep her daughter but resigned herself to the impossibility. Her mother would never allow it, and she had no means of support. Valentina would not put her precious child through an uncertain future. She agreed to the adoption for Chiara's sake, though it broke her heart.

The wind bellowed and rattled against the frost-coated window. Tomorrow, Valentina expected to find the garden covered in snow. It was rare for Florence to experience such a late spring snowstorm. Perhaps she would bundle Chiara up and walk in the garden until her plump cheeks grew red as cherries.

She kissed her daughter's brow. "I know you will have a fine life, my love. The world is changing, and it won't be long before women will be given the same opportunities as men." She chuckled to herself. "Although Mona Lisa lived more than four hundred years ago, she shared the same hopes and dreams for her daughters and all women. See how long, *piccolina,* it takes for things to change in the world and become what they should be? But perhaps yours will be the generation to make it happen."

Chiara regarded her child with a curious gaze as she continued to suckle at her breast.

By the end of her feeding, Chiara's eyes were closed, and she slept contentedly while Valentina found herself wide awake. Rather than tossing and turning, she dressed and bundled Chiara up. Valentina lit a candle and made her way to the library with her baby nestled in a basket. Her time at the convent was running out, and she wanted to transcribe as many of Leonardo's letters as she could in the days left.

Valentina had promised Suor Maria Vittoria, and even though she was not a nun, she took her pledge seriously. She would not let her friend down. She knew how important the transcripts were for posterity. Despite the care the nuns took, the letters had faded to such an extent over the centuries that the words might completely vanish one day, and so would the truth about Leonardo da Vinci and Lisa del Giocondo.

As Chiara slept in her basket on the desk, Valentina slipped on the white gloves and took out the mirror, magnifying glass, pencil, and paper. The writing was small and difficult to read, and Valentina had to proceed slowly. But she didn't mind, having become so profoundly enthralled with their story.

It pained her to know she would not be able to finish and never discover the full extent of Leonardo and Lisa's relationship. The story of the artist and muse would have to wait for Suor Maria Vittoria's successor. Hopefully, a worthy nun would continue the sacred duty of keeping the letters safe and take on the time-consuming task of completing the deciphering. Valentina would be sure to leave a note with detailed instructions for whoever the next caretaker would be.

If only I could keep Chiara with me, raise her here in this peaceful place, with the good sisters to watch over us. But it was not to be. Her brother, Rodolfo, had sent a letter informing her that Giulia had forgiven her and would welcome her home.

Mamma has grand plans for the family, he wrote.

Valentina had no idea what that meant. *I can barely think past today, let alone the future.* But what choice did she have? Her lot in life was cast. She must go home.

Home. Where is that? It was no longer Fiesole. Not in her heart. Not since her father's death. Not since *him...* Valentina gazed down at her beautiful baby and wiped the tears from her eyes.

CHAPTER 7

APRIL 7, 1503 ~ FLORENCE, ITALY

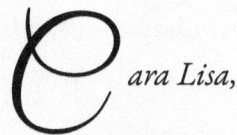 *ara Lisa,*

> *Who could imagine that I would see you again so soon*
> *after that first encounter? Do you remember our conversation*
> *at the Great Hall? I watched you approach, your beauty lit by*
> *the glow of a thousand candles...*

"She is the most beautiful woman in Florence and the most attentive and faithful wife a man could wish for."

Leonardo listened half-heartedly to the merchant boasting about his wife. The man had cornered him as soon as he entered the Great Hall, and Leonardo found himself unable to escape. The effusive cloth merchant blathered on about his credentials and even mentioned the Medici, bragging they were his best customers. Even after all these years and his memorable achievements, Leonardo's pride stung when he heard that name.

Lorenzo Medici, considered one of the greatest art patrons in Europe, had never commissioned a painting from Leonardo. Neither had his son Piero, for that matter. The last Medici who had ruled Florence as gonfaloniere, Piero, had been ousted as a traitor for capitulating to the demands of the French King Charles VIII.

After that, Florence had been plunged into four years of oppressive rule under the friar Savonarola, who'd usurped power and rained hell upon the city. The fanatical monk had practically dragged Florence back to the Dark Ages.

Leonardo had been living in Milan during Savonarola's reign of terror. But he'd wept when he'd learned of the religious zealot's atrocities in what became known as the *falò delle vanità*, the bonfire of the vanities. Everything of beauty, including thousands of paintings and manuscripts, had been burned in the public square.

Even now, Florentines were reluctant to return to the extravagant displays of opulence that had constituted a way of life before the tyrannical friar's domination.

Men such as Savonarola always meet their just ends. The friar was hanged and burned at the stake in the Piazza della Signoria, no less. Even so, the evil lurking in the hearts and minds of men like Savonarola never went away. It merely found a new host in which to thrive. Leonardo shuddered and pushed aside his ruminations. He did not want to dwell on those dark times, not tonight.

His attention returned to the glittering surroundings. The banquet, hosted by Florence's current gonfaloniere, Piero Soderini, was a feast for the senses. A hundred blazing torches cast a golden glow over the guests. Dressed in brightly colored silk and velvet gowns, the attendees mingled in small groups or danced to the melodic madrigals played on viola da gamba, cornetti, and harp.

Leonardo's stomach growled with longing as he surveyed the sumptuous feast displayed on elegant silk-draped tables. Yet here he was, saddled with this verbose man.

"I do not mean to be rude, good sir, but I must indulge my hunger." Leonardo glided through the crowd, hoping the man might become otherwise engaged. Alas, the merchant stuck to him like gesso to a wall.

Leonardo chose an assortment of vegetable antipasti, artichokes, and eggplant glistening with olive oil. He added a serving of bruschetta adorned with chopped tomatoes, basil, and garlic to his plate. Meanwhile, Francesco piled his plate high with the remains of the once-living until there was no room for anything else.

Leonardo, a fastidious eater, delicately bit into an artichoke. He tried not to look at the merchant, making loud smacking noises, skewering bloody beef cubes, and popping them into his mouth as gleefully as a child might gobble up a plate of sugar-coated almonds. Leonardo's stomach lurched and threatened upheaval, and he tried to shift his attention to far more pleasant visual diversions.

How strange that he suffered no aversion to dissecting a dead animal, or a man for that matter, yet watching people gorge themselves on meat repulsed him. When exploring his interest in anatomy, he somehow separated himself from what others considered a grotesque task. Perhaps he endured the unpleasantness because his purpose was of a higher order.

Nevertheless, he would have to ponder this curious notion further.

"I see you take no meat on your plate," Francesco said, interrupting Leonardo's musings.

"No, I do not consume meat or anything that once possessed a beating heart."

"Ah, you are like my wife. She also refrains from eating meat," he added between bites of a prosciutto-wrapped asparagus stalk.

Leonardo's curiosity was roused. *What are the odds of my encountering a mysterious woman in the Mercato Vecchio who does not eat meat, and within a few days, I meet this man who is married to a woman of the same sensibility?* Leonardo scrutinized the boastful merchant, whose graying hair and paunch made him appear much older. The degradation of the human body was another area he often pondered. It was why he strove to keep his muscular tonality by adhering to a strict regimen of walking and sensible eating.

"Maestro, you share much in common with my Lisa. I am certain that painting her will be an enlightening experience for you."

He clearly admires his wife, and no doubt wishes to please her. Perhaps he was judging this meat-eating merchant too harshly.

"I've heard about the beautiful paintings you created for Ludovico Sforza." The merchant leaned forward, the fatty glaze from roasted gristle glistening on his lips, as he said in a sly tone, "People say the portrait you painted of his mistress with the white ermine is *incomparabile*. Can you imagine a whore rising to the station of marchioness?"

On second thought, Leonardo's first impression of the merchant had been too kind. *This man is a crass buffone.* Sforza's former mistress, Cecilia Gallerani, was a dear friend. Hearing her name besmirched was most distressing. In his opinion, all women would do well to emulate the musically talented songstress who'd captured the heart of the powerful duke. So ardent was Sforza's regard that he'd seen Cecilia suitably married when their affair ended.

"I promise you, Sforza's mistress does not compare with my Lisa," Francesco added with a wink. "My wife is *bellissima* and without blemish."

"I have many commissions to see to at this time," Leonardo lied. He would rather not engage with such a man. He was inclined to find a large commission that would give him much-needed funds and the notoriety to further his career. No matter how beautiful, a portrait of an unknown lady would do neither.

Leonardo shifted his gaze elsewhere, hoping to catch a glimpse of a friend or acquaintance he could use as an excuse to walk away from the merchant. He paused his perusal of the Salone dei Cinquecento, noting the two massive walls opposite each other were still without adornment. He recalled a rumor that Gonfaloniere Soderini and the Signoria of the Chancery might commission two grand-scale murals for the walls in the great hall. Such a monumental project would bring glory to Florence and to the artist who created it. *Now, this is an undertaking worthy of my skills.* He needed to speak to the gonfaloniere.

"Maestro, of course, I am more than willing to wait however long until you are free," Francesco said, laying his oily fingers on Leonardo's sleeve. "I want to stress that I will pay whatever you ask, within reason."

Leonardo suppressed a grimace, knowing he'd have to pay his washerwoman double to remove the greasy stains. Discomfort aside, the merchant's mention of an open-to-negotiation asking price piqued his interest. *Money and patrons are the bane of artists. Both are as elusive as the Holy Grail and as demanding as a spoiled child.*

"I will think about it." With so many people dependent on him—apprentices and assistants—Leonardo always needed funds. He could not toss the promise of a fat purse out the window, no matter how ill-mannered the patron. It was far better to be diplomatic and keep the man's hopes up with the possibility his offer might be acceptable in the future. He would contact the merchant and name his price if nothing else came along. It was precisely what he did with many wealthy patrons, including the Marchioness Isabella d'Este, who had sent her representative here to Florence in pursuit of a portrait of her. Saying no would be an absolute rejection, and Leonardo avoided this path as much as possible.

Leonardo opened his mouth to form a suitable reply, but observing the muscles in Francesco's face transpose into a besotted smile made him hesitate.

"Ah, my bride approaches," the merchant said, his eyes dancing with delight. "Maestro, allow me to introduce you to my Lisa."

Leonardo turned, and a gasp escaped him.

Walking toward them with a serenity and composure that left him in awe was the *liberatrice* of the turtledoves. The woman whose smile he could not forget. She gave no sign of recognition, which caused him to finger his beard since speech seemed beyond him. She met his gaze with polite curiosity.

Had she struck him and left a purple bruise on his cheek, his pain would have been no less. Although he liked to think of himself as a man without ego, in truth, he could be as vain as a peacock.

"Lisa, my angel, *vi presento* the greatest artist in Florence, and may I dare say, all of the Italian peninsula, Leonardo da Vinci."

Lisa offered her hand, and Leonardo brought it to his lips, his gaze never leaving hers. *"Piacere di conoscervi, Signora.* Your husband has told me of your great virtue and rare beauty."

"Vi ringrazio," she replied in that mellifluous voice. "I hope you did not wear the Maestro's ears off, Francesco." Her charming reprimand drew laughter from both men.

"It is extremely difficult for me not to proclaim my ebullience over my good fortune of having a wife and mother to our children as selfless and amiable as you, *tesoro.*"

Leonardo kept his eyes on the face that had haunted him from the first moment he saw her in the market square. Up to this moment, he hoped he would cross paths with her again—and had even returned to the birdseller's stall on the off chance he might run into her. Disappointed at not meeting her again, he'd begun to sketch her face that had been etched so indelibly in his mind.

As he studied her now, dressed sumptuously in an elegant gown that displayed her décolletage so attractively, he noticed details about her that had escaped him that first time. Her hair shone like the color of leaves in autumn, and the way it cascaded in feathery ringlets to her shoulders tempted him to reach out and wrap a curl around his finger.

"Francesco," a man across the room called out, waving his hand. Francesco waved back. "You will excuse me, *cara mia.* An important customer wishes to speak to me."

"Go, my dear husband. Maestro da Vinci will keep me company."

Francesco turned to Leonardo. "Maestro, it has been a great honor, and I hope we can continue our conversation soon." With a final smile at his wife, he disappeared into the throng of guests.

Alone with the regal beauty, Leonardo found himself tongue-tied, something he was unused to. Usually, he was witty and prolific with words. His biting humor, when among friends, was often called upon to compose riddles and clever fables. *Say something, or she will think you a fool.*

Thus far, Lisa had yet to reference having met him in the market, so perhaps she did not remember. At last, the awkward silence awakened his words. "Your husband would like me to paint your portrait."

"And how did you respond?"

"I told him I was engaged in many projects."

"Then I suppose I must accept that Maestro da Vinci does not desire to paint me." Lisa's dark eyes glittered with amusement.

"You misread me."

"How so?"

"I must confess, painting yet another portrait did not spark my imagination. But perhaps I should reconsider."

"And why would you do that, Maestro?"

"*La prego,* call me Leonardo. I have a feeling that yours would not be an ordinary portrait."

"Leonardo," she said, and for some reason, it sounded like an endearment. "I am but a mother and wife," she continued. "There is nothing grand about me. I am who you see before you. Surely, there are more imposing and illustrious patrons who vie for your talents."

"Although I told your husband otherwise, at the moment, there are none." For some reason, diplomacy flew out the window, and he spoke the truth. "What you consider ordinary, I consider extraordinary. There is an elusive quality in your eyes that begs the question—"

"A question? And what question is that?"

"Is what I see who you really are?"

"Tell me, Maestro, did you return to the birdseller since our meeting in the marketplace?" she replied, dancing around his question.

She remembers.

"I have not returned to the market." His first lie to her. He could not tell her he had returned to the bird merchant several times to seek her out. What would she think of him? "But I am pleased you remember our encounter."

"Of course, I remember. I have not reached the age of forgetfulness yet."

"No," he said with a chuckle, "you are in the full bloom of womanhood. A recent mother, I imagine."

The light of a thousand candles lit her eyes. "I am recently delivered of a healthy boy. Our fourth son. Francesco is beyond joyous over the birth. As for me, my pleasure is as great to have my daughter, Camilla..." Her voice faltered, and a shadow crossed her face, and he sensed a pain she was trying to hide.

"I imagine your husband looks forward to passing his knowledge to his sons."

"I intend to enlighten the minds of my daughters as well as my sons," she countered, her voice steady once more. "My father believed in educating all of his children."

"From my studies, I find no physical reason for a woman to hold less intellectual capacity than a man."

Lisa's laughter was hypnotic, rising and falling like water

gliding over pebbles in a brook. "Does that surprise you?" she asked.

"Society's commonly held notions rarely surprise me, whether based on fact or conjecture."

"I shall look forward to our next encounter should you decide to take the commission of painting my portrait. It will provide another opportunity to continue our lively conversation. I hope you will not tire of my questions or my curiosity."

"Questioning our universe sets us apart from all other beasts. I question everything and my curiosity shows no end."

"Humankind is also set apart by its compulsion to wage war."

Leonardo frowned, remembering the horrors he had witnessed in the service of the *diavolo*, Cesare Borgia. The death and destruction wrought by the weaponry he'd designed weighed heavily upon his conscience. "War is something I pray you will never lay your eyes upon. I have seen enough to last ten lifetimes."

"I cannot imagine the horror," Lisa said softly. "You must forgive yourself for any part you played in Borgia's conquests," she said, seeming to read his very thoughts." She brushed his hand with her fingertips. "But I have taken up far too much of your time. You must mingle with the other guests."

"Time I would not care to spend in any other way. I will speak to your husband and determine a day that suits you to begin the preliminary sketches for the painting."

"So, you have decided to paint me."

Leonardo wondered at the miracle of intricate facial muscles that conspired to create her smile—a smile that was not quite a smile. "You demonstrate the antithesis of my theory that emotions require movement of the muscles of the face. In your face, less movement conveys more hidden emotions. I see a sleight of hand, a deception of what lies beneath a most pleasing façade. You have awakened my curiosity and engaged me. I must paint you."

With his mind made up, his impatience to begin took hold. Once ignited, the flame of creativity smoldered within him. Eager to start, he suddenly blurted, "May I come tomorrow? Is there a time and place where we can work undisturbed?"

Lisa opened her mouth to reply, only to close it as Francesco returned, his arm encircling her waist and his lips pressing against her temple. "My apologies for abandoning you for so long, *tesoro*. I hope you have not prevailed too much on the Maestro's time."

"I believe Maestro da Vinci is quite capable of managing his own time." She jutted her chin in his direction, her dark eyes flashing. "Excuse me, *gentiluomini*, I will leave you to the more important discussions of men."

Leonardo bowed, his lips twitching in amusement at Lisa's response. *The candle does burn hot.*

CHAPTER 8

APRIL 30, 1926 ~ FLORENCE, ITALY

Suor Maria Vittoria shivered as she stood beneath the bare branches of a lemon tree, watching Valentina and Chiara in the garden, relieved they were bundled up against the cold.

"*Tesorina*, it does not matter that you were not born of love," the girl said, cuddling the babe to her chest, her eyes full of tears. "What matters is that you *are* loved." Chiara peered at her mother as she nursed, her eyes curious as if pondering what Valentina said.

Suor Maria Vittoria's heart ached for the young mother. The dear girl had not yet confided in her about the circumstances of her pregnancy. Suor Maria Vittoria had her suspicions but hadn't pressed. Today would be hard enough for Valentina. There was no point in causing her even more pain. She understood loss all too well. What she wanted more than anything was to help the girl heal and embrace the life ahead of her.

Suor Maria Vittoria cleared her throat, and Valentina glanced up, wiping away the wetness on her cheeks with her sleeve.

"Suor Teresa and I have been looking everywhere for you. Are you all right, *figlia mia?*"

"Yes, I'm just trying to hold onto every precious second with Chiara...trying to memorize her features...trying to—" Valentina's voice broke, and her gaze dropped to her daughter's face. "She is such a perfect baby, so easy..."

Suor Maria Vittoria filled the pause. "Padre D'Angelo told our mother abbess such wonderful things about Benjamin and Gabriella Chiarelli. You know they are Jewish and live in the old ghetto in Rome. They own a bookstore, so Chiara is bound to be well educated and given every advantage."

"Yes, they are good people. It's just that..."

"What is it, my child?"

"It doesn't matter to me that they are Jewish. But what about a blessing...?" Valentina murmured, gazing down at Chiara.

"Do you mean a baptism?"

Valentina nodded. "Would it be permissible even though she will be raised Jewish?"

"I do not think God will mind."

"But how?"

"We can baptize her before the couple arrives. They need not know."

"But don't we need a priest for that?"

"No. Anyone can do it as long as it is done properly."

"Can you perform the baptism and keep it our secret?"

"*Certo.* Of course." She would do anything to bring peace of mind to the girl who had become like a daughter to her.

Suor Teresa approached at a run. "You found her, Sorella," she said, catching her breath.

"Yes, we were just discussing an important matter."

Valentina reached for Suor Teresa's hand. "Suor Maria Vittoria is going to baptize Chiara. Will you be her godmother? And promise to protect her?"

"This is wonderful news; I would be honored."

"Run to the church, little Sorella, and bring back a cup of Holy water. Meet us in the library." Suor Maria Vittoria pressed her index finger to her lips.

"Yes, Sister." Grinning, the young nun lifted her habit and took off once more.

"Bless that girl for her long legs," Suor Maria Vittoria said.

The other nuns of the convent rarely visited the library. It was a perfect place for private contemplation and an ideal place for a secret ceremony.

Valentina sat in a chair holding Chiara. Suor Maria Vittoria asked Valentina a few questions. Then she recited the prayer, "I baptize you in the name of the Father and of the Son and of the Holy Spirit. Amen." She poured the cup of water over Chiara's head. The baby's eyes widened, and a cry of protest escaped her lips.

"*Mi dispiace, tesorina.*" Valentina caressed Chiara's face and comforted her with endearments. "Hush, my angel. Hopefully, nothing worse than this will bring you tears in life."

Valentina imagined the Jewish couple felt like a fish out of water in a convent surrounded by crucifixes and nuns. Benjamin, who must have been well over six feet, wore wire-rimmed glasses and held tightly to his wife's hand. His thick, curly brown hair was neatly brushed, and his genial smile reached his kind brown eyes. Gabriella was pretty and petite, with thick black hair woven in a tidy braid nearly touching her waist. She was smiling, yet Valentina could see the nervousness in her green eyes.

Their gazes dropped to the basket she held, and despite her sorrow, her heart was touched by the hopeful joy on their faces. Valentina glanced up at Mother Superior Busnelli standing beside the young priest, Padre D'Angelo, who'd accompanied the couple from Rome. The abbess nodded and gave her a smile of encouragement.

"Would you like to meet her?" Valentina asked Gabriella.

Gabriella's smile widened, and she took a few steps forward. "Thank you," she replied in a soft voice.

Valentina set the basket on the desk and lifted Chiara from her nest of blankets.

"She's the most beautiful baby I have ever seen," Gabriella said. She looked at her husband and burst into tears.

Benjamin wrapped his arm around his wife's shaking shoulders as she buried her face in the crook of his neck. "Forgive us," he said to Valentina, "we are both so overcome with happiness. It has been a long road to get here."

Valentina nodded, biting her trembling lip, and blinking back her own tears as she cuddled her sleeping daughter for the last time.

The young man's eyes teared up as he looked at the baby. "I vow to you that she will be blessed with every ounce of our love," he said thickly, his Adam's apple bobbing up and down.

"T-thank you," Valentina managed to say.

"May I hold her?" asked Gabriella as she dried her eyes with a handkerchief.

Valentina hesitated; she'd prepared herself for this moment more than a hundred times, yet the pain was almost more than she could bear. Taking a deep breath, her lips trembled as she tried to smile at the young woman. "Yes, of course." She pressed her lips against her daughter's downy-soft forehead and breathed in her sweet baby scent for the last time. *Goodbye, my angel. You are the light of my life. I will never forget you.*

Valentina placed Chiara in the waiting arms of her new mother and stepped back, clasping her hands to keep them from shaking.

Gabriella gazed at Chiara with a look of pure adoration. "I am so happy to meet you, little one. I promise to love and care for you for the rest of my life."

Benjamin caressed his new daughter's cheek. "My beautiful child, I will devote my life to protecting you and keeping you safe."

Valentina did her best to restrain her tears. She'd promised herself she wouldn't cry. It would only make things harder for everyone. "I know you and Benjamin will be the best parents." She sucked in her breath. "I named her Chiara. I-I know you may want to change it, and it's fine with me."

Gabriella nodded. "Thank you for this precious child. We will love and cherish her forever."

Valentina's heart swelled. *I made the right decision...Chiara will have a good life. She will be loved.* "T-thank you for loving her. I-I w-wish you all the best—" Valentina could say no more. Her hand flew to her mouth to hold back her sobs as she ran from the room. She didn't want to tarnish their joy with her sorrow.

Handing over Chiara was the hardest thing she'd ever done. To witness the young couple leave with Chiara in their arms would be unbearable.

She is no longer mine...

Tears streamed down her face as she ran to her room. The physical pain of giving birth was nothing compared to the heart-wrenching agony of knowing she would never see her daughter grow up. Never kiss her scraped knee when she fell off her bicycle. Never read bedtime stories to her. Never teach her how to sew. A lifetime of 'nevers' awaited her. And worst of all, Chiara would never know how much Valentina loved her.

That evening, Valentina sat in bed, staring at a photograph of Chiara, taken by a local photographer as a gift from Suor Teresa and Suor Maria Vittoria. It was all she had to remember her precious child. She expelled a shaky breath, knowing she should get up, wash her face, and change. Her dress was wet from tears and the wasted milk from her aching breasts. Suor Maria Vittoria had told her it could take weeks for the milk to dry up. For Valentina, it would be a constant reminder of her loss.

She kissed the photo and tucked it into her bible on her nightstand. Walking to the washstand, she poured fresh water into the basin, dipped a clean cloth, and washed herself. Removing her damp dress, she retrieved the brown shift from the armoire, the dress she'd worn on that stormy night when she arrived at the convent. Slipping it on, she noticed it hung loosely on her slender frame. She would have to alter it along with her other clothes. With Chiara's adoption, Valentina's time at the convent would soon come to an end. The thought of returning to her family in Fiesole filled her with misery. It seemed as if life presented her with nothing but sad endings.

A gentle rap sounded on the door.

"Come in," she answered as she draped the damp dress over a chair to dry.

Suor Maria Vittoria entered, carrying a tray.

"You didn't come to the dining room for dinner, so I brought you some soup."

"Thank you, but I'm not hungry."

"You need to eat, my child."

Valentina sighed. "Very well, I will eat to make you happy, dear Sister." Valentina walked to the bed and sat. "But please sit with me."

The nun set the tray on the bed and sat beside her.

Valentina lifted a spoonful of the *pasta e ceci* soup and tasted it. "It's delicious." The chickpeas were tender, and the tomato broth was exquisitely seasoned.

"Suor Elena is the best cook in the world."

Valentina couldn't help but smile at Suor Maria Vittoria's oft-repeated praise of the nun who prepared all the food at the convent. "Yes, she is."

The nun reached for Valentina's hand after she finished eating. "Whatever happened, you are not to blame. Remember that always."

Valentina looked up, knowing what the older woman meant.

She had avoided telling Suor Maria Vittoria about how she came to be with child. She could not speak of it—not while she carried the baby in her womb and certainly not when she held her beautiful child in her arms. But now, with Chiara gone, she could finally unburden herself. "The memory of it haunts my dreams," she whispered. "But I need to tell you before I return home."

"Of course, my child." Suor Maria Vittoria smoothed back the errant strands of Valentina's hair.

"He's from Fiesole—the father." A bitter laugh escaped her. "It is strange to call him that, for he is everything contrary to what a father should be." Valentina gripped the napkin, letting her mind return to that fateful day. "He is a few years older, someone I knew from school. His father is an engineer and a member of the fascist party. His mother comes from a well-to-do family in Torino that owns a textile mill. They have money and are proud fascists."

Valentina could not meet the kind nun's eyes. The only way she could continue was to look out the window. "I never paid this young man any mind; however, all the other girls at school vied for his attention. He was handsome but prone to boasting one day and brooding the next.

"With no encouragement from me, he asked me to attend a dance with him. I politely refused, suggesting he should ask one of the many other girls competing for his notice. He shrugged and said any girl in Fiesole would be thrilled to accept his invitation. I heard he asked another girl, and I thought nothing more of it. But then, a few days after the dance, he started following me home with his *banda* of friends. I ignored their catcalls and whistles, hoping they would grow tired of the game and move on to other diversions..."

She paused and closed her eyes. If only she could shutter the memories, but her mind would not let her forget how she fell to the mercy of a man who had no mercy to give.

"I volunteered every Friday at our parish church—" she rasped, her throat constricting as though someone's hands were pressed tightly around her neck.

Suor Maria Vittoria poured her a glass of water from the pitcher on the nightstand.

Valentina gulped a few sips, easing her raw throat. "I took a longer way home. It was such a lovely day..."

The gentle breeze was awash with the scent of lemons ripening on the trees. Valentina walked along an old country road that cut through fields and skirted wooded thickets of olive, pine, and cypress. At times, a clearing in the trees revealed the golden glow of the Duomo. As the sun sank low in the sky, the woods came alive with the singing of nightingales.

She saw and heard only the peacefulness of the world around her as she walked. Seemingly, he appeared beside her out of nowhere— the young man who'd pestered her with his friends for weeks. Had he been following her? Had he been lurking among the trees? She had no idea, but a chill skittered up her spine, and she became wary.

He was excessively polite, remarking at the coincidence of them taking the same way home at the same time. She did not know what to do. Should she break into a run? Turn and go the other way? Ask him to leave her alone?

She decided to keep walking. Perhaps if she remained silent, he would become bored and go off in search of his friends. They continued in silence for a few minutes, and she wondered if her initial anxiety had been an overreaction. As they approached a fork in the road, he cleared his throat and apologized for teasing her those weeks since the dance.

Valentina glanced at his face to see if he was sincere. His smile seemed genuine, so she thanked him for his apology and offered him her friendship. His smile widened, and he asked for a kiss.

She politely declined and told him only her future husband would have that right.

His smile froze, and he stared at her. In the blink of an eye, his demeanor transformed from friendly to menacing.

The fine hairs on the back of her neck stood on end, and Valentina began to back away from the force of that stare. Just as she turned to run, he grabbed her and pulled her hard against him, grinding against her backside as his hand snaked under her dress and tore at her underwear.

Valentina opened her mouth to scream, but it came out as a gurgle as his other hand wrapped around her neck and pressed against her windpipe. Terror. Pure abject terror coursed through her, and she began to pray.

Ave Maria, piena di grazia, il Signore è con te...

He let go of her neck and spun her about to face him. She gasped, dragging air into her lungs before he pulled her tightly against him.

Valentina remembered something her brother Rodolfo had told her about a man's foot being the most vulnerable part of his body if one knows where to step. With a strength borne from desperation, she lifted her heel and stomped onto the top of his fine leather shoe. He stumbled back with a howl of pain, allowing her to escape.

She broke into a run.

Santa Maria, Madre di Dio, prega per noi...

A roar reached her ears, and she ran as fast as her legs would carry her.

She knew he was behind her, running after her. His vile curses echoed through the woods. But she didn't dare look back.

She kept on running.

Her heart thundered in her ears, and she sensed him gaining on her and then felt his heavy, hot breath on the back of her neck.

His hand grabbed the back of her blouse, and she felt it rip as his weight toppled them both to the ground. He wrenched her arms over her head and pried her legs apart with his knee.

Valentina fought with every ounce of strength she possessed, which only made him laugh.

He took everything from her...

Valentina covered her face with her hands, and her shoulders shook with sobs as she recalled his words, repeated over and over like a twisted mantra: *"You will never forget me. You will never forget me..."*

Suor Maria Vittoria embraced her, the nun's gentle words a soothing balm, "Unburden yourself, my child. I am here. I am here."

Valentina buried her face in Suor Maria Vittoria's shoulder, unable to hold back. The pain poured out in a deluge of tears.

When the dam had emptied, Valentina raised her face and finally met Suor Maria Vittoria's eyes. Kindness and compassion shone from them.

"I—I must tell you one more thing, for it continues to haunt me," Valentina said.

Suor Maria Vittoria gave her hand a gentle squeeze.

"After he—" Valentina took a deep breath. "H-he helped me up and kissed my cheek. Then he smiled and told me he loved me." She shuddered at the memory. "Did he think it would erase what he had done? That I would forgive him? How could he say such a thing after committing such a vile act?"

"There are people in this world incapable of remorse," Suor Maria Vittoria said.

"Please tell me, Sorella, for I have prayed and pondered this for over nine months. How could God allow this to happen?"

Suor Maria Vittoria heaved a deep sigh. "God cannot control the evil of men," she said, wrapping a blanket around Valentina's shoulders. "But in my heart, I believe God has blessed you with Chiara."

"When I realized I was pregnant, my only care was for the life growing inside me."

"Chiara will never know of the circumstances of her conception," the nun said. "She will be raised in a loving home, which is a blessing."

Valentina held the blanket around her. "It is for the best," she said, knowing she would have to be strong despite the aching hollow in her heart. "But whatever happens, *he* must never know of the child. I would do anything to protect my daughter."

CHAPTER 9

*ara Lisa,*

When I began your portrait, I never envisioned what I would discover about you or about myself. Now I cannot imagine my world without you in it...

Leonardo stood back from his easel and crossed his arms over his chest. His sketchbook was ready, and his chalk lay on the table. He'd placed a poplar wood panel cut from the center of a tree trunk on the easel. The wood gleamed from the thick coat of white that he'd heated and extracted from lead and mixed with linseed oil.

His years of painting had taught him that a white undercoat absorbed and reflected light, giving the skin and eyes a natural

89

radiance. Anxious to begin, he contemplated the paint colors he would mix. He imagined the translucent layers of oil paint he would delicately apply, glazing layer upon layer, building up depth, contour, and shadow.

In Lisa's portrait, he would bring all his mastery to bear and breathe life into it, but would he be able to imbue her inner essence onto the canvas?

As he waited in the cozy sitting room, he studied his surroundings. The *salone* was an intimate room off the *piano nobile*. On the wall hung an elegant tapestry depicting a boar hunt; the image of a unicorn woven on each side conveyed a symbol of purity. At the other end of the room, two heavily carved oak *sedia* chairs faced a large stone fireplace. Between the chairs was a table inlaid with a geometric marquetry pattern. A Venetian cobalt glass vase filled with fresh roses sat atop the table. Leonardo inhaled the sweet scent from the rose garden beyond the open glass doors. The tasteful room displayed a skilled eye for balance and symmetry, and Leonardo sensed Lisa's hand in every choice. Leonardo could not fault Francesco for effusing over his wife. He was a lucky man indeed.

Leonardo glanced at the spring-winding clock on the mantle. Lisa was late for the sitting. Even so, mothers were often distracted, and her children no doubt commanded much of her time. There was so much about her he didn't know, so much he wanted to learn.

He was nervous about seeing her again, making him impatient to begin. Perhaps he'd been premature in setting up the easel and wood panel. This commission was not one he wanted to rush to completion. If anything, he wished to draw it out as long as he could, the more time to indulge his growing fascination with the silk merchant's wife. It was why he'd refused to take a down payment. He wanted no pressure on him to finish by a specific time. He took down the easel and stuffed it into his satchel. There would be plenty to do before the painting began.

The door opened, and the lady herself swept into the room. The smile she gave him matched that of his memory and spoke of expectation and mystery. It was the smile he intended to paint. Her modest day gown of green silk velvet was without decoration or adornment. Unlike other courtly women who'd posed for him in their richly embroidered gowns, Lisa needed no embellishment. In any case, what she wore did not matter as the finished portrait would depict a gown of his imagination.

Leonardo's head filled with the fragrance of aqua vita as Lisa approached. Her eyes shone, he hoped, from pleasure at seeing him, for he felt great pleasure at seeing her. Her smile captivated him as surely as if she'd wrapped a silken cord around him and pulled him toward her.

She took his hand in hers. "Maestro, I apologize for keeping you waiting, but the children always require something." She glanced around the room. "I am both nervous and excited about our appointment. Will this room suffice for your needs?"

"The room is suitable, but I wonder if you would allow me to sketch you outside after we finish indoors. Perhaps we can take a walk on such a *bella giornata*."

"That sounds lovely. I hope we do not set the gossipmongers' tongues wagging." The teasing in her words bespoke a sense of humor and, at the same time, showed she cared not in the least what anyone said about her. *Such is her confidence and irrepressible spirit.*

He chuckled. "A young woman and an elderly man shouldn't provoke too much scandal."

"You do yourself a disservice, Maestro. You appear as fit and spry as any man I know."

"Ah, I wish it were so. I am a far cry from the man I once was."

She shook her head and opened her mouth as if to chastise him and then, perhaps rethinking, fell silent. "Where do you prefer I sit?"

Leonardo pulled one of the chairs closer to the window. "Please, Signora."

Lisa arranged herself in the chair, and he stood back, mesmerized by how the light fell onto her face and how it imbued her skin with color. *Burnt umber.* It was a color he usually applied in moderation, but for Lisa's portrait, perhaps not. Hers was not the face of a pale-skinned swan. Her palette would require dark earthen shades to better reflect her unusual beauty.

Leaning forward, his face inches from hers, he adjusted the chair's angle. He regarded the curvature of her lips and the way her eyes studied him. He tilted her chin, the smoothness of her skin an anticipated pleasure. His fingers lingered, perhaps a moment too long, for she looked down demurely, and he reluctantly withdrew his fingers from her face.

He took her hands in his and placed them on the arms of the chair. Standing back, he asked, "Are you comfortable enough to hold this pose?"

"Yes, I am perfectly comfortable."

He pulled the other chair over and sat across from her. Picking up his chalk and pad, he began to draw. They spoke little while he sketched, a refreshing change as most subjects tended to chatter on and on. Lisa seemed to understand his need to concentrate and sat in quiet repose as she stared out the window. The silence stretched out before them, and as he worked, the expression of contentment on her face never wavered, and he wondered where her thoughts took her. When she finally broke the silence, it was so unexpected he nearly dropped his chalk.

"Do you ever wonder, Leonardo, why the sky is blue? And why do the shades of blue vary? I believe a scientific explanation for this wonder must exist. I have contemplated this question my entire life, yet I fear I lack the skills to decipher it. My inability to find the answers to many things is a frustration to me." She turned to look at him. "Is it the same for you?"

"My lady, I, too, ponder these questions. But please do not assume you lack the skills to answer them. Instead, take heart that you have the presence of mind to ask them. My rudimentary education failed to satisfy my own curiosity about the mysteries of the universe. Truth exists for everything, and yet it is up to us to discover what it is. Alas, there is never enough time to satisfy that which we seek. My unfulfilled curiosity often distracts me from my other endeavors, painting being one of them. At times, I curse this flaw. And yet, I cannot stop my mind from seeking knowledge of the universe." He shrugged. "I suppose you have heard gossip regarding my various unfinished commissions."

Lisa looked down at her hands and said nothing.

"Of course, you have. Too often, I begin a project with devotion and determination only to abandon it as my interest wanes, or another project attracts my attention."

"I hope you will not grow bored with your painting of me. I hope you will think enough of me to continue until you are satisfied with the result."

"And if I am never satisfied?"

Her gaze touched his, and her lips twitched. "Then we will never have to say farewell."

"Ah, we will have as much time as God allows." He wanted to say more, longed to, but reconsidered.

"You flatter me, Maestro." Lisa resumed her pose, and yet Leonardo could see she was tired.

"My preliminary sketches are sufficient to begin the portrait. I think we both need to refresh ourselves." Leonardo held out his hand. "Let us take that walk, and I will explain my theory as to why the sky is blue."

THE AFTERNOON WAS WARM, and the marketplace bustled with shoppers. The sun shone on their faces, and Lisa realized they were both smiling. She felt so at ease in his company that sharing thoughts required no pretense.

"Your father lives in Florence, does he not?" she asked, picking up a melon and bringing it to her nose.

"Yes. You know that I am illegitimate."

"Does it bother you?" She replaced the melon, realizing it would rot before it ripened.

"Perhaps, when I was young. My father did me a favor by not legitimizing me. It allowed me to develop into whomever I chose to become. He is a notary, and sensibly realized that following in his footsteps was impossible for me. He lives on the Via dei Rustici."

Lisa sensed his discomfort, and yet her curiosity about him persisted. "Do you have siblings?"

"Yes. Seventeen half-siblings, but I see them rarely."

"Why not?"

"When the older ones were growing up, I would visit often, but after I left for Milan..." He shrugged. "They don't really know me. Perhaps I am to blame."

Leonardo picked up a melon, thumped the stem, and handed it to her. "Try this one."

Lisa sniffed it and declared, "I think this one will ripen to sweet perfection." She paid for the melon and handed it to her servant, who stood just a few feet away.

"I have always been a square peg forced into a round hole," he continued, "I have never fit in, nor have I ever followed a conventional path. My father understood this about me, so he arranged for me to apprentice in the atelier of Master Verrocchio when I was fourteen. Under his tutelage, I became an artist in the fullest sense of the word."

"Perhaps you are as much a riddle to your father as he is to you. Yet, I am sure there is love between you."

He stopped and regarded her with a curious expression that gave her pause.

"Forgive me if I overstep. Sometimes, I let my thoughts overtake me."

He took her hand and kissed it. "Never fear expressing your thoughts to me, my dear Signora. You are a woman of deep sensitivity and awareness."

Lisa blinked back tears at Leonardo's gesture and compliment.

"In all honesty, I think you have illuminated the core truth of my relationship with my father," he said. "He and I are like branches on opposite sides of the same tree. Equal to the life force and yet destined to exist apart."

"What a poignant analogy, Leonardo." They were in a crowded marketplace, yet she felt as though they were in a private garden free from the hustle and bustle around them. She looked at the sky and closed her eyes, momentarily soaking in its warmth.

"Ah, there is that mysterious smile again," he teased. "Pray, share with me the thought behind it."

She opened her eyes and turned to him. "Only that you have not answered my question."

"What question?"

She laughed. "The sky. Why is it blue?"

He joined her laughter. "The partial answer lies in the amount of water vapor in the air. The moisture acts like a veil separating what we see and what is. The blue color is visible because of the moisture that has filtered through that gauze. When I climbed Monte Rosa in the Alps, I found that the blue of the sky appeared darker and darker as I climbed. This occurred in direct proportion to the quality of the atmosphere and the higher my steps took me. If we could keep climbing, even beyond the tallest mountain, we would eventually find ourselves in complete darkness."

"What a revelation!" Lisa clapped a hand over her heart as she fully understood what Leonardo described. "I, too, have visited the mountains. Even though I did not climb to the top, as you did, I remember the sky became a darker, more vivid blue the higher I climbed."

"Signora, it is you who is the revelation." He grinned.

Impulsively, she slipped her arm through his. "Come, my perfect day will remain incomplete without a visit to our friend, the birdman."

Together, they bought several cages of birds, one of them a kite.

"When I was a child, I spent hours watching kites soar across the sky. I'm unsure if this is a real or conjured memory, but I recall waking in my cradle when a kite landed, pried open my mouth with its tail, and patted my lips. I have often wondered if perhaps this is what has made me the way I am."

Lisa sensed he was not referring to his artistic nature but to the rumors she'd heard of his romantic proclivities. "There is no shame in being different."

"Not in my world, but in yours, there is."

"Do we not inhabit the same world, Maestro? Do we both not prefer a soup of lentils over a leg of lamb? Do we both not enjoy walking in nature? Do we both not appreciate lively conversation?"

"And what of love?"

Her eyes met his, and she saw an intensity in his gaze she had not seen before. Her cheeks flushed with heat as she contemplated his question.

"Love can exist between mother and child, man and woman, and between two dear friends. It can take many forms, but perhaps it is as simple as sharing what is in our hearts."

"Perhaps you are right, Signora. Perhaps all we require is the courage to set our hearts free."

They continued their walk to the Piazza della Signoria. In full view of the imposing red-brick edifice of the palazzo, where Savonarola was burned, they gave liberty to the birds, who stretched their wings and soared into the blue sky.

CHAPTER 10

MAY 14, 1927 ~ FIESOLE, ITALY

It felt good to dig. Good to sink her hands in the rich black soil. Good to feel the roots of life beneath her fingertips when her own life felt so rootless. Valentina dropped the precious *pisanello* tomato seeds from the small paper packet she kept in an old cigar box from her father's shop. The seeds were a gift from Suor Magdalena, the nun who tended the convent's gardens. The *pisanello* resembled a flattened red pumpkin. Balanced with acidity and sweetness, the tomatoes were perfect for bruschetta or a simple sauce with pasta.

She turned over the soil and dropped a few more seeds, covering them with the rich black dirt. She soaked the ground with water from her watering can, setting the nurturing process in motion. She repeated the planting of the seeds until she completed the entire row. Snatches of a song escaped her lips as she worked.

"There's a moon in the middle of the sea. Mother, I must get married...

My daughter, who do I get for you? Mother, I leave it up to you..."

Luna Mezzo Mare was an old Sicilian folk tune about a daughter asking her mother whom she should marry. Valentina giggled as she sang the silly and sometimes bawdy lyrics about a possible match with a barber, a carpenter, and a shoemaker.

If only she could be so carefree with her mother.

In the two weeks since her return home, Valentina had pulled out all the weeds and shaped the garden beds into an organized and beautiful little oasis. She'd planted neat rows of peas, carrots, potatoes, and spinach, tending them daily, weeding and watering.

Valentina breathed a deep sigh, pleased that she'd planted several rows of Roma tomatoes, perfect for tomato paste and canning, and the *cuore di bue* tomatoes for the rich sauces her mother cooked. The herb garden would soon burst with the fragrance of basil, rosemary, thyme, dill, fennel, and sage. She brushed her hands on her apron. The garden had become her private haven and her pride.

The hours of physical labor had returned her to her prior slenderness. The nuns had given her a special oil to rub on her belly to minimize the birth scars. But her other scars were buried deep inside, and they would always be there, a reminder of what had been taken from her.

It had been a good day of planting and pruning; Valentina washed and sought her room for the quiet solitude of a book.

A sharp knock invaded her peaceful evening.

"Who is it?"

"You dare to ask such a question in my home?" her mother's voice retorted on the other side of the door.

Valentina sat up. "Come in, Mamma." She was surprised to see her mother, who rarely sought her out when the day was done. "Do you need me to do something?"

"No, Valentina, I need nothing, but tomorrow is Sunday, and you have not left the house since your return."

Her mother never mentioned the convent or why Valentina had been shuffled off to Florence. She acted as if Valentina had taken a vacation or had gone on an extended stay to visit relatives. It was beyond her reasoning, her mother's lack of sensitivity. She had hoped they could nurture a new beginning, but clearly, her mother was set in her old ways.

"I am outside in the sun and fresh air daily, working in the garden and tending the animals."

"That is not what I mean. It is time for you to return to a normal life."

"And what is normal, Mamma?"

"You have not been to church."

"Are you fearful for my soul?" Valentina wanted to laugh. Had she not spent the last five months in a convent, praying with the nuns three times a day?

"Your soul is not my concern, but your future is. Tomorrow, we will go to morning mass as a family. I spoke with Padre Garolini and volunteered you to help in the church office."

"You did this without asking me?"

"Since when does a mother need permission from her daughter? You cannot waste your life in my garden. You must venture back into the world and be among people your own age. How else will you meet a fine young man and get married?"

"I have no desire to marry."

"What a ridiculous notion!" Giulia threw her hands up in a gesture of disdain. "You will marry and redeem yourself by being an obedient wife and mother. You will not bring more shame on this family."

Valentina swallowed the words she longed to say. *You mean like you, Mamma? Were you obedient and good when you made Papà's life a misery?* She had no desire to be out in public, no desire to meet a young man, and no desire to marry. Not now. Perhaps not ever. Not with the pain of her loss so fresh.

"Valentina, as long as you live under my roof, you will obey me and take your rightful place in society. You will come with us for Sunday mass tomorrow, and that is final."

"Very well, I will go if you can get my brothers to attend church too."

"They are going, or I will box their ears." Giulia turned to leave, then added, "Oh, and there is a community picnic after the mass that we will all attend." Her mother closed the door before Valentina could protest.

The last thing she wanted to do was attend a social function. Returning to her book, she reminded herself that her father, on this point, would have agreed with her mother. Her father would expect her to hold her head up proudly and embrace all that life had to offer.

Would things have turned out differently if her father were still alive? Would he have taken his shotgun and killed Dante for what he did? In truth, she knew her father would have forced the dog to marry her and give the baby a name. At least then, she could have kept Chiara.

But the thought of Dante violating her whenever he chose

with the power of the church and the law behind him made her cover her mouth with her hand. Bile seared her throat. To keep Chiara, she would have done anything. But the repellent Dante would have been a poisonous pill to swallow. She took a sip of water from the cup on her nightstand.

Valentina picked up the book she was reading. It was about the life of Lucrezia Borgia, the beautiful daughter of Pope Alexander VI, who, legend had it, wore a ring that held poison and laid waste to any who got in her way, including her husband. *Could I have resorted to such an extreme action had I been forced to marry Dante?* Thank goodness she would not have to ponder that reality.

She flipped the page, reconciling herself to Sunday's activities. She would get through mass and the social gathering afterward. At least she would not have to worry about Dante being there. She'd heard he'd moved to Rome with his parents, doing the bidding of the fascists, and God willing, she would never have to see his detestable face again.

THE SUN HAD BURNED off the morning mist by the time Valentina and her family stepped into the church. They'd walked there as a family, although her brothers' faces betrayed their annoyance the entire way. Her fingers dipped into the ceramic bowl of holy water, and she bent and genuflected before venturing down the aisle to claim a seat in her family's usual pew.

Valentina had always loved the old Romanesque Cattedrale di

San Romolo di Fiesole. It wasn't as ornate or embellished with art and statuary as Santa Maria del Carmine, with its magnificent frescoes by Masaccio and Masolino. Still, it was filled with the memories of her childhood.

She admired the central nave, divided from the aisles by towering stone columns decorated with saints and whimsical animals. Behind the marble altar, the presbytery built above the crypt glowed golden as if it were the dome of heaven itself.

Valentina bowed her head and worried her rosary beads as she listened to the priest recite the invitation to communion.

"Behold the Lamb of God," Padre Garolini intoned. "Behold Him who takes away the sins of the world. Blessed are those called to the supper of the Lamb."

"Lord, I am not worthy that you should enter under my roof, but only say the word, and my soul shall be healed," the congregation, as one voice, chanted.

At the outdoor feast, Padre Garolini thanked Valentina for her offer of help, adding that he had sorely missed her during her prolonged visit with her relatives in Siena. Valentina did little more than nod, offering a polite smile as he reiterated her mother's words that her help would ease much of the burden on his shoulders.

When the priest finally left her in peace, she filled a cup with punch and found a shady spot under a thick-trunked oak tree. She nodded hello to her mother's friend Signora Rossi, the village gossip. The older woman wasted no time and made a beeline for her.

"Ahh, Valentina, it is so good to see you. Your mother told me about your visit to your aunt in Siena. I'm happy to hear she has rebounded."

"Zia Annunziata is a strong woman." How easily the lies slipped from her tongue now.

"Oh, look, your mother is talking with the Contis. They are visiting from Rome. Their son has a very important position with the *fascisti*. Whoever captures his heart will be a fortunate girl indeed. She will live like a queen in a palazzo."

A feeling of dread climbed Valentina's spine, and she stiffened. Her mother was engaged in deep conversation with Dante's parents. Her hands punctuated everything she said, and trills of laughter followed.

"Is he here?"

"Who?"

"The son, Dante." Valentina's chest tightened as she scanned the crowd.

"I have not seen him. I imagine they keep him very busy in Rome."

"Yes, I'm sure you are right." Valentina sighed with a breath of relief.

"Ah," Signora Rossi waved to a woman with hair dyed as red as a tomato, "I must speak with Signora Donati. Excuse me, my dear."

"Of course." Valentina was sure Signora Rossi was in pursuit of a juicy tidbit of gossip.

Her brother Rodolfo joined her beneath the shade of the tree. He slid his finger between his shirt collar and neck, trying to loosen his dress shirt, which he'd outgrown. He glared at Valentina as if she were the reason for his uncomfortable status.

"What do you think she's up to?" he asked. Valentina followed his gaze to their mother, who was still talking to the Contis.

Valentina shook her head and looked away from the trio. "I have no idea, nor do I care."

"I'm sure we'll know soon enough." Rodolfo cleared his throat, and Valentina realized he had something important to say to her, and it had nothing to do with the idle conversation they were having.

"What is it, Rodolfo?"

"I want you to know that I will be moving out of the house soon. I've asked Susanna Alfonsi to marry me."

Valentina embraced her brother. "That's wonderful news. I am so happy for you both."

"Yes, but it will mean you and Mamma...I will not be there to intervene should problems arise."

"You must not worry. I can handle Mamma."

"It's not Mamma I'm worried about."

"But what—?" Her gaze flitted back to her mother, and her throat constricted, shutting off her words. Dressed in a crisp black uniform, his black hat under his arm, was Dante.

"Valentina?" Rodolfo prodded her.

She looked at her brother as if seeing him for the first time. "Do not worry about me, Rodolfo. Get married and be happy. You are not responsible for me."

She contemplated her mother and the Conti family. Dante had just finished saying something, and her mother and his parents laughed. He turned his head slightly, and his eyes locked on hers. He'd known where she was all along. Watching her when she wasn't aware.

Dante stared at her, and his dark expression left no room for doubt: *You belong to me. And I will never let you go.*

She hated him—hated the side part in his hair, hated the way his upper lip curled in an arrogant smile, hated the way he puffed his chest like a peacock. She thrust her chin out and stared back in defiance.

I will never belong to you. And you will never have me.

CHAPTER 11

APRIL 18, 1503 ~ FLORENCE, ITALY

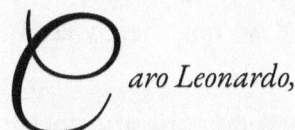aro Leonardo,

 I have heard of a religion in the East where there is no
Heaven and Hell. They believe that after death, they are reborn
into a new life where they will encounter their soul mate again.
Sometimes, I wonder if that has been our destiny, that we are
two people who have known each other in previous lives and
have met again in this one...

"Have you abandoned our portrait, Maestro?"

Leonardo swiveled around to face her. "How did you know
where to find me?"

"Finding the venerable Maestro da Vinci was not too difficult." Lisa stepped into the room and closed the door behind her.

"The Basilica della Santissima Annunziata is the site of Francesco's family crypt. The monastery here is known for providing quarters to artists, and Francesco mentioned you were in residence."

Leonardo removed his spectacles and squeezed the bridge of his nose. He seemed tired and drawn, and she wondered if his many projects were the cause or if simply his mercurial nature taking its toll.

"Tell me, what have you been up to these past few weeks?"

He gave a little shrug, his gaze skittering away, almost as though he were feeling shy. "I have been spending my nights dissecting cadavers at the Hospital of Santa Maria Nuova and recording my findings. This may sound strange to you, but I am driven to understand the underlying musculature of man and to know which muscles engage a frown and which for a smile."

"It does not sound strange at all for an artist. It sounds fascinating." She took a few steps closer. "Have we not already established that we share a curiosity about the world?"

"Yes, but to take apart cadavers goes beyond curiosity, does it not?"

"You are committed to your work." She chuckled, closing the distance between them. "I do not think there is another artist in Florence who is as committed as you are."

"Many would argue against that."

"Surely, you jest." She glanced down at the open sketchbook on the table and noticed a drawing of her face. "Aha, that smile looks familiar to me."

Leonardo moved to cover it and knocked over the inkwell. "It seems I can keep no secrets from you," he grumbled.

Lisa picked up a rag and blotted the ink. "Oh, I do not believe that to be true."

"Lisa, indulge me. Do you believe women are ignored regarding their intelligence or their abilities?"

"Do you?" she countered.

"Ah, you have answered me with another question," he quipped.

"And yet, I think you already know my answer. I am curious to hear your thoughts on the matter."

"I do not share the same prejudices of my sex. I have been privileged to know many remarkable women who are every bit the equal of any man."

"I am pleased to know you feel this way," she said, touching his shoulder. She felt him stiffen and moved her hand away. *I am too bold. Did I make a mistake in coming here today?* There was nothing to be done about it now. Time could only march forward, not backward. She cleared her throat, hoping to ease the tension she'd caused. "May I please take a look at some of your drawings?"

"Y-yes, of course." He seemed to fumble as he sifted through the stacks of papers on his table.

"May I?"

He nodded, and she reached for one of the stacks, examining and turning the pages. Her eyes widened at the sketches of skulls, skeletons, spinal cords, and the intertwining of bones and muscles. Page after page of nerves, ventricles, brain, and hearts, exacted in meticulous detail. Sketch after sketch of eyeballs, ears, noses, and other parts of the face and body. She studied each drawing in awe of his talent for detail. She turned another page, and a gasp escaped her.

"My apologies, Signora, if I shocked you." He hastily reached for the sheet, but she stayed his hand.

She blinked back tears as she stared at the ink drawing of an embryo in a womb. The fetus was curled, head resting on its knees, legs folded. The umbilical cord twined beneath the feet of the unborn child with its ten tiny toes perfectly rendered.

"I have never dissected a female cadaver pregnant with child," he said softly. "Most of what I have drawn here is based on my dissection of a cow. But the principle is the same, I believe, for all animals that produce milk for their young."

"You have drawn it with such precision..." *This is how she would have looked inside my womb. My Piera.* Lisa traced the line of the lifegiving cord joining mother and child. A bond, even when cut, that could never be broken.

"Yes, all seeds have such a cord broken when the seed is ripe, or the baby is born. Is it not remarkable that this cord delivers the life's blood between mother and child? Until birth, the embryo is still as much a part of the mother as her hands and feet."

She continued to stare at the drawing, and something shifted inside her. For some indefinable reason, seeing Leonardo's pen and ink drawing of the unborn child in the mother's womb filled her with a sense of peace. "Nature is truly wondrous. A miracle. You have captured both the physical and the spiritual aspects of birth. The drawing is beautiful and moving, Leonardo."

He smiled and inclined his head. "Though human ingenuity may devise great inventions, it will never create anything as remarkable as nature. If nature is God's canvas, I feel certain it will never be surpassed."

"Thank you for showing me your sketches," she said. "It is such a beautiful day, and Francesco is in Milano meeting with silk merchants..." She hesitated, hoping he would not think her brazen. "Would you accompany me to the countryside?" Before he could answer, she walked to the door, stepped out, and returned with a basket. "I prepared us a light lunch. I thought we might walk to Fiesole and take our meal in an olive grove. I imagine the view of the Duomo is as near to what a bird in flight might see."

"I think that is an invitation I cannot resist."

LEONARDO REACHED for Lisa's hand and assisted her over a particularly steep incline along the path. "One day, women will cast off those cumbersome harnesses and dress as freely as men. They will sit astride horses, swing a tennis racket, and play *calcio storico*."

"It cannot come soon enough," she huffed, catching her breath. "*Calcio storico!* You think women will be allowed to play sports, to kick a ball in public?"

"Why not?" He lifted her hand to his lips. "Anything and everything is possible."

They reached the summit and breathed in the vision before them. The regal beauty of the Duomo, with its red dome, adorned the sky in fiery red. It commanded the horizon, rivaled only by Giotto's bell tower. A blue-green Arno River shimmered in the distance, flowing westward through Florence as it continued its journey to the Tyrrhenian Sea. From this distance, Florence was a glorious sight. The dirty streets and distasteful odors of everyday existence were distanced, leaving a pristine vision.

They spread a cloth in the shade of a cypress tree, and Lisa laid out a feast. The woman who ate no meat had obliged their al fresco meal with various delicacies, including a bottle of crisp white wine and an *erbolata*, cheese and herb tart. Lisa's version tasted velvety, with eggs, watercress, parsley, basil, and spinach. Salt, grated parmesan, and nutmeg seasoned the pastry with such flavor that Leonardo was compelled to indulge in seconds.

"*Complimenti al cuoco.*" Leonardo took two squares of cloth from his pocket and handed her one. With his, he wiped his fingers and mouth."

"How clever," Lisa said as she dabbed at the corners of her mouth. You have fashioned special cloths to clean oneself during a meal."

Leonardo chuckled. "The idea came to me at the court of Ludovico Sforza, watching the guests wipe their hands on live rabbits tied to their chairs, a practice I found abhorrent. And so, I designed cloths with the Sforza coat of arms on them. The duke was impressed with the idea of enforcing his power with such a visual display and ordered hundreds of them to be sewn."

"How clever and yet so practical."

Leonardo patted his stomach with satisfaction. "A truly satisfying meal. Simple fare is always best."

"Our cook, Sorentina, is a treasure. I will tell her you were pleased with her cooking. This recipe is my grandmother's and one of my favorites." She took a sip of wine.

"I envy you your family. You have a close bond," Leonardo said. "Strangely, I have the finest friends, yet I lack that closeness with my family. I must admit, it weighs heavily upon my soul."

Eyes brimming with tears, she reached for his hand. "I know I cannot make up for the chasm that separates you from your family, but perhaps we can be for each other...confidants, sharing our deepest thoughts and yearnings, listening without judgment, and speaking without rancor."

"May I ask why you favor me for such a friendship?" His heart swelled in his chest at such a poignant declaration, but why would this regal and refined woman breach the boundaries and dictates of acceptable conduct. He worried about the possible consequences if her husband suspected that theirs was more than a professional liaison.

"Perhaps it is female intuition." She heaved a deep sigh. "For reasons I cannot begin to fathom, I feel that no matter where we go, what we do, or how much time or place separates us, there will always be trust between us."

Leonardo's relationship with God had eroded; even so, he did believe in the universal order of life and death. He also believed the natural world was God's perfection. Was Lisa meant to fill what had always been empty within him? Perhaps Salai, whom he loved but could not trust, was sent for one purpose and Lisa for another.

"You are so young yet wise beyond your years." He lifted her hand to his lips and kissed it. "You have already given me so much. I would be an ungrateful fool not to cherish your offer of friendship."

"Good. Then it is settled." She served them each a slice of pear tart with a golden crust. They sat for a while, enjoying the pastry, the view of nature's tapestry, and the magnificent city of Florence that had brought them together. Leonardo thought that no matter how much he perfected his art, he could never match the beauty that nature herself created. He turned to share his thoughts with Lisa when he noticed the look in her eyes. An unbearable sadness had replaced her joy. "There is something that troubles you, my friend."

She took a sip of wine as though to fortify herself. "In a marriage, one begins with the epitome of love and passion; that union can grow stronger over time. On the other hand, it can deteriorate until there is very little left to bind two people together except the tatters of a few fond memories."

"And where does your union stand, Signora?" Leonardo did not like Francesco and thought him a pompous and ignorant buffoon. The merchant publicly proclaimed devotion to his wife, but did he abuse her privately? Leonardo had never seen any bruises on Lisa, although some men had other ways of causing pain, and those scars could never heal.

"My girlhood infatuation for my husband has long since faded." She looked down and studied her hands, her face thrown into shadow. "I discovered not long after our marriage that Francesco trades in slaves. I was very young when I married, practically a child myself. I did not understand the implications of what he did."

"I understand your distress, for it is an abominable practice that I abhor."

"Some of these women work in my household. They are of dark skin, and perhaps Francesco does not see them as people because of that. He rationalizes his actions with the belief that by giving them work and a place to live and having the priest baptize them, he offers them the possibility of a place in Heaven." Her lovely face reflected the sorrow that held her in its grip. "But I do not think he does this in the name of Christ. And I cannot help but ponder if—"

"If what, my lady?"

"I do not know if Christ, our Savior, would have condoned such actions. It is one thing to preach as Christ did about God and the kingdom of Heaven, but it is another thing entirely to force people to change against their will, is it not?"

"Yes, it is, and I think you understand the teachings of Christ perhaps better than the pope himself."

"This knowledge has festered inside me for a long time, and I cannot reconcile his actions nor find excuses to condone them. But Francesco is a good provider and a caring father to his children, and I am but a wife and mother with no power or riches beyond what my husband bestows upon me."

"You feel the unfairness yet find yourself powerless to help those women and girls."

Tears welled in her eyes. "Yes. Like the birds trapped in their cages. They cry out against their captivity," she said in a broken whisper. "You and I have set some of those birds free, and yet who can liberate these women? I have not the power, and it haunts me."

"I am certain that a day will come when rational minds persevere, and the horrific practice of slavery will end once and for all. I cannot say when that will be, for man is as capable of the most extreme barbarism as he is of the most prodigious enlightenment. But you, *cara* Signora, will best serve these poor souls with your innate kindness. Neither you nor I can solve the problems of the entire world, and we can only do our best to make a difference in the lives of those closest to us. But you must not torture yourself over things you cannot change."

"Your wisdom is of great comfort to me." She took his hand in both of hers. "To know there is a kindred soul that feels as I do, makes the day brighter."

"I feel the same, *cara* Signora."

A smile he knew was meant for him played upon her lips. "Good. Then it is settled." She turned her face up to the sun, light dappling her cheeks. "We shall be dear friends for the rest of our years on this earth."

He picked up his sketch pad and reached into the pocket of his tunic, feeling the reassuring presence of chalk. "Would you care to relax for a while? I would draw you as you are now."

"I have one more request."

"Name it, and I will see it is done."

"Please do not hurry our painting, Maestro, for I desire only that we share this journey together for as long as time will allow."

CHAPTER 12

Benedetta Madre di Cristo, please guide me safely to my journey's end.

Valentina pressed her ear to the door of her room and listened. Faint sounds of snoring reached her ears. She turned the door handle, holding her breath, hoping the olive oil she'd used to grease the hinges would prevent it from squeaking. She breathed a sigh of relief when it opened with nary a creak. Tiptoeing from her room, holding a pair of shoes in one hand and her suitcase in the other, she tried not to make a sound. A floorboard creaked, and she froze, afraid to breathe. Waiting a moment, she heard only the sounds of muffled snores. Inching forward, she reached the front door and slipped from the house.

Freedom. The cool night air filled her lungs as she set on her journey. And even though it meant changing the course of her life, a sense of joy eased her racing pulse. But had her life not changed already in so many ways? When she reached the cover of trees, she set her shoes on the ground and wedged her feet into them.

Taking a final look at the house she never expected to see again, she entered the thicket of trees at a brisk pace. *I will not cry.* Whatever regrets and sentimentality she harbored were under lock and key in the strongbox of her memories. Whether she would ever, in the future, open the box again, she didn't know.

It was her future she must see to, not her past.

Moonlight filtering through the trees provided enough glow to light the path. Valentina had waited until a night when the moon would be full to make her escape. She would miss her brothers, and perhaps she would have missed her mother had it not been for her perfidy. She'd left Rodolfo a letter explaining she'd found a position as a maid for a wealthy family in Milan. She hated lying to her brother, but she could not risk her family coming after her or allow Dante to know where she was going.

Valentina had dressed as a man, taking some old clothes and shoes from her brothers. Her hair was tucked into a hat, and she wore a heavy jacket. She walked purposefully, fingering the handle of the kitchen knife in her pocket. Fear and hatred had simmered in the pit of her stomach for days after the church picnic. But she could not allow it to take root. How had her mother become so bitter? Perhaps she regretted not marrying a wealthy fascist and wanted to snag one for her daughter. Valentina would never let that happen. She'd given up her beloved Chiara to appease her mother—how could she marry the very man who'd caused her so much pain in the first place? The thought made bile rise in her throat.

Valentina pressed onward, knowing it would take approximately an hour and a half to reach the Piazza del Carmine on foot. Midnight streets in Florence held danger, but the knife was a solid companion. She walked through quavering beams of moonlight, past fig and lemon trees, their branches swaying in the wind, casting shadows on the old stone walls surrounding La Villa Medici.

She knew it well, having toured the villa and gardens as a girl with her classmates. Oh, what beautiful memories she had of the serene confines of the manicured gardens. A soothing balm after the ravages of the Great War. She shook her head at the dichotomy of a country that could wage wars on one hand and produce some of the greatest minds of the Renaissance on the other. Writers such as Mirandola, Ficino, and Poliziano, and artists such as Michelangelo, Botticelli, and da Vinci. But had da Vinci not designed weapons that were used in various battles in his time? She recalled reading about his military achievements in the letters she'd transcribed. Did the compulsion to conceive beauty with one hand and destroy it with the other exist even in the mind of the greatest artist the world had ever known?

Such clashing thoughts kept her company as she followed the path to Via Faentina that bordered the Convent di San Domenico. She beheld Brunelleschi's floating dome and Giotto's campanile. The most famous landmarks in Florence rose above the city like beacons, shimmering in the moonlight. The road took a turn, and the pathway steepened; overhead, heavy clouds shifted and moved to overshadow the moon, and she was plunged into darkness. She picked up her pace to a near run, wary of anyone she might encounter along the shadowy stretch of road.

She reached the Piazza della Libertà, the northernmost tip of Florence. A sharp stitch in her side forced her to set down her suitcase and catch her breath. A few moments later, she set off again, walking through the Porta San Gallo and the Arca di Lorena. The arch was erected in the 18th century to welcome the duke of the conquering Habsburg-Lorraine dynasty where the Porta San Gallo's old walls had once stood to prevent such conquests. Serendipitously, Leopold II, the Hapsburg Duke of Tuscany, drove through the same arch almost a hundred years later when he was deposed and exiled after a bloodless coup. Florence had a checkered history, always struggling to hold onto its free republic. Freedom always came at a price—Valentina had already paid that price in her own life. She prayed it would be enough.

By the streetlamp's glow, Valentina saw the time on her wristwatch. It was nearing two, and luckily, the streets were empty. Only the Arno River stood between her and her destination.

She arrived at the Ponte alla Carraia and began her walk over the bridge. Exhausted, she stopped halfway and breathed deeply. The clouds had shifted again, and the river glowed under a moonlit sky. She rested her arms on the stone balustrade and looked out at the Ponte Santa Trinità with its three arches and four ornamental statues, appearing like a mirage in the shimmering light.

"I am sorry, Papà, that I could not be the daughter you wanted me to be. I could not allow myself to live as a prisoner to that man, with my own mother as my warden. I don't know what the future will bring, but I will try to make you proud."

Valentina dried her tears on her coat sleeve and resumed her journey's last leg. Crossing the medieval stone bridge, she picked up her pace once again. A few more streets brought her to the Piazza del Carmine. The end of one journey and the beginning of another.

With trembling legs, she almost stumbled to the door of the convent. She pressed the bell and waited, willing her legs not to wobble.

Finally, after what seemed like an eternity, the door opened. "Pray tell me, you are not again with child," Suor Emilia scolded.

Valentina was grateful for the shadowy darkness that hid the heat in her cheeks. She was tempted to give the cranky nun a clever retort and then throw her arms around her. "I am not pregnant, Sorella."

"What brings you here at this hour of the night, child?"

"I come in search of sanctuary. I wish to consecrate myself to our Lord and take my vows in service to Him."

The nun's brows arched so high they disappeared into her wimple. "*Entra, entra.* This matter cannot be dealt with until tomorrow," she said with a sigh. "I will notify Mother Superior in the morning." The old nun glanced at Valentina. "You might as well take your old room. It's still empty. You know the way, my child."

Impulsively, Valentina kissed her cheek. "*Grazie,* Suor Emilia."

"*Va bene.* Go and get some sleep," the old nun waved her off, her gruffness gone. "We will sort this out in the daylight with God's guidance."

Valentina turned and made her way to her old room. Walking past the gurgling fountain and the frescoed wall, she breathed in the sweet scent of flowers and lemons emanating from the garden. A feeling of peace washed over her as it had on that stormy night so many months ago when she'd arrived pregnant and afraid. The convent that had initially been a strange sort of purgatory had become her haven. The sanctuary where she gave birth to Chiara, nursed her, and loved her beyond imagining. A place of learning and discovery. A place of friendship and kindred spirits.

She could not wait to see Suor Maria Vittoria and Suor Teresa again and taste Suor Elena's lemon cake. These women had become the family in her heart.

Reaching her room, she shed her clothing, tumbled into bed, and closed her eyes.

I'm home.

CHAPTER 13

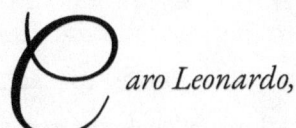aro Leonardo,

> *Our first encounter was a fortuitous happenstance, but will*
> *I rise to meet the challenge? Sometimes, I wonder if the person I*
> *am today is the same person you met so many months ago...*

Lisa sat on a red velvet cushion beside the window against the curved barrel back of the *pozzetto* chair. Her left hand curled around the arm of the chair, and her right hand rested atop.

"I wish to create an *intervallo*, a pause in time that captures the moment before the present moment and the moment to come," Leonardo said, laying out his red chalk.

Seated almost facing him, the position offered her the pleasure of watching him work. She enjoyed his company so much that a smile escaped her lips time and again before she realized her lapse and sought to compose her features in a more composed and regal expression.

At times, he would speak to her at length about anything that crystallized in his mind—a humorous story about court life in Milan under the formidable Duke Sforza or his design for a flying machine he called the ornithopter, which he explained derived its name from the ancient Greek words for bird and wing. Other times, he would lapse into silence as he concentrated. The look on his face was one of complete absorption and contentment.

Leonardo began to draw the portrait on the prepared poplar panel based on the dozens of experimental sketches he'd made of her. Tears blurred her vision as she thought about his gift to her, the lovely drawings he'd sketched at their picnic almost two fortnights ago.

That day would always be special to her, for it was the moment when they'd opened their hearts and minds to each other. She'd hidden the sketches in a folio along with Leonardo's letters, which she kept in a locked box in her wedding *cassone*. She pushed away the pang of guilt at her secrecy. *Is it wrong to have something for myself? Something private, just for me? If no one finds out, no one will be hurt...*

"The eyes are the window of the soul, Signora," Leonardo interrupted her reverie, his voice quiet and contemplative.

Lisa blinked rapidly. "Forgive me, Maestro, I am quite sentimental today."

"Sentimentality is in the heart of every nurturing mother."

"Yes, I suppose it is."

"What do I see in your eyes, Lisa?"

She wondered if it was meant as a question or merely a stray thought uttered aloud, so intent he was on his easel. "I hope you see a contented life. A mother, a wife, a daughter, a sister. A woman. A friend. Am I wrong, Maestro? What do you think you see?"

"I see a woman who is like every woman..." his words trailed away, his gaze capturing hers, "...and yet, unlike any woman I have ever known."

She felt herself tremble at such a provocative statement and was glad for the sturdy support of the arm of the chair. "You are most kind, Maestro." She wanted to memorize this precious moment and tuck it away in her heart for the rest of her days; she wanted to imprint his words into her very being and, more importantly, the transcendent glow in his eyes as he said them.

"It is the truth, pure and simple," he added. "No matter how hard we try to subvert our feelings, we are emotional beings. We carry the seeds of hate, desire, love, envy, and empathy within us, yet we struggle to deny what we feel and pretend otherwise. The truth is revealed in the muscles of the face, and yet the smile has always been the most difficult to decipher. Your smile holds a mystery, and like an unexpected twist in a story, it holds the key to solving the mystery."

"Are women not emotional creatures who wear our feelings openly in our faces?"

"Ah, well, the female child cannot help but express her emotions to the world directly. In contrast, a woman in her prime has become adept at veiling what she feels."

How perceptive he is. If only she could share the truth—all of it. She scarcely understood it herself, and yet she ached to speak of it aloud, to give voice to it. Why? Why did she yearn to share everything with him...? Because it mattered. Because he mattered.

"My lady, do you recall our agreement? You promised not to hide from me."

"*Perdonami*, I did not think I was hiding." If only she were bolder, she would speak here and now and be done with it. A bird sang in the distance, and she closed her eyes and wished she could fly and live two lives. "I think you come from a different time, Leonardo," she said, sidestepping his question. "I wonder at the miracle of the existence of such a man as you. Are you more like your mother or father? Were you close to your mother? Did you love her?"

The chalk slipped from Leonardo's fingers to the floor, breaking in two. "Why do you ask?" He bent to retrieve the pieces and set them on the table. He reached for a fresh stick of chalk from his bag and resumed sketching.

"Are there questions I am not to ask? Secrets we must keep hidden?"

"My dear lady, there will be no barriers between us. I believe our promise will survive longer than the peace treaties between nations."

"And yet some truths we keep hidden even from ourselves."

He was quiet for a few moments and then finally said, "My mother's name was Caterina. I only lived with her until the age of four. After that, I lived with my grandfather and uncle until my father brought me to Florence. Although I resemble her physically, we were nothing alike," he added with a shrug. "I was the product of an illicit summer liaison. We were estranged for many years until she arrived at my doorstep in Milan. Her husband had died, and she had nowhere to live and no one to care for her. And so, I assumed the responsibility. She died from malaria. My mother's life was directed by her circumstances. She was poor and uneducated. My father's family arranged a marriage for her. She had a better life than she would have had otherwise. I sometimes wonder what it would have been like to have the love and attention of a devoted mother. Alas, it was not to be.

"Perhaps the adversity in your life had something to do with your drive to create."

"Ah, and there is the age-old question. Does blood bond us to our fate? I have tried to live life according to my own direction, but perhaps everything would be different if I had had a different childhood."

"I believe your artistic talent is a rare gift. And while it must be nurtured, it is as innate to you as your golden hair and striking blue eyes." She smiled at the tilt of his lips and the red that flushed his cheeks.

"I thank you, *cara* Signora, for the genteel compliment," he said with a bow. "Although these golden locks have become far outnumbered by the gray ones."

She shook her head. "I speak the truth."

"Then perhaps it was the adversity in my life that sparked the drive—the need to nurture this gift, as you say."

"I am thankful that your gift and drive have led you here.

"To your home?" he said with a twitch of his lips.

"To my life. To our friendship." She giggled.

"I am thankful for that most of all," he said with a wink.

Lisa felt emboldened by their frank discussion. "What does Salai think of our friendship? I know he is your most intimate of confidants. Does he approve or disapprove of me?"

"I am as necessary to Salai as he is to me, but in entirely different ways. I am the host—and I do not mean this unkindly— he is the parasite. He will never captain the ship, but the ship would flounder on the rocks without him. He has been with me since he was ten years old. Although he is sometimes more trouble than he is worth, he is still my *famiglia*. Is my meaning clear?"

"Do you love him as a son?"

Leonardo chuckled. "Perhaps in my tolerance of his devilry; in truth, calling him my *son* is the most unlikely description of our relationship."

"Oh." Lisa's cheeks flushed. "Have you always been," —she struggled to find the words— "more inclined to the camaraderie of men?"

"My earliest memories are of men, and it is from males that I have always sought approval. My father, my grandfather, and my uncle—these men were my role models. In many ways, I tried to emulate them. In other ways, I rebelled and tried to be anything other than what they were."

Leonardo stared at the chalk in his hand, his brow furrowed. "You may have heard, although it was long ago, that my contrary nature put me in grave danger. When I was a young man, an anonymous accusation of sodomy was placed in the *tamburo* box at the Palazzo della Signoria, and it nearly brought me to ruin. It is not something I remember without anger and distress."

Lisa nodded. "I cannot imagine what you went through. I have always believed the *tamburo* made it far too easy to satisfy vendettas or ruin lives by planting rumors without substantiation." In Lisa's mind, Leonardo's sexual preference seemed built on the foundation of the world he inhabited. The world of painters, of art, was a world of men. Sensual love between men was a difficult concept for her to fully comprehend, but because of her feelings for Leonardo, she knew she must try. She partially understood because her own life reflected dependence on the will of strong figures like her father and husband, the cornerstones of her existence.

Leonardo continued working on the panel, his left hand sweeping across the canvas, reminding her of a choral conductor.

"It is curious," she continued, "that you have chosen to pour your heart into a painting of an ordinary woman."

He smiled as he regarded her over the top of the easel—a smile both charming and charismatic. It made her wonder at his assertion about her smile. Did he really think it mysterious, or was his thesis a mere projection? She'd never given much thought to her smile, yet she considered his as alluring as he seemed to think hers.

"You are no ordinary woman to me. You are an enigma—you embody the mysteries of the universe. Perhaps in painting you, I will find the answers that I seek."

She beamed at the compliment, and his answering grin warmed her soul.

"Eureka!" he declared, using the chalk as a pointer. You have finally gifted me with a smile that I can read."

"Then I assume you are satisfied that you have been able to decipher this mystery," she teased.

"Oh, do not presume that, *cara* Signora, for our journey is far from over."

"I am pleased to hear it."

Leonardo set down his chalk. "I am satisfied with today's progress. I must live with what I have done for a time and allow it to distill in my mind." He cleaned his hands with a cloth.

Lisa stretched her neck, stiff from holding the same position for a prolonged period of time. "Just as well. My neck is not cooperating."

"May I give you some relief?" he offered as he approached her.

"Please."

"In my studies of the human body, I've gleaned a great deal about the spinal column and the muscles that give it strength." He pressed into her neck and shoulders, massaging with his fingers and fists. At first, she stiffened. She wasn't used to anyone other than her husband and children touching her with such intimacy, but his strong hands moved with the skillfulness of a physician, and relief soon made her relax.

"Thank you," she breathed out a sigh.

"You are most welcome." He stepped away and began to pack his supplies.

She studied him and sensed he was pondering an unpleasant topic.

"You wish to tell me something, Maestro?"

His eyes finally met hers, and he expelled a deep breath. "I am leaving Florence for a time. Those two autocrats, Segretario Machiavelli and Gonfaloniere Soderini, are sending me on an expedition into Tuscany to map the Arno River and assess the possibility of diverting its course and directing its flow away from Pisa. I will be gone for many months."

Lisa looked down at her hands. His news upset her, but she did not want him to see her distress. "For nearly ten years, we've been at war with Pisa. Will it never end?"

"The business of war is ingrained in man's nature, but perhaps through my efforts, an end will be found. Machiavelli and I have discussed a project that might serve two functions and offer two solutions. If I could divert the river from Pisa, we would sever their supply lines. Not only would the siege end quickly, but it would provide a navigable route from Florence to the Mediterranean Sea.

My friend, Amerigo Vespucci, and other explorers could bring the new world's wealth right to our doorstep."

"Is it possible to divert a river from its course?"

"I will know better once I complete my measurements, draft maps of the terrain, and explore the ebb and flow of the river."

"Will you be safe? Perhaps you should take Salai with you?"

"It is an expedition funded by the Signoria of the Chancery for the benefit of the military. You need not worry, Lisa. I will be well protected. And as for taking Salai with me, I am safer with mercenaries than with that rascal." He chuckled. "Besides, he must remain in Florence and see that everything runs smoothly at the atelier. I am sure the *diavolo* will rob me blind while I am away. But in managing my affairs here, I trust he knows where his bread is buttered."

Lisa knew better than to ask why hired soldiers without a moral compass would be safer than being with Salai. She recognized that Salai's salacious behavior was a constant source of consternation and amusement for Leonardo. To complain about him was on par with loving him.

"I will miss you."

Leonardo took her hand and brought it to his lips. "I will try to send a letter to you from wherever I am and let you know of my progress."

"And I will try to be patient in awaiting your return."

CHAPTER 14

The cheery flame of a candle flickered on the bedside table in contrast to the feeble light filtering through the window as Valentina completed her morning prayers. She had taken the name Suor Gianna at her consecration more than ten years ago. She was nearly twenty at the time, having spent four years before that as a novitiate. No longer was she that frightened fifteen-year-old girl who'd arrived at the convent's gate, rain-soaked and pregnant. Valentina was a grown woman, a nun, and a librarian, and yet, at times, that ghost of a lost girl returned to her, and there was nothing to do but allow the tears to flow.

It was still too early to go downstairs, so she padded to the armoire, where she kept the cigar box that contained all that she held dear since the day she'd handed over her child and her heart to Benjamin and Gabriella Chiarelli. Setting the box on the bed, she carefully took out the treasures and spread them on the bed. A neat pile of letters that she'd read and re-read hundreds of times, and an envelope that held the precious photographs of Chiara. *How different would my life be if I had kept her?* She'd pondered this question many times over the past fourteen years. *I made a choice that was no choice at all.*

She gazed at her precious daughter, her dear sweet Chiara. The photograph of her holding a newborn Chiara was a cherished keepsake. A faded photograph was all she had to remember her beloved baby. The other two pictures she'd received in the mail from Chiara's adoptive parents. In one, Chiara wore a schoolgirl's uniform, her beautiful, sweet face surrounded by a cloud of dark curls. A school bag dwarfed her petite frame as she stood between Gabriella and Benjamin, ready for her first day at school. Chiara was a few years older in the other photo, her beaming smile showing two missing front teeth. Once more, she stood between her parents, holding their hands, a sunlit backdrop of towering mountains behind them. No doubt, it was taken on a holiday in the mountains.

A distant rumble of thunder drew her attention to the window just as a gust of wind blew the shutters open. Valentina jumped up, watching dark clouds roll across the sky as a summer thunderstorm threatened to unleash itself on Florence. Her bedroom was at the back of the convent and overlooked a small orchard of fruit trees and a garden shed. They would fill many baskets with fruit after they picked up the fallen fruit shaken to the ground from the storm. A bolt of lightning lit up the sky, and Valentina gasped as she caught sight of Suor Maria Vittoria emerging from a cluster of trees, carrying something in her hands. *Cara Madre di Dio, what is she doing outside at a time like this?*

Valentina secured the shutters on the window and ran downstairs to ensure the old nun made it safely inside the convent. Frightened for Suor Maria Vittoria's safety, she was frantic to get to her before the full brunt of the storm hit. Another flash of lightning, followed by a roar of thunder, greeted Valentina as she ran out the kitchen door. A strange cracking sound echoed around the garden, and she skidded to a halt just as the old oak tree split down the middle and toppled with a resounding crash. The dark clouds unleashed a pounding rain, soaking her, as she ran to the elderly nun, sheltering under a lemon tree. Suor Maria Vittoria trembled as she clutched something in the billowing folds of her habit.

"Are you all right, Sorella?" Valentina shouted above the pelting rain.

Suor Maria Vittoria looked at her as if she didn't know her and was confused as to why she was standing before her. "They are dead."

Valentina wrapped her arm around Suor Maria Vittoria's shoulders and gently guided her toward the kitchen door. It worried her that her dear friend seemed not to be thinking clearly. Lately, there were times when the elder nun slipped into the past and spoke of things that happened long ago as if they were happening now. Valentina knew it was a sign of aging, but it distressed her. Suor Maria Vittoria was like a mother to her. "Who is dead, Sorella?"

Valentina locked the door behind them once they were safely inside. Turning, she found Suor Maria cradling a nest that held a baby bird.

"What will we do, little one? Your mother and your siblings are gone?"

"We will nurture the baby as best we can," Valentina said, hoping to ease her friend's distress. "As a child, I once found a baby bird and fed it using a pipette with tiny pieces of earthworms, nuts, and fruit. It requires great patience, which I know you have in abundance. Come, let us see what can be done for our nestling."

Valentina helped Suor Maria Vittoria to a chair, keeping a close eye on her dear friend and saying a little prayer as she gathered what she would need to save the baby bird.

CHAPTER 15

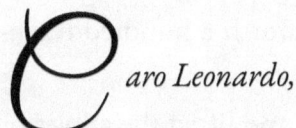 *aro Leonardo,*

> *It was with great anticipation that I received your letter. A treasure that helped fill the void in your absence. I felt the taste of honey on my tongue as I read your words; a welcome reminder you will be soon be home...*

Two months had passed before a letter arrived. The messenger brought it to her just minutes before Francesco returned from his daily business affairs. Lisa traced her finger over the letter in her pocket for the thousandth time. As they dined on their evening repast, she smiled when necessary and answered when required, but mostly, she encouraged Francesco to share an accounting of his day as he was inclined to do. The children, who had eaten earlier, were upstairs playing with the new *trottola* she purchased as a gift. They had become obsessed with the beautifully painted wooden top.

"And how was your day, *amore mio?*" Francesco finally concluded his discourse of the trials and tribulations of the silk trade. Asking her about the routines of motherhood and running a household was also part of the usual routine.

"The same as always. I oversaw the children's studies and then took the boys and Camilla for a walk to the Piazza Santa Maria Novella, and they played *maglio.*" The children loved the game played with a ball and a mallet. "Then we went to the mercato for a gelato."

"You are the best mother, seeing not only to our sons' minds but to their physical wellbeing. *Una buona madre vale cento insegnanti.*"

The old proverb, "A good mother is worth a hundred teachers," would be her legacy.

She swallowed the lump in her throat and lifted the goblet of wine to her lips. There was a time when his compliments meant the world to her. She nodded her thanks, and they fell silent as they finished their meal.

"Are you unhappy with our life, *carissima?*"

His question was so sudden and unexpected that her heart began to race. Did he suspect something inappropriate in the time she spent with Leonardo? She composed herself and gave him a reassuring smile, patting his hand. "Of course not, *amore*. What a question you ask. My day was pleasant because it was inconsequential. The gelato proved a soothing balm to those mischief-making angels known as our sons."

The letter in her pocket itched to be opened, and all she

wished for was the privacy of her bedroom. She rubbed her forehead. "But I must confess that such a full day with the children has given me a headache. I fear I must retire early with a cool compress, or I will not be able to function tomorrow."

Concern reflected in Francesco's eyes, and he raised her hand to his lips. "My darling wife. Should I send for the physician?"

"No, no, I only need to rest my eyes. Motherhood is a great joy that requires great stamina. She rose and kissed his cheek, feeling a pang of guilt in using that old yet reliable excuse of an aching head. Despite her complicated feelings about Francesco, he was a good father, provider, and a good man. She did not want to burden him with worries about her health. He had lost one wife, and she imagined the loss of another would be unbearable.

"The children will welcome their papà to their game. They adore you so."

His smile followed her out of the dining room.

The rustle of her silk skirt whispered on the russet pavers as Lisa hurried down the hallway to her bedchamber. She closed the door and leaned against it, expressing relief. Slipping the envelope out of her pocket, she studied the elegant script. The letter opener on her desk made quick work of the seal, but before she made herself comfortable and read its contents, she opened the window and inhaled the rose-scented air. Refreshed, she removed her dress and shoes and slipped on her dressing gown. Fluffing the pillows, she climbed into bed and arranged the covers over her lap.

She had waited weeks to hear from Leonardo, and now that a letter had finally arrived, she wanted to savor it and inhale the beauty of his words as if she were inhaling a fragrant perfume.

July 1, 1503
Cara Lisa,

I hope this missive finds you in good health. I beg your forgiveness, for it has been too long since my last letter, although in no way does my sluggish correspondence denote a lack of regard for you.

This grueling expedition has left me little time to myself. You expressed concern for my safety, and I assure you I am safe by most measures. I am with my military escort at La Verruca, less than 7,000 braccio from Pisa. As I have previously written, the fortress is built on a hilltop overlooking the Arno and has been Pisa's defensive fortification for a thousand years. At Machiavelli's insistence, our army conquered and veritably destroyed the fortress, and at his request, I am here to make drawings for its restoration. Alas, this hilltop aerie has only brought sorrow and grief, reinforcing my determination to end this war.

This preamble is nothing if not a digression in the wake of the tragedy now embedded in my memory. A young boy named Arnoldo was assigned to help me, and I warned him numerous times to walk with caution among the crumbling stone parapets. But, as you know, how can one stop a bird from flying? Children, by their very nature, are meant to run and play in tall grasses, clamber up trees, and steal apricots from neighboring farms. Their natural inclination is to think they will live forever. They cannot foresee an end to life, for every day is full of adventure. And so, it is, until it is not. On that saddest of days, I watched as that bright little boy plunged to his death, and I could do nothing to stop it.

How I hate this war. The price of victory is always too high. And yet, were I a son of Pisa, would I not fight to reclaim my right to determine my own destiny? A destiny free from the thumbscrews of Florence.

But I am here under the Florentine banner, as a son of Florence, and here I shall complete my esperimenti. And it is wiser that I immerse myself in these drawings that illustrate my reports to the Signoria of the Chancery and my findings of diverting the course of the Arno River. The idea is feasible by constructing a line of dams on the river and an offshoot channel. Alas, it is a costly and monumental endeavor, and I am inventing tools that would reduce the manpower needed and hasten the speed required to complete the project.

Why do I do this? Why can I not be like other artists, pursuing art with determination and a single-minded vision? Why is my vision splintered in so many directions? I have asked myself these questions a thousand times.

Perhaps, one day, I will be able to tell you.

Or, perhaps, one day, you will be able to tell me.

It matters not. Soon, I will return to our portrait, and you will find me newly inspired with ideas that I cannot wait to share with you.

Until we meet again, dear lady. And I am granted my simple wish of watching you free your birds of love once more.

Sei sempre nel miei pensieri,
Leonardo

LISA PRESSED the letter to her breast. The page was no love letter, yet the missive bridged the distance between them. To know that he valued their friendship as much as she did, meant the world to her. The boy's death pierced her heart, and she could well imagine the toll it had taken on Leonardo. Tears stung her eyes as she was reminded of her loss, the loss of her precious Piera. A loss she could never come to terms with.

Why is joy so fleeting and sorrow so constant?

Rising from the bed, she opened the chest that contained her most intimate apparel. The floral aroma of jasmine wafted from the small pouches of dried herbs and flower petals that scented her undergarments. She moved these to one side and opened the folio that held Leonardo's drawings, adding the letter to the precious contents.

Warmth infused her heart and, with it, a stirring in her breast with the newfound realization that she was the flint to light the flame of his inspiration. To be the muse of the man she admired above all others was a treasure beyond price.

Come home, Maestro, and let us begin again.

CHAPTER 16

*U*nlocking the convent's gate, Valentina walked briskly, skirting around the Piazza del Carmine and the empty streets to the Ponte alla Carraia.

"Good morning, Giacomo. Everything is well with your family, I pray." She handed the boy a coin.

The enterprising newsboy grinned. "*Non c'è male,* Suor Gianna. Mamma's headache is gone, and she is feeling better." It was their daily greeting. He handed her yesterday's edition of *Corriere della Sera,* Italy's oldest daily newspaper published in Milan. The free press in Italy had all but disappeared under the fascists. Nevertheless, it was better to be informed of the devil you knew than the one you didn't.

"Did you give her those herbs for the tea?"

"Yes, and she said it helped."

"Good. I will pray for your mamma and family today."

"Thank you, Suor Gianna. *Passi una bella giornata!*"

"*Anche tu, amico mio.*"

Returning to the convent, she entered the kitchen and set the newspaper on the table. Taking down the tin of coffee from the shelf, she scooped grounds into the *cafetiere* and added a sliver of lemon peel. Her morning routine was to read the newspaper and enjoy her coffee in solitude. Usually, she was the first one downstairs, but today was her birthday, and she'd risen even earlier.

She took a sip of coffee and unfolded the paper, knowing what would be written in the bold black and white headline, for they had already heard it on the radio the day before. Mussolini had joined forces with Germany and declared war on Britain and France. She crossed herself and said a prayer. Once again, Italy had chosen the wrong side of history. The war to end all wars did not end in 1918—neither for the wounded nor the families who mourned their dead, *lest we forget.*

She flipped through the newspaper. What would joining the German Axis mean for Italy? And what would it mean for the Jews? Mussolini and his fascist government had enacted the Racial Laws of Segregation two years ago, following similar legislation in Germany and Austria. After living in Italy for two thousand years and fully integrating into Italian society, losing their citizenship was a devastating insult to Italian Jews.

For the most part, Jewish and Christian Italians had lived for centuries side-by-side in peace. Antisemitism had never plagued Italy in the same virulent manner as the rest of Europe. Even Mussolini's long-time mistress was Jewish. Because the newly enacted racial laws, for the most part, had been ignored, Jews had flocked here from Germany, Austria, and Poland to escape the ever-tightening restrictions elsewhere.

Underground reports of what Hitler was doing in Germany and Poland terrified Valentina. Given that Mussolini had joined forces with Hitler, would Italy suffer the same atrocities? Just the other day, Valentina had heard about foreign Jews in Italy being rounded up and sent to internment camps. The cruel edicts forced them to give up their livelihoods and businesses. Even Italian-born Jews were being relocated to small towns and villages where they had to live in repurposed buildings. Life for them had become impossible with all the constraints and curfews imposed upon them.

Had Chiara and her adoptive parents been relocated, or were they still in Rome? Valentina prayed that wherever they were, they were safe. She'd wanted to write to them, but Madre Superiora had warned her that in these dark times, letters could be inter-cepted, sparking suspicion and propelling families into danger. And so, she'd refrained from reaching out.

Needing a distraction, Valentina decided to bake. After all, it was her birthday, and as Suor Elena was fond of saying, baking was the best way, next to praying, to be close to God.

An hour later, Valentina breathed in the aroma of lemon and almonds as she took the cakes out of the oven and set them on the counter to cool. Once cooled, she carried them to the dining room and put them on the table, where the nuns would gather to break their fast. Suor Teresa was already there, seated beside Suor Maria Vittoria. Her friend frowned and elbowed Valentina in the ribs, nodding toward the elder nun. Suor Maria Vittoria looked pale, and shadows smudged her eyes.

"Are you feeling unwell, sister?" Valentina asked.

"I have a headache, nothing to be concerned with. Sometimes growing old is tiring, and yet other times—*invecchiare è una benedizione.*"

"I agree that growing old can also be a blessing, which is why you should rest today."

"*I'll* be fine. Working in the library is the best medicine for me." She patted Valentina's hand.

Valentina could not help worrying about her dear old friend and kept a close eye on her while they worked in the library. Suor Maria Vittoria had been fatigued more than usual the past few days. But other than rescuing the baby bird in that thunderstorm last week, she had not ventured to the crowded mercato, nor had she visited the ailing and the sick as the other nuns did. The nuns were always careful to wash after they returned from an ill person's home to prevent the spread of contagion.

Despite her fatigue, the elderly nun sat at her desk, making notes on inventory cards. From her perch on the ladder, Valentina asked. "Sorella, do you think this declaration of war by Mussolini means the Jews in Italy will be in more danger?"

"You are worried about Chiara." The nun put down her pen and the cards and turned compassionate eyes to Valentina.

"Yes, terribly. In every country where the Nazis have taken power, the Jews have suffered greatly. Rumors abound about deportations and resettlement to far-off places." Valentina climbed down from the ladder and took the chair opposite Suor Maria Vittoria. She poured two glasses of lemonade and handed one to her friend.

The older nun took a sip and rubbed her forehead. "I, too, fear what is ahead for our Jewish brothers and sisters and for all of us, with these monsters in control. *Il male cammina mezzo a noi.*"

"You are right. Evil does walk among us." Valentina would not burden Suor Maria Vittoria with her worries about Chiara, Benjamin, and Gabriella. Even so, she could not sit idly by and do nothing. Somehow, Valentina would find a way to be helpful. She had to, or she would never forgive herself.

THE CLOCK next to Valentina's bed read midnight. She wondered how many other Italians were tossing and turning, unable to sleep because of Mussolini's declaration of war. Valentina got up to check on Suor Maria Vittoria, who'd retired early, still not feeling herself.

Cara Madre di Dio! A cry escaped her at her friend's alarming condition. She lay her hand on the old nun's head, realizing she burned with fever and struggled for breath.

Rushing out of the room, Valentina flew to the kitchen to brew a pot of willow bark tea and thyme, a natural fever remedy. She carried a tray with the tea, cold water, and compresses and set it on Suor Maria Vittoria's bedside table. Then she ran to Suor Teresa's room, alerting her to Suor Maria Vittoria's illness.

"Call Dottore Giordano and wake Madre Superiora. Tell *il dottore* to hurry," Valentina said over her shoulder as she rushed back to Suor Maria Vittoria's room.

The old nun lay on the narrow bed, her skin pale except for the dark recesses beneath her closed eyes. Valentina carefully lifted her friend and slipped two additional pillows beneath her. Sitting on the edge of the bed, she placed a cold compress on Suor Maria Vittoria's forehead.

The nun moaned, "Suor Gianna?"

"Yes, I'm here, Sister. Let me help you." She spooned a few teaspoons of tea into her mouth.

The other nuns at the convent began to arrive, clutching their rosary beads and praying at the ailing nun's bedside. Suor Elena brought fresh tea and compresses, and Suor Magdalena brought a bouquet of pink camellias, Suor Maria Vittoria's favorite flower.

Suor Teresa ran through the door with Mother Superior Busnelli on her heels, their faces stark with worry. "The doctor is on his way," Suor Teresa rasped, breathless from running.

"How is she?" asked the abbess.

"I'm giving her tea and applying cold compresses," Valentina replied, worried about Suor Maria Vittoria's rattling cough.

"Suor Gianna, take care of her until the doctor arrives." The Abbess looked around the room at the nuns who had crowded in. "The rest of you see to your duties. And pray for our dear sister." She opened the window to let in fresh air. "It is better if fewer of us are underfoot and in the way. Fetch me when the doctor arrives."

The abbess closed the door behind the last departing nuns, and Valentina was left alone with Suor Maria Vittoria. She spooned more tea past the frail nun's dry, parched lips, dipped the compress in cold water, wrung it, and bathed her forehead. She took her friend's hand and began her personal plea to the Lord. Then a miracle happened, and Suor Maria Vittoria's eyes fluttered open. It took a moment for her gaze to clear, almost as if she'd been far away and suddenly traveled a great distance. "My child, I'm so glad you're here."

"Thank God you're awake." Valentina held Suor Maria Vittoria's hand between hers. "The doctor should be here soon. Are you in pain? We're all so worried about you."

The old nun's beatific smile brought tears to Valentina's eyes.

"I am prepared for my journey," she said in a crackling voice. "God is with me."

"I don't want you to go... Not yet..." Valentina could not stop the tears pouring down her cheeks. She wiped them away with a facecloth.

"My child, you are the daughter of my heart."

A sob escaped Valentina's lips. She adored this woman who'd welcomed her into the convent and gave her a mother's unconditional love—a love her own mother had always withheld.

"Hush, my child, do not mourn for me...Rejoice, for I will be with our Lady and our Savior. I know that Alberto and our baby are waiting to welcome me with open arms."

Valentina nodded and wiped her eyes. "I love you, Suor Maria Vittoria. You are the mother of my heart. You have taught me so much about life..."

"You've matured into a strong woman, and I am so proud of you." The nun with the kindest eyes in the world took a wheezing breath. "In my Bible—" Suor Maria Vittoria's hand shook as she strained to reach her bedside table where her prayerbook lay alongside her wire-framed reading glasses.

Gently, Valentina pushed her back down. "Let me, Sister. Please, you need to rest." She set the Bible on the blanket.

Suor Maria Vittoria tried to breathe and was seized by a choking cough. "I have chosen you to continue my work." Another rattling spasm shook her shoulders.

Valentina poured a glass of water and held it to the old nun's lips. "We have no need to speak of this. The doctor will be here soon. Do not worry about the library and its care. I will see to it. You've taught me all there is to know about the books. I will see to everything."

"No, my dear. Let me speak."

Valentina nodded, as fresh tears blurred her vision. She could not bear the thought of losing Suor Maria Vittoria. The idea of living without her broke her heart.

"In my Bible, you will find a letter for you. It explains everything. I shouldn't have put it off for so long, but—" she fingered the cross around her neck and smiled. "One never thinks that time will run out."

"And it won't. Not tonight." Valentina didn't want to cry. She didn't want to face her friend's looming death. But her tears kept streaming down her cheeks, and she couldn't suppress them.

"No, of course not." Suor Maria Vittoria's smile deepened the wrinkles and hollows around her eyes. The many years of her life were etched on that beloved face.

Realizing the truth, it was all Valentina could do to contain her emotions and not cry a river of tears until the Heavens took notice and intervened.

"The treasure. You must keep it safe." Suor Maria Vittoria's voice sounded reedy and frail, as though the effort to speak consumed what little strength remained. She closed her eyes and struggled for breath.

"Sh, I understand about the letters. We have already spoken of this. I have been transcribing them for years."

"Yes, but not officially. This is what Suor Ursula did for me—"

"Yes, we spoke of that as well. I have read the formal letter she wrote you. It is a beautiful and heartfelt missive. She loved you very much."

"As I loved her."

"Rest assured, I will cherish your letter as you have cherished Suor Ursula's."

"But there are others…"

"I know what is in the *cassone* but have not had time to study everything." In truth, Valentina had wondered how she would organize all the documents and if she would transcribe them all. Some documents were not letters but merely sheets of parchment with the signatures of the nuns who'd guarded the treasure. Valentina knew that centuries ago, many nuns could barely read or write, and yet they were given charge of the priceless treasure because of their dedication and honor.

"I understand, Suor Maria Vittoria. Please do not tax yourself. I promise to read your letter and rest assured I will do as you ask. But you must rest, my dear friend. Nothing is more important." Valentina reached for the prayer book lying on Suor Maria Vittoria's blanket. Without giving the letter another thought, she slipped the prayerbook into her pocket.

Suor Maria Vittoria sighed and nodded. Her fingers clasped her cross, and she brought it to her withered lips and kissed it. "Read the letter, and then you will understand. You must promise to care for the treasure entrusted to us by that dear lady." She tried to remove the chain from around her neck.

"Let me help you," said Valentina.

"Take the key to the box and always wear it," Suor Maria Vittoria whispered.

"I promise I will." Valentina gently removed the chain with

the key from around her beloved friend's neck and slipped it over her head.

"You are a bright light, my child. No matter what happens in this war, I know you will do what you must to protect those you love."

A tapping at the window drew Valentina's attention, and she gasped as a bird flew in and landed on the bed next to Suor Maria Vittoria.

"Ah, my dear little friend, you have returned to say goodbye to me," the old nun said.

The little bird chirped and fluttered its wings in reply.

"My child, place him in my hand so I may hold him one last time."

Valentina did what the nun requested. She guided Suor Maria Vittoria's hand so the bird could hop onto her palm.

"You are brave and strong," the elderly nun told the tiny bird. "You survived that storm because you are meant for great things."

The bird tilted his head and sang in reply.

"One day, we shall meet in Heaven, and you can sing for me again."

Valentina took the bird into her hands and carried him to the open window, where he hopped onto the windowsill, fluttered his wings, and began to chirp a melancholy song.

Valentina returned to Suor Maria Vittoria's bedside. "I wish you could stay here with me."

"I will always be with you, in your heart."

Valentina bent down and gently kissed Suor Maria Vittoria's hand. Despite the cold compresses, the nun's cheeks were flushed with fever, and her breathing had become more labored. Valentina heaved a sigh of relief when Teresa rushed in with the doctor on her heels.

"I'm sorry it took so long for me to get here," the doctor said. "It seems as though Il Duce's declaration of war drove everyone to their beds with maladies."

Valentina rose. "She's running a high temperature, Dottore."

He lifted Suor Maria Vittoria's wrist and took her pulse. "If you will assist me, Sorella, I will examine her."

As the doctor concluded his examination, Valentina turned to Suor Teresa. "Can you stay with Suor Maria Vittoria while I speak with Dottore Giordano and the abbess?"

Suor Teresa nodded and continued to bathe the old nun's face and hands as Valentina followed the doctor out.

"Suor Maria Vittoria has contracted a virus in her heart." He shook his head, and white wisps of hair fell onto his forehead. His neatly manicured fingers smoothed the rebellious hair back. "I have given her an injection of morphine to make her more comfortable, and I left a bottle of syrup with morphine and herbs to ease her cough and help her rest. But I am afraid she is beyond my help. She is in God's hands now."

The abbess sent for Padre Vincenzo to administer the last rites, and Valentina and her fellow sisters gathered around their dear friend. Suor Maria Vittoria passed away two days after falling ill. The funeral was packed with mourners from the convent and the city of Florence as tears flowed for the gentle nun who'd touched so many lives with her goodness.

The little bird also returned to sing for Suor Maria Vittoria on the day of her funeral. And with a flutter of his wings, he flew away, soaring into the sky.

CHAPTER 17

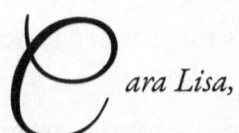 *ara Lisa,*

This painting is more than oil and water, more than light and shadow. More than the beauty that shines from within you. I have come to realize, to believe, that this painting is the melding of our souls...

"Salai, you scoundrel, where is the purple cloth I asked you to buy?"

Leonardo sifted through a pile of folded silks and velvets. It wasn't like him to be short-tempered over trivial matters but worrying and fretting over the coming exhibition wound him tighter than a recalcitrant curl.

Salai sauntered into the salon, nibbling on toasted bread

slathered with olive oil and layered with sliced tomato, cheese, and prosciutto. "I don't remember you telling me to purchase purple cloth," he mumbled between bites.

Leonardo glared at Salai, his vexation making his eye twitch.

"Of course, I told you, but you never listen." He watched a chunk of tomato fall to the floor. "Stop feeding your face and dropping crumbs all over the room. In a short while, the entire city of Florence will arrive to preview Lisa's portrait. Clean up after yourself. Heaven help you if the gonfaloniere slips on your careless droppings—your *culo* will be thrown in Stinche Prison."

"You are entirely too nervous. The cartoon is magnificent, and everyone will soon be praising your genius and vying for you to immortalize them in a portrait." The young man flicked his wrist at the swatches of cloth. "There are more than enough pieces of fabric to choose from. Pick another color."

"Always a clever answer from you. What is the matter? Have you some complaint you would like to make known?"

With an indolent air, Salai bent and wiped the tomato from the floor with a scrap of cloth and, walking to the window, flung it outside. "You act like an anxious groom."

"Bah, you speak foolishly when I am thinking seriously. Lisa and Francesco are coming to see the portrait. I haven't allowed her to see it yet, and it is important that she feel gratified. I worry that her husband won't understand what I created and will not like it. What if he decides he does not want the portrait after all?"

"You worry far too much, Maestro. I still do not understand why you chose to paint a woman of so little renown. If her husband no longer wants the painting, we will sell it to someone else. Besides, I suspect you care not at all whether he wants it."

Leonardo arched a brow. "Ridiculous. How else am I to keep

you dressed in the finest silks and velvets you're so accustomed to?"

Salai scoffed. "Your work progresses so slowly it will be a miracle if we ever see a florin from this commission."

As if explaining himself to an uncooperative child, Leonardo elucidated, "That is the reason for the atelier; from here, the work is produced in a timely manner so that I may take my time without pressure when working on a project that interests me." Leonardo turned to the drawing—in his mind, he saw the finished painting of Lisa, but he had yet to set brush to canvas. He draped a forest green swatch of velvet over the poplar board propped on the easel, fussing over each fold, making sure the cloth hung without a crease. "Please, I wish not to argue with you. Are the refreshments laid out in the studio?"

The young man offered up a contrite smile, cupped Leonardo's face, and kissed his lips in a gesture of atonement. "Everything is perfect. All we need is the citizenry."

An hour later, the studio teemed with artists and Florence's elite. Laughter and conversation staged a background chorus befitting the main event. In a city that claimed the greatest artists in the world, Florentines prided themselves on their connoisseurship of all forms of art, and it was not unusual for an artist to display his work for the public to behold before completion. Florentines understood and appreciated *disegni,* the sketches artists prepared before applying color. Leonardo hoped they would take his *disegno* to their hearts and sing its praise.

"Leonardo, you have held us all in suspense long enough. Let us see this new masterpiece," Piero Soderini, the gonfaloniere, declared.

Machiavelli seconded the statement, teasing Leonardo about

keeping them in suspense. "You are like a general who refuses to reveal his plan until the day of the battle."

Leonardo winked. "I believe I may have learned that from you, *amico mio.*"

He lifted his wine glass. "Soon, honored signori. We await the guest of honor, the lady who is the subject and inspiration of this work. It would not do for you to see one without the other." Leonardo glanced at the entrance, willing Lisa to appear. He did not know how much longer he could keep the crowd at bay. And then, as if hearing his thoughts, the del Giocondos entered the studio.

"*Mi scusi,*" Leonardo said, bowing. "Salai," he called, "wine for the signora and signore, *per favore.*"

He greeted the couple, bowing to Francesco and pressing his lips to Lisa's hand. "I bid you both welcome to my atelier as my honored guests." Leonardo kept his voice deferential and was rewarded by Francesco's broad smile. Salai arrived on Leonardo's heels and handed Lisa and Francesco each a glass of wine.

Lisa's eyes sparkled above the rim of her glass, conveying a silent message of joyful communion. He knew she was looking forward to the unveiling, but the delight in her eyes told him she was happy to see him safely returned to Florence. Until this moment, he did not realize how much he had missed her.

"I hope your trip to Tuscany was successful, Maestro," Francesco said.

"Yes, it was most informative, and the ministry is quite satisfied with my maps and suggestions. Time will tell whether my designs will be implemented. But let us not speak of that journey when there is so much excitement about the portrait you so generously commissioned."

Lisa patted her husband's arm. "Leonardo is right, Francesco. We are here to celebrate the unveiling of the *disegno*. Besides, there is enough discussion about politics, war, and commerce."

"See, Leonardo, what is a man to do when the woman he adores is always right. Let us see how well you've captured my Lisa."

"I hope you will be pleased, Signore. Now that all the actors are on stage, we can raise the curtain." Leonardo clapped his hands, and all eyes turned to him. "My friends, because so many of you are curious about my latest work, I decided to share with you *il disegno* for my next painting. The fair lady who inspired the painting joins us today." He turned to Lisa, whose cheeks brightened with a rosy hue. "I leave it to you to decide whether I do her justice."

Leonardo led the way into his *camera,* followed by the assembly of guests, abuzz with chatter. Dozens of lit candles bathed the room in a golden luminescence, and a hush fell over the gathering as all eyes focused on the velvet-draped easel elevated on a podium. Leonardo's long, tapered fingers peeled back the cloth with dramatic flair, and he stepped back.

An audible gasp escaped the crowd, accompanied by shouts of "Bravo, Maestro!" and "Congratulations!" Gratified by the favorable reception, his eyes sought the one person whose reaction he most wanted to see. *Where is she?* Lisa and her husband seemed to have been swallowed up in the thick of the throng. He sighed as his attention was captured by the exclamations in the packed room about the beautiful woman in the portrait surrounded by the magnificence of nature.

"I can see her breathe," a man remarked. "I swear her breast rises and falls."

"Imagine what she will look like when given color," a woman's voice opined. "I have never seen anything so vibrant. So alive."

"She smiles as if she knows something we would all like to know," another man quipped.

Leonardo turned back to the canvas, and serenity swirled through him as he beheld the drawing. Rivers spilled from distant mountains, flowing into the folds of her gown. A bridge spanned a river, and rock formations rose from the misty landscape like sentinels. The inspiration had come to him on his journey home after his expedition to Pisa. As he traveled through the lush Tuscan countryside, an epiphany about the painting had filled him with creative exhilaration.

He'd always regarded Lisa as one with nature and nature as one with her, so much so that a backdrop of banal domesticity would never have done her justice. Instead, he chose to enshrine her, surrounded by the splendor of primordial mountains and the surge of serpentine rivers. Her ethereal and mysterious beauty would always be inseparable from what was, what is, and what would always be.

"It's a *capolavoro*, Maestro. She lives and breathes." The gonfaloniere shook Leonardo's hand. "You must come to see me this week. I have a proposition in mind for you. It is time you were given a commission from the city of Florence equivalent to your talent and stature."

Leonardo inclined his head. "It is an honor for me to serve the republic."

And then, like a river pouring into the sea, the citizens of Florence swept into the chamber to offer their congratulations. While accepting the countless compliments and expressions of awe with gratitude, Leonardo continued to search for Lisa. She had brought about this triumphant moment. Without her, none of it would have been possible.

Having received a multitude of good wishes, at last, Leonardo stood alone, his gaze drawn once more to his vision of Lisa. A hand touched his elbow, and he turned to find her standing beside him. The truth struck him anew as it always did—that the vision in his mind's eye paled in comparison to the woman herself.

"Maestro, my dear friend. I do not know what to say..." Tears pooled in her eyes. "You have created a vision that resembles me, and yet it is so much more..."

"The drawing *is* you—*for* you. It reflects the way I see you. I hope you like it, Signora."

"I do, I do. I love it. I await our next sitting with joyful anticipation."

He wanted to take her hand, to feel its warmth and chastised himself for the thought.

"Francesco believes he has made a good investment judging by the deluge of admirers," she added with a smile.

"I am glad your husband is pleased." Leonardo was also relieved, for he worried about the merchant's opinion of his wife spending so much time sitting for the portrait. "I have good news. The Gonfaloniere Soderini has invited me to visit him at the Palazzo della Signoria to discuss a commission."

"Oh, Leonardo, this is wonderful news." Her fingers on his arm fluttered like the wings of a butterfly. "I am delighted to hear you will be recognized in an official manner. And, selfishly, I know this will keep you here in Florence."

"With the expectation of a commission here in Florence, it seems unlikely that I will divert rivers or build canals to the sea anytime soon." He leaned down and added in a low voice, "But I will continue to make time for our portrait."

Lisa's eyes twinkled conspiratorially, and her smile filled him with warmth.

"I will also continue to make time whenever you desire," she said softly.

He'd accomplished what he most desired all because of this wondrous woman who'd inspired him. Leonardo bent and pressed his lips to Lisa's hand, his heart soaring like a bird taking flight.

CHAPTER 18

JUNE 15, 1940 ~ FLORENCE, ITALY

*V*alentina took a sip of chamomile tea and set the cup down. She hadn't been hungry since they laid Suor Maria Vittoria to rest three days ago. The other sisters knew how close she'd been to the convent librarian, so she needed no excuse to take her meal alone in her bedroom.

She picked up the newspaper again and re-read the headline: *GERMANS MARCH INTO PARIS*. Complete and utter madness. Every day, Valentina read some new horror about the war.

In six weeks, Germany had invaded and conquered the Netherlands, Belgium, and Luxembourg, and yesterday they'd marched into Paris. She shook her head, hardly able to comprehend the speed and escalation of events.

Was it only two weeks ago the British named Winston

Churchill prime minister? She'd sat with her fellow sisters listening to his first speech to the House of Commons, "I have nothing to offer but blood, toil, tears, and sweat." And then, five days ago, the American president, Franklyn Roosevelt, denounced Mussolini and said, "The hand that held the dagger has plunged it into the back of its neighbor." Any hope for a peaceful remedy had vanished. The world was at war, and though the United States was not yet formally committed, she sensed it would not be long before they, too, were drawn into the fray.

Exhausted and disheartened, Valentina folded the newspaper and laid it on the desk. With Suor Maria Vittoria's passing and news about the war, she felt a growing heaviness in her heart.

A knock on the door interrupted her gloomy thoughts. "Yes, come in."

Suor Teresa poked her head in. "I wanted to see if you were all right. We missed you at supper and evening prayers."

"I'm fine, just tired and sad. Come in," Valentina invited.

"I'll only stay a moment. Perhaps a good night's sleep will help you feel better."

Valentina mustered a smile. "Yes, perhaps."

Suor Teresa fingered the cross around her neck. "I miss her, too. It was so sudden."

Valentina got up from the bed and hugged Teresa. "The unfairness of life." She thought about her father, the heartbreak of losing him without warning. "We never know when our time will come or that of someone we love.

"At least we were able to say our goodbyes to Suor Maria Vittoria," her friend said.

"Yes, a true blessing."

"I will leave you to your rest. Goodnight, Sorella." Suor Teresa left, closing the door with a quiet click.

Valentina poured a glass of water and set it on her nightstand. She pulled her habit over her head and heard something fall to the floor. She bent and retrieved a small personal Bible. An envelope slid out, and she picked it up. Turning it over, she read her name scrawled on the outside, recognizing the shaky script of Suor Maria Vittoria.

She exhaled a deep sigh, realizing she'd utterly forgotten the letter Suor Maria Vittoria had written. She prepared for bed and recited the last prayer of the day, the *Compline* from the *Liturgy of the Hours*, and with her mind at peace, she opened the envelope. A feeling of guilt settled in her stomach as she carefully unfolded the letter from Suor Maria Vittoria.

Carissima Valentina,

> *You are the daughter of my heart, the child I might have had if God had not chosen me for the Church. Over the years, I have watched you mature and blossom into a woman dedicated to your fellow sisters. Your heart is pure and giving. I know you will continue to help those who need your guidance and strength. For this reason, I have chosen you to protect the sacred promise. The same one I swore to when I was your age.*
>
> *I must explain how and why I became the keeper of this treasure. I have told you the history, but I must repeat it in writing because that is what the keepers have always done.*
>
> *Five hundred years ago, a woman named Lisa del Giocondo lived in Florence on the Via della Stufa. She was*

married to Francesco del Giocondo, a prosperous silk merchant. She had two daughters, three sons, and a stepson.

Both daughters, Camilla and Marietta, became nuns. The older daughter, Camilla, entered the San Domenico di Cafaggio convent and took the name of Suor Beatrice. She died tragically at eighteen and was buried at Santa Maria Novella.

Lisa's other daughter, Marietta, was seventeen in 1521 when she entered Sant' Orsola, a renowned convent known to take in unmarried pregnant women. Marietta took the name of Suor Ludovica.

After her husband, Francesco, passed away, Lisa del Giocondo went to live at the Sant' Orsola convent to be with her daughter. She remained there until the end of her life. Perhaps it would have been wiser to destroy the letters before her death, but they were so precious to her that she could not bear to part with them or obliterate them from existence. Instead, she entrusted them to her daughter, Suor Ludovica, and extracted a promise from her to keep them safe and not share them with the world.

Suor Ludovica vowed to uphold her mother's wishes— protect the treasure and tell no one except a trusted confidante when the time came for her to do so. And so began the sacred promise that has connected us all to the Mona Lisa.

In all the years since Signora Lisa Giocondo entrusted her treasure to her daughter, your time of guardianship may be the most precarious. The winds of war are blowing across the continent. An evil is coming that I fear will not be easily defeated, that will bring terrible suffering and profound consequences.

Over the years, you have learned much about preserving and archiving artistic and written works on paper. I encourage you to stay abreast of advancements in the field of conservation. Our duty as librarians is to preserve everything in our keeping for future generations. But in this extraordinary situation, I urge you to pursue an elevated course of knowledge and use all the tools of science to protect this treasure.

It will one day fall to you to choose your successor. I know you will choose wisely.

I leave you to your journey and wish you a long and healthy life.

I have every faith that one day we shall meet again and walk in the golden light of Heaven.

I kiss you and pray God keeps you well.

Con tutto il mio cuore,
Suor Maria Vittoria

Valentina folded the letter and slipped it back into her prayer book. Wiping her tears, she walked to the window and watched the shroud of black clouds blanketing the sky. A flash of lightning blinded her, followed by a distant rumble of thunder. The heavy clouds opened to a downpour, and rain pounded like fists upon the tiled roof. The cooling air was a relief from the humidity. Emotionally drained and physically weary, Valentina got into bed, closed her eyes, and fell asleep.

IN THE COMING days and weeks, Valentina was determined to honor her promise to Suor Maria Vittoria. She began to type out her written transcriptions to provide insight to future caretakers. Transcribing each letter was a slow and methodical process, given that they were written in Leonardo's unique coded hand. A code that Lisa had learned and used in her letters as well.

Valentina jotted down her thoughts in a notebook, which she kept in the same folder. She felt an urgency to complete the deciphering and documenting of the correspondence, worried about what the war would bring. She was determined to ensure the treasure was hidden from the Blackshirts.

Reviewing her most recent copy, she was struck by the intimacy in Leonardo's parting words to Lisa: *"I cannot wait to return to our collaboration and, if the truth be told, I cannot wait to return to you. Humbly and forever yours, Leonardo."*

A knock at the door interrupted her ruminations. "Yes, who is it?"

Suor Teresa popped her head in. "A man in a uniform is here to see you."

"Did he give a name?"

Suor Teresa shook her head. "I asked, and he said he needs to speak with you privately."

"Well, there's no sense in wondering. I will go see for myself." Valentina tried not to worry that this man knew of some infraction she'd been guilty of. Behind the scenes, she'd quietly been inquiring about a vendor at the mercato who was rumored to be in touch with the resistance.

"He is waiting for you in the cloister."

"Thank you, Sister." Valentina carefully slid the drawings and the letters with their tissue separators back into the folio, then placed the folio into the wooden box. Locking the box with the key Suor Maria Vittoria had given her before she died, she put the box in the bottom drawer of her desk. She slipped the thin gold chain with the key around her neck, a reminder of the promise she had sworn to keep. Keeping her work in progress under lock and key was time-consuming, but there was no other way to ensure its safety. The Blackshirts had spies everywhere, and although Valentina trusted every nun with her life, tradespeople were often in and out of the convent, along with lay people seeking assistance. One could never be too careful in these dark times.

Valentina made her way to the peaceful cloister with its marble benches, emerald-green lawn, and blossoming citrus trees. The stranger stood with his hands clasped behind his back under the shade of a tree.

"I am Suor Gianna. I understand you wish to speak with me?"

Slowly, he turned, and Valentina froze, recognizing him instantly. Standing before her was Dante Conti, the man who was responsible for altering the course of her life.

His black uniform, shiny knee-high black boots, and black collar flames on his tunic lapels labeled him a high-ranking member of the MVSN, the Voluntary Militia for National Security, Mussolini's army of Blackshirts. She did not think she would ever cross paths with Dante again. And yet here he was, looking at her with the same unnerving stare that she had hoped never to see again. Valentina squared her shoulders and prepared for the worst.

"Valentina Amato, it *is* you. Why, I can scarcely believe it." His eyes raked her from head to toe. "For fourteen years, I searched for you. I had heard you'd run away to Milan. And yet, here you are, practically under my feet, hiding in a convent in Florence."

"I am no longer Valentina Amato. I am now Suor Gianna of the order of Santa Maria del Carmine. I am not hiding from you or anyone else. I entered this convent sixteen years ago. Santa Maria del Carmine is my home."

The man who stood before her had changed little in the ensuing years. The softness of youth had transformed into the lean, sculpted features of a handsome man in his prime. But those black eyes still held the same arrogance as they always did, except now there was a glint of malice in his gaze as though he had learned a thing or two about revenge over the years.

"You haven't changed in the least except for that costume," he said with a smirk.

"I imagine you are married with many children by now." She ignored his disrespectful comment.

"I am not."

Valentina looked down, her fingers grasping her rosary beads. "Why are you here?"

"Now that I've found the lost love of my youth, I shall make her come to her senses, especially when she learns that I know she's kept a secret from me all these years."

Dio mio, Chiara! Could he possibly know of her existence? Or had he learned about the cache of letters hidden in the convent? She decided to call his bluff. "And what secret is that?" It was remarkable how calm she sounded even as her heart felt close to bursting from her chest.

"Rome was not built in a day, Suor Gianna. I have learned to be patient over the years." A cruel smile twisted his face, and she was transported back to that terrible day. In an instant, bile rose in her throat, and her façade of bravado disappeared. It would serve him right if she retched on his shiny black boots.

He strode toward her until his face was mere inches from hers. "Valentina," he said in a low voice, making her shudder in revulsion. "You have wasted your extraordinary beauty in this home for old nags and ugly scarecrows. You can't be more than thirty, still young enough to carry a child inside you." He leaned down and whispered in her ear, "And ripe enough to welcome a man between your legs."

Fear skittered up her spine, and she stumbled back a few steps. "Are you blind? Do you not see what stands before you? I wear a habit and veil."

"Mere accoutrements." He shrugged. "Your vows mean nothing. Easily broken." He clicked his heels together. "You haven't congratulated me on my new position."

"I do not know what your position is." *Calm yourself. He cannot harm you here. You are protected by the sanctity of the Church. A scream will bring your sisters running to help you.*

"I am now *aiutante di campo* to the Minister of Popular Culture, Alessandro Pavolini. How serendipitous to discover we both reside here in Florence. I look forward to rekindling the flame of our friendship."

More than anything, she wanted to slap the disingenuous grin off his face. "I must disappoint you, for we Sisters of Santa Maria del Carmine are far too busy with our charitable works at the convent. I'm afraid it would be impossible for us to see each other again."

"Oh, I disagree, Valentina. There is so much we have yet to resolve. I assure you we will see each other again. Count on it!" He grabbed her hand and pressed his lips to her skin before she could pull away. With a chuckle, he spun on his heel and strode away.

Like a sculpture cemented in place, she stood until he was gone. Rubbing her hand where his lips had touched, she took deep, calming breaths as her heart returned to a normal rhythm.

Of course, she knew the name Alessandro Pavolini. He controlled the press with an iron fist. The press could not publish or broadcast anything without his permission. Undoubtedly, he was a dangerous man to get on the wrong side of. Dante had snagged a powerful position, very close to the seat of power and the man who occupied that seat, Benito Mussolini. Dante Conti had undoubtedly risen in the world, which made him even more dangerous.

Valentina hoped he was bluffing. Dante could not know about Chiara unless he'd discovered the information from her mother or brothers. But she doubted they would have said anything; better to say nothing than to bring disgrace upon their own heads.

Although she'd never revealed to her family that Dante had been responsible, nor had she given them details of her daughter's name or adoption, Valentina would still need to proceed with caution. Dante now had the ear of influential people; he could easily discover the truth. She could not take his threat lightly. Even a false claim about her or anyone at the convent could prove just as calamitous.

She shivered as though the Devil had stepped across her grave. Evil stalked her once more.

CHAPTER 19

JANUARY 12, 1504 ~ FLORENCE, ITALY

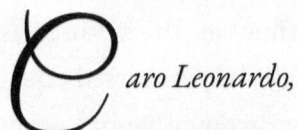 *aro Leonardo,*

*Oh, how I miss you. I know your new commission, the
Battle of Anghiari, demands the bulk of your time and efforts.
No one could be happier for you than I am, but how I miss my
conversations with my dearest friend. My days are filled with
the joy of raising Piero, Camilla, Andrea, Giocondo, and my
stepson Bartolomeo. They are my heart. However, I have come
to understand that with the passage of years, my heart has
expanded to include more. So much more than I thought
possible...*

Lisa sat in a comfortable armchair in front of a cheery fire after
a busy morning of seeing to the welfare of Francesco and the chil-

dren. It was rare for her to find the time to sit and read. A recent visit to the bookseller's stall led to the discovery of a book by a female author: *Libro della Città delle Signore, Book of the City of Ladies*, by Christine de Pizan. A growing number of printed books had become available in the past few years, but to find one written by a woman filled Lisa with delight. She was engrossed by the allegorical story about a city composed of the most famous women in history.

De Pizan's prose brought to life the stories of women such as Mary Magdalene, Helen of Troy, Caesar's daughter Julia, and dozens of female saints and royal daughters and wives. Before reading De Pizan's book, Lisa had no knowledge of the incredible feats and accomplishments of such women. What would it be like to be a woman of consequence, a woman remembered in the annals of history?

It was inspiring to contemplate a time in the future, as Leonardo had suggested when women might be considered equal to men. Lisa knew that without education, women would never advance in the ways that made a difference in the public sphere— economically and politically. She thanked Heaven that her father had made sure she was literate, and she intended for her daughter's education to equal that of her sons. She and Francesco disagreed on this point. Her husband had seen little to be gained by educating a daughter except in domestic skills, but Lisa had stood firm in her argument, and Camilla now received tutoring alongside her brothers.

A gentle rap on the door sounded, and Katerina, one of the household maids, poked her head in. "Signora, a gentleman in the foyer, carries a message for you."

"Show him in, Katerina." Lisa rose and smoothed out the

creases of her blue velvet gown. Her hand fluttered to her chest when Salai entered the study. "Is the Maestro well, Salai?" she asked in alarm.

"Yes, Signora, he is fine." Salai's face was tense and etched with a sour expression. "The Maestro sent me to bid you visit him at the cathedral. On his instruction, I waited until your husband left the house."

"Yes, yes, better not to stir up his questions. I must change. Will you wait?"

"My master instructed that I should. I have a carriage outside, and I am to escort you."

The Basilica of Santa Maria Novella was not far, but the streets were icy and treacherous. The carriage made its way slowly over the cobblestones. The young man beside her made no effort to engage in conversation. Salai held no understanding of her relationship with Leonardo, nor did she imagine he approved of her. He stared out the window; the look on his face was one of a surly dog whose master had kicked him.

She laid her hand on his. Startled, he looked at her. "Salai, I know you do not approve of my friendship with Leonardo, but you have nothing to fear from me."

He pulled his hand away, and the heavens unleashed a storm of disgruntlement. "You may not mean to harm him, but you endanger him, nonetheless. The hours he spends on your portrait waste his valuable time. It is not even you that he paints, but some vision that consumes the workings of his mind. You should not flatter yourself that you are the muse that inspires him."

Lisa was struck by Salai's malicious attack and his jealousy. She could understand he felt threatened. It occurred to her that she and Salai were probably the same age, which meant his youth alone could no longer benefit him in Leonardo's affection. "I am married, Salai, with four sons and a daughter. While it is true that Leonardo has awakened a yearning in me, it is one of mind and heart. He has become a dear and cherished friend. I mean no injury to you or your station, I promise you."

Salai huffed. "I hold as much power over Leonardo as that beggar in the street." He nodded toward a man with straggly gray hair clutching a blanket around his shoulders.

"I disagree. Leonardo depends on you and is ever mindful of your feelings. We both know he is devoted in his loyalty to you, as I am sure you are to him," she gently reminded him as the carriage clattered to a stop in front of the Basilica.

Salai climbed down from the carriage, and Lisa noted the beauty of the brocaded fur-lined cloak that graced his lean frame. He offered up his hand to help her down. "Salai, that is a beautiful cape you wear."

He looked down at himself and finally broke into a smile. "It was a gift to Leonardo from Cesare Borgia, and he gave it to me."

"I would say it leaves no doubt of Leonardo's affection for you. Thank you for accompanying me here."

Lisa followed Salai up the steps to the arched portal that framed the double doors leading into the church. As always, the harmonious proportions of Alberti's architectural masterpiece made her breath catch. She took a moment to admire the broad frieze decorated with squares and the four white and green pillars that supported it. Above the frieze was a pediment containing a round window and above that, the Dominican order's emblem of Christ as the sun god. And then, as if to crown his vision with glory, Alberti had veneered the entire façade of the Basilica with green serpentine and white marble. The Basilica tantalized like an iced wedding cake beneath a gray-laden sky.

Salai opened the doors to the church and extended his hand, inviting her in. "Signora."

She entered the austere nave, where towering Corinthian columns supported the Gothic ribs that spanned the ceiling. Crisscrossing the vault, the bones of the cathedral soared and reflected the pointed arches polychromed in black and white. Lisa glimpsed Ghirlandaio's frescoes of the *Virgin* and *John the Baptist* and Masaccio's *Holy Trinity* within the side chapels as she passed.

It was a somber winter's day, and the round, clerestory, and stained-glass windows provided little light. But even in the dim interior, she was in awe of Giotto's masterpiece, the *Crucifix of the Passion*, the moment of Christ's death when his life's blood ebbed from him. Lisa knelt in deference and made the sign of the cross.

Salai waited for her and then led her up the east aisle, where Leonardo worked with his back to them. As the sound of Lisa and Salai's footsteps echoed through the church's interior, Leonardo turned and put down his chalk.

"Signora del Giocondo, I am so pleased you could come."

Lisa knew Leonardo's formality was for Salai's benefit.

He lifted her hand to his lips. "Your hands are so cold, Signora."

"This winter's day has made them so," she said calmly. "But my hands will warm soon enough. I am honored by your request."

"Thank you, Signora. I hope to mine your thoughts about my work. But first," he turned to Salai. "Perhaps you can take care of those errands I gave you while the lady and I visit. When you return, you can escort Signora del Giocondo back to her home."

Without a word, Salai bowed and disappeared through a side door.

"He doesn't like me," Lisa said.

"Our friendship disturbs the normal order of his life. Pay him no mind." Leonardo turned to face the wall on which he was working. "As usual, I'm behind and worry that the Signoria of the Chancery will not understand my efforts. How do you respond to what I have accomplished thus far?"

Pinned to the wall were countless sheets of paper joined into one massive canvas. Lisa knew that many artists created a cartoon on paper first, and once they were satisfied with their efforts, they transferred it to a proper canvas or board, or in this case, a wall. She'd seen many of Leonardo's preparatory drawings but viewing the life-size conflagration of horses and men in conflict assaulted her senses.

The savagery distilled in the images spoke more of the horrors of war rather than its glorification. Lisa shivered at the realistic depiction of men being slaughtered by swords and trampled by hooves. Her throat tightened as if the dust kicked up from the horse's hooves filled her mouth and nose. It had never occurred to her that a horse would fight to the death, biting and kicking with as much frenzied tenacity as its rider.

It was the most chilling sight Lisa had ever seen, yet she could not look away. She knew without a doubt that Leonardo had witnessed such a battle during his tenure with Cesare Borgia and had recreated it here in startling detail.

"What do you think?" He watched her face.

"Your drawing is magnificent, and I think it will have a lasting effect on how others view war in the future." Lisa met his gaze. "I think it will be your greatest work, Leonardo."

"You think so?"

"Yes. It is so real that I feel swept away into the thick of battle. As if at any moment I will be trampled by a horse or feel the sharp edge of a sword."

"Then I have accomplished what I wished to convey." His gaze returned to the cartoon. "The greater challenge is the painting of it. I have failed with frescoes in the past."

"Have you found a method that might prove satisfactory?"

"I am experimenting with different compounds, including an oil-based pigment and glaze, but I will not know if they work until I apply them to the prepared wall. I purchased a *Pece Greca per la pittura,* a Greek pitch that I will mix with wax for the basecoat, and I have ordered a vast quantity of linseed oil."

"And this is a different approach, is it not?"

He nodded. "When I painted *The Last Supper,* I applied a base of ground white stone and white lead primer. I mixed the tempera paint with pigment, water, egg yolk, and oil paint and then added linseed oil. I experimented with varying amounts of each, but, in the end, as you know, it became a disaster. The fresco chipped and peeled almost before I finished painting. It will be a miracle from God if it survives."

"It must be frustrating to envision something in your mind and yet be thwarted in that vision because the material to execute it is lacking."

"As always, Lisa, you surprise me," he said, arching a brow. "What you say applies not only to my art but to so many of my imaginings and inventions. You, of course, are privy to my desire to fly."

"Oh, Leonardo, if only we could. I would delight in soaring across the sky with you."

He lifted her hand and brought it to his lips. "I would never risk your safety, but I have not given up on the notion of flight. In fact, I am building a new apparatus, and I plan to initiate the maiden voyage myself."

"*Per favore,* Maestro, you must assure me that you will not attempt this without a surgeon present and myself, for that matter."

"As you wish, *cara.*" His lips curved into a smile. "Are you worried that you might lose me?"

"I am worried that the world might lose you." She wanted to tell him that losing him would be the worst thing to happen to her. That she depended on his friendship, and without him, the void in her life would be impossible to bear. But she dared not say those words aloud, even though she sensed he felt the same.

What they shared made no sense to others, such as Salai, but Lisa believed what they shared was a meeting of two souls. They had carved out a precious space for each other, and it was all because of her portrait. She feared that what they shared would come to an end with its completion. Could that be why Leonardo had yet to finish it?

"I have hardly lifted a brush to your portrait recently," he said, echoing her thoughts. "I hope you are not too disappointed."

Her gaze met his. "Our friendship grows with each new line, each additional stroke to the canvas. I hope it continues as long as we draw breath."

He nodded, and she saw the reflection of what was in her heart in his dark blue eyes. It warmed her entire being.

CHAPTER 20

*M*eira Chiarelli hefted the straps of her book bag higher on her narrow shoulders and hurried down the Via del Portico d'Ottavia. The buildings of the Quartiere Ebraico turned russet and yellow in the summer light, and a slight scent of fish carried on the breeze from the Tiber River that flowed but a few blocks away.

Meira knew the history of the city she was raised in. Rome was home to the oldest Jewish community in Europe. Jews had migrated in the first century BCE, and for fifteen hundred years, her people had thrived and survived under both friendly and unfriendly emperors and popes. They had endured prohibitions, restrictions, and anti-Jewish legislation, culminating with forced tenancy within a ghetto, and yet they thrived.

The ghetto's walls were erected in 1555 by an edict of Pope

Paul IV. For three hundred years, the gates of the Portico d'Ottavia were locked every night, enclosing the Jews inside seven cramped acres of the *rioni* Sant'Angelo. The city within a city teemed with life.

A hopeful turn of events came in 1870 when Italy became a united nation under King Emmanuel Victor. Jews were granted full citizenship, and the ghetto was dismantled. For the past seventy years, Meira's people had enjoyed the fruits of this freedom.

But the dark shadow of Mussolini's rule in collaboration with Hitler's reign of terror against the Jews had again turned the tides of fate. As a student of history, Meira understood that the greedy and grasping nature of political leaders could, in the blink of an eye, cause chaos and destruction.

She turned at the Via della Reginella and picked up her pace when she entered the Piazza Mattei. The jewel of a square was cobblestoned and surrounded by orange, russet, and gold buildings lined with terracotta pots of bougainvillea and roses. In the center was the Renaissance-built Fontana delle Tartarughe, Turtle Fountain, the usual place where she met her friend.

It was easy to spot Marcello Orvieto in the crowded square. He stood tall, planted like a tree, as he waited. Her heart flip-flopped as always when his sky-blue eyes met hers. It was always this way. And it never ceased to amaze her how her entire body flushed with heat at one look from Marcello. He pushed back a rebellious auburn curl from his forehead and waved.

"Sorry I'm late, Marcello, but I had to finish a math exam." She shrugged in the way her mother did, a fatalistic gesture. "Not that it means anything with all the restrictions put on Jews. I doubt I will ever be allowed to attend university." She stood on tiptoe and kissed him on the cheek.

Marcello removed the heavy backpack from her shoulders and set it on the ground. Taking her hands, he darted a glance around the piazza, leaned down, and kissed both her cheeks. "It won't last forever, *tesoro*. I have good news."

"Good news? Tell me the war is over."

He sat and tugged her down beside him on the marble edge of the fountain. The water's gentle gurgle drowned out the buzzing conversations around them. "You remember when the Allies landed in Sicily two weeks ago, and the Fascist Grand Council issued a no-confidence vote for Mussolini?"

"Of course, I remember. I follow the news as closely as you do. So what?"

"Today, they arrested Mussolini, and Victor Emmanuel appointed Badoglio to be prime minister. I bet, even as we sit here in this lovely piazza somewhere in Rome, Badoglio is planning peace with the Allies."

"Did they announce that?"

"No. In truth, the general assured the Nazis that Italy would remain firm in its commitment to Germany."

"Then nothing has changed."

"On the contrary, rumors are circulating that it's a ruse. Now that the Allies have taken Sicily, it's a given they'll continue up the boot and drive the Germans out. Badoglio is clever. He knows Italians are sick of war. I'm sure he sees the writing on the wall."

"Oh, Marcello, wouldn't it be wonderful if peace were truly within sight?" Meira squeezed his hand. "Mamma and Papà are so worried about everything."

Marcello tucked a strand of Meira's hair behind her ear. She scooted closer to him, their bodies touching shoulder to thigh. It was a hot summer afternoon, but the heat that traveled through her had nothing to do with the weather. Marcello was the son of Rabbino Orvieto, the rabbi at the Tempio Maggiore, the Great Synagogue. They'd met a year ago at a Oneg Shabbat after services. A serious girl with a thirst for knowledge, Meira had always paid more attention to her studies rather than flirting with boys. Then everything changed when she met Marcello.

Meira didn't know if what she felt for the young man was a youthful fancy or true love—the kind of love that burned like a flame as it did between her parents, Gabriella and Benjamin. But the thought of leaving Marcello and moving to Fiesole, as her parents had been contemplating, made her queasy. Marcello was the first boy she'd kissed—the one she thought about every night at bedtime and every morning when she awakened.

"Don't worry, Meira, no matter what happens, I won't let you leave Rome," he said in his rich voice. That deep, melodious voice made the backs of her knees tingle.

She squinted at him, the blinding yellow sunlight behind him, haloing his dark auburn curls. "And what will you do to prevent it?"

"I'll marry you if I must."

"I'll *marry you if I must,*" she said, mimicking his deep voice. "What kind of a proposal is that? *Per piacere,* do me no favors." She frowned and jabbed his arm with her elbow.

"Ow," Marcello said with a chuckle. "I forget how sharp those elbows are."

"And now you add insult to injury?" She huffed, crossing her arms over her chest. "Besides, I'm only seventeen, and you're only eighteen. How do you know I even want to marry you?"

Marcello shot another glance around the piazza, then bent his lips to her collarbone. He planted kisses up her neck until he reached her ear. Warmth turned to fire inside her, and she closed her eyes, savoring the heady sensations that ricocheted through her.

Pressing his lips to hers, he made her gasp as his tongue slipped into her mouth. Not even a bomb dropping from the sky could have persuaded her to pull away. She leaned deeper into his kiss, her arms encircling him. Marcello wrapped his arms around her, pulling her close until she felt as if their bodies had merged into one. The intensity of the kiss felt like a raging fire, and a thought crossed her mind that the only way to put out the blaze was for her to lean back and pull him with her into the cool water of the fountain. When she giggled, he pulled away, a look of puzzlement on his face.

"*Cosa c'è da ridere?*"

"I'll tell you what's so funny," she said, daring to tell him the truth. "Your kiss makes me so flushed I thought about pushing us into the fountain."

Marcello gave her a slow grin, sparking a flurry of sensations that made her wriggle in her seat. He had an uncanny way of reading her as if her traitorous body enjoyed betraying her deepest secret yearnings for him.

"What a good idea," he said. Before she could protest, he tugged her backward, and they toppled into the fountain with a splash. She wanted to scold him for his childish behavior, but all she could do was laugh. The cool water felt delicious. How she loved his mischievous, teasing nature.

"Marcello, what will I tell my parents when they ask me how I came to be soaking wet?"

"Tell them the truth. After passionately kissing, we fell back into the Fontana delle Tartarughe to extinguish the flames. Or you could blame it on Duke Muzio Mattei, who legend claims built the fountain to win the hand of his lady love. Better yet, blame it on your boyfriend, the one who will be happy to marry you if he must."

She splashed him in the face. "My boyfriend. Is that what you are?"

He jumped out of the fountain and held out his arm. Meira reached for his hand, and he pulled her into his arms. Their bodies were wet, and when full against the other, the cool water had no chance of extinguishing the heat that emanated between them, and she would not have been surprised if steam rose from where their bodies touched.

"Forgive me for my clumsy words," he said. "I love you, Meira, and I don't care how young we are. I want to spend my life with you. I am old enough to know my mind, and so are you. We were meant for each other. Time or distance won't change what we feel. Our love was ordained by God." He kissed her again, and her worries about her parents and the war slipped from her like the drops of water dripping from her clothes onto the cobblestones of the Piazza Mattei.

CHAPTER 21

JANUARY 25, 1504 ~ FLORENCE, ITALY

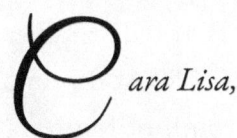 *ara Lisa,*

> *I wish I could always have you by my side, especially at times like these when I witness the rising star of another. Michelangelo is destined for greatness, and I wonder if my decline is imminent. I have never harbored jealousy toward my fellow artists—my friends. What is it about that moody sculptor that affects me so? Am I being too maudlin? If only you were here with me now to shake me out of this irrational state...*

Leonardo was thankful for his heavy cape on this frigid winter day. He lifted his hood and lengthened his strides to keep warm. Arriving at the headquarters of the Opera del Duomo situated behind the red-and-white-domed Cathedral of Santa Maria del

Fiore, he was greeted by a *pratiche,* a special committee of fellow artists and architects, as well as members of the Arte della Lana, the artisan guild for sculptors, stone masons, and woodcutters. They had gathered to discuss the "appropriate and acceptable location" for Michelangelo's *David.* Many of the men present were old friends of Leonardo. Fra Filippo Lippi, Pietro Perugino, and Lorenzo di Credi apprenticed with him at Verrocchio's studio in Florence.

As Leonardo exchanged greetings with his friends, his gaze was drawn magnetically to the statue, which towered over the room and was impossible to ignore. It was a masterpiece, much to Leonardo's dismay. The marble figure seemed to pulse with life, as though the young hero might, at any moment, leap from the pedestal and stride through the room, scattering men like chess pieces on a board.

From the corner of his eye, he spied Sandro Botticelli, another dear friend who had also apprenticed with Verrocchio. At the time of their apprenticeship, Leonardo had been a youth of fourteen, whereas Botticelli had been a young man of twenty-one. Despite the age gap, they'd formed a close bond and had remained life-long friends.

"Sandro, how are you, *amico mio?*" Leonardo exclaimed, embracing the older man. "It's been too long since we shared a meal together."

Nearing sixty years of age, Botticelli sank into Leonardo's arms.

"Leonardo, *amico mio,* do you remember when Maestro Andrea assigned you and me an angel to paint for his *Baptism of Christ?* He cleverly thought our little competition would bring out the best in us, and we would learn from each other."

"Of course. Our approach and style could not have been more different. As I recall, your angel looked dreamily at my angel as if he were in love with him."

Sandro laughed. "Sì, and with clear reason--you were the most beautiful boy in our master's workshop. We were all a little in love with you and jealous when Verrocchio chose you as the model for his *David*. Your fair curls were bewitching, but your talent seemed impossible to equal."

"Ah, *diavolo*, don't remind me of those lustrous curls that age has stolen from me. If only we could be young again and know what we know now." Leonardo studied Sandro's face, distressed by how thin and weary he looked. He wished he could have helped his friend during those dark years when Florence had been under the thumbscrews of Savonarola's ruthless reign. He'd had no knowledge that Sandro had been swept up by the friar's fiery sermons and religious fervor. He'd found out when it was too late that the gentle artist could not withstand Savonarola's spell and, fearing for his immortal soul, had become a warrior of God, and divested himself of all frivolous pursuits, including his art.

Leonardo understood well what it was like to fall under the magnetism of a powerful man. He had served two of the most ruthless, Sforza and Borgia, who wielded absolute power over the public. But Savonarola went too far when he claimed he could speak to God and that God had revealed the future to him. His downfall came when he attacked Pope Alexander VI. After he was executed, the hateful friar's ashes were scattered in the Arno River to ensure he did not become a martyr.

Word had reached Leonardo in Milan that Sandro had fallen into a deep depression after Savonarola's demise. The former artist had become a *piagnoni,* a weeper, one of Savonarola's most devoted followers who publicly mourned his execution.

On his return to Florence, Leonardo discovered a much-changed Botticelli. Sandro no longer painted the idealistic, poetic, and mythological paintings that had brought him fame. *Primavera, Birth of Venus,* or the magnificent *Venus and Mars,* were a lifetime ago. The somber work he applied himself to now found no favor. It seemed the oppressive friar had sucked the spirit out of the once-celebrated artist and bled him dry of funds. Heartbroken, Leonardo had reached out to mutual friends to see what could be done to help. He would not allow Sandro to become a beggar and be deprived of his dignity.

Leonardo grabbed a handful of *soldi* from his cloak and, embracing Sandro, slipped the coins into his pocket. "Buy food, *amico mio,* and tomorrow, come to my studio and share dinner with me," he whispered in his ear.

The glow of gratitude in Sandro's eyes warmed Leonardo's heart. He squeezed his friend's shoulder, his emotions wreaking havoc as tears clouded his vision. He was indeed lucky to have escaped Savonarola's cruel years.

The arrival of Gonfaloniere Soderini brought a hush to the gathering. Soderini called the meeting to order, and everyone took their seats. He announced to the room that everything would be recorded, *verbo ad verbum,* word for word, and he nodded to the clerk to begin taking the minutes.

"Today, we honor one of Florence's talented sons, Michelangelo Buonarotti," Soderini began, "and we decide on a permanent home for his magnificent sculpture, *David.* I now open the discussion for suggestions."

Each suggestion was met with a cheer of agreement from one

quarter and jeers of derision from another. As always, gaining a consensus in such a gathering of disparate voices seemed impossible.

Messer Francesco, the first herald, argued that the statue should replace Donatello's *Judith* on the Piazza della Signoria. He called for the removal of *Judith*, whom he smeared as an "evil constellation" and a symbol that brought bad luck to the republic. He went as far as declaring that the statue was the reason for the rebellion of Pisa and the war that cost Florence its prized possession, a route to the sea.

The esteemed architect Giuliano da Sangallo, a favorite of Lorenzo de' Medici, stood and offered his opinion. "First, considering the logistical nightmare of moving a seventeen-foot, nearly six-and-a-half-ton marble sculpture onto a rooftop makes no sense. I do see sense in displaying *David* in the corner of the Cathedral, as Cosimo suggested, where passers-by will see it—but we must acknowledge that marble, which is tender and fragile, might eventually succumb to the elements. Therefore, I suggest a more suitable location would be under the middle arch of the Loggia della Signoria, either under the vault so observers can walk around the statue and take in all its majestic beauty, or against the back wall, in the middle, with a black niche behind it as a kind of tabernacle. Unfortunately, it will deteriorate over time if it remains in the open air."

A hush fell around the room as everyone contemplated Sangallo's words. His opinion counted significantly as he was the most admired architect and engineer in attendance.

While all of this was going on, Leonardo was making a sketch of *David* in his notebook. After three other speakers agreed with Sangallo, Leonardo stood. All eyes in the room turned with interest toward him. "I support that it should stand in the Loggia dei Lanzi, opposite the Palazzo Vecchio—where Giuliano has said, and that it should be protected so that it does not ruin the official ceremonies. I would also suggest the statue be given a decent ornament so as not to disrupt or offend." Chuckles echoed around the room at his jest of desired modesty to not offend the citizenry, which was anathema to his personal sensibilities.

Leonardo sat back down and continued to doodle, sketching a pair of underpants on his caricature of *David*.

Botticelli stood and shook his head. "With all due respect, my friends, the giant *David* should stand outside the Cathedral on the steps near the Campanile with *Judith* at the other corner or perhaps on the steps facing the Baptistry. It should be exhibited as a religious icon near the Cathedral as the Operai originally intended."

Michelangelo, arriving late, strode to the front of the room. His gray tunic was speckled with white dust, and his short, curly, dark hair appeared covered in snow.

Why must he always look like someone shook a feather duster over him?

Leonardo watched with amusement as the disorderly sculptor addressed the gonfaloniere. "I will make my plea to the revered men here," Michelangelo said.

"I will allow it," said Soderini. "However, the clerk will cease recording as this statement will be *non ufficiale*." Soderini knew Michelangelo's volatile temperament well. Taking this precaution, he protected the sculptor from his worst enemy—himself.

Leonardo and Michelangelo were not on civil terms and often indulged in public disagreements. Leonardo's teasing nature was an accepted behavior of Florentine men. Like his fellow artists, he enjoyed *rompere le palle,* the Italian pastime of breaking balls with friends. With his deflated sense of humor and inflated ego, Michelangelo was incapable of jesting with his fellow artists and shunned overtures of friendship. Leonardo wanted to maintain an open mind but forming a warm opinion of the taciturn sculptor seemed impossible.

Michelangelo rubbed his scruffy beard, causing white dust particles to sprinkle onto the floor like snowflakes on a winter's morn. Leonardo inwardly cringed at the artist's lack of basic cleanliness. The artist Piero di Cosimo sneezed, and a low rumble of laughter rippled around the room. Teasing comments were shouted from all quarters, which only turned Michelangelo's face a fiery shade of red. *Rosso come un peperone,* thought Leonardo. Indeed, anger and embarrassment had turned his face the color of a bell pepper.

Leonardo was seized with a pang of sympathy for the man who seemed to throw stones in his own path. Before the meeting descended into chaos, Piero Soderini interjected, "May I have your silence." He nodded toward the sculptor. "Michelangelo, please share with us your view."

"Thank you, *Vostra Eminenza.*" Michelangelo squared his shoulders and straightened his hunched back. "My friends, for two years, I battled with the Duccio stone, struggling to give life to *David.* I barely ate, slept, or took a breath since I began. Some say," he pointedly eyed Leonardo, "that I was not worthy of the commission. But I know I am the only man who could have brought the stone to life. I have given everything to this sculpture: My blood, my sweat, and my tears, and I answered the call with a *David* that will stand the test of time.

"David bravely faced his enemy as Florentines have repeatedly done when called to our city's defense. *Il Gigante,* as some call him, speaks to the independence and strength of our republic. His existence is a warning to our enemies that no matter how great or overwhelming their numbers, Florence will stand up to them.

"Whether you place him at the Duomo as God's protector or in front of the Palazzo della Signoria, please let him stand tall among the *popolo* as an inspiration and a symbol of our strength against any tyrant or conqueror who would dare threaten our fair city. I humbly beg you not to bury *David* under some eaves where he will wither in silence. Place him where everyone will know and see that this republic will always remain free." Michelangelo looked down at his hands, which bore the cracks and scars of a common laborer. He took a deep breath, then looked up and met the eyes of every man in the room. "I leave you to your decision."

The room stilled as everyone seemed to digest Michelangelo's impassioned speech. Leonardo blinked back tears at the depth of emotion in the sculptor's gaze. A wave of shame washed over him. He denied Michelangelo his dignity and considered him a drudge because of his inability to laugh at himself or engage in friendly banter. In doing so, he had failed to see the truth.

Michelangelo, who kept to himself and rarely engaged with the artistic community, was a genius who suffered for his art. Deeply and profoundly. The man's focus was so acute that even his health and hygiene were set aside in dedication to his craft, even to the point of madness. Leonardo finally understood how personal this project was to Michelangelo. *David* represented Michelangelo's struggle to overcome his own demons. It was Michelangelo's triumph, and Leonardo suspected it would not be his last. The sculptor was young, brilliant, and at the beginning of his climb to greatness.

Leonardo envied Michelangelo's level of dedication. The sculptor was an artist whose focus did not waver until he finished what he had begun, while Leonardo's many incomplete projects were scattered hither and yon. Too many ideas pulled him in too many directions, a vulnerability his critics often exploited. Leonardo flipped open his notebook to his sketch of *David* wearing underpants and smudged it with his thumb. Looking up, he watched the brooding sculptor make his way to the back of the room, the crowd silently parting to allow his passage.

If Lisa had been present, she would have tempered Leonardo's behavior and reminded him that playing to the crowd for a laugh at the expense of someone's dignity was not done in jest. How ironic that he should empathize with Botticelli and bear such antipathy toward Michelangelo. Shame washed over him once more as he realized even at his mature age, he still had lessons to learn about life and would do well to look to that lady's grace and dignity as a beacon to embody.

CHAPTER 22

"*D*oes this mean the war is over?" Suor Teresa asked.

The nuns of Santa Maria del Carmine had gathered in the refectory after supper, listening to a radio broadcast by the new prime minister of Italy, Marshal Badoglio, who'd just announced an armistice with the Anglo-American forces.

Valentina took Teresa's hand. "No, I'm afraid not. The Germans are well embedded here and may retaliate with full force. We are now at war with Germany and must prepare for the worst."

Suor Teresa lamented, "Will this nightmare never end?"

"It will, but I fear our Jewish brethren are in even greater peril now." Valentina's concerns were focused on Chiara, Benjamin, and Gabriella in Rome. What the Nazis would do, she did not know. But she doubted they would allow the Italians to switch sides without paying a terrible price. She prayed the Chiarelli family was safe. With no end in sight, she worried that the encroaching shadow of Nazi aggression would soon cast them all into darkness. *And what of Dante?* If he found out the truth, he would use it against her, or God forbid, against Chiara and her Jewish parents.

"We must pray that our father at the Vatican will help them in whatever way he can," said Suor Teresa.

"I echo your hope," Suor Elena said, setting down a plate of fruit and biscotti. "Let us pray the pope will do what is right for our fellow Italians."

Suor Magdalena, who tended the garden, sipped her coffee and muttered, "We will pray, but prayer is not enough."

Valentina patted her hand. "You are right, Sorella. We must be prepared to act in the face of evil." Valentina believed that God worked through his human children. Action must come from those willing to take up the mantle in His name and take up arms if necessary.

"Suor Gianna is right," Suor Emilia said, biting into a lemon biscotti. "We will pray but do what we can to help those prayers be answered."

The nuns seated around the table nodded in agreement.

That night, no sleep came for Valentina. She tossed and turned in turmoil over the urgent threat to the Jews and her fears about Chiara and her adoptive parents. Should she take Suor Teresa into her confidence? If something happened to her because of Dante, Valentina would be reassured that her friend would carry on the sacred duty of guarding the treasure.

Her fears of Dante invading her life came to pass when he

returned for a second visit. Acting the consummate gentleman, he gifted her a jug of olive oil, a salami, a sack of flour, and even two bars of chocolate. Had she still been that girl of sixteen, she would have spat in his face, but the intervening years had brought practical wisdom. And so, she endured the gallant façade, the pretty words, and the courtly kiss of her hand. She swallowed the bile that rose in her gullet at his touch and managed to thank him for the supplies, knowing the nuns would put them to good use for those in need.

His third visit provided a cask of wine, a side of cured prosciutto, and a bag of ground espresso. Once again, Valentina thanked him politely, but his black eyes flashed with fury this time, wiping away any semblance of courtly manners. "I am a patient man," he growled, his hand clamped around her arm in a vice-like hold. "But my patience can only be stretched so far." Finally releasing her, he clicked his heels and strode away. Valentina had thought herself healed from the past but being forced to endure his presence with renewed vigor had torn open her scars. Would she never be rid of him?

His fourth visit was without gifts or gentlemanly pretense but simply to inform her that he'd been called back to Rome for a pressing matter.

"Do not assume you are rid of me," he growled in her ear, the heat of his breath making her cringe with fear and loathing. "I have spies everywhere who'll watch my interests while I'm away. You will not be able to escape as easily as you did before."

"I have no intention of escaping anywhere," she retorted, pulling away. "This is my home and my calling."

Afterward, Valentina sat on the bench in the garden, unable to contain her tears. Life had taught her to keep her emotions under control. Otherwise, she would not have been able to bear the pain of losing Chiara, nor of being estranged from her brothers and, yes, even the heartless Giulia. Dante had not only stolen her hopes and dreams of motherhood and the possibility of marrying a kind and decent man, but his looming presence now threatened the new life she'd carved out for herself with her fellow sisters.

Although relieved he would no longer be in Florence to menace her, Valentina was terrified that he would somehow cross paths with Chiara and her adoptive parents. They'd heard underground reports from the *partigiani* of Jewish families being stripped of their belongings and forced onto trains to camps surrounded by barbed wire in the east, where God only knew what became of them.

As she sat on the bench, weeping silent tears, a gentle squeeze on her shoulder made her look up. "You are safe here, child," Suor Emilia said, sitting beside her. "No matter his threats, you are one of us. We protect each other."

Valentina smiled at Suor Emilia's fierce protectiveness, so different from that night, so long ago, when she'd arrived at the convent soaking wet from the rain, pregnant, and afraid of the future. After comforting her, Suor Emilia and Valentina held hands in the dwindling light of dusk and prayed.

THERE WILL BE no sleep for me tonight. Getting out of bed, Valentina lit a candle and padded on silent feet down to the library. She climbed the ladder, as she had done many times, and retrieved the wooden box. Taking it to her office, she pulled a small mirror from her desk drawer and carefully extracted the letter she was transcribing.

Cara Lisa,

I have spent my life pursuing many purposes. Sometimes to serve my fellow man and other times to follow my passions wherever they may take me. I never accept absolute truths from those who claim to have found them. Instead, I follow my own observations and search for my own answers. With careful deliberation, I have laid stone upon stone, linking one discovery to the next. This journey holds me on course and leads me to whatever achievements I can claim in art and science. The thousands of pages I have written contain endless words and drawings about my experiments, discoveries, and art.

Added to these pages, and always with my mind on the future, I create various accountings of everyday life, listings of possessions, lists to remember and accomplish, or even random comments about the weather or other trivialities. But I have never revealed my inner truth unless it relates to my work or my discoveries. My reasons are nothing more than my wish to keep my privacy sacred, to keep something only for myself. These pages may survive me and provide future generations with insights into these days, this life, this place, but no one can claim to know what is in my heart. Only with you in our correspondence have I felt the lightness of spirit to record my feelings. Carissima, it is exhilarating to pour myself onto the page and to know my thoughts are embraced by your loving spirit and shall remain safely in your heart.

Alas, I feel the sand slipping through the hourglass—the shortness of life itself. Time has always meant not enough hours in the day, enough days in a year, or enough years in my life to accomplish what I aspire to, of what I seek to know. Everything distracts me from the course I have set. Everything but you.

There are days when I feel so weary. Weary of the demands of the Signoria of the Chancery, weary of their never-ending political aspirations. And although I am deeply fond of my apprentices and Salai, the pressures of providing for them take their toll. There are only two things I am never weary of—my desire to fly and our portrait. Così è la vita.

Sei sempre nel mio cuore e nel miei pensieri,
Leonardo

"You are always in my heart and my thoughts, Leonardo," Valentina repeated aloud. Profound words. Given the intentional ambiguity of his letters, Valentina could not be certain whether Leonardo referred to the painting or his friendship with Lisa.

She vowed to herself that she would not—could not—abandon this treasure, no matter what dark days lay ahead. Somehow, she would do what she must in the coming months. She would protect Leonardo and Lisa's letters with her life, just as she would do whatever was necessary to protect those she loved from the threatening evil.

CHAPTER 23

JULY 9, 1504 ~ FLORENCE, ITALY

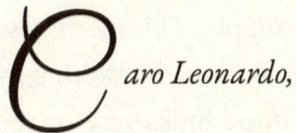 *aro Leonardo,*

> *Why can I not simply be content with my good fortune?*
> *Why do I feel this chasm between my family and my duty to*
> *myself? I love my children. They are my heart. So clever and*
> *curious yet happy and loving. They bring me endless joy.*
> *Francesco's hard work and successes have given me a life to be*
> *envied, yet something is missing...*

"*Amore mio,* I have good news," her husband said, interrupting her musings. "Our silk business is flourishing. Finally, we no longer depend on the Ottomans who control the trade routes."

"And why is that *caro marito?*" She smiled with encouragement. Francesco was fond of sharing the day-to-day details of his work with her. Shipping costs, price fluctuations, and fulfilling orders consumed much of his daily chats with her. While his business provided their family with a good life, it was fraught with shadowy practices that forced her to swallow the bile in her throat. Although she cared for her husband, she was no longer in love with him. She adored her children and would do anything to protect them, so she learned to temper her instincts in many aspects of her marriage, including questioning Francesco's business dealings.

"It seems the Tuscan countryside is a *bellissima* place for growing the white mulberry bush. The mulberry tree's leaves are the exclusive diet of the silkworm, and it is on these leaves that the worms lay their eggs. It is from the worm's cocoon that a single strand of silk is born. I am negotiating to purchase a tract of land near Siena, where I will plant orchards of mulberry trees. We will cultivate our own silk, supplementing our supply. This means less dependence on the Turkish monopoly of silk thread, resulting in lower costs for us and more profit. The future looks very bright indeed." Francesco skewered a sizeable bite of roast lamb in his mouth and chewed. Lisa looked away. The sight of a drop of blood on his lips made her stomach churn.

"Congratulations, *caro,* you are not only clever and inventive in commerce but a wonderful provider for our family."

Francesco grinned as he lifted his goblet and washed the meat down his throat with a gulp of red wine. "Soon, you will be wearing the most beautiful silk gowns in Italy, made entirely by your husband's mills. *Le signore* of the city will pound at our doors to purchase the finest cloth in Florence."

"And I will wear them proudly." She patted his hand.

"I saw something interesting today," her husband continued.

"The most inventive design for a silk loom, a warping machine that reduces the space needed to house manufacturing looms. Can you imagine this mechanical drawing was created by our friend Maestro da Vinci? The man spends his time in so many ways outside the realm of painting; it's no wonder he has no time to complete your portrait." He shook his head, chuckling.

Lisa ignored the jest. It was not the first time her husband had poked fun at Leonardo's habit of flitting from project to project.

"This loom of his has a circular shape and allows the worker to weave the silk thread into cloth using a quarter of the space needed by today's looms. It's revolutionary. Perhaps we should contact him about implementing them in our silk production." He skewered another morsel, and she waited for him to continue. "But it will have to wait under the circumstances."

"What do you mean?" she asked, taking a sip of wine to steady her nerves.

"I heard some news that I assume is disturbing to him."

Lisa studied her husband's face, wishing he would get to the point. "And what is that?"

"The Maestro's father, Piero da Vinci, died today. I understand they were not close. I learned from a man friendly with Piero's eldest legitimate son that the man died *intestato*. Can you imagine a man with twelve legitimate children not leaving a will of some kind? *Buon Dio*, the man was a notary. You would think he would have left his estate in better order."

Lisa gripped her goblet. She could only imagine what Leonardo was going through. She wished she could run from this table and go to her friend. It was nearly impossible for her to keep a stoic expression on her face, even more so to hold back her tears.

"Does this mean that Maestro da Vinci will inherit nothing from his father?"

"Most certainly, given he was born a *bastardo,* and without written and notarized stipulation from his late father, he has no claim."

"That is tragic, do you not think?" Lisa took another sip of wine to keep her lips from trembling.

"Fortunately, our friend Leonardo is a success in his own right. It should not affect him the way it might someone of lesser means." He took Lisa's hand and pressed his lips firmly upon it. Then, reaching for the carafe of wine, he refilled their goblets.

"Yes, he has done well for himself," she said, wiping her hand on the linen cloth in her lap to remove the oily film of fat transferred from his lips. In truth, she could not begin to imagine the pain her friend was going through. Leonardo kept his deepest sentiments hidden. He was a sensitive man and would surely be suffering. Piero da Vinci's death might have unforetold consequences. But she would have to wait until tomorrow to go to Leonardo. *I will have Cook prepare a lovely and comforting meal.* Knowing her friend, he would be so overcome with grief that he would neglect to eat. She would do all she could to provide sustenance and loving ministrations to support him through this sorrow.

LISA HAD BEEN CORRECT. When she arrived at the Sala del Papa, she was greeted by an agitated Salai, who was, as usual, unwelcoming.

"The Maestro is in no condition to see visitors. He has shut everyone out of his quarters and wishes not to be bothered. If you came intending to discuss your portrait with him, now is not a good time."

She had anticipated a confrontation with Salai and felt prepared to surmount his disagreeability. Lisa had learned the art of diplomacy by observing her father and honed her skills by paying heed to her husband's business dealings. "I have not come to discuss art. I heard of the passing of Leonardo's father, and I am here out of compassion for a friend." She set her heavy basket down, took out a pot of beef stew, a loaf of bread, and a bottle of wine snuggly wrapped in a cloth, and passed each item to Salai. "I brought this for you and the assistants for your repast on this difficult day."

Salai sniffed the air, inhaling the enticing aroma of aromatic spices. "Thank you, this is very kind. We are all distraught for him. Perhaps you can help ease his distress. He is most certainly not himself."

"I will try," she said, picking up the basket. "If you would be so kind as to open the door, I will do my best to help him reclaim his amicable disposition."

Making her way to Leonardo's private quarters, she knocked softly on the door and let herself in. Setting the basket down, she closed the heavy wood door. When she turned, tears stung her eyes. Leonardo lay collapsed over his desk, and a bottle of ink was spilled on the table. His quill had fallen to the floor, and sorrow hung in the air like a funereal shroud. She scanned the room and noticed the cloak draped over the mirror. It was a ritual practiced by the Jews when losing a loved one. It was said that if one should see their image in a mirror following a death, they, too, would soon die. Leonardo was not superstitious, but profound sorrow can lead to erratic thoughts. Her gaze landed on her portrait, and she was struck by its beauty. Leonardo had painted in the most dazzling azure blue sky that took her breath away.

Placing the basket on a table, Lisa gently laid her hand on Leonardo's shoulder, careful not to startle him. "Leonardo, I came as soon as I could. I am so sorry about your father." Her gaze fell upon the stationery on his desk. On it, he'd drawn some sketches and written a list of expenditures for July. She shook her head and could not help but smile at an entry of one florin given to Salai for expenses needed for the house. Her gaze settled on what had to be the last notation. Written in Leonardo's coded script, she squinted and deciphered what he'd written. On *Wednesday at seven o'clock died Ser Piero da Vinci on July 9, 1504.*

She thought it odd he'd recorded the day of his father's death as Wednesday, but yesterday had been Tuesday. It was a confusing entry that displayed no words of love or remembrance, and her brow wrinkled as she tried to decipher its meaning. Even more confusing and unusual—he'd rewritten the exact words, not in his customary mirror script, but in his easily readable cursive: *On July 9, 1504 Wednesday, at seven o'clock died Ser Piero da Vinci, notary, at the Palazzo del Popolo. My father, being eighty years old, left behind ten sons and two daughters.* Leonardo did not include himself as one of Piero's legitimate sons. Valentina attributed this lapse in accuracy to Leonardo's father having disowned him by denying his paternity. It was a rare occurrence for a man who was circumspect about his personal life and reflected Leonardo's way of declaring to the world what might be dismissed.

Lisa was so moved that she bent to kiss his head. "Oh, Leonardo, please speak to me. I cannot bear your silence or your pain."

He raised his head. Full of anguish, his eyes searched hers for a moment before he pressed his face against her breast. "How could he have been so cruel? How could he have been so uncaring in this last act of his life? To inflict a wound upon me, his son, knowing the pain I would suffer at this final disenfranchisement."

Lisa felt Leonardo's agony so completely that her heart was torn in two. Never, if she lived to be a hundred years of age, would she understand how a mother or father could be so heartless and inflict such a callous last act, such cruelty, that would stain their child's life forever, no matter their age.

"Leonardo, what has happened to you is wrong and cruel. I know that nothing can be said to heal this wound. Perhaps that is why God has gifted you in so many ways as compensation for what was denied you. When the rest of us are long forgotten, and we are but dust in the wind, you will be forever remembered and celebrated. Your father betrayed you, but you must forgive him, not for his sake, but for yours. I also pray that your father will seek redemption now that he has gone to meet his Maker, our Lord."

She kneeled on the floor and cupped his face, hoping to soothe his heartache. "You must know that I would do anything to bring you peace," she said in a voice thick with tears.

Leonardo covered her hands with his. The warmth of his touch and the love in his eyes seared her soul.

"As always, you are a balm to my heart. I know not why I have been blessed by your friendship, but I thank God he saw fit to bring you into my life, my beautiful Lisa."

"Then we are both blessed, for I thank God each day for your friendship as well." Standing, she grasped his hands. "Will you eat something? I have brought you a delightful luncheon that I would be pleased to serve you tortellini stuffed with peas in a delicate broth."

"Thank you. I will feast on your loving ministrations later," he said in a raspy voice. "I have not slept since learning of his death, and I am so weary. Would you lie with me for a time? Your presence would bring me comfort and hopefully help me rest."

"Of course." It made her tremble to think about lying in bed with a man other than her husband. But her adoration of Leonardo was far more significant than her trepidations, and any hesitancy fell to the wayside.

He took her hand and tugged her down onto the bed. She lay on her back, staring at the ceiling. Leonardo lay beside her on his side and was asleep in moments. She must have dozed off as well, for when she awoke, she was on her side staring into his eyes. Beyond the intensity of his observation, she saw something else for the first time. Something that made her face flush with heat.

"I have never lain with a woman," he confessed. "An artist's life is difficult enough without imposing that journey on another. I find great pleasure in the company of men, but a part of me has always wondered what it would be like to share intimacy with the gentler sex. The softness and delicate beauty of a woman is so different from a man."

Lisa could scarcely draw breath at hearing this confession. Leonardo had opened himself to her in a way he had never done before.

He watched her in silence as though, having made his confession, he was now afraid of what might come next. She rarely felt the flame of desire, having been married for so many years and having borne five children. Her physical needs were suppressed by the bustle of daily life and the care of her family. Francesco, who had given her pleasure in those first years, continued to seek physical release between her thighs but no longer paid the care and attention he once did.

After so many years of dormancy, Lisa's desire sparked into flames and burned like a fever. Gently cradling his face, she drew him into a kiss. Their lips met in a delicate touch at first and then with greater heat and urgency. Lisa recalled the silkworm that spins a cocoon, enclosing it in a haven. She and Leonardo were somehow woven together and bound by a silken thread. He loved her—she knew this in the depth of her soul just as she knew she loved him. This joining might have been wrong yesterday and perhaps would be wrong tomorrow as well. But not today. Not now. At this moment, it was the perfect expression of what they meant to each other.

A sigh of impossible contentment arose from him, and he kissed her as fervently as she kissed him. What was happening could not, would not, be denied. She pressed her body into his, embracing every part of him, urging him onward. She gave herself to him, body, mind, and soul, and he took the gift, opening it with delight. If he regretted this wondrous union one day, it would bring her great sorrow, but for her, it would always be preserved in that secret place of her heart where cherished memories were kept.

CHAPTER 24

*V*alentina pedaled to the Mercato Nuovo as usual on market days. Crossing the Piazza della Signoria, her thoughts returned to the letter she'd been transcribing. Leonardo's description of the unveiling of Michelangelo's *David* played upon her mind. Although the statue had long ago been moved from the Piazza della Signoria to the Galleria dell' Accademia for safety from the elements, *David* continued to represent Florence's determination to remain free. Now more than ever, an army of "Davids" was needed to stand up against the Goliath of German tyranny.

At first, Valentina didn't think she had anything to contribute to the cause, but with every report she'd heard or read, she felt the need to do something—anything to help the Allies.

Saturday had always been Valentina's favorite day. The weekly market day was usually full of excitement and activity where vendors set up stalls between the Piazza della Repubblica and the Piazza della Signoria, offering up a profusion of meats, fresh produce, and fragrant breads along with trinkets, clothing, and useful household utensils. The offerings were meager these days, but her weekly routine allowed her to engage in a different kind of exchange. Under the guise of shopping for the convent, Valentina had begun doing errands on behalf of the *partigiani*.

Over the past few months, she'd made several discreet inquiries and discovered that Beatrice, the midwife who'd delivered Chiara, had a cousin named Serafina, who worked with the partisans. Beatrice introduced Valentina to the woman who hocked her vegetables at the Mercato Nuovo. Serafina had lost her only grandson to the evil interlopers who'd crushed Florence beneath their heels. Several young men from her village had been rounded up by the Germans, lined up against a wall, and shot. She'd been powerless to save her grandson that day, but Serafina vowed so long as she drew breath, she would do everything she could to stop the bastards.

Despite Beatrice's introduction, Valentina had to earn the old woman's trust. After finally gaining her confidence, Serafina put her in touch with the leader of a small band of partisan fighters. Valentina had learned that a network of Italian civilians had been stealing munitions from the Germans whenever possible and smuggling them to the resistance fighters. Their ranks were small, and their supplies were limited. Most of those resisting were fugitives, Allied POWs, anti-fascists, returning soldiers who hated the war, and Jews trying to escape deportation. The resistance was in its infancy, and the civilian population feared reprisals from the Nazis and the Blackshirts. Accordingly, their successes were mainly ineffective, but their determination was great. They were a pesky thorn in the occupier's side, constantly slashing tires on German vehicles and stealing contraband when possible.

"Good morning, Serafina. I hope you are feeling better today. How is your arthritis?"

"*Buon giorno,* Suor Gianna. "*Beh,*" she said with a shrug, "the pain reminds me I am still alive."

Valentina handed her basket to Serafina, who placed it on the ground beneath her table.

"I have fennel, turnips, carrots, and radishes today," the vegetable seller said. "Shall I fill your basket?"

"*Va bene,* one must make do with whatever God provides."

Serafina grunted and bent down. "I'm afraid God is stingy these days."

Valentina bit back the smile that teased her lips. Both she and Serafina knew that it wasn't God that was being stingy. The Germans requisitioned everything the land produced to feed their army, leaving the population on the brink of starvation.

"*Dopo la pioggia, arriva il sole,*" Valentina reminded Serafina, "After the rain comes sunshine."

"It cannot come soon enough," Serafina grunted.

"What cannot come too soon, Valentina?" A deep voice asked behind her.

She whirled around to face the last man she'd ever wanted to lay eyes upon. He was spit and polished from head to toe, gleaming like a newly minted lira.

She was so shocked to see him that she couldn't even speak. Her mouth had become as parched as the African Sahara Desert.

He was supposed to be in Rome. For almost three years, she had not seen him, had been spared from being watched by those arrogant black eyes or touched by those insolent hands. To have resisted would have brought his wrath down upon the nuns. And now he'd returned to Florence and stared at her with that coal-black gaze as though the heavy dark cloth of her habit were nothing more than a sheer nightgown.

"Has the cat caught your tongue," he said with a smirk, "or do I need to kiss you awake, like Talia, the sleeping beauty?"

As a child, Valentina had read *The Tale of Tales*, Giambattista Basile's collection of fairy tales. *Sun, Moon, and Talia* featured a sleeping beauty raped by a king, a much scarier story than even the Brothers Grimm could fashion. The reference to the tale uttered from Dante's lips sounded like a thinly veiled threat. Valentina finally found her tongue and struck back with a barb of her own. *"Quando il diavolo ti accarezza, vuole l'anima."*

Dante barked out a laugh, making heads turn. "When the devil caresses you, he wants your soul. I suppose you are right, but remember, you will find gifts in the arms of the devil, Valentina. Gifts found nowhere else."

The thought of Dante's evil gifts struck terror into Valentina's soul, but it also made her more determined to fight back.

Serafina glanced up from beneath the table and gave Dante the evil eye, but he saw nothing as he fixated on Valentina's face. She worried the old woman might do something foolish. She would not put it past Serafina to take out a gun and shoot Dante dead where he stood.

"How are your mother and father, Signore Conti?" Valentina changed the direction of the conversation. *Please, Lord, help me distract him.*

"Getting old, I'm afraid, and despairing of not having grand-children to spoil."

"They are right. You should consider getting married and giving them the grandchildren they desire. I am certain plenty of young ladies would welcome your proposal."

He watched her like a fox eyeing a rabbit. "There is only one woman I want to be the mother of my child, and you know who she is."

It made her tremble to think of how close Dante's words were to the truth. She was the mother of his only child. "Please do not let me keep you from your busy day, Signore Conti. I'm certain you have much to do before you return to Rome."

He chuckled. "I'm sure you will be delighted to know that I have been reassigned to Florence. At present, I will not be returning to Rome. I will have the great joy of looking after you and seeing to your needs." He saluted her with the Roman-Fascist salute.

Valentina would have spit on him if she could. So, it was official. He was indeed back in Florence to menace her again. Valentina turned her back to him. *Buon Dio, let him leave.*

Dante's breath was warm in her ear, and she stiffened. "I will visit you soon at the convent. Perhaps in the garden, you will finally show some gratitude for my gifts."

She held her breath, waiting to hear his retreating footsteps. Serafina lifted the basket onto the table, the secret items covered beneath a pile of root vegetables. "That one is worse than Satan himself." Leaning forward, she whispered. "You must be careful."

"Don't worry, Serafina. I will be." Valentina slung the basket over her arm. "I will see you next Saturday. I hope God will keep you well."

The old woman shrugged. *"Dagli amici mi guardi Dio, dai nemici mi guardo io."*

Valentina nodded her agreement with the truthful old Italian proverb. *God guards me from my friends. I guard myself from my enemies.*

As she pedaled the bicycle to Miniato al Monte, a chilly wind hindered her progress up the hill. She frequently stopped to catch her breath and to ensure she wasn't being followed. She felt satisfied that with Serafina's help, she'd smuggled two revolvers and several grenades out of Florence right under Dante's nose. Hopefully, the partisans would put them to good use.

At the top of the highest hill in Florence on the south side of the Arno River rose the Romanesque green and white marble façade of the nearly thousand-year-old basilica with its brick campanile. Before the war, the basilica's bells could be heard in Florence, but the war had silenced them. Every time Valentina approached, the breathtaking view made her think of her father— how he would be proud of her for standing up against the fascists.

She left her bike beneath a tree in the cemetery in front of the church. The last time she was here, one of the monks had pointed out the tomb of Carlo Collodi, who wrote the children's story *Pinocchio,* one of her favorites from childhood. She'd included a copy of the book in the satchel she'd packed with Chiara's baby clothes when Gabriella and Benjamin had come to the convent to claim her seventeen years ago.

She wished she could have written to Padre D'Angelo to inquire if Chiara was safe and well, but one could never be sure of the mail these days. There were spies everywhere, and someone could intercept a letter from the convent to Padre D'Angelo and report her. Even a mildly worded letter could spark suspicion with the fascist authorities. Nor could she risk going to Rome to seek out her daughter to ensure she was all right. She could not risk raising Dante's suspicions. These were dangerous times. She closed her eyes and prayed for Chiara and her adoptive parents. *God keep you safe.*

She pushed open the door to the church that adjoined the monastery and stepped inside. Her footsteps echoed across the intricately patterned marble floor designed by Michelozzo. The monastery and church were run by the Olivetans, a Benedictine sect of monks. One of the friars who kept watch ushered her into the sacristy where no prying eyes would see them. As if out of thin air, a grizzled man emerged. He examined the two guns and grenades from her basket.

"Very nice. Thank you, Sorella. I look forward to your next visit." That was the extent of their exchange. Like smoke, he disappeared from the room. The less known, the better. The monk escorted her from the basilica, where they paused momentarily to take in the view. From the monastery's vantage point, the resistance fighters could spy on the strategic movements of the Nazi occupiers in the valley below.

"Thank you, Suor Gianna, for your courage in helping the cause for freedom," the monk said as they looked out at the countryside below. "Did you know this is not the first time the monastery has played a role in protecting Florence," the monk told her. "In 1530, Michelangelo Buonarroti was elected the Governor of Fortifications for Florence and was given the duty of devising protective walls for the city and surrounding monasteries. Michelangelo was a fervent supporter of the republic and designed a hastily built defensive wall around San Miniato to shield it during the siege of Florence. Taking his lead, Cosimo I de' Medici reinforced and finished transforming the monastery into a fortress. What's left of the walls surround the cemetery, and the Medici fortress continues to offer a protective haven for our partisans. We must pray these walls defend against the enemy once more and drive the monsters out."

"May God grant your prayers, Padre," Valentina said. She was in awe of the courageous men and women who risked their lives fighting the Nazis. She vowed to continue to do what she could to help them. Just as she'd promised Sister Maria Vittoria that she would guard the treasured letters of Leonardo and Lisa. But she would need to be even more vigilant under the eagle eyes of Dante Conti.

CHAPTER 25

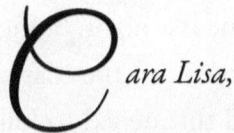*ara Lisa,*

On such a beautiful day, I would rather be with you at the mercato, watching you free your fine, feathered friends, rather than in this dingy hall...

Leonardo felt the pressure gathering like a storm upon his shoulders. Last night Michelangelo's colossal *David* had rolled out of the Operai del Duomo to begin its slow journey to the Piazza della Signoria. All of Florence was enthralled and waiting with bated breath for the "marble giant" to reach its destination and take its place as a symbol of the republic. Leonardo sent Salai to report on its journey, and Salai returned breathless with excitement.

"The Sangallo brothers designed a sling for the statue to absorb the uneven fractures and bumps in the road. They achieved an engineering feat worthy of your genius, Maestro. It took the sweat and strength of forty men to heft it into its sling and to move it onto its base of fourteen oiled tree trunks," Salai said with a smirk. "But they miscalculated the height once the statue was hoisted into the swing. They had to break down the door of the Operai to get it out. It was quite a fiasco."

Leonardo shook his head. "Well, perhaps they should have consulted me first, eh?"

"No one can match you in engineering feats." Salai nodded.

"Thank you, *amico mio*, but you don't need to grease the wheels here," Leonardo said, giving Salai a gentle cuff on the ear. "So, did *David* reach his final destination?"

"He made it halfway and spent the night under a star-filled sky, but a handful of villagers attacked the statue last night. Some pranksters hurled stones. I heard their shouts in the dark. Michelangelo became like a man possessed and threatened to kill them all if they harmed the statue. He kept watch for the rest of the night. Calling out threats in the darkness like a madman to any who dared come near."

"Dear Lord, Salai, tell me you did not take part in such a cowardly deed." Leonardo glared at his impish friend. He was certain Salai would be the cause of the last golden curls on his head turning white. "You, *figlio mio*, might think you are helping me in some way by harming my rival, but to damage art is something I would never condone. Besides, the sculptor is a little mad and would certainly *tagliati le palle*!" He made a chopping gesture with his hand to emphasize his point.

Salai winced. "Maestro, I promise, I had nothing to do with it."

Leonardo didn't find Salai's innocent look reassuring. He hoped the fear of losing his balls would temper the young man's impetuous behavior.

"And did you hear any comments from the citizenry?"

Salai dropped his gaze, avoiding Leonardo's penetrating stare. He shifted uncomfortably, and Leonardo could tell he was hesitant to speak. "*Dai*, what did you hear?"

"They speak in hushed tones of reverence. They say the giant has come to life to take its place as the protector of Florence."

"What else?"

Salai mumbled under his breath. "They say Michelangelo is the greatest artist in Florence, and this statue is the most magnificent in the world."

Leonardo stiffened from head to toe as he held his emotions in check. Anger, jealousy, frustration, sadness, and even fear battled for supremacy in his mind and heart. The brooding young sculptor had done it. He'd succeeded in eclipsing Leonardo as the preeminent artist in Florence, perhaps even the world. Leonardo turned and stared at the blank wall. Could he take back the glory that was once his? The cartoon he'd been working on for *The Battle of Anghiari* was still pinned to the wall in Santa Maria Novella. Once again, he was behind in his commission, having taken time to work on a design for a scissor lift to enable him to move up and down and across the massive painting with ease. But would his monumental mural eclipse Buonarroti's naked warriors? "When is the unveiling of the marble giant?"

"A week from now. The signoria are calling for the entire city to be present."

Leonardo nodded. The last thing he wanted to do was stand amongst a crowd of worshipping onlookers and pay homage to the brooding sculptor, but it would be unseemly for him not to be there. At least he could look forward to seeing Lisa. She would undoubtedly attend with her husband.

A WEEK LATER, the Piazza della Signoria teemed with excitement. All of Florence gathered to see the unveiling of Michelangelo's *David*. The marble giant stood in the center of the piazza draped in a giant tarp. Leonardo glanced at the towering colossus that commanded the square. Soderini had spared no expense, and the piazza was spotlessly clean and held a newly built podium for the gonfaloniere to address the crowd. Florence's heraldic red and white flags and banners waved in the breeze, adding pageantry befitting the coronation of a pope. The people were adorned in their finest silks and velvets.

Leonardo had designed state celebrations, plays, musical recitals, and balls for the Duke of Milan and was an expert at spellbinding spectators with dramatic flourishes. He understood that the art of spectacle was related more to timing than anything else. The longer the delay, the hungrier the spectators became. He didn't expect any fiascos today, and after the fanfare of trumpets and drums, the shouts of praise would begin. The gonfaloniere would rile the crowd to a frenzy, and officials would pull the tarp away to reveal the guardian of the republic. And another star would ascend to the heavens—Michelangelo Buonarroti.

On such a bright, sunlit day, Leonardo was sure *David's* white marble skin would be blinding. The youthful warrior who'd subdued a giant with a sling and a stone would shimmer like an angel from heaven, further elevating the sculptor's reputation. Stories would be told of this day's marvels for weeks, months, and perhaps even years to come.

Leonardo could think of no way to avoid congratulating Michelangelo. He could already imagine the smug triumph on the younger man's face. To cheer himself and prepare his psyche for the unsatisfactory meal of swallowed pride, Leonardo wore one of his favorite outfits, mauve silk tights and an embroidered tunic, his waist cinched with a silver belt. His matching velvet beret tipped over his forehead enough to shield him from the penetrating sunlight and any curious glances sent his way. He was always of the mind that well-appointed attire could sweeten even the sourest of circumstances.

Leonardo spotted a group of his artist friends and made his way to them. He had some satisfaction in the recognition lauded upon him as people in the crowd cleared a path for him much as the Red Sea had parted for Moses. Botticelli pounded him on the back with enthusiasm. *"Amico mio,* fortune has smiled on Michelangelo today, has it not?"

Though his own glory had faded, Botticelli was generous enough to celebrate the rise of another artist, even when that same artist publicly demeaned Botticelli's work as inconsequential and frivolous. "Indeed, it has. *É una bella giornata.* How have you been, Sandro?"

"Bene, molto bene. I hear you will soon mount the cartoon for the *Battle of Anghiari* in the Salone dei Cinquecento.

Undoubtedly, it will be equally glorious when your mural is unveiled."

"Yes, the work progresses well," Leonardo said, stretching the truth, for he was behind as usual.

"How is the painting of the silk merchant's wife coming along? You must be close to finishing it."

Leonardo gave a non-committal shrug. He would never relinquish his Lisa, but no one else needed to know. At the mention of her portrait, he surreptitiously searched the crowd for the face that gave him respite from the political machinations of his art.

And then he saw her. Radiant, she outshone the sun. He kept his eye on her, hoping for an opportunity to greet her alone. Her eyes met his, and her lips curved up. A moment later, she bent her head and whispered something to her husband, who nodded and disappeared into the crowd.

"*Mi scusi,* gentlemen." Leonardo parted the seas again as he made his way to Lisa. "Signora, the sun is dull in comparison to you. *Come va?*" He brought her hand to his lips and kissed it.

"Better now that you are here, Leonardo. I have missed you."

"On what mission did you send Francesco that he hurried away so quickly?"

"I told him I left my jewels on my dressing table."

"Did you?"

"Of course not, but he will attribute my forgetfulness to the distraction of our boys. Even with an abundance of servants to care for them, they only want their mother."

"If I had a mother like you, I would want the same." Her silk gown was the same blue shade as a peacock feather. Tendrils of her auburn hair fluttered in the breeze, and he subdued his impulse to tug one of her braids and unfurl the silky strands to run through his fingers.

The blare of a trumpet blasted across the piazza, and a roar of shouts and applause thundered around the square. Snare drums rumbled, and all eyes locked on the dais as the gonfaloniere, dressed in his robes of state, mounted the steps.

"Beloved citizens, this day is of profound consequence in the history of our republic. To our city's lasting glory, we are here to unveil Michelangelo Buonarroti's masterpiece, *David*. It is and will be a source of pride for all of us today, tomorrow, and for so long as our great city stands. Visitors will extol *David's* beauty, grace, and power to the earth's far corners. We Florentines stand proud of our native son, Michelangelo Buonarroti, and thank him from the bottom of our hearts. Let no tyrant seek our downfall lest they awaken the brave warrior standing ready to defend us. We will never be cowered or conquered! We are Florentines! Our house stands on solid ground, and we will fight to the death to keep our freedom. *Lunga vita a Firenze!*"

The shouts and cries of "Long live Florence" were deafening as Michelangelo strode up the stairs.

At least his hair is combed, thought Leonardo. The sculptor pulled the cord, and the tarp opened while a group of men dragged the screen away. Sunlight glinted off the white marble, and a hush fell over the crowd.

A wave of whispered comments floated around them.

"I can see his heart beating in his chest," one man said.

"Sì, he looks alive. The blood pulses in his veins," another said.

But Leonardo wasn't looking at bulging veins or muscles. He was looking at the gilded fig leaf that covered *David's* genitals. It had been his suggestion, for modesty's sake, and now he regretted it. *David* was a brilliant work of art, and Michelangelo's vision should have been respected. It was false and vindictive of him, as he had drawn dozens of naked men. In fact, he'd once drawn a soldier in battle with an erection astride a horse.

"Does it bother you, Maestro, to see such a fuss made over the statue?" Lisa studied his face, her brows pinched with concern.

"No. Michelangelo deserves this moment. He gave the city what he promised and surpassed their expectations."

"I hope you will not allow Michelangelo's success to become a burden on your shoulders," she said softly.

"It is a grand achievement, and the city is enthralled, as you can see. Such is the life of an artist." He shrugged. "One moment, you bask in the light of glory and admiration. Next, you stand in the shadow of someone else's triumph. I do not begrudge Michelangelo his success, even though he is such a disagreeable man."

"Leonardo," Lisa said, leaning closer to him, not enough for anyone to notice but just enough to offer him comfort. "Your entire life is dedicated to your art, to enrichment. I think one day you will be regarded as the greatest artist who ever lived."

Leonardo searched her eyes. "Do you truly believe that Signora?"

"I do. I believe your greatest achievement is yet to come. I do not know how, but I know it here." She lifted her hand to her heart, and her eyes shone with such truth and beauty that his vision blurred with tears. "Promise me you will not forget what I have told you this day," she spoke in a low voice.

Before Leonardo could reply, Lisa's husband returned, and his thoughts remained unspoken.

"Leonardo, it is some time since we have seen you," Francesco said, his voice sounding slightly sardonic. "How does Lisa's portrait progress?"

"It proceeds at a slow pace, I fear. As you might know, my commission by the Signoria of the Chancery for the Hall of Five Hundred requires the bulk of my time and effort these days."

"And now this success by Buonarroti. Very impressive. I heard a rumor that the signoria plans to engage the sculptor for other projects." Leonardo felt the sharp jab of Francesco's comment. He sensed the merchant had become impatient. Despite his many visits to Francesco's home, Leonardo had yet to complete Lisa's portrait. Did Francesco wonder if something was amiss? Leonardo hoped not, for Lisa's sake.

"I would not know, as I have my own commissions to worry about. You will excuse me. I must congratulate Michelangelo." Leonardo bowed and turned to leave.

Michelangelo frowned at his approach.

Leonardo held out his hand to the sculptor, who seemed to hesitate a moment before clasping his hand. "Da Vinci, I am surprised to see you here."

Leonardo beamed his most charming smile. Michelangelo had not even bothered to wash his hands for the unveiling. But Leonardo would not mar the younger man's glory as he surreptitiously wiped the marble dust from his fingers.

"How could I miss such an important event in the life of our fair republic?" His gaze settled on the magnificent statue. "You deserve all the accolades, Michelangelo. *Congratulazioni! David* breathes with life."

Michelangelo's coarse, dark brows arched in surprise. "Thank you, Leonardo. I appreciate the effort you must have taken to restrain your conceit, even briefly. Have you heard? It seems we will be working side by side very soon."

The man possesses no social graces. He must always rub salt into the wound. "Indeed? Pray tell me what news."

"Soderini has commissioned me to create a mural opposite yours—a scene from the Battle of Cascina."

Surely, this day cannot get any worse. To be confined to the same space for months on end with his boorish rival looking over his shoulder sparked a dread worse than the threat of being imprisoned in the Bargello prison.

Painting a smile on his face, Leonardo uttered a hasty farewell, casting one last look at the statue that towered over them. With how this day turned out, Leonardo half expected *David* to lift his sling and hurl a stone at his face.

CHAPTER 26

*M*eira's fear felt as tangible as a shroud as she walked through the streets on her errand. Every shadow threatened, and every person she passed seemed menacing.

The initial elation that Italians had felt at the armistice between Italy and the Allies was replaced by apprehension as German troops swiftly snatched the reins of power. At first, the Italian army and the carabinieri fought to hold onto Rome, but by the 10th of September, the panzer division of German tanks and mechanized infantry overwhelmed the resistance and crushed the opposition.

Two days later, Mussolini, who'd been imprisoned at Gran Sasso in the Apennine mountains, was freed by German paratroopers and Waffen-SS when they paraglided in to rescue him. Smuggled to Vienna, Mussolini met with Hitler. Then, he was taken to Salò near Lake Garda, where he became the figurehead leader of a newly formed puppet regime called the Italian Social Republic. Since then, the Germans had confiscated food supplies for their army, while Italy's citizens suffered from shortages and repression.

For the Jewish community, the changes were even more profound and life-threatening. Meira's parents worried about deportation and resettlement—the Nazi's euphemistic terms for internment camps. Nazi swastika flags now flew from every building, and armed German soldiers were overtly conspicuous throughout the city.

As she turned a corner, Meira was reminded of the omnipresent threat of arrest. Plastered on walls and lampposts were notices of the Generalfeldmarschall Albert Kesselring's chilling edicts that, if violated, would be punishable by death—either by hanging or firing squad.

Before the German occupation, Italy's government rarely enforced restrictions on the Jewish community. But now, the iron fist of Nazi rule had the Eternal City in its grip. Every Italian had reason to be apprehensive about the future, but the fear that consumed the twelve thousand Jews living in Rome was for their very survival.

Meira entered the church of San Gregorio della Divina Pietà. Built in the twelfth century, it evoked both serenity and reverence. She spotted the priest at the altar as she walked down the center aisle. "Padre D'Angelo," she said in a hushed voice.

"Sì, sono io," he said as he turned toward her. "Ah, I know you." He smiled. "You are Meira, the daughter of my dear friend Benjamin."

She smiled back. It was hard not to; the priest was known for his kindness and warmth.

"I have something from Papà." She handed him the sealed envelope. "He said you would know what to do."

His gaze turned curious, and she did not know what else to say, so she gave a little shrug. "I bid you a good day, Padre D'Angelo."

"*Buon giorno,* Meira. Stay safe."

She gave him a quick nod, then turned and hurried out of the church. She had no idea what was in the letter, nor did she give it much thought. Over the years, she had met the padre many times at her parents' bookshop and knew her papà trusted him. She'd always thought it rather odd that a priest and a Jew had such a close bond of friendship. But her father had told her he and the priest had known each other since childhood when they were members of a neighborhood soccer team.

Meira shook her head as she quickened her pace, trying to focus on her surroundings. It was hard to hold onto one thought when so many crowded her head. As she rounded a corner, her heart almost leaped from her chest as the roar of a convoy of trucks and motorcycles with sidecars carrying Nazi officers barreled past. Her heart pounding in her ears, she darted from doorway to doorway, clinging to the shadows and wishing she could make herself invisible. She pulled the collar of her coat up as she hurried along, casting quick, furtive glances in the direction of any sound or movement. She stayed so close to the stone wall along the Lungotevere de' Cenci that her shoulder rubbed against it, snagging her sweater. The walkway ran between the Tiber River and the ancient Jewish ghetto.

She looked around, making sure no one was watching, and

dashed into the Tempio Maggiore di Roma through the back entrance. She took the steps two at a time to the library situated on the upper floors of the Great Synagogue of Rome. The Biblioteca della Comunità Israelitica was the repository of seven thousand rare Jewish books and manuscripts and was considered one of the finest collections in the world. Many tomes in the library were dated from the thirteenth century and were considered priceless. The shelves contained every imaginable topic written by the most revered Jewish scholars and thinkers. Many were the only copies in existence. Most were written in Hebrew and covered a dizzying array of subjects, including medicine, pharmacology, astrology, astronomy, kabbalah, a codex on ethics, the organon of Aristotle, ritual and legal commentary, mathematics, philosophy, and writings on the two-thousand-year-old history of Jews in Rome.

A set of adjoining rooms housed the Italian Rabbinical College of Rome Library, a teaching library of ten thousand books, a treasure brought in the 1930s from Florence to Rome. Meira prayed she'd find Marcello at his usual spot with his head buried in a book.

Her parents had warned her to return to the apartment before the seven o'clock curfew. She wasn't supposed to go anywhere after delivering her father's letter to the padre, but she was desperate to see Marcello. Even so, the thought of retracing her steps home through the dangerous streets filled her with anxiety.

She made her way upstairs, her breath quickening, not just from rushing along the streets and climbing stairs but from the heady anticipation that always came over her when she thought of him.

"Marcello." Meira's breathless voice cut through the silence of the library. She knew better than to attract attention in a place where the loudest sound was the whisper of scholarly lips reciting words written by those long dead. But it had felt like an eternity since she'd last seen him. If her father hadn't sent her on the errand to deliver a letter to Padre D'Angelo, who knows when she would have been able to spend a few moments alone with him?

She pushed away the pang of guilt for not returning directly home as her parents had asked, but she needed to see Marcello to hear his reassurances about their future. Assurances that nothing would ever come between them. She was lucky the temple was only a short distance from the church; her parents would not think anything amiss if she were just a few minutes late.

"Meira, over here."

She turned toward the sound of his voice and saw him standing at one of the tables at the far end of the large room. Her heart leaped with joy, and she ran into his open arms and buried her head in his chest. Tears came to her eyes as his strong arms embraced her. "Oh, Marcello, Marcello," she wept.

"What is wrong, *tesoro?* I've missed you so much." He kissed her forehead and smoothed the wisps of hair that escaped her ponytail. He lifted her chin and grinned. "Your cheeks are red as cherries. You look beautiful, *amore mio.*"

Meira felt her cheeks flush even more and peeked around the room. The only other person present was an old man wearing a skullcap who cleared his throat in disapproval. It wasn't likely he knew her parents; besides, who in times like these would worry themselves over two young people finding a bit of comfort in each other's arms? She leaned into the welcoming warmth of Marcello's solid frame.

"Marcello, the world is falling apart. Something bad is going to happen. I can feel it. Papà and Mamma have changed. They haven't left the house since the Germans took over. They send Sofia, our maid, out to do the shopping. Sofia doesn't mind. She is Catholic and understands my parents' fear of attracting attention from the Germans." Meira swallowed around the lump in her throat. "P-Papà sits by the window day and night, peering through the sliver between the drawn curtains, watching for soldiers. Mamma wrings her hands and w-weeps, lamenting that we stayed instead of fleeing to Fiesole, where her great aunt has a small farm."

Marcello kissed her forehead. "It's okay, Meira." He pulled out a chair for her, and they both sat. Taking her hands in his, he gave them a gentle squeeze. "I agree, everyone is going *pazzo*, my parents, too. But Fiesole is no safer than here. The Nazi occupation is everywhere. Have faith, *amore mio*. The Allies will win this war and defeat those *bastardi*. It is just a matter of time."

"But how much time? Papà thought SS Colonel Kappler would keep his promise to the Jews in Rome if we raised the demanded fifty kilograms of gold for the ransom. Without a word of complaint, Mamma took off her wedding ring and emptied her jewelry box to help. But nothing has come of it. What assurances have they given us since they gobbled up all that gold?" She shook her head. "I don't know what to do, Marcello. What if they come for us? They've been rounding up Jews all over Europe. What makes us think they won't do it here? And God knows what would happen to us then."

Marcello held her tighter, pressing his cheek against her hair. "I don't believe them either, but what can we do? Maybe the pope can convince them to leave us alone."

"Do you think he can?" She grasped onto that sliver of hope.

"He gave us gold when we were short on the ransom amount. Maybe he will do more."

Meira leaned back and cupped his face in her hands. "All I want is to be with you, go to school, and live in peace."

"That's what I want too, but I'm afraid it's not what Hitler wants."

"Why does he hate us so?"

Marcello scanned the library of precious books. "Jews have been the favorite scapegoat of kingdoms and rulers since time immemorial. Although Italian Jews, by any measure, had it better. We were accepted and granted citizenship, but even here, anti-semitism exists beneath the thin veneer of tolerance. Evil people must pass the blame for their deeds onto those they victimize. And the ignorant just follow their lead. Hitler whipped up his followers into a frenzy, convincing them Jews are to blame for every ill in society, so they feel no shame in tormenting us."

"Every night, I wish we could flee—you, me, our families— board a ship bound for America. Wouldn't that be wonderful?"

"Of course—"

The door to the library flew open, and Signora Rosina Sorani, the secretary of the Community Library, burst into the room. She hurried to them, her hands twisting together as if trying to rub them clean of dirt. "*Ragazzi*, you must leave immediately." She turned to the elderly scholar, "You too, Rabbi Greco. I'm sorry, but a German convoy is on its way here. It's not safe for you."

"But why?" Marcello rose and began stuffing papers and books in his backpack. "What do they want?"

Rosina's eyes glistened with tears behind her spectacles. Her gaze flitted around the room, and she continued to wring her hands together. "The books."

"The books?"

Her head bobbed in a jerky nod. "Two men dressed in SS uniforms came here a few weeks ago. One said he was a Hebrew teacher at an institute in Berlin. He was knowledgeable, a biblio-phile, and presented himself as an academic. They spent several hours studying our collection. Then they came again a few days ago and said they would return to take all the books. They made a list of everything here. They waved it under my nose and told me that if one volume was missing upon their return, they would arrest me, and anyone connected to the library."

"But thousands of books are kept here," Marcello said, glancing around the room. "Three entire floors."

Rosina wiped her eyes. "They said they will take them all to Frankfurt. They claim it is to keep them safe."

Marcello's hands clenched into fists. "They are not taking them to keep them safe," he muttered. "They are stealing them!"

Meira had never seen such hatred in Marcello's eyes or heard such fury in his voice. Was it only a few minutes ago that he calmly reassured her to be patient? Or had he lied to keep her from being afraid?

"They intend to eradicate us," he continued, "and every trace of our existence!"

Meira began to tremble, half-expecting Marcello to drive his fist through a wall.

"Marcello, *calmati*. We must not lose faith," Rosina said. "The world will not allow them to get away with such an atrocity. But for now, there is nothing we can do." She patted his shoulder. "Go home. If anything happened to you, your father would never forgive me."

Meira wrapped her hands around Marcello's arm and tugged gently. "Rosina is right, Marcello, we must leave."

He looked at her, and the anger dissipated from his eyes, his fists unclenched, and his shoulders slumped in resignation.

"Of course, we must. I don't want you in danger." He hefted his backpack over his shoulder and clasped Meira's hand. They said goodbye to Rosina, who was helping the old rabbi gather his things. Marcello paused and glanced back at the upper floors. He heaved a deep sigh and tugged Meira out the back doors of the temple. "Come, I know where we can hide and observe the SS unseen. I want to see what happens."

"But isn't that risky?"

"No, we'll be fine. They won't be able to see us. Besides, they'll be too busy stealing our treasures."

He led her to the steps that rose to the Ponte Fabricio, the oldest bridge in Rome that spanned the Tiber to the only island in the river, the Isola Tiberina. Once on the island, Marcello guided her closer to the rambling complex of the Fatebenefratelli Hospital beneath a grove of ancient cypress trees. The bridge connected the Jewish quarter to the island and the hospital. They had a bird's-eye view of the temple's back entrance from their vantage point.

A few minutes later, a convoy of military trucks rumbled past. The vehicles made their way to the alley behind the temple and, one by one, parked up and down the street. Dozens of uniformed soldiers leaped from the trucks and began unloading packing materials.

"*Figli di puttana!*" Marcello hissed under his breath. He clutched Meira's hand so tightly she could feel his pulse pounding against her palm.

"They just keep taking from us," Meira whispered as the

German guards marched into the building with the precision of a well-oiled machine.

"They will never be satisfied!" Marcello spat. "The library's books and manuscripts are worth a thousand times more than the gold they ransomed from us."

"All those lovely books," she said.

He gripped her shoulders and spun her around to face him. "I want to join the *partigiani*," he blurted.

"No, Marcello! If anything happened to you, I would die."

"I cannot bear to feel helpless, to do nothing." Marcello pulled her into a tight embrace. "Soon, there won't be anything left for them to steal. And then they will come for us."

"But you said you had faith in the Allies," she said, her voice muffled against his shoulder. "That they would win."

"I still do, but in the meantime, do I sit like a *cappone*, waiting to be plucked for Sunday dinner?"

"I am so afraid. For you. For me. For our families. All of us are in danger."

His forehead touched hers. "Sometimes fear can be a motivating force. But I need to do something, or I will go mad watching them take everything from us." His gaze returned to the temple doors, where the first group of soldiers emerged carrying boxes.

"Marcello, promise me you won't do anything rash."

He shrugged. "What? Like get a pistol and shoot those *figli di puttana*?"

"You know what I mean. I can't lose you."

"You will never lose me, *tesoro*." Marcello dove in for a kiss, holding her so close that the heat from his lean frame drove away the chill of the night air.

"We'd better get off the streets before curfew," she said, brushing her lips against his again. "Our poor parents don't need anything more to worry about on top of everything else."

Marcello's eyes flitted back to the temple, and Meira turned in the direction of his gaze. The Germans continued to load up the trucks with the spoils of yet another Nazi victory over the Jews. "I don't think it will take much longer to empty the library," she said, in awe at how quickly they worked.

"They are very efficient, those Nazis, aren't they?" Marcello said, his voice heavy with sarcasm. Grasping her hand, he tugged her away from the bridge. "Come, *amore mio*, I'll walk you home."

CHAPTER 27

ara Lisa,

> *Is all of this for naught? More and more, I ask myself this question. What will I be leaving behind when I pass on to the great unknown? What have I contributed to art, to culture, to the world? Thousands of pieces of paper with sketches of cadavers and drafts of flying contraptions? A smattering of unfinished commissions? I cannot help but wrestle with these thoughts and with what my legacy will be...*

Leonardo stood on a platform of roughly hewn wood planks balanced over barrels in the basilica of Santa Maria Novella. The carpenters were at work on the scissor platform, but there had been delays as usual, and the complicated design required his

245

frequent presence. The back and forth between the hall and the basilica was taxing, but alas, with such an undertaking, it could not be helped.

Pressing his right hand against the paper pinned to the wall, his left hand gripping a piece of rust-colored chalk, he began to shade and contour the warriors and horses in the life-size cartoon that had occupied him for months. The center scene for the mural was nearly ready to be transferred to the wall in the Salone dei Cinquecento, but much remained to be done. He hummed, sometimes erupting into song as he worked.

He preferred to be outside on this warm fall day, but he promised Lisa that he would finish the cartoon for the *Battle of Anghiari* so that he could return to her portrait. At least then, they could spend time together again under the guise of propriety. He needed no excuse, but Signora del Giocondo must be kept above any suspicion. Not that anything indecorous had occurred since their one indiscretion unless one considered a spiritual meeting of the minds as adulterous. But the emotions of others mattered. Dealing with Salai's unwarranted jealousy posed enough difficulty, let alone a devoted husband who would undoubtedly lose his mind if he thought his wife unfaithful.

The ringing of the bells in Giotto's campanile broke the tranquility of the basilica, announcing it was half-past eleven. As if on cue, Leonardo's stomach growled. The bells at the Duomo rang six times daily, beginning at nine in the morning. Leonardo would work until the bells tolled again at noon, and then he would break for lunch.

With his fingers, he blended the curls on the head of a warrior who lay on the ground, his mouth gaping open in a death scream, eyes wide and terrified, knowing he was about to be trampled beneath a horse's hoof. The stallion looked down at the man, cognizant of what was about to happen, while his teeth locked around the muzzle of another charger.

Leonardo leaned back as he regarded his efforts. It was paramount to him that he convey his intent in every inch of the massive painting. *The Battle of Anghiari* had nothing to do with glory and everything to do with the madness of war. War and its inherent bloodlust must be displayed with ferocity. When fighting to the death, any sense of truth, honor, and valor ceases to exist, leaving only raw brutality amidst a frenzied desperation for survival.

The third ringing of the bells from Giotto's tower reminded Leonardo to lay down his chalk. He cleaned his fingers on a rag, took a last look at the cartoon, and climbed down from the platform. Sitting on the marble floor, a young man was drawing in a notebook. Leonardo observed him, impressed by his intensity of focus. With long, dark, wavy hair and no shadow of a beard, the young man seemed scarcely out of his teens. Leonardo, ever cognizant of male or female beauty, noted the lad's face resembled that of a beautiful girl, with full, curved lips pursed in concentration.

The youth finally looked up; his face flushed at being caught unawares. "Maestro da Vinci, forgive the intrusion," he blurted. "I-I didn't want to interrupt you and thought you wouldn't mind if I took a lesson from your brilliance."

"And who may I ask, am I addressing?"

The youth jumped to his feet and extended his hand. "Raffaello Sanzio da Urbino," he bowed, "I am at your service."

"*Per favore*, call me Leonardo." The youth had a firm handshake and a pleasing demeanor.

"My friends call me Raphael, and I hope you will address me the same. I am privileged to meet you, Maestro."

Leonardo glanced down at the notebook that Raphael had left on the floor. "May I?"

"I would be honored, Maestro." The youth picked up the book and passed it to him. Leonardo recognized the fine quality of the paper in the oversized book. Setting it on the platform, he began to study the pages. His eyebrows rose, and he nodded as he carefully flipped through each sketch until he came to the drawing that the young artist was sketching—his *Battle of Anghiari*.

"How old are you, Raphael? Your work is expert, and your talent extraordinary."

"Your praise is more than I could hope for. I am twenty-one. I apprenticed with Perugino and achieved my master status at seventeen."

"Your master has taught you well, Master Raphael. Would you care to join me in my *camera* for lunch?"

"That would be most agreeable, Maestro."

Raphael followed Leonardo to his private quarters. While Leonardo set out brass bowls, spoons, knives, wine goblets, and linen napkins, Raphael wandered around the studio where Leonardo's current works in various stages of progress were set on easels. Leonardo filled their bowls with tortellini and peas. "*E pronto*, Raphael, come join me."

Leonardo picked up his spoon and waved it at Raphael. "*Amico mio*, you said you are from Urbino. Tell me about yourself."

"I followed in my father's footsteps as a court painter for the venerable Duke Giudobaldo da Montefeltro. My mother died when I was eight, and my father died when I was eleven. My father's brother Bartolomeo, a priest, became my guardian. The duke and his wife, Duchessa Elisabetta Gonzaga, are exceedingly generous and supportive of me." Raphael ate a spoonful of tortellini, nodding. "This is delicious, Maestro. *Grazie.*"

"*Prego.* Our beginnings are not so different, Raphael. Though unlike you, I was born out of wedlock, and my early years were spent in the country raised by my grandfather and my uncle, a man of complete kindness who loved me like a son. My father brought me to Florence when I was twelve and apprenticed me to Verrocchio when I was fourteen. The atelier was my home. So, what has brought you to Florence?"

"You, Maestro. Your name is revered far and wide. I wanted to study the work of the greatest master. I also wish to study the work of Michelangelo Buonarotti. I have seen his sculpture of *David*, and it is a work of pure genius."

Leonardo's spoon froze in mid-air. He carefully chose his next words. "Buonarotti is undoubtedly a masterful artist, but his demeanor can sometimes be abrupt. You will find an absence of amiability coming from that quarter."

Raphael smiled. "I am aware of his reputation, but I thank you for the advice."

A knock on the door interrupted their conversation.

"*Prego,*" Leonardo called out.

Leonardo turned and was happily surprised to see Lisa enter, carrying a small hamper. He stood and went to her, reaching for her hand; he beheld her beauty, which always struck him anew.

"Signora Giocondo, what a pleasure to see you. May I introduce you to an artist from Urbino, Raffaello Sanzio. He has recently arrived in Florence, and I invited him to share my repast."

"It is my pleasure to meet you." Lisa smiled.

"The pleasure is all mine, Signora." The young man blushed.

For a moment, the three looked in silence at one another. Lisa broke the awkward lull, raising the hamper. "I brought you a lemon cake, Maestro."

"*Perfecto,*" he said. He turned to Raphael. "The Signora has done me the honor of posing for a portrait that I believe will be the finest I have ever undertaken."

Raphael looked around the studio. "May I see it?"

Leonardo strode to the cloth-draped easel and lifted the cover. "It is here for me to gaze at and ponder." He grinned at Lisa, amused that his confession had brought a rosy hue to her cheeks.

Raphael studied the painting in silent contemplation. "It is unlike any portrait I have ever seen. Truly a magnificent work of art," the young man said reverently.

"Thank you, Raphael, your compliment praises both myself and Signora Giocondo."

"Indeed, for you are a true inspiration, Signora," the young man added in a bashful voice.

"*Vi ringrazio,*" Lisa replied with a gracious smile.

Raphael smiled back and then turned toward another of Leonardo's paintings. "Maestro, would you mind if I made some sketches of *Leda and the Swan?*" His youthful eagerness glowed on his face. "It is a subject I find most appealing and have wanted to attempt for some time."

Leonardo regarded his depiction of the Greek myth of Leda's seduction by Zeus, who, in the story, transformed himself into a swan. Zeus's wing was draped around her hip as the lovers watched their four children emerge from eggshells. Leonardo was nearly finished with it. The seminude figure of Leda was a departure from anything he'd ever painted before.

The painting itself had undergone multiple changes from his original sketch. He found the present version highly appealing, focusing on the domestic bliss of father, mother, and children without sacrificing the undercurrent of erotic sensuality that factored heavily in the Greek myth. Yes, he was quite pleased with the changes.

His lips twitched as he exchanged a look with Lisa. Their time together had influenced his new vision of the painting. He turned back to the young artist and smiled. "Of course, be my guest. I ask only that you allow me to see your work when it is finished. I will be curious as to the result."

"I must take my leave of you, Maestro," Lisa said, with a light touch on his arm. "I did not mean to disturb your lunch with Signore Sanzio."

"Your visits are never a disturbance." He took the hamper from her hand. "I will return this to you very soon." He winked.

"I look forward to it."

"I will see you out."

"Thank you, Maestro."

She turned to the young artist. "I hope to see you again, Signore Sanzio."

Raphael stood before Leonardo's painting, his hand on his chin, his visage deep in concentration. As if suddenly awakened from a dream, he blinked and gave her an absentminded smile. "*Grazie*, Signora, it was an honor to meet you."

Leonardo walked Lisa to the hallway, took her hand, and pressed his lips to it. "I'm sorry, *cara*, I did not expect your visit today."

"Do not worry. I found myself free and thought I might spend some time with you. Signore Sanzio seems like a sweet young man. It is kind of you to take him under your wing."

"He is an immensely talented young artist. He will achieve greatness, I think."

"And I am certain you will give him good advice."

He shrugged. "Greatness does not come without a price. One must never forget one's humility. Sometimes, I forget this truism in my own life."

"Thank goodness that I am around to remind you."

Leonardo threw back his head and laughed. "And I am fortunate that you do."

She caressed his cheek and regarded him momentarily as though committing his features to memory.

"*Cara*, perhaps there was another reason for your visit today," he said gently, laying his hand over hers.

"Sometimes, I wish I had your talent so that I could capture every moment we spend together," she said, expelling a deep sigh. "Time is so fleeting, is it not?"

Her eyes now shimmered with unshed tears, and he was so moved he had to blink back his own tears.

"It is, *tesoro*, but we have our memories, do we not? And those are far more meaningful than anything I could render."

Her lips curved into that mysterious smile that always left him in awe. "Yes, *caro mio*. We have our memories, but the world has your art, which is more than meaningful. It is a gift for all eternity."

CHAPTER 28

OCTOBER 15, 1943 ~ ROME, ITALY

*M*eira blinked back tears as she stared at the framed painting above the piano. Lately, whenever she looked at it, it made her cry. Blending rich hues of red, the painting was a self-portrait of the artist Chagall and his wife, Bella, kissing as he floated above her in their house. Titled *The Birthday*, it was Meira's favorite painting. More so because her father had bought it for her mother on her birthday in their first year of marriage. *Happier days.*

"Papà, I made you some tea," Meira said, setting the tray beside him on the small side table next to the window in the parlor where her father sat as a sentinel, keeping watch of the piazza below. She'd drizzled some of their precious honey on a slice of bread. Her father could use the sugar. He looked haggard and worn, and it seemed he'd aged thirty years overnight. Her father had gone from a vital and confident man to a shadowy figure in baggy clothes. Meira was devastated that she could see no way to ease his burdens.

"Thank you, Meira," he said, with a ghost of a smile, as he pushed his glasses up the bridge of his nose. His gaze slid back to the window, seeming to forget the cup of tea.

Meira swallowed the lump in her throat and left her father to his night watch to check on her mother, who'd gone to bed early. She pressed her ear to the door and listened. Hearing her mother's deep and steady breaths, Meira sighed with relief. At least her mother was asleep and not weeping as she often did these days. Meira worried about her parents, worried about the future, worried they were helpless to stop the encroaching darkness from permeating every part of their lives and piercing their souls.

The war had changed Meira's happy world utterly and completely. It was as if she'd stepped through a mirror, like *Alice in Wonderland*, into a world where everything was reversed. Her mother and father argued constantly, which they'd never done before. Meira supposed it was human nature to vent your fear and sorrow on the person closest to you, the one person you should never hurt.

She vowed she would never treat Marcello with anything other than love and respect. And she was certain he would do the same. She was fortunate to have found him. Marcello was everything a girl could dream of—intelligent, handsome, caring, generous, and brave. She could go on for hours about his attributes and never run out of superlatives. And when he touched her, it felt like a fire blazed in her blood. *Please, God, I pray this war ends soon so that Mamma and Papà can be happy again and Marcello and I can be married.*

Meira returned to the parlor and sat beside her father, waiting for him to remember she was there. She longed to hear him reassure her that all would be well. Her thoughts drifted to their bookshop, now closed and boarded up, maybe forever. It broke her heart. Her earliest childhood memories revolved around the tiny bookshop on the Via Michelangelo Caetani. The sound of the cash register ringing like a musical accompaniment to the sing-song chatter of happy customers, the reassuring tactile feel of the stiff spines of the leather-bound books that lined the shelves, the sweet aroma of her father's tobacco swirling up from his pipe—all of it was indelibly imprinted in her heart and mind.

Both parents worked in the shop, and wherever they were, she was too. Meira grew up surrounded by books. Sitting on a carpet near the cash register, reading *Anne of Green Gables, The Wonderful Wizard of Oz,* and *The Adventures of Pinocchio,* her favorite book. Her parents had built the most beautiful fountain where her mind could forever quench its thirst for knowledge.

But the fountain had run dry. The thousands of books inside the sealed bookshop would turn to dust. Did those beloved tomes wonder what happened to those who'd taken such loving care of them? *Do they feel abandoned and forgotten as we do?*

Was it just last night when Marcello and she witnessed the Nazis looting the library? A sharp pang twisted her heart. Last night, she'd lain awake, unable to sleep, fearful that Marcello might join the partisans and she would never see him again. She couldn't contemplate the idea of a world without Marcello in it. She couldn't bear the thought of losing him.

Her father continued to stare out the window, the bread on his plate untouched. "Papà, please eat something or at least rest.

There's nothing outside the window that you haven't seen before."

Benjamin turned to her and pushed his spectacles up again. His once midnight hair was now threaded with silver. "I'm fine, Meira. I rest in the day. It's better that I keep watch at night, just in case..." He didn't finish the sentence, and Meira tried not to think about what *just in case* meant. Her father opened his arms for a hug, and she sank into the comfort of his embrace. He kissed her forehead and whispered in her ear. *"Vai a dormire, tesoro."*

"All right, Papà, I'll go to bed, but promise me you'll try to get some rest."

"Per te, dolcezza, farei qualsiasi cosa."

She kissed his cheek. *For you, my sweet, I would do anything.* Her father's love was a reassuring promise.

"Svegliati! Wake up, Meira! Get dressed." Meira rubbed her eyes. Was she dreaming? Her father's voice was desperate. Even in the darkness of her room, she could see he hadn't slept a wink. She fumbled for her watch on the bedside table and saw it was three in the morning.

"What is it, Papà?" What's wrong?"

"We only have a few minutes. They'll be at the door any moment. We must hurry!"

He ran from the room. Meira rubbed the sleep from her eyes and stumbled out of bed. Her parents' voices drifted down the hallway to her. Her mother was crying while drawers were being opened and slammed shut. Meira pulled on a heavy wool skirt over thick stockings, paired with a cotton shirt and her warmest sweater. She poked her head out of her room. "Papà," she called out.

Her father hurried to her. "Here," he handed her a wallet filled with *lire*, "you'll need this. The Germans are here with trucks. It can be for no other reason than deportation." He pulled her into the other bedroom, where her mother was frenetically throwing clothing into suitcases.

"Meira!" Her mother ran to her and hugged her so tight she couldn't breathe. Gabriella kissed her on both cheeks. "I love you, daughter." Her mother studied her face as if imprinting it to memory."

"I love you too, Mamma."

Gabriella nodded, her beautiful dark eyes awash with tears.

"Mamma, please don't cry." Seeing her mother cry always made her cry, too. "I love you so much, Mamma."

"I love you too, *passerota mia*." Her mother's use of her childhood endearment, little sparrow, made Meira cry even harder. Her mother had given her the nickname when Meira was six years old. It was the first day of school, and Meira refused to go, declaring she would fly right back home. "My beautiful child, whatever happens, remember we meant only the best for you. Never forget that, and never forget that we love you."

"Mamma, we'll be all right, won't we?" Meira began to tremble, frightened by her mother's words."

"Hush, my sweet girl, *coraggio* for your Mamma," she said, cupping Meira's face. "Now, it's time for you to be my strong, brave girl."

"Yes, Mamma, I love you."

"I love you too, *tesoro*." Her mother held her tight once more. "Do exactly what Papà tells you."

Meira could not control the tremors that took hold of her body. She was shaking like a dog left out in the rain. Tears splashed down her cheeks.

"Now, go!" Her mother turned her back and continued to fill the suitcases, but Meira could see her shoulders shaking and knew she was silently sobbing.

"Meira, hurry, there's no time to waste," her father said, tugging her hand.

Her father led her to a closet at the end of the hallway. "Do you remember I built another compartment for luggage at the back of the storage closet?"

"Yes, Papà." A storm was building inside her. She could barely get the words out. She was caught in a tornado of twisting and swirling emotions that threatened to overwhelm her. It was as if her father was speaking to her from the other side of the vortex. She shook her head, trying to focus on what he was telling her. There was no way forward and no way back. Everywhere she turned, darkness loomed. It pressed in on her, threatening to steal her ability to think...to breathe.

"I want you to hide in that closet and stay there until it is safe to come out. No matter what you hear, you must not make a sound or come out. I've put water, food, and candles there for you. At dawn, when it's quiet in the piazza, I want you to go to San Gregorio della Divina Pietà and find Padre D'Angelo. He will help you. Do you understand?"

"But what about you and Mamma? Why can't you come with me? We could all hide in the closet, and I know the good priest would help us all."

"It's too late for that, *tesoro*. The Nazis have lists, and they know we're here. We'll tell them you went to care for your great aunt in Fiesole. Don't worry about us, we will manage. What matters is that you are safe." Sounds of heavy boots marching up the stairs and pounding on doors were accompanied by the guttural orders of the German SS. *"Steh auf! Mach die tür auf!"* and *"Alzati! Apri la porta!"* Her father gripped her shoulders and gave her a little shake. "Promise me, Meira, you'll do exactly as I've said."

"I promise, Papà." She threw herself against her father. "I love you."

"I love you too, now and forever." He held her close, his lips pressed to her temple, and then, with a firm grip, he uncoiled her arms from around him and pushed her toward the closet. "Remember, don't make a sound."

She crawled into the secret closet, and he slid the door closed. Surrounded by darkness, she heard her father shift the clothing hanging on the bar to hide the wall panel from view.

A few moments later, their apartment door shook from a banging fist and a voice shouting, *"Apri la porta!"* Benjamin Chiarelli's last words seemed to come to her through a tunnel. "Be safe, *cara mia*. We love you." His footsteps faded amid the pounding on the front door that echoed the pounding of her heart.

CHAPTER 29

ara Lisa,

In the silence of the night, when everyone is in their beds and the piazza is empty, I sit at my open window and gaze out, thinking of you. I think about that first time I saw you at the mercato, freeing those birds from their cages, watching them fly up to the heavens. I will never forget you that way, now and forever...

Leonardo studied the wall where he would paint the *Battle of Anghiari*. Soderini and Machiavelli had outsmarted him, damn their devious hides. By giving Michelangelo the commission to paint the opposite wall in the Hall of Five Hundred, they set into motion a fierce competition that held Florence enthralled. A competition was the last thing Leonardo needed at this time. Salai reported to him that it was the talk of the city, pitting the two most illustrious artists in Italy against one another. People were taking sides and, even worse, placing wagers on who would outdo the other. Word had spread throughout Italy, and artists were journeying to Florence to witness this clash of the Titans.

As Leonardo stared at the wall, he could not help but recall another of his past failures, the equestrian statue commissioned by Ludovico Sforza to honor Francesco Sforza, his father. Leonardo shook his head at the memory. At least in that instance, it was not because he'd abandoned the project. Leonardo had completed the clay model of horse and rider, which was set to be cast in bronze. It would have been the largest equestrian statue in the world, but the fates had conspired against him. War had descended on Milan in the form of the French King Charles VIII's army, and Ludovico was forced to take the precious metal set aside for the statue and reallocate it for cannon shot. As for the clay model, France's soldiers used it for target practice, shattering it into a thousand pieces.

The statue became a thorn in Leonardo's foot, and Michelangelo did not hesitate to rub salt into the wound. One day, outside the towering Palazzo Spini, Leonardo was among friends, enjoying a moment or two of lively conversation and laughter. Michelangelo approached the group, his face a mottled red of outrage at one of Leonardo's witty quips. Leonardo could not help teasing the brooding sculptor, who was sorely lacking in a sense of humor. Michelangelo shunned camaraderie with his fellow artists, unlike Leonardo, who was generous with his time, advice, and friendship.

"You are a failure," Michelangelo lashed out. "Your grand

vision of a horse cast in bronze was a disaster. A common theme for you, is it not, Leonardo? You are the most prolific at failing than any other artist in Italy. How you keep finagling commissions is beyond me!"

At the time, Leonardo was shocked that his good-natured ribbing had caused such a reaction in Michelangelo. It had been that way ever since. And now, he was to be pitted against the man in a ludicrous "battle," for it had become that in Leonardo's eyes. When Salai informed him of Gonfaloniere Soderini's braggadocio about launching a competition for "the greatest artist in the world" that would make Florence the center of the art world for centuries to come, Leonardo was so irate that he did not pick up a piece of chalk or a brush for a week. Finally, Lisa persuaded him to climb the barrels and resume his work at Santa Maria Novella.

Leonardo shook his head, wondering if he should focus the remainder of his days painting portraits rather than chasing after these grand commissions. He chuckled. At *least then, I can fill my pockets with coins rather than chalk.*

"And what is so funny?" The melodic voice echoed down the aisle of the church. Leonardo turned and beheld the young woman walking toward him. His breath quickened at her beauty as always when he was in her presence. He hadn't seen Lisa since her surprise visit on the same day the young artist Raphael appeared and made his acquaintance.

He grinned down at her. "I was wondering which is better, wealth or fame?"

"Ah, I think neither has ever been your motivation." She gestured to the mural. "It grows more incredible each time I see it. I tremble from its realism."

"Thank you. Your praise never fails to buoy my spirits." He

climbed down from the scaffolding and kissed her cheeks in greeting. "You look lovely, Signora. Your cheeks bloom rosier than the flowers in your garden. If I did not know better, I'd say you were with child," he teased.

Her eyes widened and filled with tears.

"*Cara mia*, what is the matter?" He took her hands in his. "Have I offended you in some way? Tell me so that I might make amends."

"No, of course not." She glanced around as though nervous about being overheard. "You cannot help your powers of observance."

"Come, I want you to see your portrait. I have managed to do a little work on it."

A newly constructed door connected the Sala del Papa to the basilica, giving Leonardo direct access to the cartoon of the *Battle of Anghiari*. This way, should he feel inspired to work in the middle of the night, he could. He bolted the door behind them and watched Lisa float across the stone floor, her silk gown whispering until she stood before her portrait.

"I meant to tell you, that day, how beautiful the blue-sky background is," she said. "I love our portrait. Does it bother you that I refer to it as ours?" Her eyes reflected a worry that perplexed him.

"It is how I have always thought of it. It is you who inspires every brush stroke."

"You honor me, Leonardo. Your friendship means so much to me." She burst into tears again.

Leonardo wrapped his arms around her and drew her close. "*Carissima*, what is the matter? Tell me what troubles you, and I shall do everything in my power to remedy this pain."

She pulled back and wiped her tears with the back of her

glove, prompting him to pluck a clean cloth from his cupboard and dab at her tears.

"Leonardo, what I must share is not a trouble but a joy. A joy for me, and I hope for you as well."

"I am confused..."

She kissed his hand, and realization finally came to him.

"I *am* with child Leonardo." Her whisper of a smile mirrored the one in the painting beside them.

"Are you sure...?"

"Almost certain."

"What should I do?"

"Nothing. Just be happy. As happy as I am." Her smile widened, and her tears flowed anew.

Now, it was his turn to tear up. "I am happy. So happy, I can scarcely think." He pressed his lips to her hands.

"I felt the same way when I first realized," she said, her voice thick with emotion. "Oh, Leonardo, our child, our daughter. She will be a blessing—a true blessing, and a sister for Camilla."

He grinned. "And how do you know the child will be she?"

"Intuition."

"What of Francesco, will he be pleased?"

"Of course. Francesco will believe she is his... does that trouble you?"

Leonardo paused and turned to regard Lisa's portrait, allowing the full meaning of their circumstances to sink in. He knew it must be this way. Her life was firmly rooted in her marriage and family, and his life was firmly rooted in his work. The painting had brought them together and connected them to each other, and now they would have a child together as well. A child would be a permanent bond between them. They would be bound together in art, life, and love. It seemed a fitting evolution of their friendship.

"Leonardo, you and I will share this child together no matter what the future holds," she said, almost echoing his thoughts. You will know her and watch her grow. You will see her first smile and hear her first words. She is an unexpected but welcome gift to both of us."

"I never thought—" He shook his head, at a loss for words.

"Nor did I, but miracles do happen."

"It is a miracle. She is a miracle," he said."

"Our miracle."

"Our miracle." A lightness came over him. He opened his arms, and she snuggled into his embrace, pressing her face against his chest.

"Leonardo, God has gifted us with this child for a reason. I— after I lost Piera—I was devastated. When Piero was born, I was overjoyed. All my children bring me happiness beyond measure, yet sometimes I feel guilty for taking pleasure in life because Piera is not with me. But now, I feel I can truly rejoice because of this child growing in my womb. I don't know why or how, but I feel she is a connection to Piera somehow. And a gift. God has sent her to me. To us."

"*Tesoro*, I cannot conceive the pain you experienced in losing your daughter, but I do not think you should ever feel guilty for your happiness. You are a wonderful and loving mother, and your children adore you."

She continued to burrow in his chest, avoiding his eyes. "I thank you for the kind words."

"They are not words or a compliment," he said, lifting her chin. "I speak the truth."

The pain reflected in her eyes made his heart ache.

"Being a mother is all that I know," she said. "All that I am. But meeting you has made me believe that I can be more, and sometimes that makes me feel shame that I should even want more."

"Why do you see it as one or the other? Why can you not be a loving mother and my greatest muse?"

She chuckled, and her cheeks grew rosy again. "Leonardo, perhaps you should also ask yourself this question."

"And what is that?"

"Why can you not be a painter, an inventor, an architect, and an engineer, all simultaneously? You are all those things and so much more. But perhaps best of all, you are my dearest friend."

He breathed a deep sigh as he gazed into her lovely eyes. "*Tesoro*, I do not know why God or fate or the cosmos in all its mysteries has brought us together, but I am ever thankful that it did. And I am ever thankful that you are my dearest friend."

CHAPTER 30

OCTOBER 16, 1943 ~ ROME, ITALY

*M*eira awoke with a gasp.

"Papà! Mamma!"

Silence, emptiness, and darkness were her only greetings. Clutching her knees to her chest, she realized she was not waking from a bad dream. She was living it. She threw off the blanket and sat up. Standing up in the confined space, she bumped her head and cried out. Her hand flew to her mouth, and she began to tremble, fearful she might have given herself away. Would she soon hear thudding boots and German expletives?

The silence stretched out, and she lowered her hand. Taking a few deep breaths, she hunched over and made her way to the panel of the false wall in the secret room. Pressing her hand against the wood, she carefully slid it open. Luckily, it did not squeak; her father had cleverly oiled it. She could make out the shadowy bulk of coats and garments ahead. Slowly, she pushed them aside and crawled to the closet door. Placing her ear on the wood, she closed her eyes and listened.

She imagined hearing her father's baritone voice reading the newspaper aloud to her mother as she prepared breakfast. Her mother would reply to his clever quips with one of her own, and they would both erupt in a duet of chuckles. Finally, her mother would shush her father and tell him to keep his voice down.

"Meira is still asleep," her mother would whisper. "The dear heart was up late studying for an exam."

They would continue the rest of their conversation in hushed tones until all would go quiet, and Meira knew they were sharing a tender kiss...

Tears flowed down her cheeks as she opened the closet door, and the truth stared her in the face. A tornado of brutality had ripped everything to shreds. Climbing out of the closet, she turned in a slow circle, absorbing the destruction around her. Dazed, she walked through the tattered remnants of what was once her home. Touching every torn book, every broken vase, every splintered picture frame. Fragments of her mother's best *piatti* lay scattered on the floor. Her mother's pretty dresses and her father's crisp shirts and trousers were strewn over upended chairs. Meira's heart pounded as she bent and picked up a pair of her father's spectacles. The frame was bent, and the glass was shattered as if crushed beneath a boot. And then she saw the blood. Her father's blood, having seeped into the carpet fibers, had left a black stain. Her knees buckled, and she fell to the floor as every horrific sound she'd heard last night regurgitated in her soul.

Meira had heard everything. Every smashing plate, every snarling command by the SS officers. Curled into a ball in the secret room at the back of the tiny closet, she'd been as silent and still as a statue, just as her father had bidden her. But she'd forced herself to listen, to bear witness. It was the least she could do to honor their great sacrifice.

Her parents attempted to reason with the soldiers. Their voices, calm and polite at first, became shaky and fearful as the soldiers tore up their entire home. Meira had pressed both hands to her mouth as her father, in his halting German, offered them money, gold, paintings—everything of value they had left if only they would let them stay. The guards simply howled with laughter, saying they would take everything anyway.

The monsters interrogated her parents about where their daughter was. Her father's calm reply that she was visiting her great-aunt in Fiesole earned him a beating that made Meira scream inside her mind and bite her lip until the metallic taste of blood nearly made her gag.

In a wheezing rasp, her father repeated it again and again as the soldiers continued to kick and punch him. Her mother's begging and pleading cries tore at Meira's heart, and she had to stuff her fist inside her mouth to keep from sobbing aloud.

Dear God, why have you forsaken us?

Meira had stayed silent, rolled up into a tight ball, wishing she could wake up from this nightmare, praying for her parents who were dragged from their home and taken to God knows where. She stayed as still and unmoving as she could all night long. Just as her father had told her, until exhausted, her eyes had finally closed, and she slipped into a restless sleep.

Now, she was alone in the ragged silence of her gutted home. Wiping the tears from her eyes, she drew a brittle breath and stood on trembling legs. Holding onto the walls, she walked down the hallway to her bedroom. Pale streams of light filtered through the window. The pretty curtain twisted around the mangled curtain road. The lovely, crocheted coverlet was on the floor, the sheets pulled off, and the mattress in shreds. She slid to the floor and pulled her coverlet over her shoulders. She wept until she had no tears left, and her tears were dried patches of salt on her cheeks. *Mamma, Papà, where are you?* How would she find them? Where would she even begin to look?

Were Marcello and his parents also caught in the Nazis' net? She shuddered as she thought of the Gestapo hurting her beloved. Marcello was young, strong, and brave. Did he stand up to the Nazis as they attacked his parents? Did they beat him as well? Or worse, did they shoot him? Her life, her heart, her world was gone. Would she ever get them back?

Her hand slipped into her pocket, and her fingers found the wallet filled with *lire* from her father. She remembered her promise to her parents. She would honor her vow. It was all she had left. It was all her parents had left. At least they could cling to that hope as they were shoved onto a train and transported to some Nazi camp. She pictured her loving parents, holding each other tightly, praying, their foreheads pressed together as the train jostled, the tracks rattled, and the train whistle blew its mournful cry. How long before they reached their destination? What would become of them?

Meira stumbled back to the living room and peeked through the curtains to the piazza below. It was quiet as a cemetery, almost as if nothing horrific had occurred the night before. The turtle fountain water splashed, fed by the ancient Roman aqueduct. *Acqua Vergine*, unchanged for nearly four hundred years, the pure mountain water cascaded down from its upper basin. Rome had survived for almost three millennia, but would her Jewish family, friends, community, and people survive until the war's end?

She took a deep breath, knowing what she must do next. The only thing she could do. Rushing back to the hidden closet, she dragged out the backpack her parents had left her and the food they'd managed to save for her. She made herself eat the soft, moist bread and crumbly cheese. She bit into an apple as she sifted through the sack's contents. A change of clothes, three books, precious keepsakes, and personal toiletries. She searched for their family photographs among the wreckage in the living room. She carefully removed the precious pictures from their broken frames and slipped them into the backpack's pocket. Shoving a light coat into the pack, she tied it closed and hefted it over her shoulder. Then Meira did the hardest thing she had ever done. She closed the door of her home, locked it with her key, and walked away.

Exiting by the rear door of the building into the back alley, she stayed close to the wall as she made her way to the narrow side street, Via dei Falegnami. It was only a short walk to her destination, but it felt like an eternity. The streets were deserted, and the old ghetto had become a ghost town. Occasionally, she came across another person hurrying along the street, but everyone kept their heads down. It was as if their heads disappeared into their coats like a turtle in a shell, which made them seem inhuman. Italians were typically friendly people—quick to smile and effusive in their greetings to friends and strangers alike. Now, they offered nothing, not even a meeting of the eyes. But then, who needed to look into another person's eyes when you already knew what you would see—fear, suspicion, and sorrow.

The façade of San Gregorio della Divina Pietà rose above the Piazza Gerusalemme, a rectangular plinth bordered by relief columns. A framed oval inset resembling a cameo held a painted depiction of the crucifixion. Meira pushed the heavy wooden door open, hoping it would be unlocked, as most churches were. She paused in the entry, recalling her father telling her that years ago when the Jews were locked inside the ghetto at night, the pope required them to attend sermons outside this church on the Sabbath. Her father had laughed, telling her that the Jews had avoided listening by placing wax in their ears. But the pope must have gotten wise because a plaque was now embedded into the plaster with a quote written in both Latin and Hebrew, plucked from the words of Isaiah, where the Lord complains about the obstinacy of the Jews.

When she'd delivered her father's letter to Padre D'Angelo, Meira had hardly noticed anything about the church. Now, her gaze swept the dimly lit interior, and she paused. The inside held a central nave divided by rows of straight-backed wooden bench pews. On either side, the vault was supported by veined Corinthian columns of peach-colored marble. Hanging above the main altar was a painting framed in gold of the Madonna and baby Jesus. The image was surrounded by white sculpted angels whose hands held the ornate frame as if displaying it to the world. Bursts of gold-painted wood imitating the sun's rays radiated outward from behind the angelic reliefs, glorifying the holy mother and child. It was a beautiful work of art, and Meira felt unimaginable sorrow that the treasures of Rome were in as much danger as her people.

Not a soul was in the church. She walked up the nave, the heels of her shoes tapping on the marble floor. When she reached the front pew and looked up at the painted dome above the altar of the ascension of Mary, she could not help but think of her mother.

Sitting on the bench, her new reality engulfed her once more. Everyone she loved was gone. She was alone. Tears she thought had dried up began to flow once more. Like the Turtle Fountain fed by the aqueduct, her profound sorrow replenished her well. She covered her face with her hands and sobbed, rocking back and forth. The pain of loss was too great, almost unbearable.

She cried for her parents, whom she feared she would never see again. She cried for Marcello and their brief, doomed love. She cried for the Jews of Rome, her friends, the old, the infirm, and the children who might never live to follow their dreams. She cried for the years of peace that were no more and a war that should never have been, and finally, she cried for herself, and a future stolen from her. Her anguished sobs echoed in the nave, an unspoken accusation to God for failing her family, her love, and her people.

Her hands covered her face, and she sensed a person nearby. Her tears subsided, her fingers spread, and she peeked out, expecting to see a uniformed Nazi come to arrest her and take her away. Instead, a tall man wearing a black cassock stood before her. Compassion glowed from his kindly eyes. He reached for her hands and helped her to her feet.

"Meira, thank God you are safe. I will help you. Please do not cry."

She threw her arms around Padre Antonio D'Angelo and embraced him.

Thank you, God. Forgive me for doubting You.

CHAPTER 31

OCTOBER 30, 1504 ~ FLORENCE, ITALY

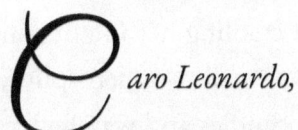aro Leonardo,

> With each passing day, my joy grows as she flutters inside
> me like a butterfly waiting to emerge from her cocoon. At times,
> I struggle with this joy. I love all my children equally, and my
> life is devoted to their happiness. My life is also pledged to my
> husband. But oh, how my soul rejoices in this child—our child.
> It is because of our friendship that she exists. Created by us, she
> is the embodiment of our devotion...

Lisa walked down the nave of Santa Maria Novella, her hand
smoothing down the front of her gown over the slight bump in
her belly. She sighed at the incongruity of life—to feel both joy

and sorrow at the same time. *Happiness for a life budding inside me. Heartbreak for a life lost before it had even begun.*

Lisa's eyes fixed on Giotto's unbearably moving tempera painting of the crucifixion. What mother, especially one who had lost a child, would not understand the agony of the Blessed Lady as she beheld her beloved son suffer to his death?

Piera, my darling daughter, how I miss you. Dio mio, why did you give her life only to take her from me?

She shivered as she glanced up at the towering black and white polychromed arches that soared above the basilica like a jeweled crown. It reminded her of the empty space within her heart that would forever belong to Piera.

Lisa entered the Cappella Tornabuoni and dropped a coin into the slot of the wooden donation box. She looked up at Domenico Ghirlandaio's wood panel altarpiece *Madonna in Glory with Saints*, depicting the Madonna cradling her infant son surrounded by Saints and Angels. Taking a small, wooden splint, Lisa touched its tip to one of the lit white candles and watched as it sparked into flame. Cupping it, she whispered, "For you, Piera." She touched the glowing tip to the wick of a fresh candle, her eyes misting with tears as she beheld the cheery flame that seemed to wave at her.

The first year after Piera's death, she would attend church every day and light a candle for her lost daughter. Gradually, it dwindled to once a week when she attended mass. Then, her busy life had stolen her time, and it had been over a month since she'd lit a candle for Piera. It grieved her that she'd been remiss.

Forgive me, tesorina. Please know that I think of you every day, even if it is not here in the sanctity of God's house.

Her hand again found the rounded bump beneath the silk of

her dress. *We will add a new member to our family in a few months. Imagine the excitement in the household. Camilla will have a beloved sister to play with and to share secrets. How I wish you were here to rejoice in this blessing with us. How I wish we could all be together.*

Lisa knelt at the altar and closed her eyes. She did not know how long she sat and prayed, but her reverie was broken by the soft rustle of a gown and the awareness of someone beside her. An old woman draped in a white veil lit a candle and knelt beside Lisa. "You have lost a dear one, my daughter," the woman said in a melodious voice.

Lisa turned to the woman whose face was obscured behind the heavy veil. "I have my lady. Have you also lost a loved one?"

The woman reached for Lisa's hand, and her touch filled Lisa with soothing serenity.

"I lost my only son many years ago," she replied in that mellifluous voice, "but I take heart that he is with nostro Signore. I am certain your daughter is as well."

Lisa squeezed the woman's hand. "That is a comforting thought, but I miss her terribly, and I worry that she is alone and feeling afraid without her family."

"No child is alone in Heaven, daughter. You must understand she is free from the trials of this world and knows only peace and tranquility. But there is much to look forward to with a new life growing within you, and she will be of great joy to you for the rest of your life."

"But...how do you know?"

The woman chuckled. "The beauty of motherhood is not such a mystery. Your eyes and skin are aglow with your grace."

"But you said *she* —?"

"Did I? Mothers have a way of knowing these things. You must look to God for tranquility, *figlia mia*."

It was unexplainable, but Lisa felt comforted by the woman's kind words. "Thank you, my lady, you have brought me peace of mind, and I am grateful."

The older woman rose as gracefully as she'd knelt. "I must leave you now, for I have many others to attend to. There are always souls in need of comfort."

"Thank you, dear lady. I bid you good day."

The woman's gossamer white gown floated behind her as she walked away, her leather sandals soundless on the marble floor. Closing her eyes, Lisa bowed her head and prayed.

How long she remained in meditation, she could not say. Opening her eyes, she found Leonardo kneeling beside her, looking intently at her. They gazed at each other in silence for a long while. Lisa's heart communed what she could not express in words.

After a time, Leonardo asked. "Have I disturbed you?"

"You could never disturb me."

He held out his hand, and she took it. "I had a beautiful encounter with an old woman who lit a candle and spoke to me. I don't know why, but my heart felt such peace from her presence. You must have seen her."

Leonardo arched his brows, a quizzical expression reflected in his gaze that surprised her. "*Cara*, no one other than you has come to pray. I saw you arrive and did not want to interrupt your prayers."

"But I saw her. She was here beside me, just as you are now."

"Perhaps I was not meant to see her." He smiled and stood, helping her up. "Come, let us go and free some birds."

Emerging from the church, they were greeted by the sun's warmth on their faces. Lisa closed her eyes and lifted her face to bathe in the light, feeling a serenity of spirit she hadn't felt in a long time.

HER COMPANIONSHIP in public was always less than he desired. Leonardo longed for their cherished time alone. A golden ray of sunshine fell across Lisa's face, burnishing her skin. She pulled her burgundy cloak more tightly around her, and her face disappeared into the shadow of her hood. The sun might as well have vanished from the sky.

"You are feeling well, Signora? The pregnancy is not debilitating?"

"Not at all. I have never felt better." Lisa reached out and patted his hand. A reminder that they were in the public sphere and visible to gossipmongers.

"And your husband, is he happy for this child?" Leonardo hated asking, but the idea was never far from his mind. He worried for her and the child.

"Yes, Francesco is very pleased to be a father again." Lisa glanced around and added in a low voice. "My dear Leonardo, soon you will feel your child growing inside me. It is a miraculous thing when she kicks."

The thought of laying his hand on her belly and feeling the movement of their creation delighted him. He chuckled. "If the child is a girl, I will truly believe in miracles and your intuition to see into the future."

"Our friendship is a miracle. But as to the future, I would not want to know what awaits us. Now, do not be stingy with your news, *per favore*. Please share everything with me."

They were nearly at the birdseller's stall, the warbling and twittering of birds becoming louder. Soon, the flapping of wings would join the complaints of flights denied and the rattling of cages from frustrated predators.

"Machiavelli informed me of a disaster near the fortress of Verucca. You recall my commission from him and my plan to divert the Arno River away from Pisa?" He shrugged. "One of my many failed projects. But this one at least cannot be laid at my feet."

"You cannot fail at what you never attempted," Lisa said in a supportive tone. "And, of course, I remember. It seemed you were away for an eternity, and I heard no word from you, and then your letter came, and I was filled with joy. But I do not understand what catastrophe has occurred?"

"Your memory and wisdom never fail to amaze me, *cara mia*. It seems they hired the wrong man to bring my design to fruition. Columbino is his name. He is a waterworks engineer who foolishly orchestrated the digging of two shallow ditches instead of one deeper ditch outlined in my drafts. I warned Machiavelli that the ditch must be deeper than the bed of the Arno, but Columbino took it upon himself to ignore my instructions."

"He changed your plans. But why?"

"I suspect it was the time, expense, or perhaps plain laziness, but the result has been far more costly. Machiavelli's secretary, Agostino Vespucci, informed me that Columbino ignored my design of a much deeper and broader single ditch and constructed two shallow ditches instead. It was a disaster."

"That sounds like a failure, but certainly not a disaster."

"Unfortunately, the failure led to a disaster. During the torrential rains last week, the ditches collapsed and flooded the bordering farms. Crops, livestock, and homes were destroyed. The signoria have abandoned the project and incurred disfavor among the landowners." He shook his head at the sheer incompetence that led to such a fiasco.

Lisa gave his hand a gentle squeeze. "I am sorry, Leonardo."

"It is a tragedy that those farmers had to pay the price for the incompetence of others. Of course, the engineer implied that my original design was to blame." Leonardo gave a fatalistic shrug. "I have learned through my many years on this earth how to deal with the consequences of failure, whether directly or indirectly. If I buckled every time disaster struck, I would have stopped working long ago. Rather than lose hope, I forge ahead to the next challenge. There will always be another inspiration, another idea, and another project. The only thing we lack in abundance is time."

Especially when it comes to our friendship.

"Time does slip away," she said with a pensive smile. "But the *Battle of Anghiari* is proceeding well, is it not?"

"Thus far, it has. Michelangelo has not completed his cartoon for the *Battle of Cascina*, so I do not have to deal with him, at least for now. I dread even the thought of having that man hovering over my shoulder as I work. His insults and snide remarks are distracting. I find his presence offensive—or perhaps it is merely his odor," Leonardo quipped, trying to make light of a situation he did not want to contend with.

"At some point, you must come to terms with his presence and focus on your work instead of his rude comments. As for the smell, perhaps you should hold your nose or leave him a gift of soap."

Leonardo threw back his head and laughed. "A most tactful remedy. As always, your practical advice rules the day."

"I am a wife and mother. Experience has made me practical," she said, laughing with him.

Leonardo sighed, wishing they could spend hours like this, sharing quips and banter. "I have more pressing news to share with you."

She looked up at him, and concern etched two fine lines between her brows. "What is it, *caro*?"

Birdsong and squawking distracted him. He placed his hand on a cage of canaries, and a flutter of wings brushed against them. The thought of leaving Lisa for what might be months made him hesitant to answer. He was caught between a sense of duty to the republic and his pressing need for funds. Just as he would have to come to terms with Michelangelo, so too would he need to bear this separation from Lisa. The birdseller's approach gave him an excuse to delay what he must tell her. *Ever the procrastinator.*

"*Per favore*, box them all up, all the finches and canaries. I will buy them all," Leonardo called out to the vendor.

The man nodded with enthusiasm. "Yes, Maestro." The bird-seller never questioned what Leonardo did with the birds once he purchased them, but sometimes Leonardo wondered if the vendor didn't capture the same birds over and over again just to vex him.

Lisa stood by another cage, whistling to the inhabitants within. "And I will take all of the love birds."

They paid the vendor, but rather than walking to a secluded

spot to release the birds, they opened the boxes in front of his stall. Leonardo felt an additional sense of satisfaction in liberating the birds as the seller sputtered in shock.

They watched the birds soar above the marketplace, chirping happy cries of freedom. Leonardo and Lisa clapped their hands with delight, encouraging their feathered friends skyward. They left the birdseller gawking and scratching his head. When barely out of the man's sight, they turned to each other and doubled over with laughter.

"Did you see the way he looked at us? Such consternation. He thinks we are mad."

"I dare say," said Leonardo, "he will tell his wife about the crazy couple who spent good money on birds and then set them free right under his nose."

"Oh, how gratifying to see his surprise as he watched those soaring birds." Lisa's hand caressed her stomach, and Leonardo wanted only to place his hand over hers.

"Shall we celebrate with lunch in my quarters?" he asked. "You haven't seen your portrait for some time."

"A wonderful idea, but you must promise to divulge this secret you so adeptly steered clear of at the stall."

"*Certamente,* there is no escaping your inquisitive mind or keen understanding of me."

A half-hour later, they sat in his quarters at a small table for two and tucked into their bowls of vegetable minestrone, white bread, and watered wine.

"You have avoided telling me long enough. What news have you?" Lisa asked.

Leonardo heaved a deep sigh. "Machiavelli has requested I leave for Piombino to assist his lordship Jacopo d'Appiani. Piombino lies sixty miles south of Pisa on the coast between the Ligurian and Tyrrhenian Seas and is a crucial port for Florence. Jacopo d'Appiani was nearly lost as an ally, and only through fierce negotiation on Machiavelli's part did the alliance hold. To reassure Appiani of Florence's support, he wants me to devise engineering proposals to build defensive protections for the castle at Piombino."

"Well, I hope this time they will at least adhere to your designs," Lisa said, setting down her wine glass. "I cannot believe that the very men who complain about the time it is taking you to complete the mural of the *Battle of Anghiari*, the same who essentially forced you into a competition with Michelangelo, now wish to drag you away from the very project they placed upon your shoulders in the first place."

"Yes, they are a manipulative bunch, are they not?" Leonardo chuckled as he refilled their glasses. "With Machiavelli, it is practically an art form."

"But this fascination with war—I cannot fathom it," Lisa continued. "Men are forever seeking reasons to wreak havoc on their fellow man for nothing more than to prove they have a bigger army or greater wealth and power. They say it is to protect the citizens, but would diplomacy not do far better than bloodshed on a battlefield?"

Leonardo could not argue her point. Lisa was more logical than any man he had ever met. She would have made an excellent queen. "Think of the bright side. It will reinforce my prestige and indispensability to the republic and allow me to work on my sketches for the *Battle of Anghiari* away from the brooding Michelangelo. Besides, I can hold this over Machiavelli's head if I find myself delayed with the commission."

"Yes, but you will be far away from me. Perhaps I am being selfish." She covered his hand with hers. "Because I care more about our friendship than your duty to the republic."

He lifted her hand to his lips and kissed her palm. "I welcome your selfishness and return it tenfold. I will write to you while I am away, and Salai will deliver the letters to you."

"When will you return?"

"Before Christmastide."

"Then I am appeased, for you will return in time to feel our child dancing in my womb."

"Something I shall look forward to with great anticipation."

"I will miss your company and the too few hours we share together."

Leonardo pressed her palm against his cheek. "It is I who will be deprived not only of your company but your wise counsel. Come, let us look at our portrait, and I will point out the changes I have made."

He showed her the lines of subtle brushstrokes and delicate glazing. It was the most successful portrait he'd ever done. Well, it would be when he completed it.

"Remarkable," Lisa breathed. "The painting is both illuminating and beguiling at the same time. It has an enigmatic quality that makes me wonder who that woman is."

Leonardo grinned. "Ah, I think that is because the muse projects that quality."

Lisa blushed becomingly. "I think it is because of the artist."

"Perhaps a bit of both," he said. Leaning down to kiss her cheek.

Lisa was right. The painting seemed to live and breathe with life. Sometimes, when he looked at it, it was as though he could feel Lisa's soul residing within.

Leonardo stood beside Lisa for some time, watching her as she studied the portrait. Memorizing every detail of her lovely face. Capturing this moment in his memory for the long and lonely months ahead when neither the lady nor his portrait of her would be near to bring him comfort.

CHAPTER 32

She could not speak. No words would come. She tried and tried, but all she heard were her raspy breaths. Frightened by her sudden loss of speech, she clutched her throat, and her breaths grew shorter and more labored. Her eyes widened in alarm as darkness began to press down upon her. *Am I to collapse and die right here in this church in front of a painting of the Madonna?*

Padre D'Angelo helped her sit in one of the pews and turned her to face him. He spoke to her in a soothing voice. "Breathe deeply, slowly. Take deep breaths and allow the oxygen to fill your lungs."

She shook her head and pointed at her mouth. She could not tell him what was wrong. She wanted to share with him about her parents and everything that had happened, but she could not get the words out.

"You are in shock. You need to rest. Do not fear. You are safe here."

She looked into the eyes of the kindly priest and followed his advice to breathe more slowly. Her heart no longer pounded in her ears, and the encroaching blackness began to fade away.

Padre D'Angelo escorted her into a small kitchen in the rectory, where he sat her down and brewed a pot of chamomile tea. Pouring the tea, he set down two steaming cups and two slices of cake.

Meira smiled her thanks. The aroma of the fragrant tea and the lemon and honey cake soothed her anxious nerves.

"I am fortunate that even in these dark times, I have generous parishioners who keep me well-fed," he said with a chuckle.

The priest joined her at the table and told her how he and her father met. "He was two years younger than me and used to follow me around like a little puppy."

Meira listened raptly to the priest's humorous story about her father scoring the winning goal in the final game of the local league's soccer championship. Her father had never told her about his aspirations to play in the professional league. "Your father was a real talent. He dreamed of playing in Serie A, but your grandfather wanted him to take over the bookshop. Eventually, Benjamin gave up his dream. At first, he was saddened to do so, but then he met your mother and soon forgot all about playing calcio." The priest laughed, shaking his head.

Knowing that her father had loved her mother so much that he willingly gave up his dream filled her heart with love for her parents. Her eyes welled with tears as she thought about her mother and father. She prayed they were together. She prayed they were safe.

"Come, I will take you to your room," Padre D'Angelo said softly. "You need to get some sleep." The priest insisted on two days of bed rest. Meira did as he asked. As soon as her head hit the pillow, she fell into a deep sleep—exhausted in both body and mind.

She awoke disoriented at first, and then she remembered where she was. She'd had the most beautiful dream. She was lying on a blanket near a small pond in Marcello's arms. They'd gone on a picnic to the Villa Borghese, something they had talked of doing before the war. Her head rested on Marcello's shoulder as they watched the clouds drifting across the blue sky, sharing all their hopes and dreams for the future... But that's all it was, only a dream.

Her vision blurred with tears, and she pressed the heels of her hands to her eyes in frustration.

Meira checked her watch and noted the time was after seven in the morning. She realized she had slept since the afternoon of the day before.

Padre D'Angelo fed her a simple breakfast of bread, dried figs, cheese, and a bracing espresso. As she ate, he asked her if she felt strong enough to hear the news about the Jewish community in Rome. She nodded, feeling more herself, even though her voice had not yet returned.

"The Germans rounded up about eleven hundred Jews the other night and held them at the Military College at the Palazzo Salviati. In the morning, they were loaded onto trains at the Tiburtina station." Padre D'Angelo expelled a deep sigh. "I am so sorry, Meira."

Tears flooded Meira's eyes as her worst fears were realized. This time, she could not hold them back. Her parents had been deported, and she suspected Marcello and his parents had suffered the same fate.

"Thank God, the rest of the Jewish population either hid or escaped over the rooftops. Rumor has it the Nazis are livid that eleven thousand Jews eluded capture, and they are determined to hunt them down. A death sentence has been ordered for anyone aiding or hiding Jews." Padre D'Angelo shook his head. "The good people of Italy will not be cowered. Our Jewish brothers and sisters are being protected all over the country—hidden in churches, convents—even at the Vatican."

Meira managed a wobbly smile through her tears. She could not, would not, lose hope.

The next day, they set out at dawn. When they emerged from Via di Monte Savello onto Via del Portico d'Ottavia, Meira felt as desolate as the streets. Rome no longer looked like Rome. Occasionally, she would see a face at a window or someone looking down from a balcony, wary eyes shadowed by fear, tormented by sorrow. The Germans seemed to be everywhere. If a person "looked" Jewish, they were stopped by the Gestapo demanding to see their identity papers. But Italians and Jews looked the same, and Meira had no idea how the Nazis could tell the difference.

Meira walked beside Padre D'Angelo, fingering the cross around her neck. A million questions filled her mind, and she wished she could express them to the priest, but no words would come forth. Padre D'Angelo had explained the trauma she'd experienced must have caused a psychological wound, stealing her voice. He assured her it would not be permanent, and she would eventually speak again.

Meira wondered if the priest would say anything to bring her peace and hope. She felt guilty about her affliction, knowing what her parents must be going through. Just thinking about her beloved mother and father and Marcello and his poor family made the palpitations start again. She practiced the breathing that Padre D'Angelo had taught her.

I must be strong. I owe it to Mamma and Papà and all they have sacrificed.

Padre D'Angelo had given her a notebook to write in if she needed to communicate. But to convey her feelings was far different than asking for a cup of water. The kindhearted priest tried to cheer her up by adding, "This is perhaps God's way of protecting you. No one can interrogate you, and your defect elicits sympathy and compassion from others—a blessing."

Blessings be damned, she thought as two uniformed German SS officers strode toward them. Meira's hand clenched in the folds of her skirt. She feared they would hear her heart thundering or see the sweat beading her brow and become suspicious of her. Her anxiety was so high she stumbled. One of the soldiers caught her arm and righted her.

"*Vorsichtig, Schwester.*"

"*Grazie. Danke.*" Padre D'Angelo thanked the officer and then turned to her. "Suor Anna Maria, you must be more careful," he gently reprimanded.

Meira wore a nun's habit and scapular. When the *priest* gave her the costume, she'd gaped at him. Her surprise must have registered on her face. He quickly explained that it was the only way to keep her safe. Father D'Angelo had chuckled as he told Meira that

Suor Concetta would not mind that he'd borrowed one of her robes as the middle-aged nun no longer fit into the gowns from her younger days thanks to her fondness for gelato.

"Suor Anna Maria is mute," the priest told the Germans. "But I know she would thank you if she could."

Meira did her best to paste a smile on her face, bobbing her head in thanks while her knees rattled together beneath the black gown. She hoped the SS guards would think her nervousness was due to the modesty and shyness of a young nun.

The officer nodded. "And where are you going, Pater, on this *schön* day?"

"We go to do God's good work at the hospital," the priest replied with a smile.

"*Ja*, I see." His narrowed eyes fell on Meira again.

Meira locked her knees together and did her best not to tremble.

"I hope all goes well for you and the good sister," the German added. He tipped his hat without further comment, and the two officers continued down the street.

"Thank God for small blessings," murmured Padre D'Angelo.

They crossed the Ponte Fabricio and entered a side door of the Ospedale Fatebenefratelli. The black-and-white tiled floors were clean and polished, and the scent of disinfectant wafted in the air. Doctors and nurses in white coats hurried past them on their rounds. Trying to calm her fears, the priest squeezed her hand.

"If you can imagine, as far back as AD 1000, this was a refuge for the poor," he told her. "In the sixteenth century, Pope Pius V wrote a papal bull conveying the hospital to the religious order of St. John. Ever since then, the friars have run the hospital. The seventeenth century brought terrible plagues to Rome, and the hospital became a sanctuary specializing in treating infectious diseases. It is a specialty of the hospital that continues to this day."

They arrived at an office where the name Giovanni Borromeo was printed on the door. Padre D'Angelo rapped softly, and a deep voice invited them to enter.

The man behind the desk stood. He had a high forehead and a receding hairline of wispy brown hair. A bushy mustache skimmed his upper lip. His smile beamed a welcome. "Padre, è bello vederti."

"It is good to see you too, Dottore." The two men shook hands.

"And who is this young lady you have brought with you today?"

"This is Meira Chiarelli, the girl I told you about."

"I see you have made your vows to God." The doctor's face was a mask of stoicism.

Meira looked at Padre D'Angelo in confusion.

Chuckling, the good padre answered. "The habit was my idea to discourage questions should we be stopped on our way here. Unfortunately, Meira cannot answer you as the trauma of what has happened to her stole her ability to speak."

The doctor's dark, expressive brows rose, and his eyes conveyed compassion. "I am very sorry, Signorina."

Meira gave him a hesitant smile. The padre had not revealed to her the reason for their visit to the hospital. She was anxious but also curious.

"Sit down, per favore." The doctor indicated the two chairs across from his desk. Meira folded her hands in her lap and looked expectantly at Dottore Borromeo.

His smile vanished, and his eyes reflected a more serious

intent. "Meira, I am truly sorry about your parents. What has happened to our brethren is a travesty. It is a stain on our history. The Fatebenefratelli Hospital will not stand by without doing what we can for you and the Jewish community. We can and will resist the German occupation and help our fellow citizens. Until a safer place can be found for you, you will be admitted as a patient to this hospital. We have created two special wards, one for children and one for adults. We know the Nazis are hunting for Jews everywhere, and we expect, at some point, they will come here."

Meira began to shake at his ominous prediction. This was different from what she had expected. She was afraid to leave the safety and sanctuary of the rectory, but learning she would be separated from the priest, the last link to her father sparked a surge of panic.

Recognizing her anxiety, Padre D'Angelo patted her hand. "You will not be abandoned, Meira. I am working on a more permanent arrangement for you. Please do not consume yourself with fear, for I will visit you every day. Do you understand?"

Meira nodded, and she wiped the tears from her eyes. Her life had changed so drastically she could barely fathom how she had reached such a terrible state. Everyone she loved was gone, and she felt so alone. She trusted Padre D'Angelo, and the thought of no longer having his comforting presence made her heartsick.

Dottore Borromeo cleared his throat. His eyes misted, and he seemed to struggle to regain his composure. "We will not let you down, Signorina. I promise we will do everything in our power to help you."

A hesitant smile was the best she could manage.

"I want you to know that my fellow doctors, Dottore Sacerdoti, a Jewish doctor who works here, and Dottore Ossicini, a devout anti-fascist, are dedicated to keeping you safe. We have devised a plan to keep the German SS out of the two wards where you will be admitted. All the patients in these two wards suffer from a highly contagious and deadly disease called Syndrome K."

Meira's eyes widened in shock. Would they infect her with a deadly disease? How would she survive?

"No, no, you misunderstand, Meira," the doctor said, comprehending her reaction. "No such disease exists, but the Germans do not know that. Rest assured, they will not want to search those wards when they hear the details about a deadly contagious disease." He grinned and tapped the side of his nose. "*Capisce?* But you and the others in the ward must be very convincing because the German SS and the Blackshirts are as wily as they are dangerous. It is perhaps a blessing that you have lost your voice because I do not have to warn you against confiding in anyone. You must trust only us. Secret conspirators and collaborators are everywhere, even here, I'm afraid. I am explaining this to you now to forewarn you—when the time comes, you must pretend to be deathly ill."

Meira wasn't sure whether such a capricious plan would work, but what choice did she have? The doctor believed it was a clever idea. He was a good man, willing to risk his life to help the Jews. For now, it was her only hope. She inclined her head and placed her hands together in thanks.

Dottore Borromeo rose. "*Bene,* I will escort you to a room to change into the garb of a patient, and we will proceed with your official admittance."

Pretending to be sick was easier than Meira thought it would be. The hospital gown was itchy, and staying in bed most of the day gave her too much time to think about the fate of her parents and Marcello, but sometimes, a few young people snuck outside for fresh air in the evening. The hospital had an inner courtyard with a garden and a small fountain that reminded her of the Turtle Fountain near her home.

She discovered she was acquainted with some of the children and young people in the ward. Still unable to converse, the doctors and nurses had explained to the other "patients" about Meira's affliction. The girls and boys in her ward shared stories of close calls and lucky breaks. Each harrowing account of that horrific night of deportations and how they found their way to the hospital sanctuary filled her with awe and perhaps a little shame at feeling sorry for herself. So many of her own age and younger had experienced far worse.

Two days after her admittance, Meira was reading *Jane Eyre*, the only novel from her home that hadn't been shredded by the Gestapo, when the doors to the ward flew open. Dottore Ossicini wheezed as he tried to catch his breath, his face flushed like a ripe beet from his exertions. "The SS are on their way," he rasped. "*Subito!* Quickly, now! You must give the performance of your lives."

Everyone scrambled back into their beds and began pinching their faces, stuffing cotton into their cheeks, and dousing their hair and pajamas with water to give the appearance of a high fever and swollen glands. The girl beside Meira grabbed a lipstick from her purse and rubbed rouge into her cheeks. The coughing and moans began at once. Meira stuck the book under her mattress and sunk into the pillow. She did not have to pretend to be feverish as her overwhelming fear made her brow slick and her skin clammy. She closed her eyes and pretended to be unconscious.

The sound of pounding boots heralded the arrival of the SS troops. A sharp, guttural voice could be heard shouting orders in German. One of the doctors replied in rapid Italian, and then another voice translated. The doctor explained this was a quarantine ward with very sick patients suffering from a highly contagious disease called Syndrome K. He warned the German officer of the mortal danger to him and his soldiers.

"If you insist on going inside, you will do so at your own risk," the doctor added in an ominous tone.

Meira cracked open one eye and glimpsed the conversation through the window of the door to the ward. Dottore Ossicini made an elaborate show of donning a long protective gown, gloves, and a mask that covered his nose and mouth. He offered the protective paraphernalia to the officer, who seemed to hesitate, and then, glancing back at his men, he cleared his throat and shook his head.

Waving his hand impatiently at the doctor, the officer gestured for them to proceed. Holding the door open, the doctor waited for the German officer to follow him inside. The Nazi took one step in and froze as his eyes swept the ward.

By now, the room was filled with the cacophonous sounds of hacking coughs, the emphatic echo of phlegm bouncing into tin buckets, the thundering honks of blowing noses, the ceaseless shrill of ear-splitting sneezes, and the discordant wails of pitiful moans.

The faces of the SS guards transmitted utter terror. They clearly did not want to enter a room filled with patients who were highly contagious and at death's door.

The Nazi commander cursed, glared at the doctor, and shouted orders to his men. Spinning on his heel, he strode away. The soldiers, without sparing a second glance at the disease-ridden ward, marched swiftly after their leader, their boots thundering down the hall as if the devil himself were chasing them.

The doctor followed the Germans out, and everyone in the ward exchanged worried glances as they waited for the doctor to return. A few minutes later, Dottore Ossicini returned and removed his mask. His serious face broke into a wide grin as he announced the Nazis had left the building, and everyone broke into hearty cheers and applause.

"Did you see the look on the faces of those *bastardi*?" one of the boys exclaimed in excitement.

"Oh, what a sight!" his friend added, enthusiastically chiming in. "I bet that Nazi pig shit his pants."

Everyone, including the doctor, burst into laughter.

"You all were very convincing," Dottore Ossicini announced to the happy group. "Let's hope they won't return to the Syndrome K infectious disease ward again."

Unfortunately, several more German commanders came to the ward in the coming days, but each time, they were repelled by the group who'd perfected their roles of patients dying from a highly contagious disease.

The doctors knew they could fool the Germans for only so long. The longer the Jews remained in the ward, the more suspicious the Nazis would become. How long before the Germans questioned why these terminal patients were still alive after so many weeks? Other arrangements had to be made, and soon.

Five days after Meira's admittance, Padre D'Angelo returned with her backpack and the nun's habit. "We are leaving Saturday, Meira."

Where am I going? she wrote in her notebook.

"Firenze. I found a place that will give you refuge."

My parents? she jotted down.

"Do not worry, Meira. Your father and mother know where I am and will contact me as soon as this dreadful war is over." The padre remained optimistic, but Meira wondered if he was merely trying to keep her spirits up so she wouldn't obsess over the dark thoughts that hovered in the shadowy corners of her mind.

"We will travel by train," Padre D'Angelo said. "I am in the process of obtaining papers for you. They are fake but, hopefully, good enough to pass muster. The Germans also occupy *Firenze.* Roundups were carried out there, but not as bad as here in Rome."

Where will I be living? she wrote in her notebook.

"I cannot tell you yet for your own safety. Just in case."

Just in case. Meira recalled those were her father's exact words the night of the raid when he'd sat by the window, watching the Piazza Mattei. His words had turned prophetic that night. She hoped and prayed it would not be so again.

CHAPTER 33

 *ara Lisa,*

I wish you were here, sitting next to me on the beach, gazing out to sea, watching the birds soaring above the water. I have enclosed a few sketches of these wondrous creatures for you. When I return, we shall visit the birdseller and liberate more of our feathered friends.

I have been remiss in my correspondence and humbly beg your forgiveness. My mission in Piombino is nearly at an end, and I will soon return to Florence. I must confess that the sea air in winter is most trying on my bones, and I cannot wait to return to our fair city. Do not fear for my health, as I know you are inclined to do when you should attend to yourself and the blossoming life within you...

Notebook in hand, Leonardo sat on the shore beneath the ramparts of Piombino, working on several things at once as he looked out at the Tyrrhenian Sea. A pair of pelicans floated on the air currents, taking turns diving into the water for their next meal. Observing them intently, he rapidly sketched the pair, delineating how they spread their wings when they ascended and folded them in when they dived.

A thought came to him, and he hastily scrawled it next to the drawing:

> *Once you have tasted flight, you will forever walk the earth with your eyes turned skyward, for there you have been, and there you will always long to return.*

The spot where he sat gave him a perfect view of the harbor where boats bobbed in the water, buoyed by the waves that raced to shore, transforming into white foam. The air was brisk, and he was bundled in a purple cloak. Had he been a few years younger, he would have leaped into the froth and foam of the sea for a swim. Although his spirit was still vigorous, his limbs were not.

Leonardo was well beyond the halfway point of his life, yet here he was poised on a philosophical precipice. How he dealt with the coming challenges would determine his future. He was not a fearful man, but some caution dwelled within him. *The Battle of Anghiari* might be the last great commission of his artistic career. And yet, the miraculous had occurred in the autumn of his life. Fatherhood. He'd never dreamed of it, but Lisa had made the impossible possible. How strange is this life? For all its bumps and frustrations, it was a miraculous journey indeed.

If only there was more time.

He paused penning his letter to Lisa to marvel at the sight of two seagulls gliding wing to wing toward him...

The past two months have added exponentially to my knowledge of hydraulic engineering and architecture. I have designed a circular fortress to be built at Piombino, and I invented a centrifugal system that will pump the water out of the surrounding swampland and deliver it to the sea. My design for the fortress includes three sets of enclosing walls. In case of attack, they can be flooded and transformed into moats. Thus, the enemy would be neatly trapped in a confined area and overwhelmed under an onslaught of smoke, flames, and other fetid things.

My calculations have also proven that a circular fortress with rounded walls is less likely to be penetrated by cannon-balls. If we have learned anything from the horrors of warfare in the last few hundred years, it is that bronze cannon and iron balls will bring down the most powerful of rulers. My former patron, Duke Sforza, is an unfortunate example. For this reason, I also designed a secret passageway should Lord Appiani need to escape. Alas, the foot soldier has no such option at his disposal.

The construction now rests in the hands of Lord Appiani and the signoria. They continue to meet, consult, and deliberate whether to embrace my suggestions and erect protective and offensive bastions, banks, and trenches or ignore what I have laid out. Ultimately, it is their decision, for they hold the reins of power, and we are but pawns in their games of war.

When I return to my mural of the Battle of Anghiari, I

shall be invigorated anew from my observations of these tenacious rulers in their never-ending pursuit of power.

On a more pleasant note, this journey to the sea also allowed me to study the interaction of sunlight on water in greater detail. It has altered my perception of the visual effect created by the absorption and reflection of light. Truly extraordinary! I have derived great pleasure from being near the sea—an ever-changing environment that validates nature's grandeur and formidable force.

I bid you farewell for now, for I must prepare for my journey home. I shall hold you in my thoughts and heart until I am in your presence again.

Be well, cara mia, and keep me in your thoughts.

Sei sempre nel mio cuore e nel miei pensieri,
Leonardo

DECEMBER HAD BROUGHT snow to Florence, and Lisa was looking forward to the holiday celebrations. But her thoughts were also filled with anticipation for Leonardo's return. In her pocket was a letter from him, which she'd read several times. *He will be here soon.* Her heart soared with the knowledge that he'd kept his promise to her and would return before their daughter's birth. Lisa could hardly wait to see his reaction when he laid his hand on her abdomen and felt their child moving inside her. That thought had sustained her through the many months of his absence.

The joyous laughter made her look up from the blanket she was crocheting for the baby. Outside, a *paradiso* of glistening snow provided endless entertainment for her active children. Camilla bundled up in a coat and gloves, ran as fast as her sturdy legs could carry her, determined to duck the balls of snow hurled by her brothers. Shrieks of delight reached Lisa in her bedchamber as Piero and Bartolomeo's well-aimed ammunition hit their target, covering Camilla with sparkling powder.

"I will get you good, you beastly boys!" she squealed between giggles.

Lisa shook her head with amusement as she remembered the same playful antics of her brothers Noldo and Francesco. Oh, how she'd relished her revenge when she came upon them unawares and lobbed two snowy missiles at their backs. Life was indeed a circle repeating itself from one generation to the next. It made her sad to think that Leonardo, who had not grown up around his siblings, had never known the childhood comfort of brotherly or sisterly affection. For this reason and so many others, she hoped their child would fill the empty space in his heart with joy.

A sudden shriek of pain echoed in the yard. Lisa jumped up, the blanket slipping from her fingers onto the floor, and ran. *Madre di Dio, the boys are too rough with Camilla. Francesco will paddle their behinds if she's hurt.* Where was Anna? She was supposed to be in the garden watching over the children.

Worried about Camilla, Lisa raced out the back door, not thinking about proper attire or footwear. She ran so quickly that she could not stop herself from falling when her slipper caught on a hidden mulberry tree root. She went flying into a snow drift.

She dragged herself up, but a sharp pain made her double over, and she cradled her belly protectively. "Please, *figlia mia,* stay inside me. It is not yet time for you to be born."

Bartolomeo picked Camilla up, and she stopped crying, but when Camilla saw Lisa in pain, she began to squirm. "Down, put me down!"

Bartolomeo did as she asked, and Camilla ran to Lisa, burying her face in her skirt. "Mamma, please don't be hurt."

The boys came running as well, their round faces pinched with worry.

"Are you all right, Mamma?"

"Forgive us, Mamma."

"We promise we will never do it again, Mamma."

Lisa did her best not to transfer her worry to the children. "I'll be fine, *my angels.* Mamma just needs to lie down." Another sharp pain struck, and she could not contain the groan that escaped her lips.

"*Basta!* Go to your rooms. Now!" Lucrezia cried out—huffing and puffing as she hurried through the snow to Lisa's side. She wrapped her arm around Lisa's shoulders and guided her into the house. "What were you thinking," her mother scolded. "You could endanger the baby and yourself. Such a *testa dura!*"

The children disregarded their grandmother's order and huddled around Lisa like chicks with their mother hen.

Lucrezia glanced around as she helped Lisa to the door. "Where is Anna? That girl is never where she needs to be."

"Do not be cross with her, Mamma." Lisa took deep breaths, hoping to ease her anxiety until the pain passed.

Bartolomeo piped in. "She went to change Andrea's diaper."

"He shit himself, Mamma." Piero proudly declared, as if this clarification was newsworthy.

Camilla lifted her face from Lisa's skirt. "Yuck!"

"Piero! I will not hear such language from you. As God is my witness, I will turn you over my lap and give you a spanking you will never forget," Lucrezia reprimanded. "*Dio mio,* what is the world coming to?"

"But Nonna, Andrea shits his diaper all the time. That's what babies do," Bartolomeo said, defending his brother.

"You two are thick as thieves, eh? Did I not tell you to go to your room? What are you waiting for?" Lucrezia bit into the side of her hand and then wagged it at the children, dramatically gesturing her wrath, but the children would not be deterred and huddled more closely around Lisa. "Hearts as big as suns and brains as small as peas."

The boys looked at each other and shrugged.

"We need to get you into bed, *subito,*" Lucrezia said as they entered the house.

Lisa gripped the banister on her right while Lucrezia buttressed her left side. Slowly, they made their way up the staircase, followed closely behind by the children who were quiet for a change. Lisa glanced over her shoulder and smiled to reassure them that all was well.

At the top of the stairs, Lucrezia threatened there would be no dessert if they didn't go to the playroom this minute. "Take Camilla with you and try to behave like gentlemen. Keep your voices down for once, and let your mother have some peace."

Lisa was too tired to argue with her mother. "Do as Nonna says. I will be fine, and you can come and kiss me goodnight after you've had your dinner."

"Daughter, you will get into bed and stay there until the pain passes," Lucrezia ordered. "I don't want to hear any argument. I will send a message to the midwife. Do not worry, I will see to everything."

Lisa would heed her mother's words, and God willing, all would be well. She could not lose this child. *Come home, Leonardo. She needed him now more than ever.*

CHAPTER 34

NOVEMBER 5, 1943 ~ FLORENCE, ITALY

*M*eira's stomach lurched as she read the newspaper headline over Padre D'Angelo's shoulder: *ITALIAN JEWS DECLARED FOREIGN ENEMIES.*

The fascists had adopted a newly revised manifesto calling for open war on Italy's Jewish population. She was now officially designated as an enemy alien in the country of her birth. All the Jews of Italy were to be arrested and deported. The Blackshirts and Nazis vowed there would be no safe hiding place.

More roundups and deportations. More lives destroyed.

She could scarcely catch her breath or hold back her tears when she thought about her parents and Marcello. The black-gloved hand of evil held the Jews in its grip.

Closing her eyes, she took slow, deep breaths—in through her nose and out through her mouth. A kind nurse had reinforced the priest's advice and taught her how to calm her panic to prevent herself from fainting.

The eight-hour train journey had been subjected to only two inspections by the fascist OVRA police, and fortunately, Meira's paperwork had cleared their scrutiny. A mute nun traveling with a priest posed no threat. At three o'clock, the train pulled into the Santa Maria Novella station, and Meira and Padre D'Angelo disembarked with their bags. Like in Rome, the German military was everywhere; however, no one paid heed to a priest or a nun.

When they crossed the Ponte alla Carraia, they stopped momentarily to rest and admire the picture-postcard view of the Ponte Santa Trìnita and Ponte Vecchio bridges that spanned the Arno River. Meira thought about the great artists, philosophers, and writers who, over the centuries, had probably stood at this very spot, admiring the beautiful sight. She wondered if perhaps they, too, had contemplated their lives as she did hers.

"Meira, I believe you will be safe at the convent. The mother superior is kind, and you will not feel alone. They have given refuge to other Jewish women and children."

Meira nodded, staring over the side of the bridge into the green water and swirling eddies below. The only blessing of being mute was that she was not expected to answer. The goodly priest was doing his best, but nothing could ease the fear that gripped her in a vise.

"I must return to Rome tomorrow, but please do not think I have abandoned you. I will send a coded message to the convent if I receive any news about your parents or Marcello and his family, and I will visit when I can."

Her eyes stung with tears, and she hugged Padre D'Angelo in

gratitude. Without him, what would have become of her? She had to remind herself that in this cyclone of insanity, there were still good people in the world, like Padre D'Angelo, willing to risk their own lives to help others.

The padre patted her back. "Meira, things will get better. You must keep faith. The Nazis will be defeated. Good will always triumph over evil."

The priest's words of encouragement reminded her of Marcello's similar unwavering belief.

Where are you, Marcello? Will you ever return to me?

If Marcello had been able to hide or escape on that awful night, he might have joined the partisans, as he'd mentioned. But would he not have tracked her down or gotten a message to her by now? But she'd heard nothing from him, which meant he must have been deported. She wished she could stop thinking these terrible thoughts. If she continued to pursue this line of reasoning to its tragic conclusion, it would crush her, and she would be liable to throw herself off the bridge and drown herself in the Arno. She felt ashamed for even contemplating such a thought. The future must hold something for her, or why else was she still free?

An hour later, she sat on a bench in the convent while Padre D'Angelo met with Madre Superiora. Occasionally, other nuns walked past, smiling as they hurried along. One nun who looked to be in her early thirties stopped and stared at her for what seemed an eternity. Meira heard her whispering to another nun but could not discern what they said. She felt their eyes on her again and wondered if perhaps they knew she was a Jew masquerading as a nun. *I hope I have not offended them.* She would need to be on good terms with the nuns to survive. What the future held for her, she did not know, but she prayed she would have the strength to survive whatever came her way.

"Who is she?" Valentina whispered to Suor Teresa. Her friend assisted the mother superior in her duties and knew every bit of convent news and gossip.

"I do not know for certain, but I suspect she is Jewish and seeking sanctuary."

Valentina glanced again at the girl, and her heart thundered in her ears. "A Jewish girl?"

"In all likelihood," Suor Teresa replied. "The deportations have caused so much terror and fear. Thousands have gone underground or have found hiding places in churches or non-Jewish Italian homes."

"I wish we could do more to help them," Valentina said.

"I know. I feel the same."

"She is so young."

"She doesn't look much older than you were when you first came to us," Suor Teresa said with a quick smile. "How time flies."

As they continued down the hall, Valentina glanced over her shoulder once more at the pretty girl who sat patiently outside the mother superior's door with her hands clasped in her lap and her head bowed as though in prayer.

"Like an angel," Valentina murmured.

Suor Teresa nodded. "How is the woman whose birth is nearing?"

"She weeps for her lost husband and family, poor soul. Thankfully, she is healthy," Valentina said. She checked on the young mother-to-be several times a day, bringing her cups of tea or nourishing broth and books to help her pass the time. "The birth cannot be but a few days away. The baby sits low in her belly. I have sent a message to the midwife to be ready."

"Then what will we do?" Suor Teresa asked, worrying her rosary. "*Madre di Dio*, how will we keep a Jewish mother and her newborn a secret?"

"Madre Superiora is clever and resourceful," Valentina replied. "I am certain she has a plan."

"I pray you are right, and I pray these *bastardi* Nazis are defeated and driven from our homeland, and we can return to a peaceful existence where children will not be torn from their mothers' arms."

Suor Teresa never cursed or wished misfortune on anyone, and yet even the most tolerant and well-wishing among them were being tested in these horrific times. The devil himself seemed to be guiding the Nazis.

"God will deliver us and bring His justice to all these evildoers." Even as she said the words aloud, Valentina questioned whether she genuinely believed them. Dante had not paid for his sins. He suffered no consequences for what he did to her all those years ago. He continued to work for the Blackshirts, enjoying all the privileges of power, including his ongoing threats against her. Her last encounter with him still haunted her.

Suor Teresa's comment comparing the Jewish girl's tender youth to Valentina's when she'd first arrived at the convent echoed through her mind. Valentina had spent years envisioning what Chiara might look like. Could she be seeing similarities that were not actually there? She'd already made that mistake when another orphaned Jewish girl arrived at the convent with her aunt two weeks past. The girl also looked about Chiara's age with the same coloring. The aunt was only twenty-four years old, and they were the only two in their family who'd evaded deportation from Rome. But it turned out not to be Chiara, and the women left three days later for Grassina.

And what of Gabriella and Benjamin? The stories about the fate of the deported were too horrific to contemplate.

"Tomorrow I must go to San Miniato. They will be expecting me," Valentina said, *sotto voce*, as they entered the library.

Suor Teresa shook her head, her heavy brows furrowed. "You risk too much, Suor Gianna. I worry about you constantly."

"Please do not distress yourself; you already have a sensitive digestion, and worry gives you *agita*. Besides, I'm getting quite good at sneaking about. These little things I do are not so risky to me, but if I can be helpful to the *partigiani*, I will do what I can."

"But you already do so much. You have the treasure to protect," Suor Teresa said in a low voice as they unpacked a box of books left anonymously at the gate. They'd received many such secret donations since the war began, perhaps to keep the books from being stolen or destroyed. They made a notation of each one, including the date they'd received it, in case the owner returned to claim it one day.

"Yes, and the letters will remain hidden. If something happens to me, the promise to Suor Maria Vittoria must be kept." Valentina had convinced Teresa to help in the library and enlisted her as a co-protector of the secret correspondence between Lisa del Giocondo and Leonardo da Vinci. Teresa had declined to read the letters or even glance at the drawings, but she agreed to help protect the secret cache as so many had done before them. Valentina was grateful for the dear nun. Their friendship was a blessing that neither took for granted.

Valentina pinched Suor Teresa's cheeks affectionately. "Why don't we go to the kitchen and make a pot of tea? Nothing soothes a worry like a cup of chamomile."

"Ah, *tè e biscotti, perfetto.*"

Valentina chuckled. Suor Teresa made no excuses for her sweet tooth.

AN HOUR LATER, Valentina was back in her office transcribing another letter. Hearing a knock at the door, she quickly slipped the missive into her desk drawer and called, *"Entrate, vi prego."*

The door opened, and a priest with graying hair and lines around his eyes stepped over the threshold. She recognized him immediately. "Padre D'Angelo," she said, her heart thundering. She gripped the edge of the desk and stood on wobbly knees. *"Buon Dio,* Padre, please come in. What brings you here?"

"I am here to inform you that I escorted Meira to the convent from Rome. We arrived only a few hours ago."

"Meira?" Valentina could scarcely breathe.

"Your daughter. That is the name the Chiarellis gave her. It means *light* in Hebrew."

"Please sit, Padre, and tell me what has happened," she said. "Why have you come here with Meira? Where are Benjamin and Gabriella?" Valentina's hands began to shake, and she clasped them tightly on the desk. Dear God, had her worst fears come to pass?

Padre D'Angelo sat across from her and cleared his throat, "Benjamin and I were boyhood friends, and over the years, we remained close. He wrote to me weeks ago and told me that should anything happen to him and Gabriella; he wished me to watch over Meira and keep her safe." The priest paused to pull a handkerchief from his pocket and wipe his teary eyes. "They were taken in the roundup two weeks ago and deported. Benjamin and Gabriella hid Meira in a secret closet in their home, and miraculously, she was not discovered." He shook his head. "The poor child heard and had to bear in silence everything the SS did to her parents as well as the pillaging of her home. The next morning, she crawled out of the secret room her father had built and came to find me. The girl was in shock, to say the least, and has not been able to speak since that terror-filled night. But I am hopeful her words will eventually return to her."

A sob escaped Valentina, and she covered her mouth with her hands. "C-chiara." Tears spilled down her cheeks at the stark realization of what her beloved daughter had endured. Swiping her tears away, she rasped, "Benjamin and Gabriella? Did you find out what happened to them?"

The priest shook his head. "I do not know, and there has been no word. But as I have said to Meira, we must never give up hope."

"You brought her here, my Chiara. Does she know who I am?"

"Sorella, she has been through so much, such trauma. Meira does not know she is adopted, and for now, I believe it is best that we keep the truth from her. Otherwise, it might be more than her fragile mind can bear."

"Yes, I understand." Valentina gave a jerky nod. "Of course, you are right. I am thankful she is safe, and I am grateful to you for bringing her here. Maybe in time, I can help her recover her voice."

"That would be a blessing."

"Yes, Padre, a true blessing."

CHAPTER 35

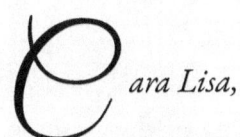ara Lisa,

I send you good tidings—our portrait awaits you. Given this dismal weather and the risk to the painting, it would be best for you to visit my quarters. I cannot wait for you to see it, and I cannot wait to see you...

The seemingly endless days of rain had finally ceased, giving Leonardo a precious reprieve to resume work on the *Battle of Anghiari*. Leonardo stood with his hands on his hips, watching the carpenters complete the scissor lift and scaffold while his assistants were busily attaching the cartoon sheets to the wall. When he was in Piombino, there was no one to oversee their work, but now that he'd returned, they could forge ahead at a faster pace.

Leonardo's spirits soared with anticipation as he contemplated putting brush to paint at long last.

Even with the sound of hammers hitting nails and clouds of sawdust floating in the air, the business of Florence circulated around them. The noise reminded him of a hive of bees and made him grumpy and short on humor. Merchants and dignitaries swarmed in and out of the center of government, buzzing about as if Leonardo and his crew were invisible.

Salai returned from an errand and sidled up next to him. "Soon you will begin to paint, Maestro."

Leonardo's brows knit together, reflecting his frustration. "Yes, but how will I paint in this *maledetto* place? I might as well set up my easel among the fishmongers in the mercato."

"Perhaps you can place wax in your ears to drown out the noise."

"The muted buzzing would be just as irritating."

"I bring news to brighten your mood."

"Really?" Leonardo arched his brows. Judging by the gleam in Salai's eyes, he'd been indulging in his favorite hobby—spying and eavesdropping. "Well then, what morsel of gossip have you brought to charm me?" Leonardo ruffled his young friend's curls affectionately.

Salai held up a hand and scanned the hall as if he were about to make a confession that might land him in the Bargello prison.

Leonardo crossed his arms over his chest as he waited. *People who spy on others always worry that someone is spying on them.* This was why he was so careful about his own privacy.

Salai leaned forward and murmured, "One of Michelangelo's assistants told me the brooding master finished his cartoon for the

Battle of Cascina, and when he returns, they will be ready to mount it on the wall here."

Leonardo frowned, anticipating his reaction to the surly sculptor breathing down his neck. It distressed him that Michelangelo, who received his commission from the signoria long after he did, was so far along already.

"Not only will I have the distraction of every merchant and politician parading through here daily, but I must also contend with that moody sculptor. *Cavolo!*"

Salai's grin reminded Leonardo of the proverbial cat who swallowed the canary.

"*Aspetta!* You said when he returns. I can see you are dying to tell me, so where did he go?"

"*Roma.* The pope requested his presence." Salai's brows wriggled teasingly as if he knew yet another secret he could barely contain.

"You think this might be a papal commission from Julius II and that our friend might abandon his mural?" Leonardo asked.

"The winds seem to be blowing in that direction."

"And why has the pope set his sights on Michelangelo?" Leonardo had never received a call from His Holiness, let alone a commission. Unlike Michelangelo, who was the darling of the Medici, Leonardo had no favored patron or family member to pave his path with flowery praise. How he hated nepotism in the world of art. *Why must everything come down to political machinations and affiliations?*

"The pope is eager to leave his imprint on history and summoned the architects Antonio and Giuliano Sangallo. Perhaps they recommended Michelangelo. I also hear your friend, the architect Bramante, is in Rome." Salai's eyes twinkled with this juicy tidbit, an intentional rub.

Leonardo was all too familiar with Salai's love of flexing his mischief-making muscles, especially when Leonardo himself was the target. How could Leonardo not be offended by these rumors? He'd been overlooked time and again by the Medici and the pope. He felt the sting of the snub, like brine pouring over an open wound.

And now, the sulky sculptor would surpass him once more. Even without the Sangallo brothers' endorsement, Pope Julius II was already familiar with Michelangelo's previous sculptures in Rome of the *Bacchus* and his highly acclaimed *Pietà*. Leonardo had never seen either creation, but he had heard effusive praise about Michelangelo's marble sculpture depicting the sainted Mary cradling her crucified son.

Despite the accolades, Michelangelo constantly stirred up drama wherever he went. Rumors abounded that the temperamental artist had carved his signature into the sculpture when he heard people mistakenly attribute his work to another artist from Lombardy. What should have been the end of the incident was exacerbated when the moody Michelangelo, regretting his action, declared in a temper tantrum that he would never sign another work of art.

Leonardo blew out an exasperated breath. Michelangelo's delay in Rome would at least give him extra time to work ahead. He patted Salai on the back. *"Grazie, sei stato bravo."* He knew Salai like the back of his hand, and the smug grin that adorned the young man's handsome face told Leonardo that the impish troublemaker was still holding something back. "But I think there is more. What nugget of gossip are you hiding, *diavolo?*"

Salai chuckled as he reached into his pocket, pulled out a sheet of fine art paper, and unfolded it with great care. "The apprentice made a copy of Michelangelo's cartoon. I thought you might like to see it."

Leonardo's curiosity was now so piqued that he nearly grabbed the sheet from Salai's hands. *Scoundrel!* "You would have kept this from me had I not called you out. Perhaps you were hoping for some payment? Hm?"

"And why not? Spies are always paid for their efforts."

"But friends are not. And you get more than enough compensation for your duties."

The young man shrugged indifferently.

Leonardo examined the drawing and could not believe his eyes. "*Cazzo!* This is not the depiction of a battle. It's an orgy of naked men bathing in the Arno River." He smacked the paper with the back of his hand. "And it's not even an interesting orgy. It's nothing but an anatomical rendering. He's drawn them devoid of any grace and form. They look like sacks of walnuts rather than men." Leonardo shook his head. "What can one learn from these naked warriors about the horror and hardship of war?"

Salai laughed. "I think the only battle he had in mind is that of foreplay, and then—" Salai whistled as he slid the index finger of his right hand through a circle he made with his left. "He will take it in *il culo.*"

Despite his irritation, Leonardo burst into laughter and lightly smacked Salai on the back of his head. "*Basta!* You are incorrigible, *amico mio,* but I think not too far off the mark." It was time to shake off his gray mood. And it was best not to become embroiled in the petty politics of his profession. He had to focus on the single most important commission of his life. At least as far as the public was concerned.

Privately, Leonardo believed his portrait of Lisa was his best work. How could it not be with her as his inspiration? Leonardo was relieved that Francesco had not rescinded his commission of the portrait; spending time with Lisa would be next to impossible if he did. Leonardo would no longer be able to visit her at home. And they would have to be even more careful in public.

For that, I am truly thankful.

Aside from the gleefully disparaging comments at the unveiling of the statue, *David* in the Piazza della Signoria, Francesco had not sought out Leonardo nor made any demands about the completion of the portrait. Nor did Lisa convey anything of that nature.

But would she tell me if she and her husband were in discord?

He checked his pocket watch and noted that if he did not make haste, he would not be on time to greet her in his quarters. He wanted everything perfect for her private viewing. Indeed, he was far more anxious about Lisa's reaction to the portrait than he was of a mural about a bloody battle.

LISA WAS BARELY able to tear her eyes away.

"Signora." Leonardo handed her a goblet of wine.

"*Grazie.*" The power of the portrait had stolen her ability to speak. She could feel the intensity of Leonardo's gaze and knew he was anxious to hear her thoughts. Leonardo was a patient man in most things, but he was also vulnerable to his emotions.

Taking his hands in hers, she lifted them to her lips, kissing his knuckles. She raised her eyes to his, unable to stop the tears from spilling down her cheeks. "Leonardo, it is the most beautiful painting I have ever seen. There are no words that do justice to what you have created."

Leonardo pulled her close and kissed her forehead. "I thank you, but my humble abilities do not do justice to your beauty. Yet, I am most fond of this painting. It represents all that you mean to me."

"I wish there were something that I could give you that would equal what your friendship means to me, Maestro, but..." She shook her head, so overcome was she.

"What is it, my *tesoro?* What troubles you?"

"I-I fear that the impending completion of the portrait means our time together is nearing an end as well."

"To be honest, I am not completely happy with it." He tossed a sly wink at her. "Perhaps more can be done to bring it closer to perfection." He perused the portrait as he rubbed his chin in contemplation. "Yes, I think you should not fear that it is finished. I'm afraid you will have to put up with me for a while longer."

Lisa was overwhelmed by both laughter and tears. Leonardo wrapped his arms around her again, and she buried her face in his chest, her protruding belly pressing against him. The soothing scent of lavender and lemon verbena calmed her. How would she ever survive being parted from him?

"Oh...did you feel that?"

Leonardo's eyes were wide with concern. "Feel what? Are you all right, Lisa?"

"Give me your hand." She pressed his hand lightly against her stomach. "There! Do you feel her?"

Leonardo's face transposed into awe and wonder. "Yes, I feel our *piccolina* is making herself known." He knelt and kissed her belly and then pressed his ear to her. "She is a miracle dancing inside your womb." He chuckled. "I think she will be as curious of the world's wonders as you and I are." He sighed and stood. "I am humbled, for she has already wrapped me around her little finger."

"As it should be, Papà."

The painting was a masterpiece, but it paled in comparison to the beauty of their friendship and the precious life they'd created. The portrait had brought them together, but it was their friendship that she treasured. It was a sacrilege, but the words slipped from her lips without her thinking about how presumptuous they were. "Will you sell the portrait one day?"

"Never. Your portrait is priceless to me. I will never part with it."

Her heart soared. Everything they shared mattered to her. Someday, she would have to find a safe place for Leonardo's letters. One thing she was sure of: she could never part with them, nor would she ever destroy them.

CHAPTER 36

Cold and hunger fought for dominance as winter came to Florence. Valentina shivered, drawing the gray blanket tighter around her shoulders as she wrote in her notebook at her desk. Few of the sisters volunteered in the library or had time to read these days as they were occupied with preparing for winter and ensuring they had enough food stores, clothing, and supplies for their community and the fifty Jewish women and children who'd sought sanctuary at the convent.

The Jewish women stayed hidden for the most part, keeping to their rooms as much as possible. To protect their secret flock, the nuns kept the convent doors locked day and night and barred visits from strangers. They hoped and prayed that the Nazis would continue to ignore them.

The German occupiers conducted frequent roundups of

young men, deporting them to work camps and the Eastern Front, where they were forced to toil in factories and the back-breaking labor of building trenches and roads.

Tragically, Italy was a divided country at war with itself. Half were fighting with the fascists, and half supported the Allies. The Italian peninsula was once more engaged in a battle that broke the bonds of blood and family as the war raged on without end.

Valentina's efforts to help the partisans slowed because of the weather. The muddy country roads were impassable by bicycle due to frequent rainstorms. With her activities curbed, Valentina was inspired to keep a journal interpreting the story of Lisa and Leonardo via their letters and his drawings. She also utilized the library's reference books about the Renaissance and creative works from that period.

It might have been considered breaking the sacred trust passed down to her, but who would it hurt? She did not intend to share her journal with anyone. The world was dark and filled with despair, and Valentina struggled not to let it smother her—writing kept her sane.

So much about Leonardo and Lisa's story reminded Valentina of Shakespeare's *Romeo and Juliet*. Leonardo and Lisa's love burned as bright as the star-crossed lovers, but like the doomed lovers of Verona, there was no future for them. Their relationship, intentionally hidden from history, had no tragic ending, but neither did it have a happy one.

Who was Leonardo da Vinci? she wrote.

He was a scientist, engineer, inventor, artist, and polymath who had no time for traditional marriage yet nurtured the camaraderie of fellow artists, students, and admirers. The historical record had fashioned a man who lived for intellectual pursuits. A mind forever questioning, thinking, creating, and building. A genius by every measure.

But his letters to Lisa and the personal sketches he drew for her reveal another story of a man who bore deep feelings and yearned for more...

Who was the Mona Lisa? she wrote.

Mother, daughter, and wife who was inquisitive and questioned the world she lived in.

But her letters, like Leonardo's, revealed another story of a woman who yearned for something beyond what her life could give her. A woman who experienced a love that could never be fully realized. A love that created a child whose true father would forever remain unknown.

Valentina could well understand the turmoil that Leonardo must have felt. The necessity of harboring such a secret and the agony of carrying it in your heart. It was the same pain Valentina lived with every single day.

Since Chiara's arrival, Valentina had kept a respectful distance but also maintained a watchful eye on the girl. She knew Chiara was not mute from illness nor from birth. She'd cried, cooed, and babbled like any other baby. Padre D'Angelo had shared a little about Chiara's circumstances. But Valentina wished she knew what Chiara had gone through. Perhaps then she could help her recover her voice. But the girl was as closed off as a dam with no spillway.

Even so, the girl was generous with her affection, and her

goodness poured from her without reservation. Chiara spent her days with the Jewish children who'd been thrown into a world of imposed containment without the benefit of sunshine and with little physical activity. Children are not meant to be silent and imprisoned; they are meant to explore and embrace the freedom of youth.

It seemed that Chiara derived as much comfort from playing with the children as they did from her. They didn't care that she was silent. They were delighted to be with an adult who never reprimanded or hushed them. She couldn't read aloud to them because of her muteness, so they read aloud and sang to her, and she clapped her hands, keeping rhythm with their voices.

As Valentina concluded her entry in her journal, she heard the library door creak open. Looking up, she saw Chiara take a few hesitant steps inside. The girl's eyes widened at the tall shelves of books. Valentina, who could not keep the tears from springing forth, grabbed a handkerchief and dabbed the corners of her eyes. "It's all right. You're welcome here," she called, blowing her nose for good measure.

Chiara gave her a shy smile and took a few more steps into the room. Valentina's chest constricted at the longing in the girl's eyes as she perused the rows of books. "Is there a particular book you're interested in?" As she spoke, she closed her journal and slipped it into the accordion folder along with the photographs of her daughter. Sliding the folder into her desk drawer, she locked it with one of the keys that hung from the gold chain she always wore around her neck.

"My name is Suor Gianna, and I am the librarian." Picking up a pencil and paper, she offered it to Chiara. "Perhaps you could write your name down, and we can get to know each other better.

I don't often have visitors in the library these days, and I appreciate the company."

The girl seemed to hesitate but then accepted the offering and sat on the chair opposite the desk. Valentina watched her write in beautiful slanting penmanship: *My name is Meira Chiarelli, and I am from Rome.*

"I have never been to Rome," Valentina said, clearing her throat as emotion flooded her heart. "Is it as wondrous as everyone says?"

The girl smiled, and the dimple in her chin deepened as she wrote. Then, she turned the notepad toward Valentina.

"There is nowhere in the world more beautiful than Rome," Valentina read. *"It is the marriage of the ancient and the new. From the crumbling coliseum and the crowned dome of St. Peter's Basilica to the magnificence of the Tempio Maggiore, it truly is the Eternal City. My parents owned a bookshop in the old Jewish ghetto. I miss being surrounded by books. That is why I came to the library, to be reminded of them."*

Meira's pensive brows came together, and she seemed to gather her thoughts as she wrote:

"I miss the bookshop. I miss my parents, my city, and my friends. I am afraid I will never see them again."

Meira sniffled and wiped her eyes with the back of her hand. She took a slow breath, and her back straightened as if fearing her lapse in composure would earn her a scolding.

Without thinking, Valentina came around the desk and dropped to her knees, taking Meira's hands in hers. "My dear child, you must not lose faith. You must keep hope alive in your heart."

At first, Meira stiffened, but Valentina smiled compassionately and gently laid her hand on Meira's cheek. "I do not know what you have gone through, but if I can help you in any way, I will. We all need someone we can trust."

Slowly, the girl's shoulders relaxed, and the tension seemed to ease from her slender frame. It was all Valentina could do to refrain from embracing her daughter, as she did not want to overwhelm her.

Meira picked up the pencil and resumed writing. "*Thank you, Suor Gianna. You are very kind. I'm sorry to have burdened you.*"

"You are no burden, Meira. Tell me, have you always been unable to speak?"

Meira shook her head.

"May I ask what happened?"

Meira wrote furiously, her pencil making a loud scratching as it flew across the page.

"*My parents made me hide in a secret closet, and when the Gestapo raided our home, they dragged my parents away, but they did not find me. That night, I could hear what they did to my mother and father, but I could do nothing. My parents made me promise not to make a sound. When I crawled out of the secret room the following day, our home was in utter shambles. The Gestapo took my parents, and my voice went with them.*

I followed my father's instructions and went to his childhood friend, Padre D'Angelo. The kind priest took me in. He says my voice will return to me eventually and that it is a blessing from God that I cannot speak should the Germans try to question me. Padre D'Angelo brought me here and told me I would be safe."

"Padre D'Angelo is a wise man. I am sure your voice will return to you, and the other nuns and I will do everything we can to keep you safe."

Suor Teresa suddenly burst into the library, her hand holding her side as she caught her breath. "Sarah is in labor. Hurry!" Teresa's gaze darted from Valentina to Meira. "*Sbrigati*, there is no time to waste."

Valentina ran from the library with Suor Teresa and Meira on her heels. She reached the stairs leading to the upper floors and stopped momentarily, listening to the cries coming from above. The screams were so loud that Valentina feared they would be heard from the street. She glanced back at Meira, whose complexion had turned bone white. There was no time to comfort the girl as they would need to act quickly to avoid drawing the attention of the authorities.

Rushing up the stairs, Valentina hurried into Sarah's room where the elderly midwife, Beatrice, the same woman who'd delivered Chiara, and two of her fellow nuns were doing their best to calm the laboring mother.

"*Per favore, respiri profondi, signora.* Breathe in and out." But try as she did, Beatrice's soothing encouragement had little effect. Sarah writhed and twisted on the bed as if possessed by the Devil himself.

Valentina reached for Sarah's hand as she combed back the heavy, damp strands of black hair clinging to her forehead. "Shh, Sarah, you must try to pant like a dog through the contractions. It will help you get through it. Do not fight the birth. You must help your baby be born. You are causing undue stress on yourself and your child, and I know you would not want to hurt him or her."

The mother bit her lip, trying not to scream as another labor pain shook her. "Dear God, take this baby from me!"

"Pant Sarah! Pant like me." Valentina demonstrated, and Sarah began to follow her lead.

Mother Superior's forehead was grooved with worry. "Is there anything we can do to ease her pain?" She nervously rubbed her rosary beads. "Do we have any laudanum? Perhaps a few drops will relax her."

Beatrice massaged the woman's stomach. "I don't like to use opiates, but under the circumstances, it might be a blessing." She carefully slid her hand between Sarah's thighs, closing her eyes as she examined her. "Thank God the baby is not in a breech position."

Valentina glanced at Meira, wondering what effect this was having on her. Seeing the suffering of a woman in labor was not healthy for the girl. These were the kinds of memories that could haunt a young mind and spark an inordinate fear of childbirth. "Meira, go to the kitchen and ask Suor Patrizia for the laudanum. She keeps it in a locked cabinet."

Meira stared back at her as if in a daze.

"Go, child. Now!"

Meira blinked as if she'd been awakened from a deep slumber. Spinning on her heel, she ran out the door.

"And bring some sherry," Valentina called after her.

Valentina bathed Sarah's forehead with a cool compress and murmured soothing words in her ear between contractions. After what seemed an eternity, Meira returned, and Valentina leaped from the bed, taking medicine and a wine bottle from the girl's hands. She handed Meira a compress. "Here, you sit beside Sarah and wipe her brow."

Valentina poured a glass of sherry and added three drops of laudanum into the glass. Lifting Sarah's head, she held the glass to her lips. "Drink, Sarah. This will help you."

Sarah nodded and drank deeply. Another pain hit, and Meira

jumped as Sarah squeezed her hand tighter. The opium tincture soon began to take effect, and Sarah's breathing grew even, and her body relaxed before the next contraction came. Her eyelids grew heavy, and her parched lips formed an O as she inhaled deeply.

"That's it, Sarah. Breathe and push," Beatrice instructed.

Sarah took a deep breath through her nose and clenched her lips together. A groan escaped her, and her face flushed a deep red from the strain of pushing. Then she panted again. The process repeated until the contractions became more frequent. A few minutes later, Sarah gave one more keening cry as her baby finally emerged from the womb.

"It's a boy!" Beatrice announced, cutting the umbilical cord. "Congratulations, Sarah, you have a beautiful, healthy boy!"

The newborn's wail brought tears of relief to everyone's eyes. The new mother sank into the pillows and closed her eyes, unaware that her ordeal was over. Beatrice packed her with clean rags while Valentina washed the child, making sure his throat and nose were free of mucus and secretions.

"Most mothers say they don't remember the pain of childbirth afterward," Valentina spoke in a hushed tone to Meira, who stood beside her, watching her swaddle the baby. "We remember only the beauty of the moment because the elation of holding our child for the first time erases the memory of the pain." Catching herself, she added, "I have no firsthand knowledge, of course, but that is what I have heard from mothers after they give birth."

Valentina avoided looking at Suor Teresa and the midwife, who both knew the truth. Meira seemed not to notice, and Valentina could see she was caught up in the moment. Valentina had assisted in many births over the years, and she never ceased to be amazed at the beauty of such a miracle.

She blinked back tears as Meira, her cheeks aglow, leaned down and gently kissed the baby's downy head.

How contrary life is that most people witness death many times over, but few experience the joy of watching a soul enter the world.

"Sarah, here is your son." Valentina laid the baby in his mother's arms, blinking back tears as she recalled the happiness she'd felt all those many years ago when Beatrice handed Chiara to her. "What will you name him?"

Tears filled Sarah's eyes as she beheld her son. "Isaac. His name shall be Isaac."

Sarah guided his tiny bird-like mouth to her breast, and Isaac hungrily began to suckle. Everyone in the room shared a chuckle, forgetting for a moment that they were in the midst of a war.

Valentina never took these precious moments for granted. Glancing around the room at the disparate group of women bonded by the sanctity of life, she realized what they shared was more potent than any petty dictator's speech from a balcony. In each other, they would find the will to defeat their oppressors. Long after the Nazis were vanquished and their evil regime was no more, new lives would be born, and the world would go on. Every day they survived was a victory for humanity.

CHAPTER 37

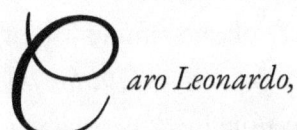*aro Leonardo,*

How I wish you were here. How I wish I could hold your hand as my time draws near. I feel as though I am a first-time mother, ripe with child and heavy with worry. I cannot fathom this darkness that hovers over me. I should be rejoicing, and yet I am afraid...

"Save her!"

"No, Mamma!" Lisa whimpered as another wave of agony overtook her. Her fingers clawed at the sheets as she tried to push the child from her body. It felt like she was being torn in two, the pain making her nearly insensible. She gritted her teeth and breathed through her nose. "Please, no matter what, you must save my daughter."

Her mother squeezed her hand. "*Tesoro,* you have five children who love you. They need their Mamma. You cannot abandon them. Please do not give up your life to save this unborn child. If it is God's will, you must let Annunziata save you," her mother sobbed. "Think of Francesco."

Francesco was the last thing on her mind as another birth contraction gripped her body in a vise. All Lisa could think about was her devastation if she lost another child. *This child.* Her miracle with Leonardo.

She bit her lip so hard she tasted blood as she concentrated on pushing the baby from her body. She would not lose Leonardo's only child. She knew what it meant to him. This baby would be his family. He would be her father. Lisa wanted him to have that gift because his childhood had been bereft of the simple joy of knowing he was loved. *Please, God, do not punish this child for my indiscretion. Forgive me for loving him. I promise I will never break my marriage vows to Francesco ever again. Should I outlive my husband, I will go into a nunnery for the rest of my days. Blessed Virgin, I pray to you, as the mother of the son of God, please save this child.*

Lisa loved all her children, but the fact that this child fighting to be born had been conceived from her one and only union with Leonardo made her believe it was a gift bestowed by God. A gift that meant goodness and hope. She regretted breaking her vows to her husband, but she could never regret what she felt for Leonardo or the child they conceived together.

He'd ignited a light inside her that she had never felt before. The light of possibility, being understood and sharing her thoughts and dreams with someone who listened. Leonardo treated her as an equal. Her opinions mattered to him and were duly considered. Beneath those tender rays of sunlight, she had blossomed. And perhaps, in some small measure, she had also helped Leonardo. She knew he would be shattered if this child was not born, did not breathe, did not flourish.

"I will do what I must to bring this child into the world."

"You stubborn girl!" Her mother kissed her forehead and gripped her hand.

Lisa hadn't realized she'd spoken her thoughts aloud. She was healthy and young. Her love for her unborn child and for Leonardo gave her strength. *I can do this. I know I can. Buon Dio, I will not lose this baby.* She screamed as another excruciating pain ripped through her as the midwife pressed down on her abdomen.

"Breathe, my lady, breathe," Annunziata said. "The child is breech, Signora," the midwife murmured to Lisa's mother. "It is in a difficult position. I will do what I can to turn the babe. But if it is impossible, I will need your permission to do what must be done."

"I will tell you what must be done," Lisa cried out. "I am the mother of this child. Annunziata, you will turn this child inside of me so she will be born. No matter what!"

"For God's sake, Lisa," her mother said, tears streaming down her face. "You cannot do this. It is God's will, not yours."

"Do not speak of God's will. I know in my soul this child needs to be born. Please, help me do that! I can bear the pain. Just do what must be done."

"All right. All right," Lucrezia agreed as she made the sign of the cross. She turned to Annunziata and nodded. "Let us do what my daughter asks."

A moment later, Lisa closed her eyes and gritted her teeth as the midwife reached inside her to turn the baby while her mother pushed down on her abdomen. She pictured Leonardo's happy face when she presented him with their daughter. From the first moment she'd discovered she was *incinta*, she had known it would be a girl. Leonardo's world was abundant with males; most of his friends were artists, and his apprentices were boys. His longest relationship was with Salai. But it was the female spirit that was missing from his life. Perhaps, unconsciously, he imbued it in several of his paintings, including her portrait. Leonardo had poured his heart into it more than any other work.

"Lisa." Her mother gently slapped her face, making her snap out of her reverie. "I know you are exhausted, but you must not close your eyes. You must stay with us, or this baby will never be born. Push daughter. Push!"

"Sì, Mamma," Lisa groaned as another wave of torture took hold. She bore down with all the strength she had. She and her daughter would live, and she would share this joy with Leonardo.

"Push, my lady," Annunziata shouted. "We're nearly there."

Lisa felt Annunziata's hand inside her as Lucrezia pressed on her abdomen.

"Dai, Signora! Dai!"

Lisa screamed in agony as she gave one more push—and felt a rush of release as the baby slid out into the waiting hands of the midwife...

"My baby. My baby. I want to see her," Lisa cried, trying to reach for her child.

But everything went silent.

She blinked and tried to focus.

But darkness enveloped her.

And everything went black.

SHE WAS FLOATING, no longer tethered to her body. Her first thought was how wonderful it felt to soar. Leonardo would be so envious that she was flying without him. And then she saw her—a little girl sitting beneath an olive tree in a beautiful garden surrounded by roses and lavender that perfumed the air.

"Who are you?"

The child looked up, and the joy of recognition filled her. Could it be?

"I am someone who loves you," the angelic girl said, a smile lighting her face.

"Piera, my heart, we are reunited." Lisa wrapped her arms around her daughter, the daughter she had lost. "My prayers have been answered. I am here. This is meant to be."

"But Mamma, you cannot stay here."

"But we are both here together in this beautiful garden. Surely God has willed it so."

"One day, we will be together again, Mamma, but not today. You still have much to do. You have a family to nurture."

"I wish you could be there too. Laughing and playing with your brothers and sister."

I do miss Bartolomeo and Piero, and one day I will meet Andrea, Camilla, and Giocondo." She crooked her finger. "Mamma, I have a secret to tell you."

"Tell me, my love."

Piera cupped her hand around Lisa's ear and whispered, "Sometimes I sneak away to watch them play calcio in the garden. I sit beside Giocondo and tickle him."

"So that is why he giggles so much when he watches his older siblings play."

"He's a good baby. But a very stinky one. When he poops, it is time for me to leave."

Lisa laughed through her tears. "My Piera. Heart of my heart. I lost you once. How can I bear to lose you again?"

"Mamma, you never lost me. We will spend eternity together. I promise."

Lisa looked about, admiring the garden's beauty. A profusion of colors bloomed brightly, and the sun was warm on her face. "It is so peaceful here. Why can I not stay?"

"You know why, Mamma."

"I know. My family, Francesco, the children, Leonardo…I could not bear to leave them either."

"Yes, Mamma. But there is more, so much more…. You will become an inspiration to millions of people all over the world for centuries to come. It will be your destiny, Mamma. You will be the most famous woman in the history of the world," she declared, jabbing her index finger in the air.

Lisa gasped and crossed herself. "Is that blasphemy you speak? What of the Blessed Virgin?"

The child cupped her hands over her mouth and giggled.

Lisa couldn't help but hug her daughter close. Oh, what a lovely imp she was.

"Aside from the Blessed Virgin, Mamma." Piera laid her hand on Lisa's cheek. "Who do you think brought you here."

"Oh, my darling child—"

"You must go back but know in your heart that we will see each other again. I love you, Mamma."

"I love you, my daughter. I love you..."

"And your daughter loves you too. But she needs to eat. Lucrezia's voice intruded, and the garden disappeared in a mist. "Wake up, Lisa. *Madonna mia!* You always were a sleepy head."

Lisa's eyes blinked open, and she beheld the face of her newborn as Annunziata laid the child in her arms."

"Oh, what you put me through," Lucrezia reprimanded, and then her gaze softened as she looked at her newest grandchild. "She is surely an angel sent from Our Blessed Lady, Herself."

"She is, Mamma."

Lisa kissed her daughter's downy-soft hair, and Lucrezia and Annunziata breathed the same relieved sigh.

CHAPTER 38

NOVEMBER 12, 1943 ~ FLORENCE, ITALY

On the Sabbath, the nuns of Santa Maria del Carmine encouraged the small community of Jewish women and girls to practice their faith in prayer and song, as the nuns did their best to supply only the foods that observant Jews were allowed to eat.

A group of Jewish women baked the egg bread they called challah on Fridays, and the convent was supplied with wine so that at sundown, those in hiding could say the prayer over the wine and bread and observe their religious traditions.

A feeling of peace and harmony descended on the convent following Isaac's birth. Both mother and baby were doing well, and thankfully, Sarah's screams during her labor did not bring the Gestapo to their door. The tranquility of convent life continued. Meira visited the library, and Valentina felt their bond deepening.

She watched her daughter shelve the last of the books on the trolley and breathed a deep sigh. How could one's heart be so full of both joy and sorrow at the same time? And yet, that is how Valentina felt to be physically reunited with her daughter but unable to share that happiness with her. She was tormented by the tragic circumstances of their reunion and heartbroken about the fate of Meira's adoptive parents.

"Thank you for your help, Meira. It is good to have someone working in the library again. It can get a little lonely sometimes." Valentina slipped the letter she had just finished translating into the archival envelope in the accordion folder and locked it in the box on her desk.

Meira's stomach growled as she pulled up a chair across from Valentina. She blushed and shrugged at the same time.

"Sometimes, I lose track of time and forget to eat." Valentina stood. "I could use a cup of *caffè,* and I think there is still some of Suor Elena's *Pan di Spanga* in the tin on the counter. Would you like some, too?"

Meira's face lit with a smile.

Valentina chuckled. "I see you have a sweet tooth, as I do."

Meira nodded.

"Good, we will both have a little *merenda.*" She plated two slices of the sponge cake and poured two cups of coffee from the thermos flask. *Caffè e dolci.* How often had Suor Maria Vittoria used coffee and sweets as a prelude to calming her fears and offering Valentina some sage advice? How she missed her dear friend. And now, she was trying to do the same for Meira. Life was undoubtedly a circle that oft repeated itself.

"Do you think Isaac's birth is a good omen?" Valentina read aloud from Meira's notebook.

"Yes, I do," she replied. "Where there is renewal of life, there is hope."

Meira sighed as she continued writing in her notebook and passed it to Valentina.

"*Shabbat was always special in my home. My mother cooked a special meal, and we celebrated by singing songs and sharing stories. I miss them so much. Do you think they are alive?*"

Valentina thought for a moment about how to answer Meira. "I pray for them and for you every day that it will be so. I am sure your parents want you to stay strong and believe in the future."

Meira picked up the pencil and hesitated before scrawling another note. She slid it toward Valentina.

"*I also pray for someone else,*" Valentina read. "*I never got the chance to tell my parents about him. His name is Marcello, and we were*—she'd scratched out "were" and wrote "*are in love.*"

Meira's cheeks turned pink with her confession.

Valentina laid her hand over Meira's. "Don't be embarrassed, my dear. To share love with a man is a gift."

The girl sighed and wrote again.

"*Did you ever share love with a man before you became a nun?*"

Valentina sighed and shook her head. "No, I was never given that blessing. But I know it is something precious. I am certain Marcello is a special young man, and God willing, you will find each other again."

Tears filled Meira's eyes. She swept them away and wrote furiously in her notebook.

"*With every fiber in my being, I pray you are right. I believe that Marcello and his parents must have been deported, or he would have come to me after the raid. He would do anything to find me. He swore it to me.*"

Valentina hoped Meira was right and the young man had somehow survived. She'd heard from her partisan friends that thousands upon thousands of Jews had been deported to internment camps from Italy, Germany, Poland, and other conquered countries, where many had met a horrific and unspeakable fate. Valentina would never share this knowledge with Meira. "And I'm certain your Marcello is brave and strong, and he will move heaven and earth to be with you again."

Meira bit her trembling lip and continued to write in the notebook.

"I never told him I love him, and now it is too late. I don't know why I never said the words. I cannot bear him not knowing how I feel. And now, wherever he is, he has nothing to hold onto. No way for him to know that I'm waiting for him. That I would wait my whole life for him. Maybe I am not worthy of him, and now I am being punished? When I had the chance, I did not say: I love you, Marcello. I did not say those precious words aloud. And now my chance is gone. I no longer have a voice to tell him."

"I am certain he knows, Meira," Valentina whispered. "I'm sure Marcello knows how you feel, and he holds that love in his heart. I believe that love is stronger than hate, just as I believe the Allies will bring an end to this war." Valentina tucked a strand of Meira's dark hair behind her ears. "My darling girl, please never think you deserve this punishment. Yours is a pure heart. You must believe in yourself and believe in Marcello. You must be brave. You must have hope."

Meira nodded as the tears streamed down her cheeks.

Valentina was heartbroken by Meira's confession. She was so young, and her declaration of love so profound that Valentina worried about her heart and mind if Marcello did not survive.

Her own spirit had nearly been broken by the past—by Dante. His threats still loomed over her, casting a terrifying shadow. Thank goodness she had found a welcoming family among the nuns at the convent. Otherwise, she did not know if she would have survived.

She prayed for Marcello to make it through, but no matter what the future held, Valentina vowed to do whatever it took to protect her daughter. "Come, let us visit Sarah and Isaac and see how he's doing. If anything can lift our spirits, that sweet baby can."

They entered Sarah's room to find both mother and child doing well. Isaac's eyes were open, and he gurgled happily. Meira didn't answer with words, but her smile glowed as she bounced him gently in her arms, and he cooed in response. His dark eyes sparkled, and his plump cheeks puffed with his efforts to talk. Dark wisps of hair lay flat on his round, mostly bald head, making him look like a miniature old man.

Sarah beamed from the bed where she still lay as she recovered from the birth.

"He really has taken to you, Meira," she said.

Valentina replied, "Isaac has the disposition of an angel and the wisdom of a sage. I never hear him cry or complain."

"Yes," Sarah agreed, "he is an easy baby. Maybe he is making up for having caused his mother such pain during labor." She chuckled, and then a shadow fell over her face. "I wish his father could see him," she whispered, her eyes filling with tears.

Valentina squeezed the young woman's hand. "I pray fervently that he will." No one knew the fates of loved ones who were arrested and deported. The tragic losses of this war were written on every face and felt in every heart. The price they paid would affect their lives long after the guns stopped firing and the bombs stopped falling. For the time being, they were safe and together. A small blessing. It would have to be enough.

CHAPTER 39

APRIL 23, 1505 ~ FLORENCE, ITALY

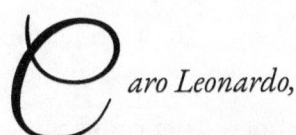 *aro Leonardo,*

You are the father of a beautiful girl! I cannot wait for you to meet her. Her name is Marietta. She is beauty incarnate and bears a remarkable resemblance to you. I could see her awareness and inquisitiveness from the moment she opened her eyes. Her chubby little hands are in constant motion as if trying to capture the stars. It reminds me of your fascination with seeking the secrets of the universe. I am completely in love with her and treasure this time of holding her to my breast.

Con tutto il mio cuore,
Lisa

The sweet fragrance of roses and freshly tilled soil wafted through the open window. Lisa inhaled their heady scent as Leonardo stepped into the *salone*. She stood and smiled. "Welcome, Maestro. Welcome. It is so good to see you." No verbal endearment passed her lips in case a servant should overhear, but she hoped her eyes conveyed everything in her heart.

Leonardo quickened his pace as he crossed the room, reaching her side in moments. "My lady, you are a dream come to life. I dare not move lest this vision of loveliness standing before me disappears. What an exquisite painting you would make." His eyes twinkled as he spoke.

Lisa arched a delicate brow. "You mean in addition to the one you are currently working on?"

Leonardo chuckled. "Ah, were I to spend the rest of my days painting portraits of you, Signora, I could never capture all the myriad facets of your lively personality—not in a thousand portraits."

Lisa felt the heat of a blush. She would never tire of his witty banter and his clever compliments. But in truth, Lisa was pleased to look her best for him. Her mother had fretted over her paleness before taking leave of her two days ago. With that in mind, Lisa had chosen a bright turquoise gown of the sheerest of silks to brighten her complexion. It pleased her that she'd made the right choice. Lisa set aside her thoughts of the difficult birth. Today was a day of joy and celebration.

"Maestro, I want you to meet your daughter," Lisa said softly. She wished she could freely speak and express her feelings, but they were not in his private rooms. She bent down over the cradle she'd set between their chairs near the open glass doors leading out to the garden. It had been so warm and humid for several days that cooler air was a welcome respite, and Lisa had opened the doors to let the gentle breeze usher in the scent of the flower garden.

She lifted the baby and turned to Leonardo. "Marietta, I want you to meet your father, Leonardo da Vinci." She placed the babe in his arms, and Leonardo let out a small gasp and blinked back tears as he cradled the infant.

"She is perfection," he said in a husky voice. "She is the epitome of beauty and looks just like you."

Lisa watched Leonardo's eyes as he beheld Marietta. She saw the love and devotion of an adoring father, but she also saw an inner light—as though he were committing this moment to memory. His gaze seemed to take in every particle of Marietta's being. Lisa understood utterly, for she had felt it too from the first moment she held Marietta in her arms. It was the same feeling she'd experienced with all her children, and it humbled her and filled her with awe.

"My lovely angel, Marietta. It is a great honor to meet you." He touched her lips with a gentle finger.

Lisa swallowed the lump in her throat as she watched him speak sweet, fatherly words to his daughter. Leonardo was unlike any other person she had ever known. In truth, she was in awe of him, not just because of his artistic genius and talent. No, it was his curiosity about everything around him that Lisa loved most. Leonardo was the most knowledgeable person she had ever known, not because he knew the answers, but because he asked the questions. He sought to learn as much as possible about the universe and all its mysteries.

"I predict you shall have a life full of beauty and wonder," Leonardo continued, "Not because you are my daughter, but because of your gracious and intelligent mother."

He looked up, and his gaze met Lisa's. She was about to tell him how much she loved him when a gurgling fart erupted from Marietta.

They both chuckled as Marietta's slight frown of concentration transformed into a smile after releasing a few more gaseous notes.

"Aha, I now see the truth of it," Leonardo said. "That mysterious smile is merely an expression of relief from passing gas."

"Oh, stop, you are incorrigible." Lisa took Marietta from his arms and lay her in the bassinet. She checked her daughter's swaddling, ensuring she had not soiled herself.

"Children and the elderly have only three cares in the world," Leonardo declared. "Sleeping, eating, and pooping."

"And is this something you plan to study and write about in one of your notebooks?" Lisa grinned as she sat in the chair and gestured for Leonardo to do the same."

"No, for it is a simple fact of life. Besides, I think Marietta has no patience with my philosophizing." He bent down and tickled Marietta's feet, making her giggle and coo.

"I should say not. She prefers a more tactile interaction, as you can see."

Leonardo caressed his daughter's face as she gurgled as if trying to speak.

"Look at how she gazes at you," Lisa said. "She knows you." Forgetting where they were momentarily, Lisa reached for his hand and gently squeezed it. "This is an auspicious day and one I will never forget. You see with the artist's gaze and the keen eyes of a scientist, yet you do not say who our perfect child resembles."

"The bone structure of the brow is me, but the nose and lips are you. The clever cunning in the eyes could only be me, whilst the sweet mystery of her smile could only be yours."

Lisa tilted her head as she regarded her daughter. "Yes, I can see that. She is already beginning to change. I think her hair will be curly and lighter in color, as you described yours as a young man."

"Must you remind me of my advanced age, *cara mia?*"

"*Sciocchezze!* Nonsense, I will not feed your insecurities. You are in your prime. What does it matter that your once golden locks are threaded with gray? Does it not fascinate you that hair turns gray over time? Is there no scientific theory to be discovered in that? Gray is simply another color, is it not? Does it not add depth as well? You are an artist; you should know that better than anyone."

He threw back his head and laughed. "Oh, my dearest. One of the things I love best about you is you do not indulge my ego nor my predisposition to seek praise."

"There are enough people around you who do that already; besides, we do not need to seek reassurance from each other. I will always be truthful with you, *caro.*"

Why was it so simple to be honest and forthright with Leonardo, and yet with Francesco, so difficult? She had promised God during her arduous labor that she would never stray from her vows again...*But how can I stop my feelings from straying?*

Leonardo regarded Marietta and then Lisa. "When the light catches her eyes, the hue changes and becomes identical to yours. She will have eyes the color of fossilized tree sap. They will be amber."

Lisa wrinkled her nose. "Only you would equate eye color with some ancient, preserved matter. But amber does bring good fortune, does it not? We all can use a dose of that."

"My good fortune came when I met you, Signora. That is a truth I will never seek the answer to, for it is as settled as the sun rising in the east and setting in the west."

Lisa's eyes filled with tears at his lovely words.

"*Carissima,* I did not mean to make you cry."

"You did not. I am just overjoyed to see you meet Marietta at last."

"I am truly sorry for not venturing here sooner, but I was awaiting your letter of invitation. I simply assumed you were enjoying this time with your family. Forgive my transgression." He reached out and kissed Lisa's hand.

A sob escaped her despite her attempts to suppress it.

Leonardo knelt at her feet, his hand cupping her face. "Dearest, are you in pain or discomfort from your recent labor? How can I help you? Shall I fetch your maid?"

"No, no. Please, I am fine." She inhaled a deep breath.

He took a handkerchief from his pocket and gently wiped her damp cheeks. "Do you know the reason why our portrait is so striking?"

"Because you are the most talented artist in the world?" She chuckled through a fresh wave of tears.

"Well, I cannot argue with you on that point," he said as he continued to dab at her cheeks. "But the secret of the painting lies within your beautiful eyes. The extraordinary depth of feeling in your gaze that you hide behind that mysterious smile. I can see something is troubling you. Please unburden yourself."

Lisa took a deep, shuddering breath. "It was a difficult labor..." She dared not tell him she almost died, for it would cause him deep distress. "It took more from me than my prior births."

"*Cara*, I am so sorry." He reached for her hands. "How are you feeling?"

"I must admit the recovery has been much slower than with my other children, and I have been suffering from an inexplicable melancholia when, in truth, I should be the happiest woman in the world."

"Why did you not share this with me? I would have come to you without delay."

"At the time, I could not—my mother was here, and Francesco had returned from his travels. The other children were overjoyed to welcome their little sister, especially Camilla. But I think I am through the worst of it. I have six beautiful children and one sweet angel in heaven watching over us. I am truly grateful for my blessings," she gazed down lovingly at Marietta and then up at him. "I am also grateful for you, Leonardo, more than you will ever know."

"I am in awe of you," he said.

"Me?" She blinked in surprise. "You are the Maestro, and your talent is beyond measure. How can you be in awe of me? I am just a wife and mother."

"Ah, you said those words to me when we first met, and even then, I knew the truth. Your capacity for love is beyond measure," he said, using her own words. "You have taught me what love truly is, and for that, I am forever yours."

Leonardo's eyes glimmered with unshed tears, and Lisa saw, reflected in their depths, the love she carried for him in her heart.

"I shall cherish your words for the rest of my life," she said.

"And I shall cherish your gift of this beautiful child." He closed his eyes. "I have already completed a new portrait."

"What? When did this happen? And why did you not tell me—"

He placed a finger to her lips. "Hush, *cara mia*. It is a portrait I shall always carry in my heart—a portrait of the Mona Lisa and her daughter."

CHAPTER 40

NOVEMBER 15, 1943 ~ FLORENCE, ITALY

*D*espite the war that raged outside the doors of Santa Maria del Carmine, Valentina, her sister nuns, and the Jewish women inside the convent had forged a daily rhythm to their lives. Meira came to the library each day to help Valentina sort through the boxes of books that continued to be left outside the gate. They noted the titles in each box and the day the books arrived in case the owners returned to claim their treasures after the war.

After the war, Valentina repeated the mantra that never left her or anyone else's thoughts. The end of the war still seemed so far away. Yet, with each passing day, with each underground report about the movements of the Allied troops or news of another skirmish between the partisans and the German occupiers, another ray of hope shone in their hearts that their prayers would be answered.

Valentina and Meira had taken a few minutes from their busy morning to have an espresso and a biscotti. Meira jotted down a note and passed it to Valentina.

"I hear the older women—the mothers talk when I am playing with the children. They hide their tears from the little ones, but I see their fear. I hear them whisper about the horrific atrocities the Jews are suffering at the hands of the Nazis. Why is God allowing this to happen?"

Valentina looked up and saw the fear and anger in her daughter's eyes.

"I do not know the answer to your question. Wars have been fought since time began. Humanity is capable of the worst atrocities. And yet also great beauty, and kindness, and love. Perhaps that is what God wants us to realize. That even in the darkest times, there is always goodness. There is always a light shining somewhere. There are always courageous people who will stand up against evil and tyranny."

The girl wiped her eyes with the back of her hand and sniffled.

Valentina pulled out her handkerchief from her pocket and handed it to Meira. She might not be able to reassure Meira of Marcello's survival or that of her parents, but perhaps she could help take Meira's mind off the fears that plagued her, at least for a little while.

"I know you have been curious about my work here that consumes so much of my time."

Meira blew her nose and picked up the pencil.

"I have noticed that whatever you are writing must be a secret. I admit I am too curious for my own good. I am sorry about that."

Valentina shook her head. "No, Meira, you misunderstand. I am pleased that you are curious. You have a bright mind." She patted her hand. She knew Meira like she knew her own heart. Her beautiful baby had grown up to become an intelligent and inquisitive young woman. Just as Suor Maria Vittoria had entrusted Valentina with the secret all those years ago when Valentina had arrived at the convent scared, pregnant, and alone, so too would Valentina entrust the secret of Leonardo and Lisa's letters to her daughter. She hoped the letters would buoy Meira's spirit as they had hers.

Valentina unlocked the box and took out the accordion file. She slipped on the gloves and extracted the letter and the translation she'd been working on for the past few days. "I want to read you this letter, but first, I will tell you a story..."

Meira's eyes were wide with wonder as Valentina shared with her the history of the treasure and the deep and abiding love between Leonardo da Vinci and Lisa del Giocondo.

"*Tesoro mio, forgive me for not putting into words how much you mean to me,*" Valentina read. "*As engrossed as I am on the mural, it is a miracle that I can think of anything other than this challenge that saps my strength and patience. But at the end of the day and long into the night when I finally seek my rest, my thoughts are only of you...*" Valentina stopped. "That is as far as I have gotten on this letter. There are many others."

Meira's pencil flew across the page of her notebook. "*Shouldn't these letters be in a museum?*"

Valentina sighed. "I said the same thing at your age to Suor Maria Vittoria, and she said the same to Suor Ursula before her. Long ago, it was decreed that the letters would be kept secret.

Never to be shared with the world. I cannot break my solemn promise, the same vow that so many sisters made before me."

Meira paused for a moment, then continued to write.

"*I understand about solemn promises. I will never tell a soul about this treasure. Perhaps it is for the best that it remains a secret. It would be horrible if the Nazis found out about the letters. They would do what they did at the Tempo Maggiore to our precious books. They confiscated all the belongings of the Jews that were of value. I am certain they plundered so much more.*"

Valentina nodded. "They are butchers and thieves. Soulless creatures without regard for human life. I will fulfill my task and keep this treasure from their thieving hands. Perhaps one day, many years from now, when the world is safe once more from these atrocities, the nun who guards this treasure will feel compelled to bring the letters to the attention of scholars and the world, but until that day, my duty is clear. I will preserve it with my life." Valentina returned the letter to the box and locked it with the key she wore on the gold chain around her neck.

Meira's pencil resumed its frantic pace across the page. When she was done writing, she turned the pad toward Valentina for her to read. "*I am in awe of you, Suor Gianna. You are a hero.*"

Valentina's cheeks flushed, and she blinked back sudden tears. "I am no hero, my child."

Meira grabbed the pad, and her words flew across the page again. "*I know you risk your life helping the partisans.*"

Valentina shook her head. "I just help a little here and there. What I do is nothing, and the danger is not great."

Meira blew out a breath as if in frustration and continued to write.

"Every time you go to the marketplace to see the old woman who works with the partisans, you risk your life. What if the Blackshirts or Nazis follow you? What if you are accused of collaborating with the partisans?"

Meira dropped the pencil and covered her face with trembling hands.

"Please don't cry, *cara*. I am very cautious." Valentina enfolded Meira in her arms. "You are safe here—my fellow sisters have the courage of lions. Everything will be fine, I promise."

Meira looked up, eyes brimming with tears. Valentina's heart ached with sorrow and the unfairness of life. She yearned to tell Meira the truth that she was her mother. But she could not break her promise to Padre D'Angelo. Nor could she bear to cause her daughter any more pain. So many promises, so many secrets, so much suffering. Valentina took Meira's hands and was about to offer reassuring words when Suor Teresa barged through the door.

"Suor Gianna, excuse me for interrupting your work," Suor Teresa breathlessly announced. "But a young boy is waiting for you downstairs. He says he bears an urgent message from Serafina."

Meira's gaze swept from Suor Teresa to Valentina, her brows raised in question. There was no time for explanation. Whatever Serafina wanted; it was not for Meira to hear. "I'm sure it's about the eggplant. I've been after her for weeks to get some. Is that not so, Suor Teresa?" she said for emphasis so that Meira would not worry.

"*Mannaggia!* I should have known the little scoundrel was seeking a tip for his efforts in getting you to the marketplace," Suor Teresa said, slapping her knee and shaking her head in such an exaggerated fashion that Valentina had to suppress a smile. Thank goodness Suor Teresa had had a calling as a nun. She would not have made a convincing actress.

Valentina patted Meira's hand. "I must go and resolve this pesky problem. Nothing to worry about. I hope we can continue our conversation later?"

Meira nodded, but Valentina could see the worry in her daughter's eyes.

A HEAVY BLACK wool cloak hid Valentina as she followed the boy dressed in a ragged coat over the Ponte Vecchio. Valentina's breath condensed in the frigid air as she hurried to keep up with the youth who'd provided no clues regarding the calamity that demanded her attention. Beneath her cloak, her heart drummed rapidly in sync with the basket bouncing against her leg. She wondered what had provoked Serafina to reach out to her publicly. Something was undoubtedly amiss for the old woman to break their established routine. And now Meira had also been alerted. Valentina worried about the girl carrying yet another burden on her shoulders.

Valentina took a few minutes to wander through the stalls and make a few purchases. She tried to calm her racing pulse and appear as innocuous as possible. When she approached Serafina at her vegetable stand, the older woman whispered, "What took you so long, *cara* sorella?"

"I didn't want to draw any attention," she whispered back,

placing her basket on the table and glancing around, ensuring no one was watching them. "Is anything wrong?"

Serafina picked up a bunch of radishes and placed them in the basket. She leaned forward. "A young resistance fighter named Marco got into a skirmish with some Nazi *bastardi,* and there was an exchange of gunfire. He was shot while getting away. He's at the home of one of the commandos, but he can't stay there because he needs medical attention. They could not risk contacting il dottore. You know how sneaky the Blackshirts are. They have spies everywhere and watch the doctors like hawks."

"Dear God, how badly is he wounded?"

"I'm not sure, but they tell me it is serious—" Serafina's voice suddenly took on a sing-song quality as her eyes cajoled with humor, "Sorella, the *asparagi* are very tender." The old woman lifted several bunches of asparagus wrapped in twine and placed them in the basket.

Valentina felt the hairs on the back of her neck stand on end. She bent to examine the vegetables in her basket, and out of the corner of her eye, she spied two of the feared and hated members of the MVSN striding down the aisle toward them. Their *colbac capomanipolo,* the black tasseled fez hats, made them easily identifiable.

"*Grazie,* Signora, we are always grateful for your advice on the best vegetables. And these asparagus look delicious," Valentina replied, joining the charade.

Serafina cackled, "*Ogni pazzo vuol dar consiglio.*"

Valentina responded with laughter. *Every fool is ready with advice,* was a well-known witticism. "You remind me of Suor Maria Vittoria with your clever sayings."

"Ah, how I miss that gracious nun," Serafina said, doing a

quick sign of the cross. No one could haggle like Suor Maria Vittoria."

They continued their light banter until the henchmen were well out of earshot. Valentina breathed a sigh of relief.

"You are the only one who can help, but it will put you and the sisters in danger," Serafina warned.

"I am not afraid, and I know the mother superior will feel the same. I will go to her as soon as I return to the convent. Men are not allowed in the sleeping quarters, but I know of a safe place where I can nurse the young man away from prying eyes. Suor Teresa and I will prepare one of the storerooms in the cellar."

"Then it is settled. After sundown, our brothers will bring him to the convent hidden beneath a straw-filled cart. It will look as if they are delivering hay for your donkey. In your care, perhaps the boy will recover. *Se Dio vuole*." Serafina shrugged, packing up the basket. "*Eh, beh,* we are all just living on borrowed time."

Valentina's heart went out to the old woman. Since losing her grandson at the hands of the Blackshirts, Serafina had become even more fatalistic than she already was. Valentina worried the old woman would one day take two loaded pistols and gun down as many fascists as she could, knowing she would be signing her own death warrant. "With God's blessings, he will recover." She also prayed that Serafina might one day rediscover God's light to guide her through the darkness in her heart.

VALENTINA LED two burly partisans down the back kitchen stairs to the supply rooms, the silence broken only by the men's grunts. She carried a candle to light the way. The young man lay motionless, his eyes closed, his face as pale as a cadaver. He wasn't much older than a boy. Blinking back tears, she prayed she could help him, prayed he would survive.

Valentina had propped open the door to the storeroom with a jug to allow it to air out. She and Suor Teresa had rushed to make it suitable for Marco. She didn't even know his last name, but what did that matter? All that mattered was saving his life. The mother superior had granted her blessings for the endeavor. Her only caveat was that no one was to know about the partisan except Valentina, Suor Teresa, and herself.

Valentina showed the silent partisans out and hurried back to the room. She carefully removed the bandages and discovered the bullet in his side had been crudely removed. Valentina bathed the wound with mild soap and warm water that had been boiled earlier. Next, she applied antiseptic and sulfa powder to kill the bacteria. She did not know if her ministrations would work, given that the wound had begun to fester, and Marco had a temperature. Making a poultice of elm leaf and blackberry, known to be effective at preventing infection, she packed it over the wound and covered it with a clean bandage.

As she tended to him, Marco mumbled incoherently. Occasionally, she heard him call out to his mother, begging her to forgive him. His pleas tore at Valentina's heart. He was so young, perhaps eighteen or nineteen years old. If not for the war, he would be filled with dreams of his future—of falling in love, getting married one day, having children, and building a life for his family. Wiping her tears, Valentina thought about all these things as she tried to save Marco.

Dear Lord, help this boy.

Valentina had prayed harder than she'd ever prayed. She and Suor Teresa took turns nursing him, but after three days, there had been no improvement, and she was almost at her wit's end. Marco's high fever had not broken, and he continued to slip in and out of delirium. She wished she knew more about him, who his family was, what he enjoyed doing, what he dreamed about.

Blessed Virgin, please don't let this boy die.

She rinsed a cloth in cool water and pressed it against his forehead. Marco had been restless and mumbling incoherently all morning. Even though she wasn't sure he could hear her, she brushed his cheek with her fingertips and murmured, "I'll be right back, Marco. I will get you a cup of Suor Elena's homemade *brodo*."

A short while later, Valentina balanced a tray with the broth and a few supplies as she descended the stairs to the sick room. She stopped, suddenly alerted to the sound of a male voice. Marco was speaking to someone. She tiptoed closer, her ears pricked up as she tried to make out what was being said. It took her a moment to make sense of the boy's breathless words.

"Am I in heaven? Are you an angel?"

Valentina could hear the scratching sound of a pencil on

paper. *Meira.* She must have wondered why she and Suor Teresa kept disappearing for hours and followed them.

"*Sei così bella.* Like an angel. Did Mamma send you?"

The pencil lead scratched against the notepad in reply.

"I was with the partigiani. We snuck out to slash the tires of the Nazi fiends. What is your name?"

The one-sided conversation continued with its written responses.

"Meira—pretty name. Pretty girl." Marco drew in a breath and groaned. When he finally spoke, his voice was barely above a whisper. "The pain.... It is unbearable. I-I must try to be brave—try to be strong... I wish... I wish..."

The scratching sound from Meira's pencil echoed off the walls.

"Meira, please, can you hold my hand?"

Valentina heard the scrape of a chair being moved.

"I-I will die never having kissed a girl. If only I'd met you before this—" Marco gasped. "*Ti prego,* don't cry, *sei un'angelo.*"

The silence that followed was more than Valentina could bear. She set the tray down and tiptoed to the doorway. Peeking into the room, she saw Meira bending over Marco, her hands cupping his face. Slowly, Meira lowered her lips to his and kissed him. Tears slipped from the corners of her eyes and onto his cheeks, but she did not pull away.

When she finally sat back, his eyes were closed, and a gentle smile graced his face. "*Grazie,* my angel, you have saved me..." Marco whispered with a breathy sigh and then grew still. Meira laid her head on his shoulder as silent tears streamed down her cheeks.

Valentina leaned against the wall and wept for Marco and all the lives lost in this cruel, unforgiving war.

CHAPTER 41

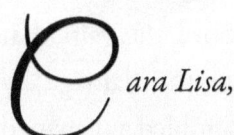ara Lisa,

I pray the day finds you and Marietta well. The afternoon
I spent with you and our daughter was like a dream and
warms me even now. It is all that keeps me from despair. This
commission has been one calamity after another. The technique
I employed, using distilled turpentine, resin, and melted candle
wax to coat the wall, refuses to adhere. I am burning braziers
around the clock to enable the pigments in the wax to set. I pray
the rain is behind us, for should the weather turn malignant,
all this effort will be for naught. The other night, I dreamed it
would end in disaster, and now I fear the Battle of Anghiari
will be lost...

Leonardo stood on the scissor platform at one end of the massive mural and Salai at the other as they tried to nail a tarp to the wall to divert water that poured from the ceiling away from the mural. The summer storm had unleashed a deluge, overwhelming the ceiling and walls of the Hall of Five Hundred. While he and Salai struggled with the covering, his assistants frantically tried to sponge and dry the wall's surface.

Leonardo saw his premonition delivered with a vengeance as if the storm's only mission was to destroy the *Battle of Anghiari*. He watched with a sinking heart as portions of the cartoon began to dissolve, sliding down the face of the mural and landing on the floor in piles of pulpy mush. The transparent layers of oil paint streamed down the wall, like blood seeping from an open wound. Dizzy from the sight, he gripped the scaffold to keep from falling.

The only thing more destructive than man is Mother Nature.

"Bring more braziers," Leonardo yelled above the rain that pounded the ceiling, "maybe we can mitigate the damage by drying the surface." He glanced at Salai, who resembled a drowned rat. He would have laughed had the situation not been so desperate. The heat from stoking the additional braziers did nothing to dry the cartoon. Instead, it began to melt the wax coating, causing the colors to bleed even more.

Amid the frantic effort to save the mural, Leonardo heard a familiar voice call up to him.

Looking down, he saw Lisa standing at the base of the scaffold. "You should not have come," he said as he climbed down. "The weather is terrible, and you put yourself at risk."

"I came by carriage, and I am fine." She pushed back her hood and stared up at the mural. "Oh, Leonardo, I am so sorry. What will you do?"

He rubbed his forehead. "It is beyond repair. I fear an ominous message is being sent."

"What do you mean?"

"Come, you are shivering." He took her elbow and led her closer to the heat of one of the braziers. "My efforts to create an adherent surface for the mural have failed miserably."

Behind the smoky haze of the braziers, the paint continued to drip down the wall, the imagery reminding him of a sad clown whose painted face is smeared by tears.

Perhaps I am the sad clown.

"But you can recover and begin again," Lisa said, gently squeezing his hand. "The signoria will surely understand this destruction is no fault of yours."

"That does not matter. There have been too many failures in my past and too many abandoned projects. I was hoping, with this mural, I could redeem myself in the eyes of potential patrons. But alas, I fear my star has already reached its zenith, and there will be no more grand commissions in my future." He took out a handkerchief and wiped the perspiration from his face. "All I have ever wanted was to create and share my work with the world. Not to be forever at the mercy of the powerful and the rich who seek to control everything we do."

"I beg you not to speak with such pessimism," Lisa said, her eyes reflecting the glowing flames of the brazier. "Your work is a shining example of your artistry, and the public knows that. So do your fellow artists. You have helped so many along the way. I recall that time in the church when you offered sage advice to the young painter Raphael. Although the world may never know of your kindness to your fellow artists and the knowledge you have shared with your apprentices over the years, your wisdom will be seen in their work, which will be felt for centuries."

He regarded her with wonder and once again felt a sense of peace enfold him whenever she was near. "*Tesoro*, forgive me. I hope I did not give you the impression that our portrait is insignificant. Alas, I speak of these patronages and how we artists are twisted into knots of worry each time we undertake such work."

She reached up and caressed his face. "Leonardo, I understand. We share something precious that has given us both such joy."

He knew she alluded to more than the painting and their friendship that had grown and blossomed; she also referred to their beautiful daughter, Marietta.

At the sudden shouts of his assistants, they turned to witness a massive section of the cartoon give way.

Lisa gasped and gripped his hand.

"I should have known this would happen. I should have anticipated it." Leonardo shook his head as he beheld the destruction of his work.

"My heart is breaking for you, *caro*," she said in a husky voice.

He lifted her hand and kissed it. "It cannot be helped. Nature is only fulfilling the wishes of the signoria."

"What do you mean? How could Soderini have known this would happen?"

"He may not have known, but he will certainly be pleased."

"But why did they award you the commission in the first place?"

Leonardo shrugged. "There is nothing Florentines love more than a *concorrenza*. By stoking the fire of competition between Michelangelo and myself, perhaps they thought to focus the attention of the entire Italian peninsula on our greatness. Soderini and Machiavelli's plan has always been to bolster public support for their war against Pisa in the name of the Republic. They made that clear when they placed Michelangelo's *David* in the center of the Piazza della Signoria as if he were Florence's protector and warrior, ready to step off his pedestal and slay any monster who threatened her."

"But Michelangelo is in Rome working on another commission for the pope, is he not?" Lisa said. "Besides, if this has happened to you, the same fate could befall him. We cannot predict the whims of nature."

"Yes, but that does not matter at this point. Michelangelo has already fulfilled the wishes of the signoria. His planned mural played right into Machiavelli's scheme. *The Battle of Cascina* is no battle at all, created by a man who has never witnessed the brutality of war. Michelangelo prefers to depict frolicking naked men with beautiful bodies whose muscles resemble walnuts. There are no scars or wounds to detract from the myth of the glory of war because the truth is far too ugly. The blood and gore that drenches the ground, the screams, and pleas for mercy from the dying are nowhere to be found in Michelangelo's work."

"His approach sounds more fantasy than fact," Lisa mused. "But surely, your vision will resonate far more with the public, will it not?"

Leonardo shrugged. "Our two interpretations of war constitute a battle in and of itself; our visions will never align. My mural would have dissuaded any sane man or woman from supporting an effort that caused so much death and destruction."

"Wars are fought on faraway battlefields, and the public only knows what officials tell us," Lisa said.

"Indeed, *cara mia*." Leonardo wrapped his arm around her shoulders and held her close. "Michelangelo's glorification of war is what Soderini and Machiavelli want, whereas my depiction of war's gritty truth will only put fear in people's hearts." He heaved a beleaguered sigh, knowing he would experience the consequences of the failed fresco long after today. "Michelangelo wins the battle once again." He flicked his arm at the ravaged mural. "Bah, let him claim his victory. He is welcome to it. I am done with all this nonsense. For me, the taste is too bitter to bear."

"*Caro,* I pray you do not give up hope for the future. Yours is the vision of truth. Perhaps one day, more artists, poets, and playwrights will carry this banner, and then the world will know as well."

"My dearest, I hope your wish will come to pass for the sake of humankind."

"Do you know what you will do next?"

He forced a smile. "I will do what I always do. I will find a way to move forward, or I will find a way out."

CHAPTER 42

NOVEMBER 27, 1943 ~ FLORENCE, ITALY

*T*he bell rang and rang, and the pounding on the door was enough to wake the dead. Valentina jumped out of bed and threw on her habit. The door to her room burst open, and Meira ran in and wrapped her arms around her. The terror on the girl's face told Valentina everything she needed to know. She ran to her closet and grabbed another habit. "Put this on. Whatever happens, stay close to me."

Gunshots erupted outside, followed by shattering glass and splintering wood. Heavy boots thudded on the main floor as shouts in both German and Italian echoed throughout the convent. "*Aufstehen! Schnell! Schnell!*" they shouted. "All occupants of this convent are hereby ordered to descend to the main hall with identification papers. No exceptions."

Valentina and Meira ran into the hallway and saw a Blackshirt fire his pistol up the stairway. Thank God no one was hurt, although if the curses from the outraged nuns came true, the SS guards would suffer a lifetime of digestive ailments.

Valentina and the other nuns followed an established protocol they'd planned with the madre superiore. Should the fascists storm the convent, the Jewish women and children would hide behind stacks of boxes and blankets in closets, and only the nuns would emerge from their rooms and gather on the main floor. They hoped with this plan, they could calmly convince the Blackshirts that the convent was inhabited only by the Carmelite Sisters.

The Gestapo commander stood like a statue as the mother superior took him to task. His eyes remained unblinking as her finger pointed accusingly at his face.

"What is the meaning of this?" Madre Superiore demanded like an avenging angel. "How dare you storm into the sanctity of Church grounds? This is Vatican property. Our order is under the protection of the pope."

Valentina suppressed a gasp and moved closer to Meira as she recognized the man who stepped forward to translate for the SS officer. It was Dante Conti.

"You would do well, Madre Superiore, *not* to interfere," Dante said with a sneer. He scanned the group of nuns who'd gathered. His eyes collided with Valentina's, and he added, "We are here to take into custody the Jews hiding within these walls."

"You are illegally harboring enemy aliens. You will be arrested if you do not step aside," the commandant barked.

"I do not fear you, for God is my witness, and he will protect me," the abbess declared. "I will not stand aside, and I will not be silenced!"

Dante and the SS officer pushed past the mother superior, causing her to lose her balance. Valentina was grateful that Suor Teresa was there to steady the elder nun.

"All the Jews hiding in this convent are ordered to show themselves," Dante shouted up the stairs. "Bring your identity papers and report downstairs to the meeting hall right away!"

The guards stormed up the stairs, kicking open doors and shouting orders.

Valentina sensed Meira trembling beside her and reached for her hand, reassuringly squeezing it. Her heart wrenched, knowing the guards would find the women and children. She wished they'd had an underground tunnel or a secret room where the Jewish mothers and children could have hidden. But they had relied on the hope that the fascists would respect the sanctity of the Church. She'd been naïve to think so. These men possessed no moral fortitude, no reverence for their eternal souls.

Dante had been menacing her since he'd discovered her whereabouts and had no doubt been biding his time until he could cause as much pain, fear, and destruction as possible.

The Jewish women and children were herded downstairs into the main hall. They were in every imaginable state of undress. Children cried, clinging to their mothers. Valentina felt a surge of fury, wishing she had the strength of a hundred men to vanquish these fiends from their midst.

From the corner of her eye, she saw Sarah slip into the hall holding Isaac wrapped in a blanket. The young mother's eyes seemed wild and panicked as her gaze skittered around the room. Meira moved as if she intended to run to Sarah, but Valentina held her back. "*Aspetta*," she whispered. "Let us see what she does."

Sarah hesitated as though considering her options. Her eyes

locked on Suor Teresa, and Valentina watched as the young mother took a deep breath. Amid the shouts and screams in the main hall, Sarah's demeanor seemed to transform from shaky to serene. Her eyes, no longer showing panic, now reflected a deliberate focus. She inched her way to Suor Teresa, who stood at the back of the room. Sarah knelt and laid the bundled boy at Suor Teresa's feet. In the confusion, no one noticed. The young mother and nun looked into each other's eyes in a moment of silent communication.

Tears streamed down Sarah's face, and she bit her lip as she walked away and joined the other Jewish women. Valentina watched, mesmerized, as Suor Teresa took a step forward, and then as if it was the most natural thing to do, she lifted her skirt, and Isaac disappeared beneath the folds of her habit. Meira squeezed Valentina's hand. The girl had also seen.

A woman's screams snapped Valentina's attention toward the entrance to the hall. Two guards dragged a Jewish woman by her hair. *"Lasciame andare!* Let me go!" She fought like a tigress, struggling to free herself.

The Blackshirt yelled, "I found this one trying to escape through a window." Giving her a vicious slap across the face, he kicked her, making her stumble into a group of huddled women.

The commandant SS officer pulled out his Luger pistol and aimed its barrel around the room, causing shrieks and cries of terror as mothers shielded their children. With a cruel smile, the Nazi fired the gun at the ceiling.

He shouted in German and Italian, *"Ruhe! Silenzio!"*

A hush fell over the room, and the women clung to each other. Even the wailing children were silenced into sniffles and whimpering, the littlest ones sticking their thumbs in their mouths.

The abbess bravely approached the SS officer in charge. "Many of these women have identification papers protecting them. Others are Hungarian workers without permits. I will not allow you to arrest them."

Dante translated for the German officer, who regarded the mother superior with a narrowed-eyed stare. "We will check all these so-called papers. But first, abbess, where is your telephone?"

"In my office. But why—?"

"Go with her," he ordered one of his men, "and cut the line." The German soldier saluted his commander, aimed his pistol at the abbess, and gestured for her to lead the way.

The Nazis set up a table, and the women were lined up in front of it. The processing was quick and efficient. Some women held work permits and paperwork that excluded them from being deported. They were shuffled to one side of the hall. The rest of the women pleaded, begging for mercy. "I have tuberculosis and medical papers that protect me," begged one woman, and another swooned and fell to the floor, but the soldiers lifted her and hauled her away.

When Valentina arrived at the front of the line, she held tight to Meira's hand.

The SS officer looked her over and waited for her to speak. She handed him her identification papers and Meira's. "I am Suor Gianna, and this is Suor Anna Maria. Suor Anna Maria is mute. I will speak for her."

Dante, who stood next to the table, stared at her. His eyes seemed to burn as they roamed over her from head to toe. And then she realized she'd forgotten her veil, and her hair spilled down her back to her waist.

Valentina cursed her forgetfulness, recognizing the look in Dante's eyes—the same look etched on his face each time he'd visited her at the convent. The look of a hungry wolf intent on his prey.

Meira, who'd kept her gaze glued to the floor, trembled like a leaf in the wind. Valentina held tight to her hand, hoping to calm the girl. But she couldn't stop the fear and anger from swirling through her veins as Dante shifted his focus to Meira. Standing side by side as they were, did Dante notice their resemblance? He was clever and devious. How long before he guessed the truth?

The Nazi commander frowned as he perused their papers. "It says here that this young nun is from Rome."

Valentina held her head up and maintained her composure. "Yes, she joined our order a month ago." Valentina forced a serene smile. "She is a blessing to our order."

The Nazi's reply in German was lost to her.

"Are we done, sir?" She needed to get Meira away from Dante. It wasn't the Nazis who presented the greatest danger to Meira. It was the demon who'd haunted Valentina since she was barely sixteen. God help them all if he ever figured out that Meira was his daughter.

Before the SS officer could answer, the mother superior returned and marched to Valentina's side. The abbess said in a voice filled with indignation and righteousness. "I demand that you leave this convent now! These women are ordained Sisters of Mary. Your jurisdiction does not extend to our order. We answer only to God."

The SS officer threw his head back and laughed. "We will leave when I say it's time to leave. I am sick of your interference, you old hag. You are a traitor and will be treated as such." He flung his arm out dismissively. "Arrest her!"

The other nuns cried out in protest. "Please! You cannot take Madre Superiore!"

"It's all right," the abbess said calmly.

"Schweigen!" the commandant barked.

The nuns fell silent, and even Dante looked surprised as the mother superior was strong-armed out of the convent. Valentina prayed they would let her go. They would contact the Archbishop of Florence as soon as possible and ask him to intervene on behalf of the beloved nun.

The SS officer waved Valentina and Meira away. Desperate to get her daughter out of harm's way, Valentina led her from the main hall and out of Dante's sight. They ran down the hallway to the kitchen, where several nuns were preparing food bundles for the Jewish women taken into custody. Valentina told Meira to stay in the kitchen until she returned, then she snagged a potato sack and ran back to the main hall.

Suor Teresa hadn't budged from her spot, but her face was dotted with perspiration. Isaac, God bless him. He had made no sound and was likely still asleep, but how long before he began to whimper from hunger or cry because of a wet diaper? How long before he fussed for a cuddle from his mother? They would be found out. The SS would take Isaac, and God only knew what would become of the infant. Valentina brought a chair to Teresa and said in a low voice, "Sit, Teresa. I have an idea."

Teresa nodded and sat. Valentina scanned the hall to make sure they were not being watched. She kneeled behind Teresa's chair and pulled the sack from beneath her habit. Reaching under

Teresa's gown, Valentina scooped Isaac into the burlap bag and stood.

"Rest easy, my friend," she whispered to Suor Teresa.

The baby did not stir, another miracle she would thank God for later. She gently slung the sack over her shoulder, walking past the rows of women waiting to be processed.

As Valentina calmly walked across the room, her eyes met Sarah's. The young mother gave an almost imperceptible nod; her eyes glistened with unshed tears, and a faint smile hovered on her lips before she turned away.

Just a few feet left to go. Valentina held her breath as she approached the door and cast one last look over her shoulder. She wished she hadn't as her gaze locked with Dante's. His lips curled up in a mocking smile, and he inclined his head as if in a brief salute. A chill skittered up her spine. Had he been watching her? Did he see what she'd done? She prayed he hadn't, but she refused to be cowed by him. She straightened her shoulders and shot him an icy glare, answering his arrogance with defiance. Turning her back on him, she disappeared down the hall with Isaac.

CHAPTER 43

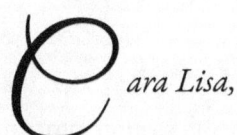

ara Lisa,

Forgive me, cara, I would not leave you for the world, but alas, every artist is only as worthy as his last commission. I will never finish The Battle of Anghiari, and I fear it will be the last important commission offered to me. The King of France has invited me to Milan, and I dare not refuse. Leaving Florence will be difficult, but leaving you and Marietta will break my heart...

The *mercato* was bustling with Florentines eager to enjoy the balmy spring weather as Leonardo and Lisa strolled once more past the crowded market stalls with their beloved daughter toddling between them, her hands grasped firmly in theirs.

Leonardo had been looking forward to this outing and yet dreading it at the same time, knowing his time with them was coming to an end.

Despite his anger over the disastrous collapse of his mural of *The Battle of Anghiari* and his frustration over the political machinations behind the scenes, Leonardo had attempted to restore what had been destroyed in that dreadful rainstorm and complete his painting in the Hall of Five Hundred. But after spending nearly a year toiling at the task, he had to finally admit defeat. Leaving Florence was his only way forward.

With a little huff, Marietta stretched her arms upward and wiggled her chubby little fingers at Leonardo. "Zio Leo, carry me," the golden-haired cherub demanded.

"Ah, did you hear that, *caro*?" Lisa smiled indulgently at her daughter.

"Well, what more can I say? I find it impossible to resist the two loveliest ladies in Florence." Grinning, he picked up his daughter, who promptly laid her head on his shoulder, her plump little legs swinging back and forth. The bond between him and his child was something Leonardo had never imagined he would experience. And now that he had decided to move to Milan, he feared that perhaps he was making a mistake.

But the truth was Soderini, Machiavelli, and the rest of the signoria would never publicly absolve him and would make his life miserable. The city of his youth had given him much but had also taken a great deal. Perhaps more than he could bear. He would not leave Florence with regrets, for she had been a mercurial mistress. But leaving Lisa and Marietta, the two most important people in his life, would cleave his heart in two.

The squawking of caged birds greeted them, just as it had so many times before. Marietta's hazel eyes grew round with curiosity as she pointed at the noisy birds. "Mamma, *volare uccello!*"

"Yes, *tesorina,* you are right. Birds do not belong in cages." Lisa winked at Leonardo. "Is she not the cleverest child? She questions everything as you do. Her mind is like quicksilver. She observes, she assesses, and she correctly concludes."

"Each time I see her, I discover a new facet to her personality," Leonardo mused. "But she is also like you, *cara.*"

"How so, *amore mio?*"

"Ah, well, she has your smile, of course. And a particular twinkle in her eyes when she is about to say something mischievous."

Lisa threw back her head and laughed. Seeing her mother's exuberant laughter, Marietta did the same, perfectly mimicking her. Leonardo planted a kiss on Marietta's cheek. She puckered her lips and kissed him back, and then swinging her legs, she demanded, *"Giù, giù, giù!"* Down, down, down!

"Sì, piccolina, you are like a little starling who demands to be free. I will put you down for no other reason than to watch what you do." Marietta ran to a cage, where two lovebirds sat so close together, they appeared to be one." A tear traced its way down her cheek, and Lisa bent and kissed it away.

"Don't cry, *tesorina.* We are going to set the birds free," Lisa said in a soft voice.

The heavyset shopkeeper joined them. He gently pinched Marietta's cheek, and the child glared at him.

"I see you are training the next generation of customers for me," the birdseller said with a good-natured chuckle.

It was likely none of his other customers paid good money to buy birds and then set them free. If the shopkeeper thought them *eccentric,* he had the decency not to vocalize it. Business was business, and the stout birdseller clearly did not care what they did with the birds after they purchased them.

A few minutes later, Leonardo carried Marietta in one arm and a box of squalling birds in the other. The child held a small box to her breast with a pair of lovebirds inside, while Lisa held two boxes with several doves. They walked until they found a quiet, open area with a clear view of the sky.

"I think this will do," said Leonardo, stopping and putting Marietta down.

Lisa knelt in front of their daughter. "*Tesorina,* would you like to open your box first?" Marietta nodded, her expression solemn as if she'd been tasked with guarding the republic.

"Let me hold it for you, *angioletta.*" Leonardo helped Marietta lift the lid. For a moment, the birds looked up at the child and then at the sky, most likely not realizing their good fortune.

"*Vola, vola, vola,*" the little girl chanted, waving her hands. The lovebirds looked at one another, flapped their wings, and made for the sky. Marietta clapped her hands and hopped up and down in celebration. The ritual was repeated until all the birds were free.

Leonardo tickled Marietta under her chin, bringing forth a glissando of giggles. Smoothing back her golden curls, he said, "Marietta, will you promise to be a good girl for your mamma and take care of her for me?"

Marietta gave his beard a gentle tug and nodded, her now somber expression mirroring the sadness he was trying so hard to hide. He wrapped his arms around her, hugged her, and pressed his lips to her forehead. "May God bless you, *my angioletta.*" He stood, taking her hand in his. "I wonder what you will do with your life, my darling daughter," he murmured half to himself. "I do not know if I will be around to see it. But something tells me that your purpose will be very special. Very special indeed."

"Soon, you will be as lost to us as these birds are," Lisa said thickly, her eyes glistening with tears.

"But we have liberated them," Leonardo replied. "Do we not rejoice as they soar up into the Heavens? We have released them from their prisons. Is this not the most joyous gift we could have given them?"

"Has this city been such a prison for you then?" she asked softly.

He considered her question for a moment as he watched the birds in flight. "Perhaps not a prison. But there have been too many walls in Florence. Walls that have restricted me, walls that have crumbled at my feet, and walls that will never ever come down."

"Perhaps I, too, have erected some of those walls," she said. "I am a woman who is not free. A woman who has made life-long vows."

"Never, cara mia." He lifted her hand to his lips. "You have given me the greatest gift I have ever hoped for. Our daughter."

"And you have given me a love I never thought possible. And now you are going away for good."

"Never, amore, Milan is not so far away. I promise I will return as often as possible to visit you and Marietta. And my letters to you will keep us close until my hand can no longer hold a quill."

"Oh, how I will miss you." She breathed a deep sigh. "I doubt I shall ever see our portrait again."

Glancing around to make sure no one was watching,

Leonardo bent and kissed Lisa. "You are wrong, *amore*. One day, the portrait will be yours."

Lisa gave him one of her mysterious smiles. And he knew she did not believe him. *Beh*, for now, the portrait would stay with him. He could not part with it. Not now. Not for many years to come. But not because it had yet to be finished nor because it was perhaps his finest portrait. He would not part with it because as long as the painting was with him, so was she.

"Before I die, I will arrange for the portrait to be sent to you," he said. "After all, it is as much your creation as it is mine."

"Do not speak of death," she said in a voice as solemn as he'd ever heard her speak. "Do not speak of finality. Do not speak of goodbyes." She looked at him, and he thought he could see everything in her eyes in one timeless moment. "We shall never say goodbye. We shall say, *arrivederci*."

"Until we meet again," he whispered.

CHAPTER 44

DECEMBER 25, 1943 ~ FLORENCE, ITALY

*V*alentina sat at her desk and wept. It was the saddest Christmas anyone in the convent had ever experienced. Since the horrifying raid of November 27, a blanket of grief shrouded them. Of the eighty Jewish women and children, only thirty had been spared. The others had been arrested and taken to Verona. Only yesterday, Valentina learned that on December 6, the first trains filled with Jews had departed from Verona and Milan, heading east to a destination unknown.

What will become of them?

She'd prayed for most of this holy day, hoping they would survive.

At least one prayer had been answered. Thanks to the intervention of the Archbishop of Florence, Cardinal Elia Dalla Costa, the mother superior, was released and returned to the convent. In standing up to the SS and the Blackshirts, she'd shown true strength and valor. Valentina admired the sainted abbess immensely.

Saving baby Isaac had been a miracle, but Isaac was too young to be weaned and was placed with an Italian woman who'd recently lost her baby. Isaac's mother, Sarah, was among the women arrested and deported.

The arrests and deportations had left Meira devastated. The shell she had tentatively begun to break free from had been erected once more. Rarely did she emerge from her room, and she ceased visiting the library. Valentina tried to talk to her and brought books and notebooks to her room, but the books sat unread, and the notebooks remained blank.

Valentina's failure to help her daughter left her heartsick. Her own fears about the future made her anxious and short of temper. Even with Suor Teresa, who was as dear to her as a sister, she could not control her acerbic tongue or rebukes.

After a meager Christmas supper, the nuns retired to their rooms early. The convent was quiet, and Valentina sought refuge in the library, expecting not to be interrupted. She climbed off the ladder and set the folio with Leonardo's letters and drawings on the desk. She opened the drawer to take out her mirror and spied the pistol Serafina had given her.

When the old woman had heard about the raid, she insisted Valentina be armed. Serafina's words replayed in Valentina's mind: *It is better to die fighting than surrender to these fiends.*

Shuddering, she took out the mirror and closed the drawer. She slipped on a pair of gloves and carefully picked up one of Leonardo's letters. She held the mirror over the letter to view the reflection of his lefthanded backward handwriting and focused on the slow process of translating his words.

The story of Lisa and Leonardo had emerged bit by bit from the shadows of nearly five hundred years. Although their love had broken the bonds of society's mores and the dictates of the Catholic Church, Valentina did not judge them. Her discovery of the love between Leonardo da Vinci and Lisa del Giocondo had been a revelation, a beacon of light in the darkness of war.

Valentina blinked back tears as she re-read the transcription of Leonardo's farewell letter to Lisa...

> *Our leave-taking left me feeling wretched. Your tears are forever etched upon my soul. You who have become my dearest friend, the other half of my heart... Alas, we have always known the time might come for our paths to diverge. As for our hearts, they will always remain as one. Milan is not far away. I promise to return as often as possible to see you and our dear Marietta. Please kiss her sweet cheeks for me and know that you are always with me, as I am with you.*
>
> *Sei sempre nel mio cuore e nel miei pensieri,*
> *Leonardo*

Valentina wiped the tears from her eyes and glanced at the clock on her desk. She'd spent two hours completing the transcript. So many letters, so many shared experiences, so much love, and so much sorrow. But she was so very grateful that Suor Maria Vittoria had bestowed upon her this gift, for it had sustained her throughout these dark and desolate years of war.

She pulled her shawl more tightly around her shoulders in

answer to the chill seeping through the window. Valentina picked up one of the drawings of Lisa holding a cherubic Marietta on her lap. She studied the child's face, trying to discern Leonardo's paternity in her features. So engrossed was she in the sketch that she jumped up from her chair when the door suddenly flew open. Taken by surprise, Valentina didn't at first recognize the man whose face lay in shadow from his hat pulled low over his face.

"Who are you? What do you want?" She stood on trembling legs as she confronted the stranger.

"I want *you*, my beauty."

He removed his hat, and Valentina saw the face that had given her nightmares for the past seventeen years. The face of Dante Conti.

"How did you get in here?" she said, her mind racing as she tried to figure out what she should do.

"When your sainted mother superior was arrested, she was searched, and her keys were confiscated. Of course, they were returned to her when she was released. But by then, I'd had a duplicate set made." He chuckled as he lifted the ring of keys, swinging it back and forth. "I simply bided my time until I could pay you another visit. A private one."

"*Bastardo!*" With so much turmoil and tragedy happening around them, Valentina had not even considered changing the locks, nor had the mother superior.

He wagged his finger at her and tsked. "I think my parents would be most offended by your vulgar insult."

"And what of you?" she countered. "Sweat beaded her brow as she slowly eased open the drawer where the pistol was kept. "Are you not offended as well?"

A slow smile spread across his face, and she couldn't help but wonder at how a man with such an ugly soul could possess such a handsome face.

He took a step closer. "Of course not. I know how spirited you truly are. Despite how hard you try to hide your passionate nature under the guise of being a nun, just as you hide your voluptuous body beneath that drab black sack you wear."

"You have no right to be here," Valentina said, realizing that Leonardo da Vinci's letters and drawings were still on her desk. She tried to gather them up, but her hands shook, and one of the drawings flew up like a bird, slowly floating to the floor.

Valentina's heart froze as Dante bent to pick it up. She ran around the desk to grab it from him, but he held it high above her head, and she felt like a child jumping to take back a doll snatched by a bully.

"Stand back, Valentina, or I'll tear it to pieces."

Her heart pounding in her ears, she backed up a few paces.

"What have we here?" He studied the drawing, his brow furrowed.

Dante's education and interests did not extend to the history of art, and Valentina hoped he would not comprehend the value of what he held.

"A drawing done by a nun who stayed with us for a time," Valentina said in as calm a voice as she could muster. "We kept it in case she asks us to mail it to her."

But Dante continued to examine the sketch, and she could see by the gleam in his eyes that he was considering what to make of it.

"It's very good." He shot her a sharp glance. "Maybe too good for some unknown nun to have made." He looked at the desk where the folio lay. "You have more?"

Valentina flicked her wrist in a dismissive gesture, trying to keep her voice even. "One or two, but as I said, we will most likely be mailing them to her. May I have it back, please?"

He held the drawing up to the light. "I've seen this style before, and the paper looks old."

"The nun copied it from a book. She kindly gave a few drawing lessons to some of the sisters who'd expressed an interest. It's a mere trifle, nothing more."

He regarded her in silence for a moment before handing her the drawing. "Perhaps, I'll return tomorrow with a few SS officers who can better assess these mere trifles, as you call them."

A cold sweat dripped down her back, and her mind whirled with panic, knowing that she was putting everyone at the convent at risk. She returned to her desk, slipped the drawing into the folio, and placed it back in the drawer. Even if she managed to find a place to hide the letters, the Nazis could easily tear apart the entire convent to find them. Her carelessness had put them all in danger, especially the Jewish women and children under their roof. Her pulse thundered in her ears—what if they discovered who Meira truly was?

Valentina looked up and saw him regarding her with a narrow-eyed stare.

"I saw you take that baby and hide it," he said. "I could have had you arrested on the spot, hauled you off to jail. I doubt the pope would have interceded on your behalf as he did for your precious mother superior. I think you owe me a debt of gratitude. Don't you agree?"

"I think you should thank God for your act of mercy," she countered. "You spared the life of a child. Maybe he will grow up and thank you one day."

He shrugged. "What do I care about a brat and a Jew no less?

Besides, it's your gratitude I crave..." The smiling mask vanished, and Valentina knew the devil possessed him.

Dante stalked toward her, trapping her behind the desk. Before she could react, he tore her wimple and veil from her head, and her dark hair tumbled down around her shoulders. Lifting a dark strand between his fingers, he probed the depths of her eyes. She recognized that look. It had been imprinted in her brain more than seventeen years ago. The face of a man who revels in inflicting pain, a man driven only by his arrogance and hubris, a man who doesn't care about anything or anyone except himself.

Terror invaded her chest with the memory of leaves crushed beneath her back from the weight of his body pressing down on hers—suffocating her, violating her...Valentina took a deep, shaky breath as her hand moved toward the drawer for the gun, but it was just out of reach.

He edged closer and she caught the soured stink of alcohol on his breath.

"Stop this, Dante! Stop this and leave now."

His face twisted into the smile of a beast about to leap on its prey as his fingers wrapped around her arms, digging into her flesh. He lifted her like a rag doll and slammed her onto the desk, knocking the wind out of her. The back of her head hit the hard wood with a thud, blurring her vision as her hands flailed, desperately searching for something she could use as a weapon. She struggled beneath his heavy weight, her strength ebbing as her mind reeled with the stark realization that it was happening again.

His hot breath invaded her ear. "Stop fighting, and I won't harm the girl. I know she's a Jew."

Valentina froze.

Meira.

He gripped a handful of her hair, yanking it hard, pulling her head back. "Mine!" he growled as his teeth grazed her vulnerable throat. "You are mine." His eyes burned with a feverish gleam as he ripped her habit from hem to neck, exposing her completely to his ravenous gaze.

"Don't do this, Dante, I beg of you. If not for me, for the sake of your immortal soul."

He barked out a laugh. "Don't you know, Valentina, I sold my soul to the devil the first moment I laid eyes on you." He straddled her hips and released her hands as he unbuckled his belt.

Her hand inched toward the drawer, feeling for the handle.

"We both know this is the only way it can be," he rasped. "Why can't you see it?"

Her index finger hooked onto the drawer handle but faltered as he spread her legs and dragged her closer.

"You are mine. Since the first moment I laid eyes on you. No woman has ever equaled your beauty, your spirit—"

She stiffened, squeezing her eyes shut as his hand pushed between her thighs. He tore at her underwear, his fingers invading her. She swallowed her cry of pain and finally managed to open the drawer.

"Stop, Dante! Please!" She gasped as Dante pinched her breasts, rubbing himself against her.

"I can't," he grunted. "I've waited long enough. Too long," he muttered, fumbling with his zipper.

Keeping her wits about her, she managed to hook her finger around the handle of the pistol in the open drawer.

Valentina slowly lifted the gun, trying to conceal her movement, but the metal flashed under the glow of the lamplight, drawing Dante's notice.

"You bitch!" He slapped the pistol out of her hand. The momentum made him stumble, giving her a split-second to slide out of his grasp and run for the door.

She made it barely a few steps before he dragged her back by the torn hem of her habit. She fell to her knees, and he shoved her onto the floor. She struggled like a fish caught on a line as he flipped her onto her back and pinned her hands over her head.

"You think you're helping your cause by fighting me?" he hissed. "This makes me only want you more."

"Please, for the love of God, stop this madness!" she sobbed.

His hand gripped her chin. "Yes, I am mad, but you have made me so. You deny me with your words, but your lips and body have taunted me since you were a girl."

He leaned down and captured her lips in a punishing kiss, drawing blood.

When he pulled away, Valentina was aghast at the sight of her own blood staining his lips. A macabre grin contorted his features into an ugly mask. His fingers dove between her legs once more, making her cry out in pain. "I will have you now and any time I want," he spat out. "Or I'll burn down this entire place along with those crow-faced nuns and your precious Jews."

A shot rang out, and both Valentina and Dante froze.

Their gazes locked on each other for a moment, but it seemed like an eternity.

Dante's eyes widened in surprise, and his hand clutched his chest.

"Why?" A gurgling cry erupted from his mouth as he fell on top of her.

Both shocked and horrified, Valentina rolled him onto his back and looked up to see her savior. Meira stood above her, holding the smoking pistol with two hands, still pointing the muzzle as if to fire.

"Dear God, Meira." Valentina slowly got to her feet. "It's all right, child. It's all right." She raised her hands slowly palms facing outward.

Hearing footsteps fast approaching, Valentina glanced at the doorway just as Suor Teresa and the mother superior rushed into the room. Valentina gave a slight shake of her head, warning the nuns to do nothing. Any sudden movement or sound might cause Meira to discharge the weapon again.

Meira trembled like a leaf in the wind, the gun shaking in her hands. Valentina reached out and eased the pistol from the girl's stiff fingers and passed it to Suor Teresa.

"I'm s-sorry. I-I didn't m-mean to kill him," Meira said as tears streamed down her face. I'm s-sorry. I j-just wanted to s-stop him hurting you..."

You saved my life," Valentina whispered. "It's all right, Meira. You saved my life." Valentina embraced her daughter and held her close, unable to stop her own tears as Meira wept on her shoulder.

CHAPTER 45

APRIL 27, 1519 ~ CHÂTEAU DU CLOS LUCÉ ~ AMBOISE,
FRANCE

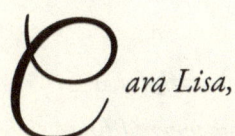*ara Lisa,*

*How I have loved you. How I have cherished our friendship.
My time is nearly spent, and my only regret is that you are not
at my side. Ever near me is your portrait, your beauty captured
for all time. It is the most precious thing I possess. Only in death
will I relinquish it.*

*Please forgive me for leaving you and Marietta in
Florence. The years after were prosperous, if only partially satisfactory. Milan, Rome, and now France, where I will take my
final leave. Between my wanderings, I kept my promise to you
and visited when possible. Those treasured hours with you and*

*our daughter sustained me and gave me a measure of peace I
have never known.*

*As you so wisely predicted, adopting Francesco Melzi as my
son has lightened the burdens in my life, freeing me from
Salai's bickering and stressful antics. Though I still care for
Salai, it is from a distance, which is better for both of us. I do
not think he is the sadder for it or for being free of me. As they
say, our friendship ran its course long ago.*

*With his immense generosity and devotion, Monseigneur
le Dauphin, Francis I, has granted me serenity and contentment in the winter of my life, and I am forever grateful. If only
you were here to sit with me and share a peaceful walk in the
exquisite gardens surrounding this chateau. I often think of our
picnics in Fiesole. If only I could have flown from the peak of
Swan Mountain with you by my side. That pleasure has
forever eluded me. Perhaps in another lifetime if such a notion
exists.*

*Most of all, I miss our trips to the birdseller's stall, for it is
there we had our first encounter sixteen years ago, where I first
beheld the wonder and beauty of your grace. And it is there I
acquired my most treasured memories of the times spent with
you and our precious daughter Marietta.*

*Over the years, your friendship inspired me, but more
importantly, it opened the door of my heart to feel a love so
profound it transformed my life. You and Marietta have
become the family I was denied as a boy. As I leave this world, I
leave it knowing that I have been loved and that I have loved
in return.*

*You asked in your previous letter why I have written about
death in my last few letters. Because my dearest, my once*

vigorous frame withers, and pain has become my constant companion. It is only when my weariness manages to overcome the pain in my limbs that I am able to slumber for a few blessed hours. Even as I write this missive, which is of such import to me, I can barely lift the quill.

But I must share with you a genuinely illuminating occurrence. Twice now, I have been awakened by a blinding white light that fills me with such wonder—that should it appear to me a third time, I must explore and discover its origins. To that end, I can only say that I am ready when God calls me.

One task remains to me. When Salai last visited, I entrusted him with this letter to you. I am also returning all the cherished letters you wrote to me over the years. I entrust them to your safekeeping. Perhaps one day, many years from now, when I am long gone, you will give them to Marietta so she might know the love between her mother and father.

My will is complete, leaving most of what I possess to Salai and Francesco, but to you and Marietta, I leave my treasure— your portrait. No one is more entitled to it than you. You inspired my greatest work and the light that filled my heart. It is only fitting that the painting should be yours. Kiss my sweet daughter for me. Oh, what I would not give to see her one last time.

I close this letter, my last to you, with my eyes gazing on the face I have adored so well. It is the last face I shall look upon when I take leave of this world.

It is the face of the Mona Lisa.

Con tutto il mio cuore,
Leonardo

Lisa's eyes blurred with tears as she pressed the letter to her breast. The chirping of birds drew her gaze to the open window. She watched two sparrows take flight, and a sigh escaped her. She'd received news of Leonardo's passing the same day his final letter arrived.

Salai had delivered it and imparted the news that Leonardo took his last breath, dying in the arms of the King of France, on the second of May.

Salai handed her a lovely wooden box with a carving of two birds in flight. The box contained her letters to Leonardo over the years. Leonardo had made it himself, and Salai had been kind enough to allow her to keep it. But he denied her Leonardo's final bequest. He knew she would not fight him on this matter. She could not and would not lay a legal claim to the painting, for to do so would expose her entire relationship with Leonardo and their daughter, Marietta. She would not jeopardize Marietta's birthright as the legal child of Francesco del Giocondo.

The painting, although she longed to see it, held no determination on her future. Lisa lived a comfortable life and wanted for nothing. She suspected Salai would sell the portrait to the highest bidder, the king of France being the likely buyer. At least it would be in the possession of someone who'd cared about Leonardo, someone who would always treasure and preserve it.

Leonardo, my love, no grand commission, no mural in the Hall of Five Hundred, no patronage from king or pope ever equaled what you achieved in our portrait. I believe, my dearest, that it is your greatest work—a work of such astounding beauty that it will stand the test of time and elevate you to who I always knew you would become... the most significant artist the world has ever known.

A gentle knock sounded on the door. *"Sì, accomodi."*

A girl with golden curls and wide hazel eyes peeked around the door. "Mamma, are you unwell? You promised we would go to the mercato and set the birds free."

"*Scusami, cara,* I nearly forgot." Lisa rose and straightened her gown. Catching a glimpse of herself in the looking glass, her lips curved up in a small smile as she wondered if she was even recognizable as the same woman who, sixteen years ago, had posed for the greatest artist in the world.

Taking Marietta's hand, she bent and kissed her on the cheek. *"Vieni tesorina, ora ti racconterò una storia.*

Come, my darling, let me tell you a story...

EPILOGUE

MAY 20, 1945 ~ FLORENCE, ITALY

The war was finally over.

Valentina wanted nothing more than to sing and dance, but instead, she gave a prayer of thanks each day since Germany's surrender on April 29, 1945.

The nuns and the remaining Jewish women and children at the convent had celebrated with a joyous feast, a repudiation of all the long years of conflict. Everyone was humming with anticipation as they talked about what life would be like now that the nightmare was over.

But some nightmares would continue to haunt Valentina for the rest of her life. Although Dante's death was behind them, Valentina would never forget the events of that horrific night. With the help of Suor Teresa and the mother superior, they dragged Dante's body to the cellar. Concerned about leaving

Meira alone, Valentina asked her to carry the lantern to light their way.

The next day, Valentina sought help from Serafina, and arrangements were made for three resistance fighters to remove the body. The old woman later informed her that Dante had become an offering to the river gods—the currents of the Arno would carry him out to sea and his final resting place. Valentina prayed for Dante's soul and hoped he would seek the light of atonement and finally be at peace in death.

In the weeks following Dante's death, they'd walked on pins and needles, terrified the Nazis and Blackshirts would come pounding on the convent's door once more, but fortunately, no one did, and they were blessedly left alone for the remainder of the war.

The garden bloomed with a profusion of roses, herbs, and bougainvillea, scenting the air with a sweet fragrance. Valentina sat beneath a fig tree reading, while nearby, Meira knelt in the grass with shears, snipping herbs, roses, and lavender and placing them in a basket for drying.

Valentina yawned, stretching her arms toward the bright blue sky. "You have a real talent for gardening, Meira. Suor Magdalena does not trust just anyone with her precious herbs and vegetables. As for the flowers, she guards them as if they were a priceless treasure. Yet she seems content to give you free rein in her kingdom of greenery."

The young woman gave her a slight smile. "I feel peace here in the garden," she said in a soft but ragged voice. Although that terrible night had brought Meira's voice back to her, the young woman continued to write her thoughts down in a notebook that she kept in her pocket.

"Even as a young girl, I have always found a sense of peace while gardening," Valentina agreed, her heart hurting for her daughter. It was as though speaking her thoughts aloud felt strange and foreign to Meira. "We are fortunate to have such bounty and must rejoice for what we have."

In truth, Valentina did have much to be grateful for. The treasure was safe, and Valentina's promise to Suor Maria Vittoria had been kept. One day, she would pass the torch onto a young nun who would promise to safeguard the beautiful letters between Lisa del Giocondo and Leonardo da Vinci.

She was thankful for the war's end and hoped the world would eventually heal from its wounds. She prayed the malevolent serpent that had wreaked such evil in its murderous rampage across Europe in its quest to annihilate the Jewish people would slither back into its black hole, never to emerge again.

But she worried about Meira. Her daughter was safe and physically healthy, but the young woman carried a profound sorrow within her. As she watched Meira work in the garden, she prayed for God to help heal her daughter's heart and mind. Valentina vowed she would always be there for Meira no matter what the future might bring.

I will do everything I can to help you, tesoro.

The bell ringing at the convent's entrance announced a visitor, and Valentina rose from the bench to see who it was. Opening the door, she beheld a tall young man with his hands shoved in his pockets. His trousers were baggy, and his thin frame was all sharp angles. His blue eyes were striking despite the shadows beneath them, and his shaved head sprouted an auburn fuzz. Valentina knew immediately the young man had most likely survived one of the appalling internment camps. Since the end of the war, grisly details about the heinous camps run by the Nazis had begun to emerge. She and her fellow sisters had been helping survivors and those who had gone into hiding as they began to return to their homes and reclaim their lives.

"*Posso aiutarla*?" she asked the young man.

"*Sì, per favore.* I am searching for someone. I was told she may be here."

Despite the war's end, Valentina remained cautious about strangers who came to the door, especially regarding anyone inquiring about her daughter. "Who advised you on this matter?"

"A priest from Rome. His name is Padre D'Angelo. I came at his urging."

Valentina's heart galloped in her chest. It seemed impossible, and yet... "Who is it that you seek?"

The young man wrung the cap clutched in his hands. "Meira Chiarelli, we were—" He swallowed and hesitated, seeming to search for the right words. "Friends...close friends, Sorella."

Valentina beamed at him. "Are you Marcello Orvieto?"

"*Sì, sono io,*" he nodded, his sky-blue eyes wide, reflecting surprise that she knew his name.

"Welcome, welcome." Valentina offered her hand, and he grasped it like a lifeline. "Follow me." She led Marcello through the cloister to the garden, where Meira knelt among the flowers, her back to them.

"Meira, you have a visitor."

Meira dropped the garden shears and sat frozen for a few seconds. Finally, she rose, brushed the dirt from her dress, and slowly turned.

For a moment, Marcello and Meira stared at one another as if in a dream.

Then, as if suddenly shaken awake, Meira cried, "Marcello." Her legs carried her like a colt racing to the finish line as she flew into the young man's open arms.

Marcello swung Meira around and around as if she were a mere feather.

Valentina blinked back tears as she watched the joyous reunion.

"Meira, *amore mio,* a thousand times I have prayed to God to keep you safe. Thinking of you gave me strength. It kept me alive." He buried his face in her hair, his shoulders heaving. He held her so tightly their bodies seemed to merge as one.

"Marcello, you came back to me. Nothing else matters," Meira sobbed into his shoulder.

They kissed as though they were the only two people in the world, but after a few moments, they pulled apart, their faces flushed.

Valentina had returned to her spot beneath the fig tree, giving them privacy, but she could not stop the flow of tears streaming down her cheeks. Tears of joy for the miracle of Marcello's reunion with Meira. Together, they would help each other heal.

Valentina would weep again when it was time for Meira to leave the convent to return to Rome with Marcello and reclaim what was left of their families and homes. Those tears would come later. For now, she would rejoice in all that was found.

Meira ran to Valentina, embracing her. "Thank you for everything you have done for me, Suor Gianna. How will I ever repay you?"

"Your happiness is thanks enough, but if I could ask anything of you, please come back for a visit from time to time."

"Of course, we will visit you. And promise me you will come to Rome to visit Marcello and me when we are settled."

That was a promise Valentina would gladly keep.

MEIRA AND MARCELLO held hands as they stopped midway across the Ponte Vecchio, the only bridge spanning the Arno that the Germans did not destroy when they evacuated Florence. From the Ponte Vecchio, they saw the destruction the Germans had wrought on the beautiful ancient bridges.

Still, the sight was beautiful. Meira's heart was so full of love for Marcello that she couldn't bear to be apart from him, not even for a second.

Marcello cupped her face in his hands and kissed her, and time fell away. She recalled before the war when she wondered if she was really in love with him or even knew what love was. How foolish she'd been. But, along with her joy, there was immense sorrow. She and Marcello had wept, holding each other close, as he told her what had happened to their parents.

Both their families had perished in Oświęcim, Poland, in a death camp called Auschwitz.

Together, they'd said the mourner's kaddish, the prayer recited for the dead. The years of war and the loss of her parents had transformed Meira from a girl to a woman. She was ready to claim her new life.

She and Marcello breathlessly broke from their kiss. His face was thin and lined, but she knew he would eventually regain his strength, and his easy smile and confidence would return. She would love him back to health.

"Meira, I have something to ask you," Marcello said as he got down on one knee, taking her hands in his. "I asked you once," he said softly, "and now I ask you again—Meira Chiarelli, *sei la mia vita. Amore mio, vuoi farmi l'onore di diventare mia moglie?*"

"Yes! Yes! Yes! I will marry you, Marcello Orvieto. You are my heart and soul. You are the love of my life. *Non riesco ad immaginare la mia vita senza di te.*"

Marcello gave an exuberant shout and swept Meira up in his arms. Jubilant cheers and applause resounded around them from passersby as Marcello spun Meira around and around. A bubble of laughter escaped her, and she realized it was the first time she'd laughed in many years.

Tears streamed down her cheeks as she said a silent prayer of gratitude to her beloved parents for their sacrifice, courage, and boundless love.

Carissima Marietta,

Tesoro, if you have paid heed to my final wishes, you are reading this letter, and I am now in paradise with your beloved sisters Piera and Camilla, and your dear brother Giocondo. I expect to be busy for quite some time, greeting our dear family members and loved ones.

I rest peacefully, knowing that my precious treasure is in

*your care. In your official capacity as Suor Ludovica, I know
you will guard and keep it safe. Leonardo would be pleased to
know I entrusted the treasure to you. He loved you well, daughter. I pray I have taught you that love should be cherished, no
matter what form.*

*Sometimes, the road for those who love deeply is a chal-
lenging one to travel. It has been so for me, but I regret nothing.
How could I, for it brought you into this world.*

*Both your fathers were good men who loved you. Never
forget that.*

*I shall miss you, my darling daughter, and my dear sons
and grandchildren. Know that I will always keep watch over
you, and one day, we will see each other again. But in the
meantime, I plan to spread my wings and soar across the
Heavens with my dearest friend.*

*Life is a brief dream, and love is the only thing that makes
it worthwhile.*

Addio,
Con tanto amore,
Mamma

VALENTINA WIPED the tears from her eyes as she re-read the
final lines of Lisa's letter. Slipping the delicate paper into its tissue
sleeve, she returned it to the soft burgundy leather folio. She
placed the folder back in the carved wooden box and gently traced
her fingers along the etching of the birds in flight. She hoped the
translation of the letters would bring light and understanding to
the next nun who received this precious gift of guardianship.

Completing the deciphering of the letters had been bittersweet. But the experience had inspired her to keep writing in her own journal. Perhaps, one day, she would write a book about courage, faith, and love that would end happily. But in the meantime, she had much to look forward to. Next month, she and Suor Teresa would travel to Rome for the joyous occasion of Meira and Marcello's wedding. Valentina's eyes misted as she recalled the sweetness of the young couple's reunion.

She'd received a letter from Padre D'Angelo explaining how Marcello had found him and the good father had conveyed to the young man that Meira was safe at the convent of Santa Maria del Carmine. Valentina had written back to thank Padre D'Angelo for the letter and asked him to help with the arrangements for their upcoming visit. She also informed him that she believed it would be best if Meira were not told the truth about her parentage. Her adoptive parents had made the ultimate sacrifice for Meira, and it would be wrong to diminish that.

After all, Valentina had learned from Leonardo and Lisa that some secrets are better kept safely in the light and love of the heart.

Dear Reader:
Thank you for reading *Mona Lisa's Daughter*.
If you would like to leave a review,
please scan the following QR code:

SCAN HERE TO LEAVE A REVIEW FOR
"MONA LISA'S DAUGHTER"

Keep Reading for a Free Preview of
The Last Daughter.
All the best,
Belle Ami

Based on a True Story of
One Girl's Courage in the Face of Evil

The Last
DAUGHTER

From the bestselling author of
THE GIRL WHO KNEW DA VINCI

BELLE AMI

FREE PREVIEW

THE LAST DAUGHTER

I awaken in the middle of the night to an explosive rumbling and screaming sirens.

Blinding bursts of light fill my room in between the roar of bombs, a frightening man-made thunderstorm. Everything in our bedroom rattles and shakes, and I am terrified our building will collapse, killing us all. Above the wailing sirens, I hear glass shattering, my mother screaming, my brother crying, and my father in the next room trying to calm them both. My poor grandmother shrieks with each detonation then lapses into a mournful litany of crying and prayers in Yiddish to God and my grandfather to intercede and halt the firestorm threatening to consume us. Another explosion shakes the building, drowning out the pleas of my family. "Nadja, what is happening?"

"I don't know!" Her arms fly around me, and we shudder against each other so hard we can feel each other's bones. With her hand clutching mine, we jump from the warmth of our bed and run to the window. The sky has turned a blistering red from the glow of fires burning throughout the city. We hear the drone of planes overhead, punctuated by ear-rattling explosions.

In the week leading up to this horror, my family and relatives had made a commitment to each other's survival, sharing whatever we have. The adults agreed that if given the opportunity to emigrate, we would all go. But in the face of such destruction, the slim hope I carried in my heart of my family escaping this war has shattered into tears.

Gripping the windowsill, I stare at the chaos below. The scene unfolds like a movie reel from America, and all I want to do is stop it. Horses run up and down the street in confusion, their wild neighs echoing in the night. They must have escaped their stalls when the bombing began. But there are people in the streets as well, and they are wailing as loud as the horses.

"Why are people in the streets?" I ask Nadja. "Is it not safer to remain inside our homes? They will be trampled!"

"Those men are chasing after the horses," she replies, her arm tightening around my shoulders.

"But some of the people are not. They are just screaming and running around."

"They are afraid," Nadja says. "I imagine people do strange things when they fear for their lives."

I have never thought about the true meaning of fear before. I have feared not doing well on an exam. I have feared that I would sully the new dress that Mama and Papa bought me for Hannukah. But I realize those fears are not fears at all. Those fears are little flies that buzz about my ears. But the fear that surrounds me now is a thunderous roar, and I wonder if even worse fears will come?

Every minute, another deafening explosion shakes our home,

and we hear terrified shrieks from the other apartments. People stand at their windows as my sister and I are doing. My father runs into our room shouting, "Girls get away from the window! It isn't safe!"

Nadja and I run into my father's arms. "*Tata*, what is happening?"

"Come, come with me into the other room. The war has begun. Germany is attacking."

As flashes of light illuminate his eyes, I see the truth of it, the reality that is now upon us. We run with my father to the safety of our parents' bedroom, where my mother, brother, and grandmother are huddled under the bed. I don't know why my parents' bedroom feels safer, but it does. My brother's arms are locked around my mother's neck as he whimpers, "*Tata, Tata*, make them stop."

"Please God, help us," my grandmother prays over and over again. Her prayers feel like dust in the wind. In the face of madness, they have no consequence.

Another explosion shakes the building, and the room is filled with a pellucid white light that turns night into day. My mother holds us tight, her arms wrapped around us like a shield of armor.

"Don't cry, children, don't worry, it will stop," my father says. "We are safe. The building is strong. Be brave, my darlings." But my father's words tremble on his tongue, and I know he is trying to convince himself as much as he is all of us. Under the bed, we cling to each other, frozen with terror, as the attack continues for what seems like hours.

I feel certain we will not survive the night. Perhaps this is the end. In a terrible final collapse of wood, iron, and glass, we will be buried beneath the rubble of our building, forgotten to the world.

Several times during the night, the bombing stops, and we slip into a troubled slumber, but then it begins again. We awaken and begin to pray once more.

We remain prisoners in our home for the next five days while bombs intermittently strike our city. After the second day of bombing, during a lull, my father ventures out in search of any news. When he comes back, we run to him, relieved that he has returned safely.

"*Tata*, *Tata*, you're back!"

My mother rushes to him, interrupting our questions, "Joel, what have you heard? Is there any hope?"

Looking at our pleading faces, he responds, "Yes, yes, there is good news. England and France have declared war on Germany."

"Thank God!" my mother exclaims. "What else? Tell us more."

My father seems to weigh his words. "Unfortunately, the Nazis are moving rapidly. The Polish army is fighting valiantly, but they are heavily out-armed and undermanned. Germany is pounding the cities and transportation lines. There have already been hundreds of deaths and injuries. I must be honest. I can't imagine any other outcome than the Nazis conquering our country."

"How long?" my mother asks.

"How long what?"

"How long before the British and the French come to our rescue?" my mother's voice sounds shaky and impatient.

"I'm afraid—it's likely we will have to endure a German occupation. It will take time for the allies to prepare for war."

My mother's face conveys what we all feel as her eyes flood with tears.

Putting his arm around her shoulders, he says, "Come, dear, let us make some tea and listen to the radio."

We gather around the radio. The steady flow of news is disheartening. *"We will take Lodz today and tomorrow, Kielce, and on and on until we take Warszawa!"* Hitler declares, his voice harsh and guttural. He yells like a madman, and I wonder why he is filled with such hate.

My father turns the dial in search of something other than the hysterical boasting of Hitler. Finally, we hear the voice of a Polish reporter crying out his dismal news, "Countrymen, the sovereign nation of Poland is being bombarded. The Germans have thrown an immense force against our beloved country. We estimate nearly 2,400 tanks organized into six panzer divisions have rolled across our borders, striking with rapid precision through our defensive lines. The Germans are surrounding and destroying our troops with a legion of foot soldiers and mechanized infantry. The tanks are scorching the earth and leaving a path of death and destruction in the wake of this *blitzkrieg.* This lightning strike is an organized attack of such surprise, speed, and strength, it is impossible to defend against. Pray for our brave soldiers who are fighting for their lives and yours!"

In horror, we hear guns firing and explosives detonating in the background of the announcer's report. His voice fades in and out with the crackle of radio static and interference until there is only the hiss of a severed transmission.

I sit at the window in my bedroom during a momentary lull, staring down at the street. It is deserted except for an occasional person darting from doorway to doorway, furtively making their way to some unknown destination. I scrunch my eyes to see if I can recognize the people who dare to go out, but their faces are covered, and they stay in the shadows.

I beg my mother to let me go downstairs to Fela's apartment to see her. Her answer is an unequivocal "No!" My mother, who never raises her voice to scold any of us, has begun bursting into tears and holding us close. At other times she rails against this unfairness.

I wish my mother had not been the force of nature she was before the bombing. I wish she hadn't been so strong, so attached to our home and our lives here. Perhaps we could have convinced her that we should all leave. Perhaps my father would not have acquiesced so quickly to my mother's objections. Perhaps we could now be living safely in Palestyne or even America. A tightness builds in my chest, and guilt washes over me for thinking such thoughts. I love my mother. She had no way of knowing what would happen. None of us did.

The radio drones its endless blitz of bad news. We are overcome with shock and fatigue. We find out the roads are clogged with refugees heading east in a desperate attempt to outrun the Germans, who are conquering the towns and cities in their path. As I sit at the window, it occurs to me that even the birds have flown away. I have not heard a bird chirp or seen one hopping on my windowsill since the bombing began. At least they have wings to carry them away. I wish we did, too.

How did the refugees decide what to take and what to leave behind? How do you pack up a lifetime into a cart? I wonder why my parents have decided to stay instead of joining the refugees on their trek.

My sister comes to sit beside me at the window, hugging me in her arms, offering a bit of solicitude and affection. "So, what do you see, Dinale?"

"I see the end of our world, and it breaks my heart," I answer as tears well in my eyes.

"You mustn't lose hope!" Nadja kisses my forehead. "There are good people in the world. They will come to our rescue. We will have to be strong and resilient." She stares out the window, her skin as pale as the clouds in the sky. "It is our fate." Her words sound strong, but her eyes look like she is trying to convince herself as well as me.

"Since when do you believe in fate and not free will?" I grumble.

"I'm afraid that freedom for all Poles disappeared when the Nazis crossed our border. I don't know what the future will bring, but I do know we are in for difficult times, and Mama and *Tata* are going to need us in ways that I can't even imagine." She squeezes my shoulders to emphasize her words. "Right now, they could use your sunshine smile. Maybe you could comfort Abek and play a game with him. He is so frightened and could use a little distraction from his fears. I've tried, but he won't respond to me."

I nod and turn from the window. Nadja holds my hand, and we walk into the parlor. My brother Abek is playing quietly on the floor with his jacks. I smile at him and tousle his blond curls, asking if I can play jacks with him. My once jolly brother, now subdued, hands me the ball. Taking it, I whisper, "Are you afraid? It's okay if you are. I know I am."

My question is met with silence as Abek looks down at the jacks on the floor.

"Abek, I know sometimes I am not the best sister in the world.

I'm truly sorry about that. But I am so glad you are my brother. Please talk to me and tell me what you feel."

He looks up at me then, his blue eyes glistening with tears. My heart is breaking as I grab his little hands in mine and squeeze them. "Abek, we are all here together, and that is a good thing." I lean into him and touch my forehead to his.

I bounce the ball and begin to play. But everything is different now. Abek is a little boy, but I see in his eyes that he knows what I know. No matter how much my parents try to reassure us, our world of Radom and a thousand other cities and villages like it has vanished. Not for a month, or a year, but forever.

Dear Reader:
I hope you enjoyed this FREE PREVIEW of
The Last Daughter.
If you would like to keep reading please scan the following
QR Code.
All the best,
Belle Ami

SCAN HERE TO GET
"THE LAST DAUGHTER"

AFTERWORD

BELLE AMI

This book has been several years in the making.

I spent hundreds of hours researching Leonardo da Vinci and Lisa del Giocondo, Renaissance Italy, and the history of Italy leading up to and during World War II. A few notable standouts include Walter Isaacson's brilliant biography, *Leonardo Da Vinci*, and *Leonardo's Notebooks* by Leonardo da Vinci and H. Anna Suh, and Jonathan Jones' *The Lost Battles (Leonardo, Michelangelo, and the Artistic Duel that Defined the Renaissance)*. In preparing to write about Italy during WWII, many books influenced me, including Mark Sullivan's breathtaking saga *Beneath a Scarlet Sky*, and Rick Atkinson's monumental *Liberation Trilogy*.

I am grateful to all the writers who continue to write about what occurred under the Nazi's reign of terror and barbarity.

Authors of historical fiction have the challenging task of weaving a fictional story with factual information about real people, places, and events. I hope that in *Mona Lisa's Daughter*, a happy balance has been attained, one you will find engaging, intriguing, and poignant.

Although some historians and academics might disagree with my interpretation of some of the facts about Leonardo da Vinci and Lisa del Giocondo's relationship, the timelines of their lives in Florence seamlessly mesh, and their relationship could easily have evolved in the way I portrayed in the novel. As far as the historical record is concerned—there is nothing tangible or specific recorded about their relationship, but to be truthful, there is very little recorded about any of Leonardo's relationships or his personal life.

The thousands of pages of notes and drawings that Leonardo da Vinci generated do not reveal a great deal in terms of intimate details about his life, however, they are certainly indicative of his incredible creative output. What cannot be disputed is that Leonardo worked on and off on the portrait of Lisa Giocondo for 16-17 years. He never received any payment for the commission, and he never sold it, even though he was often in need of funds. He also kept Lisa's portrait with him until his dying breath. I kept asking myself why he would do that. Many reasons have been hypothesized, none of which I found satisfying or compelling. The only explanation for me was that Lisa's portrait held a special place in his heart.

I have interwoven many truths about Leonardo's life into the story. His difficult relationship with his father, Piero da Vinci, his illegitimacy, and the ultimate rejection from Piero, who left no will or testament acknowledging Leonardo as his son.

The acrimonious relationship between Leonardo and Michelangelo and the competition fueled by the Signoria of Florence all of which is well-documented became a dramatic element in this story and reflected the nature of Leonardo's often volatile and complicated relationship with his "hometown" of Florence and art in general.

The World War II storyline during the years up to and including the German occupation of Italy, weaves in historical facts and true events, including the Nazi's theft of the entire collection of books from the Temple Maggiore in Rome (books that have never been found to this day). There were so many stories of heroism that I discovered in my research, including the hiding of Jews at the Benefratelli Hospital in Rome during WWII and the hiding of Jewish women and children at the convent of Santa Maria del Carmine in Florence.

And yes, an assassination attempt was made on Mussolini by a woman—an Irish Catholic aristocrat whose gunshot grazed his nose.

Although Valentina is a fictional character, she is representative of the valiant spirit during World War II when so many good people did what they could in the face of evil. Chiara/Meira, Marcello, Benjamin, and Gabriella are also representative of Italian Jews at the time, many of whom were deported to Auschwitz during the Nazi/Fascist raid of October 16, 1943.

Sincerely,

Belle Ami

ABOUT THE AUTHOR

BELLE AMI

Belle Ami writes breathtaking historical fiction, captivating historical romance, and gripping romantic thrillers. Creating unforgettable characters and complex stories, Belle's writing reflects the redemptive power of love and the strength of the human spirit. Her series and stand-alone novels include the following:

MONA LISA'S DAUGHTER: A 500-year-old secret protects a priceless cache of letters between Leonardo da Vinci and Lisa del Giocondo hidden in a convent in World II, Florence, Italy. A young nun is sworn to protect it, but secrets from her past come back to haunt her and potentially destroy everything she holds dear.

THE LAST DAUGHTER is a compelling and heart-wrenching World War II historical novel based on the life of Belle Ami's mother, Dina Frydman, and her incredible true story of surviving the Holocaust. The story begins at the dawn of World War II and follows the Nazi invasion and occupation of Poland, focusing on the Nazi's six-year reign of terror on the Jews of Poland, and the horrors of the death camps at Bergen-Belsen and Auschwitz, where more than six-million Jews along with other vulnerable innocents were slaughtered.

OUT OF TIME SERIES: A time-travel, art-thriller series with romantic elements. Includes the #1 Amazon bestsellers *The Girl Who Knew da Vinci*, *The Girl Who Loved Caravaggio*, and *The Girl Who Adored Rembrandt*.

THE BLUE COAT SAGA: A three-part serial, time-travel, suspense thriller with romantic elements set in the present-day and in World War II. Includes *The Rendezvous in Paris*, *The Lost Legacy of Time*, and *The Secret Book of Names*.

TIP OF THE SPEAR SERIES: A contemporary, international espionage, suspense-thriller series with romantic elements. Includes the acclaimed *Escape*, *Vengeance*, *Ransom*, and *Exposed*.

LOST IN TIME SERIES: A riveting and romantic time travel historical romance series published by Dragonblade Publishing that follows three female friends who time-travel from modern-day America to late 19th century London, Paris, and Tuscany where they must unravel an ancient mystery, battle evil, and of course, fall in love.

LION'S DEN CONNECTED WORLD series: *Luck of the Lyon*—A highly successful and beloved series published by Dragonblade Publishing, comprising over 60 novels and novellas. Belle Ami's *Luck of the Lyon* is one of the most recent installments. A 5-Star reviewer writes: *This book had everything: a real hero, a beautiful widow, and, of course, Mrs. Dove-Lyon.*

NIGHT OF LYONS: A LYON'S DEN WORLD ANTHOLOGY (THE LYON'S DEN) —A selection of novellas by bestselling Historical Romance authors including Belle Ami. *"It's a night to remember at the notorious Lyon's Den where anything goes..."*

A former Kathryn McBride scholar of Bryn Mawr College in Pennsylvania, Belle, is also a proud recipient of the RONE, RAVEN, Readers' Favorite Award, and the Book Excellence Award.

Belle's passions include hiking, boxing, skiing, cooking, travel, and of course, writing. She lives in Southern California with her family and her brilliant Chihuahua, Giorgio Armani.

Belle loves to hear from readers. You can reach out to her via her website: **belleamiauthor.com.**

SCAN HERE TO SIGN UP FOR THE BELLE AMI JOURNAL

Sign up for Belle's newsletter: **The Belle Ami Journal** by scanning the QR code above for exclusive giveaways, contests, sneak peeks, and no spammy stuff. You can also connect with Belle on social media by visiting **belleamiauthor.com.**

ALSO BY BELLE AMI

BELLE AMI COMPLETE BOOKLIST

HISTORICAL FICTION

The Last Daughter

Based closely on the remarkable true story of author Belle Ami's mother, Dina Frydman, one of the youngest survivors of the Holocaust, *The Last Daughter* will reaffirm your faith in the indomitability of the human spirit.

Mona Lisa's Daughter

Two remarkable women discover their courage and strength, during the golden days of the Renaissance and the darkest days of World War II.

TIME TRAVEL HISTORICAL FICTION

OUT OF TIME THRILLER SERIES

She can see into the past. She can see the truth.

But the truth can be deadly.

When art historian Angela Renatus pairs up with former Navy Seal turned private detective Alex Caine to recover stolen and missing art, she begins to have strange dreams that take her into the past where danger threatens her life.

The multi-award-winning and bestselling author Belle Ami brings us a compelling and mesmerizing time-travel historical romance, mystery-thriller series that will leave you breathless.

The Girl Who Knew da Vinci — Book 1

The Girl Who Loved Caravaggio — Book 2

The Girl Who Adored Rembrandt — Book 3

THE BLUE COAT SAGA

A unique, three-part, time-travel mystery thriller weaving together the lives of two extraordinary women and the destiny they both share.

The Rendezvous in Paris — Book 1

The Lost Legacy of Time — Book 2

The Secret Book of Names— Book 3

Boxed Set: The Blue Coat Saga (Books 1, 2, 3)

LOST IN TIME SERIES

Published by Dragonblade Publishing

Three paintings, three best friends, three time-travel portals, three incredible cities:

London Time — Book 1

Paris Time — Book 2

Tuscan Time — Book 3

HISTORICAL ROMANCE FICTION

Part of the Bestselling Lyon's Den Series World published by Dragonblade Publishing

Luck of the Lyon

Night of Lyons

CONTEMPORARY THRILLER FICTION

TIP OF THE SPEAR THRILLER SERIES

Mossad agent Cyrus Hassani and his elite team of courageous men and women embark on dangerous missions to thwart the ever-looming threat of deadly terrorists and nuclear attacks. Award-winning and bestselling author Belle Ami delivers a fast-paced and thrilling international espionage series interwoven with complex and compelling love stories about the heroes and heroines who work deep undercover to keep the world safe. Guaranteed page-turners you will want to read all the books in this series.

Escape — Book 1

Vengeance — Book 2

Ransom — Book 3

Exposed — Book 4

www.ingramcontent.com/pod-product-compliance
Lightning Source LLC
Chambersburg PA
CBHW022238020726
47496CB00004B/959